The Stolen Twin

By Michele Pariza Wacek

The Stolen Twin Copyright © 2015 by Michele Pariza Wacek.
All rights reserved. Printed in the United States of America. No part
of this book may be reproduced or transmitted in any manner or by
any means, electronically or mechanically, including photocopying,
recording, retrieval system, without prior written permission from the
author, except in the case of brief quotations embodied in a review.
For information, address Michele Pariza Wacek, PO Box 10430
Prescott, AZ 86304.

This book may be purchased for educational, business, or sales promotional use. For information, please email
info@michelepw.com.

ISBN 9780996826020

Library of Congress Control Number: 2015917800

DEDICATION

To my mom, who I know is smiling down at me right now (and probably saying to my grandparents "it's about time") and my dad (who has already told me "it's about time"). Thank you both for believing in me and encouraging me.

Chapter 1

My life has been dominated by two dreams.

In the first, I see my twin sister Cat at seven, the last time I ever saw her. She is all pink and golden – hair hanging in yellow ringlets, dancing blue eyes, rosy cheeks. She is beautiful, my sister. Light, sweet, charming. My opposite.

My father is pulling her as she sits in a little red wagon, laughing and waving. They're in a wild, grassy field. Birds are twittering, crickets chirping. A butterfly flits by. Gently swaying grasses and colorful wild-flowers brush against her, stroking her soft skin, loving her. She laughs and caresses their long, flowing stems.

But there is more in this field than plants, insects and birds. Fairies live here too – although they usually hide when people walk by with their heavy crushing footsteps, unnatural smells and callous voices. My father, plowing through with bent back and plodding footsteps, sends them cringing and scurrying away as well.

But then they hear the tinkling sound of my sister's laughter.

Peeking from behind brown-eyed Susan's and pebbles, they see Cat in the wagon, clutching a dandelion in her fist, rubbing the yellow petals against her face. She astonishes them, seduces them, hypnotiz-es them. They've never seen anything like her before. Gradually, they creep out and move closer. Cat virtually sparkles in the sunlight, bright and shining. As she catches sight of the fairies, she laughs and blows them kisses.

The fairies, now completely under her spell, swarm over to her, nuzzling her face, soft arms, slender neck. She smiles, touching them back – fingers grazing over delicate wings not much more substantial than a cobweb.

More fairies emerge as my father guides her deeper into the field. The grasses become thicker, taller. The fairies cling to the blades, reach-ing their tiny hands out to caress Cat as she drifts by.

Finally, the queen herself comes forward, tall and majestic. She wears a dress made from white tulips and daffodils, sparkling with dew-drops. Her long, silky, golden hair is entwined with white daisies. Large green eyes peer out from under her mass of hair. Her face is cold, all sharp angles and pale skin, but beautiful.

"This is the one," the queen says, her voice like breaking glass.

Cat looks up, fairies tangled in her hair. She blinks as her gaze meets that of the queen's. They stare at each other, each mesmerized by the other. Then, slowly, the queen reaches down and gathers my sister into her arms. The fairies dart out of the way, hovering above them like a cloud of gnats. The queen turns, Cat cuddled in her arms, and they disappear, vanishing into the thick grass.

My father pulls the wagon a few seconds longer before realizing something is wrong. Seeing Cat missing, he drops to the ground and begins searching fruitlessly through the grass. "Cat," he yells over and over. "Cat, come back. Come back!"

Nothing answers him, not even a chirp from a bird. He cries her name over and over, begging her to come back, while the fairies croon over their newest prize.

My second dream is completely opposite - much like the difference between Cat and me. It begins with me and my parents in the car. We're going to Milwaukee to visit my grandparents, but suddenly my parents take a detour. We drive down an old country road filled with potholes and thirsty cracks. My chest begins to take on a familiar heaviness.

We're at a church, a white country church with a tall steeple and an elaborate stained glass etching of Mary and Jesus in the manger. A bell rings, deep and melodious. I'm having trouble breathing.

We walk to the graveyard behind the church, my parents in front of me, talking quietly, ignoring me (as usual). The bell continues to ring, the sound growing louder, echoing in the stillness. I stumble, trying desperately to breathe, to draw air through lungs now shrunken into a tight ball of twine. I need my inhaler, but don't know where it is.

My parents continue to ignore me. I gasp and start to fall, but now I'm floating, floating, toward the graveyard. All I can hear is the tolling of the bell. I can't breathe at all. My lungs burn, a bright fireball in my chest. This is it, I realize. This is the end. This is where I die.

I wake then, gasping and reaching for my inhaler. As uncomfortable as it is, I prefer it to the hot tears and heavy sick feeling that follows the fairy dream. Cat is the chosen one. I'm the disappointment.

These were the dreams that dominated my life. If I had other ones, I never remembered them. Only these two. I never told a soul about my dreams – they were my penance, my burden, my personal hell.

Until the day Cat came back, turning my life into something worse than any nightmare I ever could have imagined.

Chapter 2

I was busy admiring my gun when the voice of Brandi, my roommate, floated toward me.

"Kit, a Halloween party generally takes place in October."

"Almost ready."

I holstered the gun and took one last look in the mirror. Not bad for something thrown together in an afternoon. A short brown cashmere skirt, fringed leather vest, white shirt, tall brown high-heeled boots and cowboy hat. The perfect cowgirl. None of the browns matched, but that just added to the overall ragtag charm.

My hair I left loose – it hung like a black curtain almost down to the middle of my back. Normally, I wore only blush and lipstick to add color to my pale complexion, but tonight I went all out, dabbing on eye shadow and liner. My dark brown eyes were such a contradiction to my colorless skin, I often felt like a waif out of a Dickens' novel.

I took one final glance, then scooped up my purse. Yes, I definitely liked this costume. Especially the gun.

I found Brandi in her immaculate bedroom, poking at her hair. The rich, musky scent of her expensive perfume drifted toward me. Her eyes met mine in the mirror. "You make me sick."

I did a little pirouette. "I didn't think I looked that good."

She rolled her eyes. "Like I believe that." She adjusted the pale gold scarves on her harem outfit.

"I thought you wanted to get going."

"I do. The cab will be in here in a sec."

"Cab? The party is two blocks from here."

"Two long blocks. It's windy and I don't want my costume blowing away."

Typical Brandi. Rich and liked to flaunt it. "Is Martha coming?"

Brandi snorted. "The mole? Hello. Are we talking about the same person here? It's past her bedtime."

Martha was our third roommate, nicknamed "the mole" by Brandi because she lived in the downstairs bedroom. Our original roommate, Martha's cousin Elena, had moved out of her sorority house and into our apartment for the sole purpose of seeing her boyfriend more. After three weeks, she decided she would rather live with her boyfriend than us. Because she didn't want her parents to know, we kept her name on the answering machine. As a consolation prize, she offered us Martha.

"She's really very nice, very sweet, no trouble at all," Elena had insisted. "She's a little strange, but harmless, really."

"Harmless?" Brandi had replied. "You make her sound like a would-be serial killer."

Elena laughed nervously. "No, no. I didn't mean it like that. She – just – she has a little trouble finding people to live with her. Nothing else. She's really quite sweet."

Brandi rolled her eyes at the second time the word "sweet" fell from Elena's mauve-colored lips. A former beauty queen, Elena had a tendency to call everyone sweet.

In the end, what we wanted didn't really matter. Elena needed someone to take over her share of the rent and Martha needed a place to stay. So three days later, we found ourselves living with our new roommate. Our new, very odd roommate.

"It IS Halloween," I said. "You'd think she might have something to do."

Brandi rolled her eyes. "Yeah, I think I saw her wearing some sort of costume today. She had on all black and her face was dead white. Oh, that's right. That's the way she always looks." She swept her purse off the rose-colored bedspread. "We're out of here."

As usual, Brandi looked fabulously seductive in her harem outfit. The thin, silky material strained at her ample breasts, yet still managed to minimize her rounded hips and thighs. Her dark brown hair glowing with blond highlights was piled on top of her head, emphasizing her high cheekbones, pouty lips and huge hazel eyes. I know my thinness bothered her, but in my opinion, I had nothing on her. Men spent more time gazing at her curves than they ever did mine.

She looked sideways at me from under her lashes. "I like your gun."

"Thanks. I do too."

"Planning to do away with Tommy?"

"If only."

We both laughed. Brandi shook her head. "Yeah, I know if I had the quarterback and captain of Riverview's winning football team drooling over me, the first thing I would do is reach for his gun. Oops, I meant my gun."

"Yeah, I bet you did."

She opened the door to the apartment, letting in a gust of cold wind. "Girl, you need your head examined. You do know that, don't you?"

I shrugged. "Don't do commitments. He wanted to get serious. I wanted to have fun. Had no choice."

She shut the door behind us and locked it. "Fun. You're talking to the queen of fun. You're a complete idiot."

"And that's why you broke up with Ted, is it? Or maybe it's Fred? Gee, I can't remember the last one."

"Don't get cute, sister. We're comparing a bunch of losers to the football god."

I rolled my eyes. She shook her head again, her smile exasperated.

We hurried to the cab, the wind sporting a knife-edge that turned it from crisp to cold. The air smelled of dead and dying things – leaves, plants, insects – and a touch of snow. I shivered. I hated fall. It felt like death to me. Cold, rotting death.

A hint of moisture brushed my cheek. Brandi licked her lips. "Crap. It's probably going to rain."

"It always rains on Halloween. You know that. Besides, what do you care? We're in a cab."

She settled in the car. "And you doubted."

"Never again."

Brandi smiled and told the driver our destination. I sat back as she straightened her outfit. "How do I look?"

"Hot enough to kill."

"Perfect." Her eyes narrowed. "Chuck better be there."

"I'm sure Chuck and Violet both will be there."

She glared at me. "Don't even go there."

I merely smiled and looked out the window.

By the time we arrived, the frat house was packed. An INXS song boomed throughout the house -- apparently it was an eighties Halloween party. Beer and shots flowed freely, mixed with the scent of cigarettes, perfume, sweat and the faint, but unmistakable sweet aroma of pot. I headed for the keg.

A few beers later, someone I barely knew dragged me into a strange drinking game. I appeared to be the loser since I ended up consuming shot after shot. Finally, I couldn't stand it anymore and decided to stumble off to the bathroom. I lurched to my feet, swaying, the world tipping, and wobbled across the room and into the hallway.

A line. Of course there would be a line. There would always be a line at a party like this. I groaned, wishing I hadn't waited until using the bathroom had become something of an emergency. At least it was quieter in the hall - the brown paneled, stained walls muffling everything but the thudding bass and drums of AC/DC's "Shook Me All Night Long."

A woman wearing an angel costume stood in front of me, her wings brushing my face. Clumsily I knocked them away.

The woman turned. "Sorry," she said and smiled.

I smiled back. "No problem."

Someone in a sexy witch costume stumbled into me, giggling, her breath stinking of Jack Daniels and tequila. "Oops," she said and started to hiccup. I stepped closer to the angel. The witch collapsed against the wall. "I have to pee so bad," she hiccupped.

The angel continued to study me, her eyes a clear sky blue. Golden wavy curls framed a face made up of delicate features and creamy skin. She looked like a porcelain doll.

"That angel costume suits you," I said, unable to drag my eyes away from her almost unworldly beauty. She reminded me of someone, but I couldn't think of who.

She raised a perfectly shaped eyebrow. "Angel?"

I blinked. No, not an angel. It was a fairy costume, pink and fluffy. "Oh, you're right. Fairy. Pretty cool."

Behind me, the witch groaned and slid to the brown tiled floor. "I don't feel so well," she mumbled between hiccups.

The fairy tilted her head and smoothed her dress. Even under the dim hallway lights, it sparkled. "Yes, it is."

She seemed so familiar, especially the soft, fluid way she moved. The hiccups behind me turned to retching. I smelled the faint odor of vomit. People started yelling about taking care of another sick one. I stumbled closer to the fairy, trying to focus my blurry vision. "What's your name?"

She tossed her hair. "Cat."

I staggered, nearly falling. "Cat? My sister's name was Cat."

Cat smiled again, showing white, even teeth. "Short for Catherine I'll bet."

"No, short for Catalina. Can you believe it? Is that even a name? It always sounded like a car to me."

"Really? I'm a Catalina too." Her smile widened.

The world unexpectedly tilted sharply to the left. I put my hand against the wall. "No way. Actually, now'd you say it, you look a little like her. Actually, you look a lot like her. At least I think she'd look like that, I mean you, now. I haven't seen her for awhile."

She cocked her head. "Why not?"

"She's been gone, kidnapped. When I was seven. She was seven too, we were twins." A part of me couldn't believe the words tumbling out of my mouth. I so rarely talked about my past, but somehow it felt right telling her.

She reached up and twisted a lock of hair around her finger. "Maybe she was kidnapped by the fairies."

I gasped, the corners of my vision turning black. "Why … how … why would you say that?"

She leaned forward, almost touching me, her blue eyes so clear, so direct. "It's the dreams, isn't it, Kitrina? The dreams of the fairy queen. And the dreams of the church. Where you die."

The alcohol in my system turned to ice. My brain went numb. I couldn't breathe, couldn't think. "My name," I stuttered, the only thing I could grab onto in this sea of unreality spinning around me. "How did you know my name?" Even my fingers were cold and unresponsive. Blackness roared in my ears. I blinked to steady myself, but all I could see was the blue of her eyes, like an anchor in an ocean of madness.

Ignoring my question, she leaned even closer, so close I could breathe in her scent. She smelled wild, free, a combination of fresh-cut grasses, wildflowers and the bitter cold wind of Halloween night. So different from the smoke, liquor and sweat of the party. "Listen to me, Kitrina. There's danger here, lurking in the shadows. It hasn't seen you yet, but it will. Tonight. It'll seize you in its jaws and never let you go, unless you can stop it. You must be strong, stronger than you've ever been in your entire life, if you are to prevail. And prevail you must, for there's more here at stake than you can possibly imagine. The innocent depend on you. You must save the innocent, because by saving the innocent you save yourself. It's the only way you can set yourself free."

She drifted back. Her pink dress shimmered in the half-light, twinkling like a thousand stars. The wings fluttered, suddenly looking real. Living and breathing, their touch as soft and insubstantial as cobwebs. Actually, the dress seemed alive too, alive and glowing and winking at me in the dimness.

She smiled, her face golden and glowing. "Don't be afraid, Kit. I'll take care of you. I'll always take care of you."

Blackness swamped me. I closed my eyes, thrust back to a time when I was six, taking swimming lessons at the YMCA, before my sickness, before Cat disappeared. Cat, as usual, had jumped in, fearless and tough. But I had hung back, terrified of the water, at the loss of control. The teacher tried to reason with me, but that just made it worse. I shook my head and flattened myself against the wall. The idea of water covering me, holding me down, keeping me from breathing, petrified me. That fear was so strong I could taste it in my mouth, coppery and thick, mixed with the sharp chemical scent of chlorine. Cat, seeing my plight, hoisted her tiny body out of the pool and ran to my side, nearly slipping on the slick surface. She took my hand and squeezed it. "Don't be afraid, Kit," she said in her authoritative voice, so odd in a six-year-old, yet somehow so comforting. "I'll take care of you. I'll always take care of you."

But she didn't take care of me. A year later she had disappeared, vanished, kidnapped by the fairies, leaving me almost dead in a sterile hospital room, never to fully recover. Not in body or in soul.

Tears pressed against my lids. I opened my eyes in anguish, searching for her. But she had disappeared, along with everyone else. I was completely alone in the hallway.

Chapter 3

The bathroom door stood open. Empty. I tottered in, shutting the door behind me and collapsing against it. Silence. Not even the stereo. My ears rang in the stillness. What the hell was going on?

My chest tightened, my breathing short and choppy. Fumbling, I reached into my purse for my inhaler. Take slow, deep breaths, I thought, sucking on the plastic instrument. Slow, deep breaths. Finally, my airways relaxed. Air rushed into my lungs, so sweet it hurt. I closed my eyes and would have toppled to the floor if the pain in my bladder hadn't reminded me why I started this trip down the rabbit's hole in the first place.

Could it really have been Cat out there, alive and well, after almost fifteen years? No. Not possible. Yet she knew things even Cat wouldn't know.

Dreaming of fairies. Dreaming of churches. Dreaming of dying.

I shook my head, trying to clear it. Everything was blurred and unreal, yet my drunkenness seemed to be draining away. Quickly. Frighteningly quickly. I needed another drink and fast.

Maybe Cat really had been kidnapped by the fairies, and now a fairy herself after years of living with them, she had returned to warn me.

But warn me of what? Impending danger? Death? I've lived with that my entire life. And what about this innocent thing? Saving the innocent? Right. I couldn't even save myself.

It's the only way you can set yourself free.

Sighing, I flushed the toilet and straightened my clothes. The place stunk of vomit, beer and urine. Stepping around piles of wet and suspicious-looking wads of paper towels, I twisted the faucet and glanced into the cracked mirror. Positively ashen. Oh God, I couldn't deal with this.

Someone banged on the door. "Excuse me, this bathroom is to share. It's not for your own private use."

Another voice piped in. "The bushes outside are adequate for puking, you know."

I washed my hands in the rusted and chipped sink, washed the tears off my face, dried off, dropped my paper towel on the floor to join its brethren, and opened the door.

Obviously I had suffered some sort of alcohol hallucination. That was the only rational explanation. The girl in the fairy costume probably had resembled Cat to some degree, thus triggering me to imagine the rest.

Outside, the stereo blared Tears for Fears' "Shout" mixed in with the dull roar of slurred voices. People were packed in the narrow hallway. A woman in a cat outfit with streaked black eye makeup gave me a dirty look before shoving past me into the bathroom. I blinked and tottered down the hallway, picking my way over and around the gaggle of bodies littering the area. Where had all these people come from? Or maybe a better question would be where had they all been a few minutes ago?

My head spun. It was the alcohol. Just the alcohol. Never mind that I now felt completely, stone-cold sober. Never mind that I may have just seen my sister for the first time in fifteen years. Never mind that she looked like a real fairy. Never mind that she even sounded like a real fairy with her cryptic messages. I closed my eyes. Alcoholic hallucination, I chanted under my breath. Only an alcoholic hallucination.

I crashed into a wide male back. "Sorry," I said, attempting to step aside when I smelled it. That unmistakable combination of Irish Spring soap and clean sweat.

Tommy.

Oh no. I tried to back up before he saw me and promptly bumped into someone behind me. The person pushed back and I fell into Tommy again. I tried sidestepping away, but Tommy had already turned around, a beer in each hand.

"Kit," he exclaimed, throwing one arm around my neck, his southern accent even more pronounced than usual. Beer sloshed down the front of my shirt, the wet cold jolting me out of my haze. "Where the hell you've been? I've been look'n all over for you."

"Been around," I said vaguely. Yeah, been talking to a fairy who resembled my kidnapped sister. Sure, I've been around. I decided not to think about it anymore. I studied Tommy instead.

He was so gorgeous. Thick, wavy dark blond hair that curled around his neck, dark green eyes with startling long lashes, high cheekbones and a full, sensuous mouth (not to mention his lean, muscular athletic body without a trace of fat). University of Riverview's star quarterback, breaker of several national records, rumored to win the Heisman Trophy this year. Despite his college successes, I thought him to be a bit too small for the NFL. The NFL, however, didn't appear to agree with me as he had already spoken to scouts.

In addition to his physical prowess, Tommy even had a brain, maintaining a solid B average. I privately referred to him as my Golden Boy, although due to our recent breakup, he wasn't mine anymore.

His gaze lingered on my body. "Cool costume. You look incredible."

I pulled away, feeling the familiar shivers tingle across my skin. Damn him. If he weren't so good in bed, this breakup would be a lot easier. "Just keep in mind I'm armed." I showed him my gun with a flourish.

His eyes widened. "An armed woman. I think all my fantasies are coming true, right now."

"Oh, you fantasize about having your dick shot off?"

He choked. "Well, actually, no. My fantasy doesn't involve a gun going off."

"I see." I made a point of looking him up and down. "So, what's this depressed existentialist thing you got going?" He wore black jeans, a black shirt and had a black cape tied around his neck.

He tried to look hurt. "Whad'ya mean? I'm Dracula."

I plucked one of his beers from his hand and drank. Christ that tasted good. Maybe I could get some of my numbness back. I still felt shaky and vulnerable. "I'll let you in on a little secret. Dracula has fangs."

"Can't drink with fangs."

"You're supposed to drink blood, not beer."

He grinned, wildly and lustfully. "Is that an invitation?"

I tossed my hair back. "Hardly. Virgins are what you're after."

He pondered this. "The blood of virgins. This definitely has some possibilities."

I finished his beer. His nearness both disturbed and excited me. "Well, before you set off on that virgin quest, Count, did you happen to notice someone wearing a pink fairy costume around here?"

He frowned. "Fairy costume? How non-PC."

The music switched to a Duran, Duran song. I rolled my eyes. "Not that kind of fairy. A real fairy, you know, like in fairy tales? Wings and magic and everything."

"Oh, like Tinkerbell and shit."

Someone squeezed past me, forcing me to step closer to Tommy. "Something like that."

He thought for a moment. "No, no Tinkerbells."

"How about Tinkerbells wearing pink dresses?"

"Nope, none of them either."

I sighed, deciding I had better get out of this conversation and over to the bar. Fast. "Okay, thanks anyway."

He grabbed my arm as I started to turn away. "Kit, wait a sec. I was hoping we could talk."

Not fast enough. I closed my eyes. "We've already talked."

His hand slid up to my neck, fingers brushing against my bare skin. I began to have trouble breathing. "I still don't know what I did wrong. Or why you don't want to see me anymore."

"Nothing. We just want different things, that's all."

He leaned closer, his breath faintly misty and warm against my cheek. My stomach felt hot and twisty, like a nest of serpents had moved in and taken control. His hand kept rubbing my neck, slowly, sensuously, sending delicious tingles down my body. "What's so different about what we want?"

The serpents squirmed about. My mouth felt dry and hot. "I told you. You want a relationship. I want to have fun."

"I want to have fun, too."

I opened my eyes. His face was so close it was out of focus. The want, the need to have him lead me out of here and take me to his apartment was so powerful it almost overwhelmed me. Not just for the sex, but for the connection to another human being. I felt so empty, so alone. So utterly and completely alone. I saw now how detached I was from the human race. Sure, I had plenty of friends, acquaintances mostly, but no one I could really talk to, really connect with. After

Cat, after almost dying, I never allowed myself that luxury. I couldn't. I didn't want to hurt anyone the way I had been hurt. I refused to get involved. But now I could painfully, agonizingly, feel what I missed, and how desperately I wanted that bond.

But I knew I never could. It wasn't meant for me.

I tried to lean back, tried not to show the devastation in my eyes. "You want to get serious, too."

"I told you we can go slower. We can go as slow as you want."

Like the beer he splashed down my neck earlier, that one sentence shocked my senses, broke through the enchantment he had been weaving around me. It didn't matter how slow we went, the ending would be the same. I wasn't normal. I would never be normal. He was the Golden Boy with a Golden Future. I had no future. I could not, would not, let myself drag him down.

I backed out of his grasp. "You win. We can talk, but later. Right now a beer's calling my name."

He stepped forward. "I'll get it."

I waved him back, deftly stepping into the crowd. "My name, my beer. Now's not the time to talk anyway. We're supposed to be having fun."

"But, Kit," he called, looking so plaintive, so forlorn. I hardened my heart and gave him a cheery wave, trying to put as many people between us as fast as possible. He started toward me, but then one of his teammates grabbed him by the neck. I slunk into the crowd.

He would get over it, get over me, soon enough. There was no shortage of golden girls with golden futures who would be more than happy to console him. He could have his pick. He would be fine. Never mind how hollow, how ill I felt to think of him with another girl. This was for the best. I knew it.

"Hey, Kit. Wow, you look fab. Have you checked out Brandi?"

The fresh, wholesome, all-American and apple-pie face of Elena beamed up at me. "What?" I said, inwardly giving myself a shake. Enough about Tommy. Time to focus on the present.

She grabbed my arm and swung me around. "See? Brandi." She pointed.

My mouth dropped open. "Oh, God."

All hips and scarves, Brandi swayed seductively to a song I didn't recognize, although I suspected it wasn't from the eighties. It looked like some sort of snake dance – actually more of a cross between a snake dance, belly dance and striptease. She had managed to capture the attention of more than a dozen drooling and panting boys, but she had eyes for only one – Chuck.

"What's Violet think of all this?" I asked, as Brandi wrapped one of her scarves around Chuck's neck.

"Well, I'm no psych major, but I don't think she's a happy camper right now. What's your diagnosis?" Elena nodded to the side, her words slightly slurred. Violet stood by herself, eyes glued to the Brandi and Chuck Show. She appeared to be turning as violet as her name.

"Yeah, no happy camper there. That's my official diagnosis anyway."

Brandi blew Chuck a kiss as she swung her hips for the next salivating guy. "She's gonna get him back," Elena said.

"Think so?"

Chuck clapped his hand to his heart and mock staggered back. Brandi tossed her head, one gleaming lock twirled in its own dance, and whirled away.

We looked at each other. "Oh, yeah," we both said at the same time.

Elena noticed my empty hands. "Where's your poison?"

"On my way to refill."

Elena's gray-green eyes widened. "What? You've been reduced to getting your own beer? I don't believe it. Why haven't you snared some unsuspecting guy to fetch it for you?"

"Because they've all been snared by Brandi."

Elena giggled as she swallowed and ended up in a coughing fit. I pounded her helpfully on the back while Gloria Gaynor belted "I Will Survive" out of the speakers, which I knew wasn't from the eighties. Brandi switched to "tough yet sexy girl" and started acting out the beginning of the song for Chuck. I wondered if she had promised the DJ a little something special at the end of the night – these songs seemed a bit too perfect for chance. Not to mention from the wrong decade.

"Come on, I'll get my snared guy to bring you a beer," Elena said when she could talk. "At least I will unless he's fallen under Brandi's spell."

"So far, so good," I said as Brad picked his way through the crowd toward us. "At least for the moment."

Elena gave me a dirty look. Her curly, copper-colored hair had been replaced by a black, straight-haired wig that didn't work at all with her skin tone. She wore a black leotard covered with some sort of silky material, high heels, and a sign that said "Do you believe in life after love?" When she turned to plant a passionate kiss on Brad's lips, I saw the sign that hung on her back. "Gypsies, tramps and thieves."

"Hey, Cher. You look fantastic for being a hundred and fifty years old."

She turned back to me and smirked. "The power of plastic surgery."

"Hey, we leavin' or something? What'd I do to deserve that?" Brad asked.

"Please get Kit a beer. There's someone I have to introduce her to," Elena said.

Inwardly I groaned. Another setup. Exactly what I didn't need.

"Elena," I started to say, but she pounced before I could get another word out.

"He's cute and he's sweet. Perfect for consoling. Although, I haven't figured out exactly why you need to be consoled, but that's a discussion for another day."

"Thanks, I think."

Brad shook his head. "Definitely gone. Don't want to be anywhere near this."

"Just bring Kit back a beer," Elena said.

"Elena, really," I said as the crowd swallowed Brad up. "I think I need a little alone time right now. You know, find myself and all that shit."

Elena snorted. "You? Right. Like I can see you sitting around smoking pot and listening to Nirvana or Pink Floyd and discussing the finer points of the meaning of life."

"Nirvana or Pink Floyd? We're talking two distinctly different drug trips here."

Elena rolled her eyes. "Whatever. Let's go meet David." She took my arm and led me across the room. I thought again about protesting, but then I saw Tommy doing shots with a group of beefy guys and changed my mind. Maybe if I started seeing someone new, he would move on faster. Certainly worth a try.

"Hello, David," Elena cooed, tucking her hand in the arm of a werewolf. "I've brought you a special treat."

"Special treat?" I started to sputter, but then the werewolf turned around and I forgot my ire.

Large turquoise blue eyes, high cheekbones, dark blond hair curling against his forehead and under his collar. I sucked in my breath. At least Elena had the cuteness part right.

He held his hand out. "You must be Kit."

"And you must be David." His hand felt cool and dry. "So, what nasty things has Elena been saying about me?"

"I never," Elena said indignantly.

"Believe me, it was all good." He still held my hand, eyes gazing into mine. I deliberately broke the grasp and leaned closer to him.

"Don't believe a word of it." I smiled my most enigmatic smile.

He grinned back. "So, should I believe the nasty things then?"

I opened my mouth to answer, but something in his eyes stopped me. Maybe it was the angle, or a reflection of the light, but they suddenly looked like monster eyes – cruel and calculating, gleaming at me with a kind of hunger.

There's danger here, lurking in the shadows. It hasn't seen you yet, but it will. Tonight. It will seize you in its jaws and never let you go.

The room went eerily silent, exactly the way it had right after the fairy disappeared. My blood froze, my breathing stopped. My lungs felt like a huge icy hand was clutching them, squeezing the life out. Panic was like icicles exploding inside me, frozen particles imbedding themselves in my internal organs.

Never let you go.

"Kit, are you okay?"

I blinked. The room swayed, came back into focus, smelling of sweat and smoke, sounding of laughter, voices and Michael Jackson. Normal. Completely normal. For the second time that night, I felt as if

I had fallen into Lewis Carroll's LSD-induced nightmare misleadingly named "Wonderland."

David was staring at me with more than a hint of concern. My breathing hitched in my chest and I coughed. "I'm fine." I dug into my purse for my inhaler. "Just a little asthma attack, that's all."

What was going on with me? Why would I have imagined David a monster?

Why would I have imagined seeing my sister again, tonight of all nights?

And why would she be warning me against some undefined danger?

Alcoholic hallucination. That was the explanation. My breathing returned to normal and my insides thawed out. Alcoholic hallucination. Nothing else.

I put back my inhaler and smiled. "So, now what were you asking me?"

Chapter 4

I awoke the next morning with a horrible headache and a sick feeling in my stomach that I regrettably couldn't attribute only to alcohol. Pain is good, I thought as I often did when something hurt. Pain lets me know I'm alive. Sometimes that chant worked. It didn't today.

I rolled out of bed. My mouth tasted like something had crawled inside it and died during the night. At least I had remembered to turn on my humidifiers before tumbling into bed.

Unfortunately, I hadn't managed to get myself drunk enough to forget. Much to my dismay, I remembered every gory detail. Disgusting. If I had to suffer from alcoholic hallucinations, at the very least those hallucinations should have the decency to be forgotten by the next morning.

Never let you go.

I shook my head, changed into sweats, pulled my hair back in a ponytail and did my exercises. Then I turned on my computer and checked my email. A couple of jokes, a new petition, nothing urgent. I sighed, rubbed my face and turned off my computer. Time to face the world.

Brandi was sitting at the white Formica kitchen table drinking coffee and flipping through a textbook. She had twisted her hair into a loose knot at her neck. A couple of strands fell across her pale and drawn face. "Sleeping Beauty arises." She blew a lock away. "Or, did you have a prince in there to keep you company?"

I opened up a dark brown cupboard and took out a blue glass. "No prince, charming or otherwise."

"So Mr. New Wonderful struck out, huh?"

I busied myself at the sink, reluctant to tell Brandi the truth. Although David had walked me home, I didn't kiss him goodnight. That creepy moment at the party had stuck with me, even though I knew it was all in my head. I just couldn't see letting him touch me.

"Not necessarily." I turned to lean my back against the sink.

Brandi cocked her head, her eyes sharp and penetrating. "He just isn't Tommy, is he?"

"What's that supposed to mean?"

Brandi tapped her pen on the table. "Well, let's think about this for a moment. Tommy's gorgeous, smart, funny, obviously head over heels in love with you and, oh yeah, did I forget to mention star quarterback of our winning football team? Yeah, he's no keeper, is he? I'd definitely choose David over him."

"Why are you so fixated on this breakup? Last year alone he must have gone through all of Kappa Kappa Gamma's sorority sisters. I'm surprised he hasn't gotten around to sleeping with you. What's the big deal if I break up with him? He won't be lonely for long."

Brandi slammed her hand on the table. "That's exactly why. Because he's never gotten serious with someone, and when he finally does – you – you throw him back. Why? It doesn't make any sense. And don't give me this bullshit about needing different things. Anyone with half a brain can see you're just as crazy about him."

I took a long drink of water, trying to think of an answer she would accept. Of all people to live with, why did I choose someone obsessed with finding a husband? "I'm just not sure what I want," I said. "I was feeling uncomfortable in the situation and needed some space. That's the truth."

Brandi eyed me, clearly not believing me but not pursuing it either. Instead she went back to flipping the pages of her textbook.

I decided to change the subject. "As official dancing queen of the night, I'm surprised you didn't come home soaked with drool from those poor mesmerized boys."

She shook her head in disgust. "I don't want to talk about it."

I walked across the faded yellow linoleum floor and sat down at the table. "Didn't go so hot with Chuck, huh?"

She savagely ran her fingers through her hair, releasing the smell of perfume trapped in its thick folds. "I had him right where I wanted. It was perfect, even better than I expected. Then she throws a fit and he goes running off to comfort her." She yanked at the ends of her hair. "What did she do to get that kind of hold over him?"

"Probably some disgusting, perverted act."

She half-smiled. "Not Chuck. He's not interested in disgusting, perverted acts. Believe me, I tried."

"Ah, so it's the Catholic school girl he wants. Maybe she has a kick-ass costume."

"Yeah, and she's probably a prude to match." Brandi sighed. "Oh, David sent you roses. They're in the living room."

"David?" I stood up. "How did you know David sent them to me? Did you open the card?"

"Of course I did. Duh. How did you think I knew who you were talking to last night? I thought maybe the florist had the name wrong."

The flowers stood on the coffee table. How could I have missed seeing them this morning? A dozen yellow roses in a vase, just beginning to bloom. I picked up the card. "Dinner tonight?" Signed with his name and phone number. How sweet. No trace of creepiness here.

"Oh, did I mention he wants to have dinner tonight?" Brandi's voice floated from the kitchen.

"No, but I figured it out."

"Are you going to say yes?"

"Haven't decided."

"Well, he *is* cute."

"Thanks for the high approval rating." I went back into the kitchen.

"In case you hadn't figured it out, I'm trying to be a supportive roommate here. You could give me something better to work with."

"Oh, sorry. Forgot to memorize my lines this morning." I plucked my glass from the table and went to refill it. Now that I was up and moving, I was beginning to feel more like a person and less like two-week old leftovers. "By the way, last night at the party, did you happen to see someone dressed as a fairy?"

"A fairy? And he didn't get beat up?"

I sighed. "Good God. Why's that the first thing people think of? I meant a woman dressed in a real fairy costume. Pink dress, wings, the whole bit."

Brandi frowned. "No. Not that I recall. Why?"

I shrugged, moving back to the table to sit down. "Just wondering who she was. We talked a bit last night, but I don't remember seeing her around before."

"And you didn't think to ask her her name while you were talking?"

I studied my water glass. Maybe I shouldn't have started this conversation in the first place. Had I ever told Brandi my sister's name?

Had I ever told her I even had a sister? "Her first name is Cat, but I don't know her last name."

I risked a look at Brandi from under my lashes. Brandi's face registered no recognition. Thank God.

"Sooo ... what? You throw up on that pink dress and now you're feeling guilty about it?"

"Something like that."

Brandi twisted a strand of hair around her finger. "Right. Whatever. By the way, remember I have to go home this weekend."

"Funds running low?"

Brandi looked indignant. "And Ellen is being very unsympathetic to my plight. She won't even put me on the phone with Daddy."

Brandi always referred to her mother by her first name. Needless to say, nobody would ever nominate them for the mother/daughter relationship of the year. Brandi was fond of saying that she knew her mother loved her because she had named Brandi after her most affectionate and enduring relationship.

"So, you'll take care of Jezzy for me, right?"

I hated it when she asked me that. What if something happened to me and I ended up in the hospital? What would I do about Jezzy? "Just as long as I'm around." I kept my voice light.

She rolled her eyes. "I know, I know. Just as long as you aren't hit by a bus or have an aneurysm or get smacked in the eye from a ruler thrown by some disgruntled professor."

"Hey, my one lit professor got so agitated once he spilled coffee all over himself."

"And everyone knows that spilling coffee is just the first step down that slippery slope of flying rulers." Brandi sauntered across the kitchen to refill her coffee cup. Even hung over, she still moved with her trademark slinky, sensual grace.

"We all have our little quirks. Mine is I don't like making plans more than a day in advance because you never know what might happen. You can always ask Martha to take care of Jezzy."

"Martha? Hello. I'm not sure Martha's figured out there's a cat in this house much less take care of her."

As if on cue Jezzy, short for Jezebel, appeared at the door and meowed. A beautiful cat, striped with shades of gray with huge blue eyes,

Jezzy's moods swung from loving when she got her way to annoying when she didn't. Like owner, like pet.

"See, even she's saying she doesn't want Martha to take care of her." Brandi stirred fat-free cream into her coffee while the cat curled up on my lap.

"Oh, is that what she said?"

"So, you going to take care of her or what?"

Jezzy regarded me with her unblinking stare. "I told you, just as long as I'm around."

Brandi shook her head. "I must be the only person on this campus who has not one, but two roommates, yet still has to consider getting a cat sitter to go away for a friggin' weekend."

The front door slammed shut, accompanied by Martha's trademark muttering. Jezzy leaped off my lap and streaked out of the room. Brandi mouthed "I told you so."

The front door opened onto a small landing with stairs leading both up and down. Normally when Martha came in, we would hear her stomping down the steps that led to her bedroom. Instead today, we heard her heavy footsteps trudge up the stairs and across the living room, her feet making this odd clumping noise. One good thing about Martha – we never had to worry about her sneaking up on us.

She appeared in the doorway, arms full of books. Martha spent her life studying. She wanted to be either a history or a philosophy professor. Brandi and I couldn't figure out which one she muttered the day we met her. Come to think of it, half the time we couldn't tell if Martha was muttering to us or to some inanimate object in the room.

Today she seemed to be giving us her complete attention. Nodding, she hoisted the books on the kitchen counter.

"Cold." She rubbed her hands together. Her chapped red nose had started to run and she reached for a tissue.

"Yes, it does tend to get a bit chilly in November," Brandi said.

"Can't believe it's November already. So behind in everything. I have three papers due and another midterm and a project and then finals. D'you mind if I have some coffee?"

Brandi moved away from the coffee maker. "Be my guest."

Martha marched to the cupboard, feet clumping all the while. Unlike Brandi, her movements were jerky and unsure, as if she had just gone through a growth spurt and didn't know the limits of her body. Her lank brown hair hung limply against her pale and unremarkable face. It wouldn't take much to turn Martha from plain into pretty, but either she didn't know she could be more attractive or she didn't care.

On second thought, maybe pretty was overstating it.

"Nice roses," Martha said, after swallowing half her cup. "Think I'm allergic though."

"To roses?" I asked.

Martha sniffed. "Something's got me all stuffed up."

"Maybe you're allergic to the cold," Brandi said.

Martha shook her head. "No, something in the apartment's been bugging me. Been like this a few days."

"I'll put them in my room." I stood up.

"Won't matter if they're in your room if I'm allergic."

"I'll keep the door shut." I ducked out before I could hear her explanation of airflow in apartments.

When I returned, Martha and her books had disappeared, leaving Brandi alone with her coffee and disgusted expression.

"When do we get to vote her off the island?" Brandi flicked her hair out of her face, one hip leaning against the counter. Faint strains of Jane's Addiction floated up the stairs.

I helped myself to coffee. "Maybe she really is allergic. Maybe it's Jezzy."

Brandi shot me a sharp look, eyes filled with daggers. "Don't even go there. Don't you dare put that thought into her head."

"Oh, and we should ignore the possibility that one day she may actually notice the litter box."

Brandi banged her mug on the counter and crossed her arms. "Cats eat moles."

I put the coffee pot down and faced her. "Yeah, but this mole pays rent."

Brandi pursed her lips, picked up her coffee and flounced out of the room. "She may pay rent," she called over her shoulder, "but I'll bet even if this cat went away, the mole wouldn't play."

She did have a point.

Chapter 5

I ended up going to dinner with David on Saturday. I needed another day to recuperate and get some perspective on Halloween. He offered to pick me up, but I told him I'd meet him there.

When I arrived at the Indian restaurant – his choice – David was already seated and had ordered a bottle of wine. I slid into the chair across from him. The smell of curry and exotic dishes permeated the air. The one-room restaurant was simply and elegantly decorated with dark gray carpet, black chairs, crisp white tablecloths and delicate candles.

"Wow, a whole bottle of wine," I said. "Usually I'm lucky if I get a bottle of beer."

He smiled and poured me a glass. "I find that hard to believe." If anything, he looked better than he had the night of the party. He wore a maroon and black sweater, which brought out the blue in his turquoise eyes, and his dark blond hair curled around the collar of his sweater. With a sharp pang, I thought of Tommy and how good he looked in red. I swallowed the lump in my throat with a sip of wine. Chardonnay. Not my favorite, but as long as it had alcohol in it, it would do.

His eyes followed my every move. "You look very beautiful tonight," he said.

Beautiful? I tried not to make a face. Cute I could buy, or pretty, or sexy, but not beautiful. Besides, he said it the way my father would. "Thanks. You look pretty good yourself."

He smiled again and sat up straighter. "I took the liberty of ordering seekh kebab for an appetizer. It should be here any minute."

First he ordered wine without consulting me, then an appetizer. What century did this guy come from? "Did you order my dinner as well?"

He stared at me for a second, before dropping his eyes to his plate. "I didn't think you'd mind. I was trying to make the evening special. I figured you're the kind of girl who'd be used to guys treating you special."

He looked so hurt, so crestfallen, I instantly regretted my words. "I didn't mean anything by it," I stammered out. "I guess I'm just used to taking a more active role in relationships. You know, women's lib, feminism, all that. It sort of changed things like relationships."

The appetizer, lamb and vegetables on skewers, arrived before he could answer. "It looks good," I said, taking a skewer, ignoring the fact that lamb wasn't my favorite. He finally met my eyes and smiled a little. I took that as a good sign.

While he served himself, I dug into my purse for my pills. "Just digestive enzymes," I said, as I always did when eating with someone new. But he was staring at me with this strange, almost frozen look of shock.

"What? You've never seen a girl take pills before?" I said, attempting to lighten the mood. He had such an intense, odd look in his eyes, it was starting to frighten me.

He swallowed hard. "You have Cystic Fibrosis, don't you?"

I dropped my pill container on the table. Digestive enzymes flew everywhere, bouncing on the table, the chair, the floor. "What? How did … "

"I know?" he finished my sentence. "Do you?"

I started retrieving my pills, my hands shaking so much I could barely pick them up. "Yes, I do. But how did you guess? My roommates haven't even figured it out."

He knelt down on the floor to help me. "My sister died from Cystic Fibrosis. She was four."

"Oh, my God, I'm so sorry," I stammered. I had never met anyone outside of those god-awful support groups who had lost someone to Cystic Fibrosis. And to lose a sister? Before I could stop myself, I heard myself saying, "I lost my sister, too. But not to Cystic Fibrosis. She was kidnapped when I was seven."

He had been picking up my enzymes, but now he became very still. "Really? Kidnapped at seven. Did she have Cystic Fibrosis as well?"

I shook my head. "No. She was the picture of health. Golden curls, big blue eyes. She was perfect."

Something flashed across his face, some unreadable, peculiar expression. It disappeared so fast I wondered if I had imagined it. All I could there now was deep sympathy.

"I'm sorry. I know first-hand how horrible it is to lose a sister."

"Yeah."

David reached over and put his hand over mine, gently squeezing. We were quiet for a moment. Then he straightened, rising to his feet and sitting back down. "I don't mean to pry, but do you know what happened to her?"

I shrugged. "No, not really. My parents never talked about it. But I keep having dreams that she was kidnapped by the fairies." I laughed a little self-consciously. For the second time in two days, I was telling people I barely knew secrets I didn't even acknowledge to myself. I wondered what that meant.

David looked puzzled. "Fairies? What a fanciful notion."

"Yeah, I'm not sure where it came from either."

"What kind of fairies, do you know?"

"Just your garden-variety fairies. My father is pulling her in a wagon through a field, and the fairies come out and, well, take her."

"You saw this?"

"No, no. It's in my dream."

He nodded, sipping his wine. I swallowed my pills. Across the room a guy wearing an oversized red plaid shirt was arguing fiercely with the man across from him, jabbing his finger repeatedly into the table.

"But," I said, folding and unfolding my napkin, "what I really want to know is how you guessed I had Cystic Fibrosis. I mean, I know about your sister and all, but … " I trailed off.

He busied himself with the skewer on his plate. "It's okay. I know what you were going to say and it's okay to say it. My sister died as a child and you, well, didn't. So, how would I know what to look for in an adult?"

The guy with the plaid shirt became more and more agitated, his face turning the same red as his shirt. "Yeah, something like that."

"After she died, I did some research on it, learned as much as I could. I don't know what keyed me off to you - maybe it was the combination of asthma attack and taking those enzymes, plus your thinness. But something just clicked in my mind."

I tapped my fork against the table. "So, how much do you know then?"

He looked at me sideways. "I know that sixty percent of people with Cystic Fibrosis die before they're twenty-five."

I shifted in my seat, unable to meet his eyes. "So, you've kept up with the research."

David leaned forward, his hand caressing mine, his touch light, gentle. "That means forty percent live past twenty-five."

I reached for my wine, swirling the gold liquid around the glass. "I've never had the best luck. Never came out ahead at betting games, never won the lottery. The odds have usually beaten me."

He continued to study me, his eyes intent, the blue in them deepening. "You've outlived my sister."

I swallowed most of my wine at once. "Sorry. I didn't mean … "

He grasped my hand. "It's okay. I didn't say it to make you sorry. I said it so you'd know that you are lucky. I mean, look at you. You look pretty healthy to me. There's every chance in the world you're going to beat this thing."

His hand was warm, the pressure soothing. "But anything could take me out. A bad cold or flu could turn into an infection like that." I snapped my fingers. "The infection could become bronchitis or pneumonia and that would be that."

"Or, you could continue to take good care of yourself and outlive all of us."

I raised my eyes to his. He smiled slightly and reached over to push the hair out of my face. The waitress appeared at our table, pad in hand. He released me and sat back. "Do you know what you want or do you need a minute?"

My mind was spinning like the tornado that had dropped Dorothy off in Oz. The guy in the red plaid shirt shoved his chair back so violently it flipped over, smashing into the man next to him. That man then leaped to his feet and started yelling. While the waitress turned to deal with this new situation, I smiled at David.

"Why don't you order for both of us?"

***

After dinner, I invited him back to my apartment. I had all these strange emotions coursing inside me – shaken by his revelations, yet also intrigued by this new bond. He lost his sister as a child, he understood my disease – these things made me feel connected to him in ways I was just beginning to grasp.

I offered him a beer, and turned on the television. With Brandi at her parents and Martha's room as silent as an abandoned cave, I hoped we would have some privacy.

As it turned out, we didn't need any. He acted like a perfect gentleman, both entertaining and interested. We talked about our majors – he was a grad student in computer science – current events and other relationships. I was vague about Tommy, only sharing that I recently broke up with someone. He didn't press it.

I couldn't help comparing it to my first date with Tommy, where we couldn't wait to get to his apartment and tear each other's clothes off. Well, to be honest it wasn't really a date. We were at a party and discovered that, for the first time since we met four years ago, neither one of us was seeing someone else. There had always been an intense sexual chemistry between us, held in check only because one or the other had some sort of relationship going on at the time. When we finally acted on it, the results were explosive – no pun intended.

When David decided to leave, I accompanied him to the door. He brushed his finger down my cheek "I had a really good time tonight."

"So did I."

"Does that mean I can see you again?"

"What do you think?"

He smiled and bent to kiss me lightly on the mouth. He had an interesting smell to him – a sort of dark combination of salt and spice. Not unpleasant, just different. Unique. Intriguing.

I looked into his eyes, now more green than blue, and blurted out, "You know, the reason why I was so surprised that you knew about my Cystic Fibrosis is because no one knows."

He looked surprised. "No one? Not even your roommates?"

"No." I studied the floor, the dull beige linoleum looking cheap and dirty, feeling more and more uncomfortable. I trusted him, yet I still felt like I needed to say this. "And actually, they don't know about my sister either." I took a deep breath and raised my eyes to his. "I don't like to talk about my past or my problems. So please keep it to yourself, okay?"

For a moment he didn't say anything. Then he pressed his hand to his heart. "Thank you for your trust. You don't know what that means to me. And, yes, your secret is safe with me."

"Thank you," I breathed. I took his hand and squeezed it. "Thank you."

He kissed me gently again, and opened the door. "I'll call you."

I nodded. He started to step outside, but I reached out and put my hand on his chest.

"You know all my secrets," I said. "And I just realized you've never told me your last name."

He hesitated. The light was behind him, turning his eyes into dark pools of shadows.

"Naughton," he said. "David Naughton."

I smiled. "Pleased to meet you, David Naughton."

He smiled back, caressed my cheek, then turned and disappeared into the night.

I shut the door behind him and leaned against it. The wood cooled my flushed face. I was jittery and exhausted at the same time, like the night I had consumed five triple lattes cramming for finals. I knew I wouldn't be able to sleep, so I went back to the kitchen for another beer. I settled myself on the brown plaid couch and watched old reruns of *Seinfeld*.

I wondered why he didn't try to do more than kiss me. After all, we had that bond. Or at least I thought we did. He must have felt it too. The evening, however, was so chaste, almost like being with a brother. With a bond like that, wouldn't we be drawn to sleep together? Yet he didn't even try.

After a couple of beers, I started drifting off, so I moved to the bedroom and collapsed on the bed. When sleep finally came, I ended up slipping into the church dream. But something had changed. There were people in the graveyard. People grouped around a grave. And something else. Something black and evil standing within the group. Something waiting for me with hungry eyes and gnashing teeth …

I gasped for breath, my terror a living thing in my chest, blocking my breathing as much as the mucus in my lungs.

I awoke, thrashing uncontrollably, coughing and choking, before my flailing arms seized upon my inhaler. I sucked on it, my coughing quieting and my breathing returning to normal.

My dreams have never altered. Not once. Ever. So why now?

My entire body dripped with sweat. I fished around for a clean tee shirt and stumbled into the bathroom.

It wasn't until I had calmed down, a cool washcloth pressed against my burning face, that I realized what had truly petrified me about the dream. It was completely irrational and unexplainable, but even thinking about it with all the bathroom lights on made my breath freeze in my throat, nearly causing another attack.

Mixed in with the ringing of the church bell, so subtle I almost missed it, was the distinctive, unmistakable howling of a wolf.

Chapter 6

"Hey, Kit. Looking for a study partner?"

I was sitting at a table in the student Union, hoping popcorn and a Coke would make reading my lit book less painful. So far, the results had been disappointing.

Studying was difficult for me under the best of circumstances – I could never shake the feeling of it being a colossal waste of time. Chances were high that I would never have the opportunity to use the knowledge I gleaned in these hallowed halls. But it beat being stuck in a nine-to-five I detested.

I looked up to see Tommy gazing at me, smiling his easy-going grin. Inwardly I groaned. I didn't need this today.

"I don't think so," I said, as he shrugged off his backpack and plopped his books down on the table. Around us I could see people glancing up from their studies or conversation to stare at him. Even without his football jersey, everyone knew him. It didn't hurt that he was cuter than hell.

"Why not? We used to study together." He dragged a chair over and sat next to me, so close I could smell his Irish Spring soap even against the backdrop of hamburgers, burritos, beer and smoke. The background music morphed into yet another U2 song.

"We used to do a lot of things together, but now we don't. That's what breaking up means."

"We could get back together. Then we could start doing all those things together again. I wouldn't object to that."

I sighed. I was tired and behind in my classes. After the church nightmare, I couldn't fall back asleep and ended up watching bad movies and paging through my books for hours. Needless to say, nothing much got done.

"Tommy, I have a lot of studying to do, so if you wouldn't mind … " I made a shooing gesture with my hands.

He sprawled out in his chair. "I thought you said you wanted to be friends."

"I did."

"And don't friends study together?"

I shot him a disgusted look. "That's not the point."

"You study with Elena a lot. She's your friend. You study with Brandi. Well, actually I don't know if I've ever seen Brandi study, but I'm sure you would if she did."

"Fine. Point made. Stay. Just be quiet so I can get something done."

He flashed his grin again and retrieved his books from his backpack. I shook my head and opened mine.

Unfortunately, I couldn't concentrate. He was making me absolutely crazy. I kept darting glances at him from beneath my lashes. Elbow on the table, he had propped his head up with his hand, blond hair falling forward. He wore a loose-fitting dark blue shirt that emphasized his broad shoulders and lean, muscular figure. Occasionally he would chew on his pen, a habit I found disgusting. I finally couldn't stand it anymore and reached over to shove his pen up his mouth. He almost choked.

"I thought you said you wanted to study," he said when he could talk.

"You know how much I hate that."

"In case you haven't heard, we aren't dating anymore. I have no reason to impress you."

"Fine." I held my book over my face to show how little I cared. When I glanced at him again, he was back to chewing the pen. Pretty deliberately, I thought.

I turned my attention to my novel, *Clarissa* by Samuel Richardson. Unfortunately, this thousand-page monstrosity of a book was failing to capture my interest no matter when or where I read it. I should have taken eighteenth century poetry instead – the readings would have been shorter.

"So, how was your date last night?"

I lowered my book. The music switched to Pink Floyd. Tommy was gazing intently at his textbook. "Excuse me?"

"Date. How was it?"

"How did you know I had a date last night?"

Now he turned toward me. "Oh, come on, Kit. Everyone walking by on State Street could see you. That Indian restaurant has a huge picture window."

"You saw me?"

"What does that have to do with anything? I was just asking how your date went."

I picked up *Clarissa*. "Fine. Just fine." A girl sitting at the next table was eying us. Eying Tommy, actually. Her long blonde hair shimmered. Probably colored it.

"Good." I could hear him tapping his chewed-up pen on the table. "Want to tell me about it?"

"Why would I want to tell you about it?" I said from behind the book.

"Because that's what friends do. They talk about things like dates."

"I don't think you care at all about the date."

"You don't?"

"No." I closed *Clarissa* with a snap. "I think you just want to know if I screwed him or not."

He gazed into my eyes. "Well. Did you?"

I thought about lying. Maybe he would leave me alone then. But something in his expression stopped me. I looked down. "No."

"Did he try anything?"

"Jesus, Tommy. It was a date, that's it. No more, no less. Do you really want a play-by-play of the evening?"

"Since you brought it up, sure."

The blonde shifted her chair closer to us. Better to listen in. "Sorry. Forgot my television crew. You're going to have to settle for the TV guide summary: we had a nice time."

"And you didn't sleep together."

I started putting my books away. The blonde kept darting glances at Tommy. Cute and perky. I hated her. "And we didn't sleep together. Happy? Now, if you'll excuse me, I need to go find an unoccupied corner so I can actually get something done."

He leaned his arm against the back of the chair. "Ah, running away. You've certainly perfected that move."

I froze, one hand on my notebook. "What the hell is that supposed to mean?"

He shrugged. "Just that every time anything comes up that makes you uncomfortable, you split."

I renewed my efforts, shoving my books into my backpack. "You don't know anything."

He reached over and snatched my arm. "Is that why you broke up with me with nothing but that lame-ass explanation? Because I was getting too close to something?"

I snatched my arm away. Now other people, not just the blonde, noticed our arguing. The blonde had a small smile on her face. I wanted to scratch it off. "You're a fine one to talk. You've never told me anything either."

Now it was his turn to freeze. "I don't know what you're talking about."

"Oh, so it must be my imagination that I only know two things about you – you're rich and you're from Louisiana. Oh, maybe three if I can count inferring you played football in high school."

His face closed, hardened. I had seen that expression often enough before, when other people mentioned his past. Until this moment, we had never discussed it. I had always respected his reluctance to talk as he had mine. "I don't talk about that because there's nothing to tell. Very boring story."

People were openly staring at us now. I half stood up, leaning over my chair to look into his face. "Newsflash: I don't talk about anything either because there's nothing to tell. Very boring story."

He half stood as well. "Is that why you broke up with me? Because I wouldn't tell you about my past?"

"Goodbye, Tommy." I pushed away from the table and strode off. The blonde watched me go. I shot her my dirtiest look. She smiled sweetly in return. Bitch.

I was trying to block out the picture of the two of them together when Tommy grabbed my arm.

"Kit, I didn't want to fight. Really. Can you stop for a second?"

I didn't want to stop. I didn't want to talk. I especially didn't want to look at him anymore. But somehow I found myself turning to face him. "What do you want?"

He released his grip on me and took a step backwards, jamming his hands into his pockets. "I want to be friends. Truly. I miss talking to you, Kit. We always had such a good time together. I miss that."

He looked so sincere, so forlorn, my resolve began to melt away. "Is that all you miss?"

He raised his eyebrows. "What do you think? Seriously though, even though we aren't dating, I'd like to be friends."

I shifted my backpack to the other shoulder. "I said I'd like that too and I meant it. Okay?"

He backed away another step and flashed me that grin. "Okay. See you around?"

I nodded and walked away. I didn't believe a word he said. He didn't want to just be friends. But Tommy was the Charm King. And against my better judgment, I had given him leverage, right back into my life.

Cold air hit me like a wall as I pushed open the doors and stepped outside. Damn Tommy. Like I would be able to get anything done now. Maybe I should just go home and go to bed early and leave the trials and tribulations of Miss Clarissa for another day.

Chapter 7

Stepping into my apartment, I had the distinct impression I had accidentally walked into a flower shop.

Mondays and Wednesdays were my longest class days. Today had felt even longer since I had spent most of it mulling over Tommy and David. Although Tommy and I did have things in common, it was the superficial stuff – books, music, that sort of thing – whereas David and I shared a bond more difficult to find – two people who understood what it was like to live with a terminal illness. However, while I found David attractive, we didn't have the chemistry Tommy and I had.

But sex isn't everything. Everyone says you shouldn't base a relationship on sex. So I should probably focus on David because we had more of the important things in common. Right?

And would Tommy, could Tommy, even comprehend what it even means to have Cystic Fibrosis? What it means to make a commitment to someone with CF? Wasn't that too much to ask of someone unfamiliar with the disease? David already knew what to expect. Wouldn't I be better off with him, in the long run?

I had been going around and around like this most of the day, and instead of finding answers, all I found was a nasty headache. Then I walk into my home and find it transformed into a flower garden.

"Kit, get your butt up here. You aren't going to believe this."

Brandi's voice floated down to me, obviously back from her parents.

Roses. That's what greeted me when I finally made it up the stairs. They were everywhere, along with their rich, moist, distinctive scent.

"Brandi, who's sending you flowers?" I asked, examining the red, yellow and pink blossoms.

Brandi smirked and winked at me. She still wore her sucking-up-to-Daddy outfit, navy blue dress, pearls, hair pulled back in a French twist. "Not me. You. What did you do with David while I was gone?"

I stood in the middle of the living room, surrounded by roses, my mouth dropping open. "David? David sent these to me?"

"Unless you got back together with Tommy and didn't tell me. Yes, I'm pretty sure they're from David."

"Oh, so you didn't read the card."

"Honey, this is one card I thought I better not read."

An uneasy sensation snaked its way inside me. Something wasn't right here.

"Aren't you going to look at it?" Brandi waved the card at me with a flourish.

I took it from her, but didn't open it. That uneasy sensation slithered, sending out tendrils throughout my body, squeezing my insides until I thought I might burst. I circled the room again. What wasn't right here?

"Kit? What's with you?"

"Brandi," I said, my voice taking on this dreamy quality. "How many roses do you think he sent me?"

Brandi glanced around. "Well, there's five dozen here and what looks like a half-dozen. How weird? I wonder if the florist ran out of flowers."

Five and a half dozen roses. The uneasiness froze inside me, the tendrils breaking into thousands of crystals. Suddenly I knew exactly what was wrong. I tore open the card.

"Sixty-six roses. What a strange number. What do you think it means?"

I stared at the card, my fingers like ice. "Not sixty-six. Sixty-five." I said before I could stop myself.

Brandi came over and looked over my shoulders. "'Sixty-five roses just for you.' How sweet, I think. Did you guys do it sixty-five times or something?"

"I didn't sleep with him." I lowered my hands before Brandi could see them shake.

Brandi laughed. "Yeah, right. And I'm going to be taking a cruise in a great big boat with Leonardo DiCaprio."

My hands curled into fists, squeezing the card into pulp. "Brandi, I'm not kidding. I did *not* sleep with him." My voice sounded louder and harsher than I wanted it to.

Brandi gave me an odd look. "If you say so."

I took a deep breath. "Yeah, I do. I'm sorry. This is just so weird."

Brandi nodded and glanced around again. "Well, maybe this is an extreme reaction to playing hard to get."

I let my breath out. "Probably."

Brandi caressed one of the pink petals. "If this is what you get when you play hard to get, maybe I should give it a try. Think Chuck would go for it?"

The front door slammed shut before I could answer. Brandi rolled her eyes. Martha's heavy footsteps clumped up the stairs.

"Roses," she said, and immediately sneezed. "See, what'd I tell you?"

"Martha, I refuse to accept this rose-allergy thing you have going on," Brandi said. "It's the cold. Or maybe a little green-eyed monster is paying you a visit."

"Brandi," I warned.

"You think I'm jealous?" Martha asked, her voice starting to rise. "Not likely."

"I'll throw out the roses," I interrupted before Brandi could continue the argument.

"What?" Brandi gasped, spinning toward me.

"Look, Martha's obviously suffering, and I'll just get rid of them. See? Simple solution." I put my bag down and started gathering them up.

Martha looked relieved. "That'd help."

Brandi clutched my arm, pink manicured nails digging into my green sweater. "You can't be serious. You can't throw out all these roses just because Martha here is claiming to have some ridiculous allergy. He just sent them."

"It's not a big deal. Don't worry about it."

"If you don't want them, I'll put them in my room."

"Won't get rid of the allergy." Martha sneezed again. Brandi glared at her.

"See? Can't put them in a room. Nothing more to do except get rid of them." I swiveled my head toward Brandi so Martha couldn't see and mouthed "Tell you later." I had no idea what I was going to tell her later, but it bought me time to think of something.

Brandi shrugged. "Fine. Be a rose-killer for all I care. I'm going to go change."

"Actually," Martha called out. "Those roses are already dead. They were dead when the florist cut them."

"Whatever." Brandi flounced out of the room.

Martha half-smiled at me. "Need help?"

"No, I can take care of this. You go take some allergy medicine so you'll feel better."

"Okay." Martha clumped down the stairs.

It took me two trips, but I threw them all out, vases and all, even the one from two days ago. I wanted no reminders anywhere.

I couldn't believe he had done something so crass, especially with what we had shared the other night. I felt so stupid – here, I had been thinking about this bond and feeling close to him, and all he wanted to do was throw it into my face.

Well, we would see about that.

He had told me which apartment building he lived in the other night – the tall red and white brick one near the corner of North Main Street. I didn't know the actual apartment number, but figured I could find it once I was there, even if it meant banging on every door in the building.

As it turned out, that wasn't necessary. The apartment had a directory, and I easily found David's name stuck on with a little piece of tape. A man with a tangled and untidy beard happened to be leaving right when I arrived, so I managed to slip through the security door.

David lived on the fifth floor, apartment 5D. I ran up the stairs that stank of urine, stale pizza and pot. I was too agitated to wait for the elevator, but I ran too fast and ended up having a coughing fit. I wasted several minutes getting my coughing under control before heading for the apartment.

It took several minutes of pounding before he appeared. "Kit, how nice to see you." He wore a dark blue sweater and jeans, and looked cool and collected. I was so angry I could only stand there, glaring and shaking.

David's face took on an expression of concern. "What's wrong? Did something happen?"

"Can I come in?" I managed through gritted teeth. I didn't want to do this in the hall. He held the door open and I pushed my way through.

"Kit, what's going on?" He shut the door.

I whirled around. "Why the hell did you send me sixty-five roses?"

He looked surprised. "Because I wanted you to know what a good time I had the other night."

I started shaking my head. "Bullshit. If that's what you wanted, you would've sent me a dozen, like before. No, you sent me sixty-five roses because you knew that was the fund-raising campaign for Cystic Fibrosis. 'Sixty-five roses, Cystic Fibrosis.' Some kid thought that's what the doctor was saying when he told him he had Cystic Fibrosis, and they named the whole damn fund-raising campaign after that. You knew that."

He scratched his head. "Can we sit down and talk about this? I didn't mean … "

I flung my hands in the air. "You didn't mean what? To tip my roommates off? I told you nobody knew but you. I asked you to keep it a secret. I thought we had a connection here, something built on shared experiences and trust. And you betrayed it! I told you my roommates were from wealthy families. I'm sure they received letters from the Cystic Fibrosis foundation, asking for donations. How could you be so sure they wouldn't figure it out?"

He came toward me. "Kit, look, I'm sorry. I wasn't trying to tip your roommates off. Honest, it never occurred to me that anyone but you and I would know what that meant. I just wanted to let you know that I, too, felt that same bond, and that it didn't bother me that you had Cystic Fibrosis. I thought it'd be kind of a code between us, you know? So you knew I didn't care about it."

I backed away before he could touch me. "If that's really what you were trying to do, it was a very bad idea. Someone could have figured it out." But my voice had started lowering, the anger draining. The way he explained it, it did make a certain amount of sense.

His voice had become soft, caressing. "I can see now that it was a bad idea. And I'm truly sorry about that. I just wanted you to know how special I think you are. That's all."

I glanced away. His living room was small but immaculate. Nothing like any other guy's apartment I had been in. But it seemed almost sterile. No posters or photos or CDs scattered around. A small pile of books sat on the coffee table next to a neat stack of mail – the only indication anyone lived here.

The fury inside me had dissolved, leaving a sort of uneasy ache. I felt empty and exhausted. I turned back to David, catching a whiff of that odd, salty spice scent of his. "Okay. I accept your apology. I better go, I have a lot of studying to do."

He shifted to the side, blocking my path to the door. "Look, I'd like to make it up to you. Can I take you to dinner? We can study afterward."

All I wanted to do was get away from him. "No, I can't. I have to attend a couple of meetings tonight, and before I do that I need to get a few things done as well as study," I lied. "Raincheck?"

He continued to block my path. "Tomorrow then? I really want to make it up to you."

I saw that I wasn't getting out of his apartment unless I agreed to something, and I was too tired, too confused, to fight him anymore. "Okay. Tomorrow."

He smiled, wide and bright and full of teeth. "Great, I'll see you then." He went to the door and held it open for me, giving me a quick kiss on the cheek as I went by. I think he may have wanted more but didn't want to press his luck.

The door shut behind me with a firm click. As I slunk down the hall, I started to wonder what the hell I had gotten myself into.

Chapter 8

"So, how was your date with the Sugar Daddy last night?" Brandi asked, standing by the counter, examining her pale pink nails and pouring coffee at the same time. She had small elegant hands, and the perfect oval of her nails made her fingers appear even more graceful.

"Fine." I pushed my toast spread with both butter and peanut butter around my plate. Jezzy watched me intently from her perch in the chair next to me.

I wasn't in the best mood this morning. Haunted by the metamorphosed church dream, I hadn't slept well. I was already tired and still had my long day of classes in front of me.

David had been charming and attentive. We ate dinner at Lacie's Café then studied at my favorite coffeehouse, The Student Grind. Afterwards, he walked me home, gave me a gentle kiss on the mouth and left. This morning he sent me an email message from a Yahoo account: "Enjoyed last night. Can't wait to see you again." Although I wondered about the Yahoo email – why didn't he just send it from his university address? – I couldn't have asked for a more pleasant or polite date. So, why did I still feel a strange sense of unease when I thought of him? And what was up with the eerie church dream I kept having, even more so lately than before?

Brandi glanced at me from the bottom of her eyelashes. "Fine? That's more of a parent-friendly description than a date-with-a-man-who-sends-you-dozens-and-dozens-of-roses description."

I took one last bite of toast and tossed a piece of crust to the cat. "There's nothing wrong with the word 'fine.' I had a nice time. He seems like a nice guy." Jezzy delicately sniffed my offering as I placed the chipped, sunflowers on mint background plastic plate in the sink. I think it was Martha's.

Brandi raised her eyebrows. "Seems?" she started to say, but was interrupted by the doorbell ringing.

"Gee, I wonder who that could be? Maybe more flowers?" She winked.

I sighed. "Can you get it? I'm not dressed yet."

Eyeing me, she picked up her mug and sauntered to the door. When she returned, she held a small package with my name on it in big letters. "Guess I was wrong."

I turned it over in my hand. "Who left this? It's too early for the mailman."

Brandi shrugged. "It was just sitting on the stoop."

In the background I could hear Martha clumping around the apartment. Feeling that same sense of uneasiness creeping over me as I did with the roses, I opened it.

Inside was a small box, the kind you'd get from a jeweler. Brandi crowded closer, eyes bright, like shiny hard pebbles. The smell of her perfume mingled with the scent of coffee – a strange but not unpleasant combination wafted over me. "Go on. Open it."

Still I hesitated. The unease swirled inside me like a tornado.

"Is this supposed to be some savoring-the-moment thing? What're you waiting for?"

Martha chose that moment to clump her way through the kitchen muttering something unintelligible.

"Good morning," I said. She sort of waved in my direction.

I turned back to Brandi's impatient face, sucked in my breath and snapped open the box.

Inside, nestled in black satin, was an elegantly constructed rose pin set with diamonds.

Brandi gasped as she leaned over. "Those are real, sweetie. Take it from a diamond expert. What the hell did you do to him – dress up like a dominatrix and fulfill his S-and-M fantasy?"

Martha brushed past us on her way out. I barely looked at her, unable to tear my eyes away from the beautifully wrought pin. "So, it's expensive."

"Let me put it to you this way – as far as boyfriend gifts are concerned, you hit the Wheel of Fortune jackpot. Though I wonder about this rose-fetish."

I snapped the lid closed. "I have to return it."

Brandi gaped at me. "No, you don't. You never have to return any gift a guy gives you, even if you break up the next day, because it's a gift."

I put the box on the counter. "I'm not interested in gift-getting etiquette 101. I can't accept something that expensive. We haven't even slept together yet."

Brandi snorted. "Right. Why the protesting? Like I care."

I started pacing around the kitchen. "Brandi, I'm serious. This is an insane gift. We've known each other less than a week, had exactly two dates and exactly two kisses. Yeah, we've had a good time and all that, but we've barely reached the roses-and-candy level, much less the expensive-gift level."

Brandi sauntered over to the table and slung her black book bag over her shoulder. "Well, if that's the case, I'd nip this thing in the bud, pun intended. Otherwise, you may end up with an obsessive stalker boyfriend on your hands."

The room temperature dropped twenty degrees when she said that. The uneasy feeling twisted violently in my stomach, and I swallowed hard to keep from being sick. "Gee, Brandi, maybe you should teach a class in reassurance, you're so good at it."

Brandi shrugged, swinging her hair over her shoulder. "Hey, if you want sappy platitudes, go talk to Elena. I'm in the business of truth-telling, even if it's unpleasant. And I think in this case you'd rather hear the truth, wouldn't you?" She raised her eyebrows at me as she strolled past. As usual, she had a point.

***

In my first class of the day, half of my brain listened to the professor while the other half pondered Brandi's words. If she was right, then I had to put a stop to this relationship immediately. But maybe she was wrong. Maybe David hadn't dated many women and didn't know what was deemed "acceptable dating behavior."

Either way, I needed to have a serious talk with him before things progressed any further. Hopefully after that, I would know what to do.

My class ended, but my brooding hadn't. As I walked outside, I heard a familiar voice behind me say, "Good morning, Kit."

David? Here? I spun around and saw him standing off to the side, clutching a coffee container and a small bag, wearing a huge smile.

At first I could only stare, convinced that my deliberating had either plunged me into some sort of hallucinatory nightmare, or conjured him up. David couldn't really be standing there – he was in computer science. He belonged on the other end of campus.

"What are you doing here?" I sputtered.

He came forward and thrust the coffee and bag at me. "I brought you breakfast. Coffee and two chocolate-filled croissants."

I took them both, although the idea of sweets in the morning made me nauseous. "David, you didn't answer my question. What are you doing here? How did you know where I'd be?"

He adjusted his backpack and slid his hand up my arm, hooking his fingers around my elbow. "Here, I'll walk you to class. It's in Bacomb Hall, right?"

I automatically began to walk, although I felt like the edges of reality had started crumbling away. "Yes, but … "

"Computers," he said smugly. "I just found your class schedule on the computer, and since my next class doesn't start until noon, I thought I'd come over and surprise you."

"Well, you certainly accomplished that."

He paused for a moment, brushed the hair out of my face and looked into my eyes. "Kind of scary what you can learn about people on the computer."

Again he reduced me to simply staring. The way he said it – it almost sounded like a threat. "Yes, it truly is," I choked out.

He smiled and resumed walking. "I can show you how to better protect your identity. I'm writing my thesis on it."

"Sure," I said, baffled. Was he trying to keep me off guard on purpose?

My next class was my least favorite class – not because of content, but because of location. It was on top of Bacomb Hill, a pretty ambitious climb - especially in the morning when I needed my energy just to stay awake, let alone hike up a hill.

We started up the tree-lined path at almost a trot, much faster than my normal pace. The trees, leaves long gone, waved their bare branches at us. Fat squirrels searched for leftovers while equally robust rabbits scampered about. All the animals that lived on campus were fat and tame – squirrels would perch right next to students on the grassy hill, waiting to be hand-fed. And the ducks – they had long crossed the tameness line and were fairly ravenous: one could lose an arm, eating in front of them.

David continued to smile. "Did you get my gift this morning?"

At least he saved me the trouble of bringing it up. "Yes, I did. We need to talk about that."

He frowned. "Why? Didn't you like it?"

I shook my head, my breath starting to wheeze in my throat. "No, that's not the problem. Can you slow down a bit?"

David's stride never changed. "Then there's nothing to talk about. I'd hoped to find you wearing it this morning."

I began to cough. "David, I can't accept it. It's way too expensive for the point we're at in our relationship. Can you please slow down?"

"What do you mean you can't accept it? Of course you can. It's my gift to you."

Was it my imagination, or was he walking even faster? "But it's too much. That's the problem." I started coughing in earnest, my chest clogging up. I wanted to ask him to slow down again, but I couldn't catch my breath.

"Look, Kit. I didn't give you that present to make you uncomfortable. I gave it to you to show you how special I think you are and how much our relationship already means to me. I know we only met last week, but I already feel like I've known you much, much longer. I wanted you to know how I felt, and also I wanted to apologize for sending you sixty-five roses."

"You already apologized for the sixty-five roses. You paid for dinner last night," I said between coughs. "Can you please slow down?" We had almost reached the top of the hill, which was good because I could feel the mucus rising up my throat. My chest burned.

"Yes, but I didn't feel like I really let you know how sorry I was for that misunderstanding and how much I already care about you."

I couldn't answer him. We had finally arrived at Bacomb Hall, and I hurried to the bathroom, coughing the entire time.

Locking myself in a stall, I prayed nobody would pay any attention to me hacking up the mucus in my lungs. It was terribly embarrassing. Usually I could make it up Bacomb Hill with only a little coughing, I kept myself in pretty good shape, walking and with yoga. But this was too much for me.

"Asthma," I offered as an explanation to the women gathered in front of the mirrors. The concern in their eyes turned to sympathy. I left the bathroom, chest aching, and found David waiting for me.

"Are you okay?" he asked, deep concern in his eyes.

I grabbed his arm and yanked him to the side, away from the crowd. "Why the hell didn't you slow down? You know I can't exert myself that much."

"I thought you were supposed to exercise more to strengthen your lungs."

I glared at him. "Yes, you're supposed to exercise, but not like that. You must know that."

He held his hands up in supplication. "No, I didn't. I thought you wanted a good workout."

"A good workout?" I half-yelled, unable to keep my voice down. "I asked you to slow down three times!"

He shrugged his shoulders. "I didn't hear you."

"You heard me cough."

"I thought that was normal."

Was he trying to make me crazy? What the hell did he want? I could feel a blood vessel in my head start to pound. "Whatever. I have to get to class."

He reached out to touch me. "What about tonight? You want to grab something to eat, then do some studying?"

It took every bit of willpower to turn and face him. I just wanted to get away. This situation was becoming entirely too weird for me. I needed to think, to try and figure out what the hell was going on here. "Not tonight," I lied. "I have plans."

He looked hurt. "What kind of plans?"

"What business is it of yours?" is what I wanted to say. Instead, politeness reared its proper head and I said, "A study group. I'll be busy most of the night."

"Then how about tomorrow?"

I started edging away. "Look, I have to get to class. I'll call you later." I ducked into the crowd before he could protest again. Hurrying up the steps to the second floor, I ran into the bathroom, rubbing my sore chest. I needed time to pull myself together – besides, I had this irrational fear he would follow me to class, begging for an answer.

Why the hell did I allow him to drag me up the hill in the first place? I should have just stopped. Too polite for my own good. Maybe I should be asking what was wrong with me.

Along with a place to hide, the bathroom also offered an unexpected benefit – a receptacle to throw out my untouched coffee and croissants. I suddenly had this vision of him pulling the food out of the trash in the hall and running after me yelling, "You forgot to eat this!" Right now that didn't strike me as the slightest bit far-fetched.

Chapter 9

"So, let me get this straight." Elena picked at her salad with her fork. "David has given you several dozen roses, an expensive piece of jewelry, taken you out for dinner twice and met you at class with coffee and croissants in hand, and you find this unacceptable behavior."

We were eating lunch at the student Union, surrounded by the dull roar of conversation, laughter and U2.

I forced myself to swallow a bite of cheeseburger. Although losing my appetite wasn't unusual during stressful times, I had to maintain my current weight so I selected the most fattening thing I could find. Not to mention nibbling more than usual on cheese, trail mix, peanut butter and crackers and nuts throughout the day. I had learned early on the dangers of becoming too thin – sickness.

"You don't think it's the slightest bit of creepy that he accessed my school records?"

Elena shrugged. "He's a computer geek, right?"

"Well, yeah."

"That's what computer geeks do. Take it as a sign of love."

I dipped a fry into some ketchup. Next to us, a couple of girls burst into noisy giggles. "Yes, but what about him not slowing down while we were walking? You know I'm subject to asthma attacks when I exert myself too much."

Elena speared a piece of lettuce and gazed longingly at my lunch. "Maybe he really didn't hear you."

"The coughing should've been a big clue."

"Nobody should ever accuse boys of being observant."

"Yes, but this goes beyond that. It's borderline creepy. At least that's the way it feels to me. It honestly doesn't strike you as the least bit odd?"

A couple of guys bumped into our table as they lumbered by, making everything shake. Elena steadied her Diet Coke. "All right. It does seem a little weird. He appears to be a bit heavy in the money-spending department and a bit short in the observant department. But maybe he's trying to impress you and doesn't know any other way to do it. Are you trying to tell me you don't find this even the teensiest bit romantic?"

"I don't know," I muttered, making myself eat more cheeseburger. When Elena put it like that, my fears sounded almost silly. But only almost. Elena didn't understand the full implication of the roses, nor had she experienced the altered church dream after the dates. She also hadn't seen the creepy, shiny light in his eyes when I asked him to slow down the third time. Almost like he enjoyed seeing me cough. Even now it chilled me. But how could I possibly explain all that to Elena?

"Okay, maybe you're right. Maybe I am overreacting. But I'm curious; who invited him to that party anyway?"

Elena shrugged and nibbled at her lettuce. "Who knows? Who invites anyone to those parties?"

"How did you meet him?"

Elena thought about it. "You know, I can't really remember."

I smothered another fry with ketchup. "Great."

"I'm sure it was your usual, run-of-the-mill party meeting, nothing too terribly sinister."

"No, of course not," I said. Across the room, under the arch that provided the exit and entrance to the dining area, a woman stood talking to a group of people. Long, wavy blond hair drifted down her back, golden against her dark brown coat.

"Look, Kit, this isn't brain surgery," Elena continued to speak, although I only had half my attention on her, the other on that oh-so-familiar blond hair. "If what he's doing bothers you, tell him to stop. No big thing. I'm sure if you told him you didn't like expensive gifts, he'd stop giving them to you."

That hair tantalized me. I flashed to the woman at the party who called herself Cat. "Elena, do you remember seeing a girl at the Halloween party wearing a fairy costume?"

"Fairy costume?"

The woman half turned toward me, and I leaned forward to catch a glimpse of her face. "Yeah, fairy costume. You know, something out of a fairy tale, pink fluffy dress, wings, that sort of thing."

"Nooo, I can't say I recall anyone wearing a pink fluffy dress and wings. Kit, what are you looking at?"

The woman said goodbye to the people, adjusted her books and tossed her thick curls out of the way. At that moment, I saw her face.

It was definitely the woman at the party. Cat.

And then she was gone, disappearing down the hallway.

I stood up so fast I knocked my chair over. "I'll be right back," I said over my shoulder and started weaving through tables and chairs and people, all seeming set at odd angles. I had to backtrack twice before finally reaching the entrance.

She was nowhere in sight.

It must have been the same woman I saw on Halloween. It looked just like her.

Did that mean Cat really had returned? After all these years, could she really still be alive?

After searching the hallways and lobby with no success, I headed back to the table and a confused Elena.

"Uh, Kit," Elena tapped her fork on the edge of the plate. "What just happened here?"

I straightened my chair and sat down. "I thought I saw that woman again. The one I asked you about."

"The one in the fairy costume?"

"Yeah, that one."

Elena stopped tapping her fork and regarded me like one would a cornered wild animal, cautious and unsure what its next move would be. "So, let me get this straight. You sprinted out of here to chase a woman you talked to once at a drunken Halloween party?"

God, did my life sound stupid. "Uh … yeah. But it was a very … odd encounter. That's why I wanted to talk to her again."

Elena leaned across the table. "Kit, what's going on with you?"

I played with my napkin. "What do you mean?"

"I mean, first you break up with Tommy with no explanation to anyone. Then, you start accusing another guy you're dating of being some kind of nutcase, because he's showering you with attention. Now you're chasing some woman through the Union who you talked to once at a party? And I haven't even touched on how you've been all super-distracted and barely pay attention. You're starting to scare me."

I slumped in my chair. "It sounds worse than it is."

Elena wiped her hands off with her napkin. "For your sake, I hope you're right." She started piling her dishes, including her half-eaten salad, on her tray.

"What are you doing?"

"What does it look like I'm doing? I'm cleaning up so I can get to class."

"But we still have time before classes start."

Elena paused, one hand poised in mid-air, and stared at me. "Are you going to tell me what's going on?"

I rubbed my temples, swinging my hair so it concealed my face. "I thought I did," I said weakly.

Elena went back to cleaning up. "Yeah, well, I have to get to class."

I reached over to clasp her arm. "Elena, stop. I'm not trying to be difficult. It's just hard to explain."

Elena looked directly into my eyes. "Try me."

I sucked in my breath, trying to form the words, but they eluded me. I wanted to tell her, but I couldn't see myself blurting out the secrets of my life between classes at the Union. "I will," I said finally. "But not here, not now. Just give me a little time to sort things out. Okay?"

Elena sighed and stared down at her tray, her partially eaten salad staring back at her. "All right," she said, meeting my eyes and smiling a little. "I can do that. We'll talk soon, okay?"

I nodded. She picked up her tray and left. I studied the remains of my lunch and suddenly remembered Elena had mentioned she had something to talk to me about. Some friend I was. I had never gotten around to asking her about it.

***

I left the Union and went home, skipping all of my afternoon classes. Why bother? I knew I wouldn't be able to concentrate.

I closed the off-white drapes and lay on the lumpy couch with a wet cloth draped over my eyes. Horrible headache.

After a while, Jezzy settled herself purring on my stomach.

My muddled thoughts whirled through my head, scattering the old comforting ideas of how my life worked. Was that woman at the party really Cat, my sister Cat, returned from the fairies or whoever had kidnapped her? Was that who I saw today at the Union? But how did she know the things she did? How did she know about my dreams? And why did she warn me of danger?

And what about David? Was it coincidence I met him after the warning or was he the danger? And what about this Jeckyl-and-Hyde inconsistent bullshit? One minute, Dr. Charming and the next Mr. Asshole?

To top it all off, none of my friends took me seriously. Well, to be fair, maybe they would if I told them the truth. But I had built my life behind a wall of secrets and misdirection. While I kept outright lies to a minimum, I had become a master at evasion. How could I tell people the truth now? How would I even start? Would they take me seriously then? Would they believe me? Maybe I didn't believe me. This whole past week was starting to take on an unreal, dreamlike quality, like reality had simply gotten off at the last bus stop, before the Halloween party, and left me with a leering monster masquerading as my new boyfriend, a fairy sister granting me nightmares instead of wishes, and the faint but unmistakable sound of wolves' howling.

The click of a key unlocking the deadbolt jolted me out of my thoughts. I held my breath, hoping it was Martha. I willed her to clump down to her bedroom without disturbing me. No such luck – Brandi's distinctly lighter tread tripped up the stairs.

First a pause, then Brandi's disembodied voice floated across the room. "You've taken up performance art I see. Let me guess, this is your rendition of *Life*. I bet you call it 'In the Dark.'"

Jezzy leaped off my stomach. "You're funny."

I heard another click and the darkness under my lids lightened to a maroon color. I caught of whiff of her musky perfume. "So, what is this?" she asked.

"Performance art. You already guessed."

"Your creativity certainly knows no limits. Are you sick or something?"

Sighing, I rolled over and removed the washcloth from my eyes. "I wish. It'd be simpler if I were."

Brandi swung her book bag off her shoulder and knelt to pet Jezzy. "Did you talk to David?"

"Sort of." I sat up. "He showed up after my psych class and walked me to English."

"How romantic."

I flung the washcloth on the floor. "That's what Elena said. It's not romantic. It's creepy. He looked up my schedule on the computer and found me."

Brandi raised her eyebrows. "Really. So what did he say about the jewelry?"

"Just that he wanted show me how special I was."

"Hmmm." Jezzy sauntered away and Brandi sat down in the orange-brown chair, crossing her legs. When we had first moved in, Brandi had spent the better part of an hour pacing around the living room with its mud brown paneled walls, industrial brown carpet and hideous furniture, trying to decide if it was worth it to redecorate. Eventually she decided it wasn't. "I swear that cat likes you more than me. So, Elena thinks this is romantic."

"Actually, she thinks I'm overreacting."

Brandi nodded. The vee-neck of her black sweater set off the delicate diamond and gold necklace "Yeah, I can see that."

"So, you think I'm overreacting as well? What about this morning when you said he could be an obsessive stalker?"

Brandi scooped up the mail and began thumbing through it. "Obsessive stalker is still a possibility. Another one is that you're overreacting. And a third possibility is that you're blowing this whole David thing way out of proportion because you want a reason to get back together with Tommy."

"Stop anytime you want with the Tommy references. The sooner the better, I might add. I swear, you and Elena have been worse about this breakup than Tommy has."

Brandi sighed, separating one envelope from the rest. "Probably because we both want to see true love win in the end."

I twisted my hair in a ponytail and snorted. "You? Right. Maybe Elena, but the only reason you'd be kissing frogs is because of the prince's money."

Brandi clucked her tongue. "That's harsh, Kit. And entirely untrue. Haven't you heard? It's just as easy to fall in love with a rich man as a poor one." She hurled an envelope at me. "Your Sugar Daddy has graduated to love letters. Maybe it really is true love."

A cold, sick knot tied itself up in my throat. Trying unsuccessfully to swallow, I reached down for the envelope. It was plain white, my name and address either typed or printed from a computer.

"What makes you think this is from David?" I flipped the envelope over. There were no other markings except for the stamp and my address.

Brandi shrugged. "What makes you think it's *not* from David? Of course, you could open it. Then we'd know for sure."

The knot swelled in my throat. I slid my finger under the flap, tearing it slightly, and eased out the piece of paper inside. With it came a shower of sparkling silver confetti.

"Festive," Brandi commented as the confetti blanketed the floor. "Wonder what the celebration is."

I unfolded the paper. The letter was fashioned like a ransom note with words cut out from magazines.

Kit Cat. First there were two, then there was one. Soon there will be none.

Kit Cat. Open your eyes and see, because the truth will set you free.

The note was unsigned.

"I'd say David needs a little help in the love-letter writing department," Brandi said, reading over my shoulder. At some point she had moved to sit next to me, but I had no memory of when.

I lowered the note so Brandi wouldn't notice my hands shaking.

Brandi continued to speak. "Did any of that make sense to you?"

I flashed to Cat's words Halloween night. *You must save the innocent, because by saving the innocent you save yourself. It's the only way you can set yourself free.*

I shook my head, not trusting myself to speak. Terror had lodged itself in my chest, blocking my breathing. The glittering confetti winked at me from the floor, mocking me. I saw it then for what it was – fairy dust.

Sprinkle a little fairy dust, cast a spell. Works like a charm. Now I was under its spell. Some strange, secret, mysterious spell.

Brandi stood up. "You've certainly caught yourself a good one, Kit."

"It's not from David," I said, through parched lips and throat.

Cat's face taunted me from the Union, turning as it disappeared into the crowd. "This isn't from David." My voice cracked.

Brandi eyed me. "Who do you think it's from then?"

"I'm not sure, but not David."

"Sooo … you have two people sending you strange and unexpected gifts now? Whatever. For myself, I'd want to keep the guest list small and focused, but if you want to start inviting new and strange paranoia in, then have at it."

I stood up. "You think I want this? Any of this? Newsflash! I want it all to go away."

Brandi put one hand on her hip and raised an eyebrow at me. "Then maybe you better do something about it."

Chapter 10

I decided to study.

I knew it wouldn't solve my problems. But school I could control. Kidnapped-sisters-who-have-recently-returned sending me vaguely threatening letters and Dr. Charming/Mr. Asshole were an entirely different matter.

I went to the Mary R. Black Library, also known as MRB, one of the few libraries I felt comfortable studying in. It had a lounge-like atmosphere and large windows overlooking the giant, winding Ohtawakee River – the "river" in Riverview. Faded lime green cushiony chairs, many with their springs broken, were interspersed with wide, straight-back beige chairs around circular tables. I wanted a cushiony one, but other people had already snagged them, so I settled for two straight-back chairs at one of the tables – one to sit on and one to stretch my legs over.

All things considered, I managed to plow through quite a bit of *Clarissa* before Tommy interrupted me.

"You look like you need a study partner." He made himself comfortable at my table.

I eyed him over my book. "You look like you need new friends, or at least more of them."

"Ouch, Kit. That wasn't necessary." He pulled a notebook and gnawed pen out of his backpack.

"That's reality."

"You're making me reconsider my offer of friendship."

"Whatever." I tried to go back to my novel but Tommy wouldn't let me. Although technically a library, MRB had pretty lax talking restrictions.

"What's with the bad mood?"

I held my book in front of my face. "No bad mood here. Just trying to get some studying done."

"Lover's spat?"

I lowered *Clarissa*. "Didn't we already cover the David-and-I-aren't-lovers thing a few days ago?"

He shrugged. "Things change. And you are here all by your lonesome."

"By choice." I tried to raise the book again, but Tommy nudged it away.

"Are you and David having problems?" He had managed to arrange his features into a sympathetic expression.

I let *Clarissa* fall into my lap. "Are you out of your mind? Why would I tell you even if we were?"

Tommy looked hurt. "I'm trying to be a supportive friend here."

"What you're trying to do is pry into something that's none of your business."

Tommy dropped his gaze to his books, the picture of an injured little boy. Against my better judgment, I felt myself softening. I tried reminding myself that it was kinder to cut our doomed relationship off now, before things became even more complicated, but it didn't work. Not with him in front of me, looking so sad, so confused. I sighed loudly. "All right. Look, we had two dates and he was very polite after both of them. Nothing physical has happened; it's a very platonic relationship."

He opened his mouth as if he were going to say something, but then fixed his gaze back on his books instead.

"Take it from me, there's nothing yet about this relationship you have to be jealous about, okay?"

His head snapped up. "Yet?"

"You'll be the first to know if or when there's something to be jealous about." I patted his hand. "Okay, maybe the second, or third, but I won't keep you hanging. Agreed?"

He nodded, studying the table and worrying a corner of his notebook.

"Chances are by the time that happens, you'll be so wrapped up in some cheerleader you won't even remember having this conversation." Although my tone was light, a bolt of white-hot pain seared my heart. I covered my face with my book in case any of that pain was reflected there.

Tommy muttered something and flipped open his notebook. I sighed in relief. Maybe we were finally done with this conversation.

I had just reached a point where I almost cared about Clarissa's problems when Tommy interrupted again.

"Okay, I'm not trying to start a fight here," he began, dropping his chewed-up pen on the table with a thunk.

I rolled my eyes. "Yes you are, or you wouldn't have just said that."

"No, really. I know something's wrong in your life."

"What're you talking about?"

"Are you denying it?"

"Since I don't know what you're talking about, it's kind of hard for me to deny it."

"Well, I know things are … a little peculiar with David, and … "

I slapped my book on the table. "Where did you hear this?"

At least he had the decency to look sheepish. "From Brad who talked to Elena … "

I shook my head. "I should've known."

"She's just worried about you, that's all. And so is Brad, which is why he told me. And how you ran after that girl in the Union –"

"Oh, for God's sake. Elena is blowing this way out of proportion."

He laid his hand on my arm. "Then tell me how it really is."

"Why?"

He looked at me like I was an idiot. "Why? So, I can help you. Duh."

That suggestion was so appealing. To actually have someone to talk to. But where would it end? Would I find myself telling him everything? Could he handle it?

"The David thing is a bit peculiar," I said hesitantly. "That's why I told you not to be jealous. But, Tommy, come on. Do you really think I can talk to you about it objectively?"

"Point taken. But what about this girl? Elena mentioned something about her being dressed up as a fairy at the Halloween party. Is it the same person you asked me if I saw?"

I sighed. "Yes."

"So, what gives?"

I turned away, unsure of how to answer. A guy dressed in a faded, ratty sweatshirt stood up from one of the low-slung chairs and began an elaborate stretching routine. At another table, two girls with cropped shiny brown hair sat hunched over note cards, quizzing each other at a frantic pace. The guy at their table, dressed in a UW sweatshirt, dug through his backpack.

"Kit?" His voice was so gentle, so full of concern that I allowed my eyes to meet his. I saw only sympathy and caring reflected in the dark-blue depths.

"She was at the party," I said. "We spoke for a few minutes."

"And … "

I propped my elbows on the table and buried my face in my hands. "It sounds crazy though to just say it. You're going to think it was just a drunken episode."

"Try me."

I raised my head. "She … she warned me."

"Warned you? Of what?"

"She just said I was in danger."

Tommy folded his arms across his chest. "From what?"

"She didn't say. But then a few minutes later I met David, and, well, I don't know."

"So, you think she was warning you away from David."

"I don't know what I think."

Tommy rubbed his chin, studying me. "And that's it?"

I sat back. "Isn't that enough?"

He didn't answer right away, just kept studying me. "Then why do I get the feeling you're holding something back?"

"Maybe because you're frickin paranoid." I started shoving my books into my bag. How dare he say that to me? Tommy, the king of never opening up, accusing me of holding out. How rich was that?

"Why are you getting mad?"

The guy in the UW sweatshirt brushed past me gently as he ambled by. "Why do you assume I'm not being honest with you?"

Tommy held his palms out. "Whoa. I said nothing about honesty, merely that I thought you weren't telling me everything. And judging by your response, I'd say I was probably right."

I stood up. "Fine. Whatever. I'll see you later." I snatched up my coat and stalked to the door. Never mind that deep down I knew he was right. Never mind that I knew I was being irrational. Never mind that a part of me wanted to tell him everything. Waves of anger rolled though me. I should have stayed at the apartment.

I shoved open the door to the cement steps leading down and to the outside. The building had eight floors altogether – the bottom four were part of the library and the top four classrooms and offices. I liked the fourth floor best because it had the nicest view of the river.

It was almost as cold here as outside, so I paused to put on my coat and adjust my backpack.

A hand seized my arm as I started toward the steps. "Tommy, I don't want to talk to you right now." I tried to wrench my arm free.

"It's not Tommy," a voice said. I snapped my head around. David stood there, still clutching my arm, his eyes smoldering embers, his mouth a straight pinched line.

"Oh, David. Sorry, I thought you were Tommy." Could I sound any lamer?

"Yes, I gathered that," he said coolly. "Who is he?"

"My ex." I tried again, more subtlety this time, to free my arm, but David gripped it even tighter.

"Your ex, or your current boyfriend?"

I glared at him, exasperated. "He's my ex. I don't play those sorts of games. We're still friends, that's all. Now, if you'll please let go of my arm, I want to go home."

He leaned closer, eyes blazing. "You lied to me."

"I did not."

"You said you had a study group."

I gritted my teeth. "Look, I don't have time for your jealousy-over-protective issues right now. Let go of me."

He grabbed my shoulders and shook me roughly. "You lied. You didn't have a study group at all. You just wanted to get together with your football boyfriend."

My head snapped back, teeth clicking together painfully. I couldn't believe this was happening. "Stop it. You're hurting me."

He shook me again. "Answer me."

I tried to push him away. "Stop it."

His hot breath on my cheek smelled foul and stinking, like something rotten. I shuddered, struggling not to gag. He was such a neat freak – why was his breath so horrible? And where did all this violence come from? How could he be doing this to me? Me? We had a bond! How could this be happening?

He jerked me closer, hissing into my face. "What? I'm not good enough for you because I don't play football?"

I gaped at him, the full meaning of his words becoming clear. "Football? I didn't tell you he played football. You were following me."

He shook me a third time, sharp bursts of pain exploding in my face and neck. "I'm the one asking the questions here." His bright-red face loomed over me, ugly and monstrous, his eyes hot and burning.

He's going to kill me.

The words came out of nowhere, numbing all other thoughts in its path. My anger dissolved into terror – suddenly, explosively.

"Let go of me," I screamed and shoved him violently. My voice echoed crazily, bouncing insanely against the cement walls and steps, as twisted as my reality had become. He stumbled backwards, releasing his hold. Quickly, before he regained his footing, I spun around and fled down the stairs.

Immediately I knew I had made a tactical error. I should have gone back inside, at the very least opened the door. And screamed. Tommy would have helped me. Now I had no choice but to outrun him.

Above me, he swore and started the chase. His pounding footsteps echoed and boomed, sounding as though he had me completely surrounded. I would never escape him. The familiar bands tightened around my chest – my breathing began to hitch. Oh, God, not yet.

The stairs were deserted. Where was everyone?! Just like a clichéd nightmare, I was alone and defenseless against the monster. Any minute now I would be unable to move, my body weighted down by unseen entities, forced to run in slow motion, struggling to breathe.

The booming grew louder behind me as the coughing began to rise in my throat. I would never be able to outrun him …

Where the hell was the bottom? I was only on the fourth floor. Why hadn't I reached the first floor yet?

Maybe I had passed it. Maybe I was heading toward the parking garage in the basement. Oh God. This was a nightmare. I had never been in the garage. Could I even find my way out?

I had almost decided to turn around and run up a level when I spotted it: the outside door, on the landing below me. Thank God. My chest felt like it had turned into a fireball. Ignoring it, I summoned a fresh burst of speed and dove toward the door.

"Kit," David yelled, his voice taking on a sinister, eerie edge. "You can't beat me. You know it and I know it."

I slammed into the door before remembering I had to pull it open. Struggling not to cough, I wretched it open. David's voice continued taunting me:

"Kit, you know you can't outrun me. You're probably using all your energy to keep yourself from coughing. Just stop. All I want to do is talk."

I managed to stumble outside before surrendering to my coughing fit. But still I kept moving, kept going forward. Through the coughs. I couldn't stop. My lungs had transformed into tiny, burning straws. Every breath was agonizing. Excruciating. But I couldn't stop.

This is how it must feel to die.

The words tumbled in slow motion through my head. With incredible effort, I pushed them away. No, I would not die today. Today is not a good day to die.

People moved in the distance, but no one was close. How could this be? Maybe I really was trapped in a nightmare.

The Union loomed from across the street. Sanctuary. I started toward it, moving in a sort of shambling half-run. The wind whipped around me, icy fingers eagerly digging their way past my open coat to my sweating body underneath. This air was even harder to breathe. The bitter cold mixed with the fire in my lungs, and turned it into a scorching, blistering disaster.

Uncontrollably coughing now, chest burning, I staggered to the street. Have to keep moving, have to keep moving, I chanted to myself. Although maybe it would be easier just to let him catch me.

Shadows from the streetlights stretched around me, dark and twisted. Everything looked mutated. Distorted. Like I had stepped into a funhouse mirror reflection. David yelled my name again. I fought to run faster, terror and pain blending seamlessly.

Cross the street. One foot in front of the other. Mind over matter. The pain wouldn't kill me. Pain meant I was alive. Hold on a little longer. Almost to the Union. Find someone, anyone. Maybe I would get lucky and run into a campus cop. Oh, why couldn't I bump into Tommy *now*?

"Kit, I just want to talk to you. Come on, Kit. I don't want to hurt you."

Across the street. Finally. Now for one final flight of steps. A car sped by, its headlights flickering strangely off the trees and brick walls of the Union. Hopefully it would slow David down long enough for me to find some help.

I hurled myself down the steps, flung open the door. A beefy guy passed me on his way out – finally a person. He didn't stop, just eyed me a little strangely.

"Kit," David howled as I ducked inside. The warm air caressed my cheek, soothed my tortured throat. Still coughing, I wound my way around the hallway. Wasn't there a campus police station in here somewhere? But where? I had never looked for it, never thought I would need it. Still, somebody should know. I could ask someone, maybe the person who sold the popcorn and ice cream. The bartender might not believe me, might think I'd had too much to drink.

I stumbled through the hallway – passing the dining area, passing people who turned to stare. Eyes wide, mouths open. Who could blame them? A coughing, hysterical female scuttling through the halls.

"Kit." A familiar voice. Brandi. She was sitting at a table with a couple of her sorority sisters. Relief washed over me, so sweet it burned.

"Kit, what the hell?" Brandi jogged toward me.

I tried to tell her. I wanted to tell her. But now that relief had replaced terror, my lungs decided they had been ignored long enough. I started coughing so hard I almost fell over.

"Jesus, Kit," Brandi put her arm around me and patted my back.

"Bathroom," I managed to gasp. "I … bathroom."

Propping me up, she half led, half dragged me to the bathroom. Right then, David appeared, running, coat open, eyes wild, hair sticking up all over.

"Kit," he exclaimed, stopping abruptly, skidding on the slick floor. "Kit, didn't you hear me call out for you? Why were you running like that? Did someone do something to you?"

He righted himself and came toward me. I jerked away. "Him." I gasped to Brandi, my coughing preventing me from saying more. Brandi studied me for a second. Whatever she saw in my face must have convinced her, because she nodded and pushed me toward the bathroom.

"I don't believe we've met," I heard her say coolly. "I'm Brandi, Kit's roommate."

As soon as the bathroom door swung closed, I collapsed on the floor. Between coughs, I crawled into one of the stalls and locked the door. Luckily the bathroom was empty.

It seemed to take forever to clear out my lungs. It took even longer to stop coughing. Finally I unlocked the stall, washed my hands, washed my face and combed my hair. I still looked pale and my chest hurt horribly, but at least I could go out and deal with David.

He had turned on the charm big time for Brandi, smiling and talking animatedly. I couldn't tell if she had bought his act or not – her expression was flat, neutral.

"Kit," he called, his voice warm, concerned, caring – absolutely nothing like his shouts from the library stairwell. It was as though it had never happened at all.

He held his hands out, stepping toward me. "What happened to scare you so? Why didn't you stop? Didn't you hear me calling you?"

I marched over to him. "You know damn well why I didn't stop. I was trying to get away from you!" I slapped his hands away.

He looked mystified, his eyes darting back and forth between Brandi and me. "What are you talking about? I never –"

"Stop right now with this innocent act. I'm not in the mood for it." I advanced toward him, jabbing with my finger. He would *not* sweet-talk me into believing this was some sort of misunderstanding. "You attacked me in the stairwell of the library, you shook me –"

"He attacked you?" Brandi cut in, incredulously.

David held both palms up, a gesture of surrender. "I didn't attack you in the stairwell, you misinterpreted –"

I interrupted, my voice rising. "David, I don't want to talk about this right now. In fact, I don't want to talk to you at all right now. Please leave."

He gazed at me plaintively, his eyes soft, begging me to listen. "But –"

"If you don't leave right now, I'll call campus police."

David's eyes narrowed. "You wouldn't dare."

I folded my arms across my chest. "Try me."

He looked down, but not before I saw anger flash in his eyes.

The same anger I saw in the stairwell.

When finally he raised his eyes, he had smoothed his features into a neutral, emotionless expression. "I can see you're not in the mood to listen to reason, so I'll go. I certainly don't want to add to your distress. I'll give you a call later to see if you're ready to talk."

He started to walk away, but my voice stopped him. "Don't bother calling me. I'll call you when and IF I'm ready to talk to you. If I were you, I wouldn't spend a lot of time waiting for the phone to ring. That's just a friendly piece of advice, since I wouldn't want you to waste your time or anything."

The color drained from his face – such a contrast against the anger brightening in his eyes. He closed his eyes and gave himself a little shake, as if he was collecting himself. When he opened them, his expression had returned to neutral. He smiled thinly and strode away.

I watched him disappear before turning to Brandi. She was studying me, arms crossed, one hip jutting out. "He really attacked you?"

"What, you think I'm making it up?" I rubbed my neck. Along with the agony in my chest, my neck had started to throb. With my luck, I had whiplash.

"No, of course not. I'm just … I'm surprised. That's all."

"Why are you surprised? You're the one who thought he could be a mad, obsessed stalker." I waved at Brandi's sorority sisters. Needless to say, they had been mesmerized by the David-and-Kit Show. No sense in trying to keep this a secret from Tommy.

"Yeah. Guess I was right." She smiled ironically. "Lucky you."

Chapter 11

"We should drive down that road," my mother said, her finger pointing out the window. "That's the right road."

My father turned his head, slowly, deliberately. He nodded, quietly, leisurely. My mother's finger never stopped pointing.

I turned my head as well, my movements as sluggish as my father's. Cat was sitting next to me. "Kit Cat," she said. "First there were two, then there was one." She was seven, the same age as me.

"What did you do with my doll?" I asked.

She smiled. "Don't worry. They can't see me." She tilted her head toward my parents.

"You did something to my doll. What was it?" I was fretting, sure I was missing something important.

She patted my hand. "Don't be afraid, Kit. I'll take care of you. I'll always take care of you."

The car jerked, as if it had made the transition from pavement to dirt. "Almost there," Cat said. "Kit Cat. You can never go back."

The church loomed in front of us. My parents stepped out of the car. "Hurry, Kit," my mother said.

"Yeah, hurry," Cat echoed, and started to slide out. I clutched her arm.

"What did you do with my doll? You have to tell me. What did you do?" Her arm melted out of my grasp. Then I was outside the car, trotting behind my parents.

To the church. To the graveyard. My chest tightened, filled with fluids.

The bell started ringing, low and melodious.

"Ahh, the bell has rung. It has begun." Cat fell into step beside me. The wolves yipped and howled, sounding like children – children playing, children dying.

I could see the graveyard now, just a piece of it, peering out from behind the church.

My breathing hitched in my chest. I started to cough. "Tell me what you did with the doll. I have to know. Before it's too late." My coughing worsened. More of the graveyard appeared. People were standing around a grave, a freshly dug grave. It was so fresh I could smell it – wet, dank, earthy. Any second now the black evil Being will appear. I will be powerless against it without the doll.

"Ahh, the doll," Cat said. "What about the innocent? Why aren't you concerned about the innocent?"

I gasped, tearing at my chest, my lungs burning the air I so desperately needed. "What innocent? I don't know about the innocent. Only the doll." I could now see the shadow of the evil Being – long, black, misshapen. It started stretching, bending and twisting, falling over the grave. The dirt beneath the shadow began to swell, to ripple, like someone or something had been buried alive and was now clawing its way out. I tried to scream, but all that came out was a pathetic whimper. I collapsed, fighting to breathe.

Cat towered over me as I lay huddled on the ground, but she was no longer seven. Now she was the age I saw her at the Halloween party, her pink dress glowing, her wings sparkling in the weak sunlight. She was all brightness and color, especially vivid against the gray, cloudy graveyard. Even her scent was so much more alive – wild, green and growing – masking the dark, damp smell of the grave.

She stared down at me, sadness radiating off her. "Oh, Kit," she sighed. "Don't you understand? The doll is a liar."

I awoke with a jolt, gasping for breath, my head slipping off my propped arm and almost hitting the desk. Fumbling for my inhaler, I struggled to find my bearings. Where the hell was I?

"Don't worry," Joe whispered from the seat next to mine, trying unsuccessfully to hide his smile. "You didn't miss anything important."

Now I knew. I had fallen asleep in Abnormal Psych class.

In between sucking on my inhaler, I returned Joe's smile, then faced my professor. Last night I had been too wound up to even attempt sleep for several hours. When I finally did crawl into bed, all I could think about was the transformed church nightmare, since it seemed to go hand-in-hand with my David encounters. I ended up snapping on the light and studying instead – reading *Clarissa* of all things. At least I had finally almost finished it. Then I could start *Evelina*. I had high hopes for *Evelina*, since a woman wrote it. With any luck, it would portray women a bit more positively than Richardson had.

Returning my inhaler to my purse, I fished out a bottle of water and a couple of pieces of beef jerky to gnaw on. The more calories the merrier. Besides, eating would help keep me awake.

I took a big bite of the jerky. Early this morning I had fallen into a restless sleep – no dreams, but not very refreshing either. Then, I drift off in class and have the church dream. If I didn't know better, I would think the church dream had a mind of its own. It wanted to have its say regardless of what I wanted, or what I did. Great. I get to be stalked by both David and a scary dream. Must be my lucky day.

Why did the dream change in the first place? It didn't make sense. And why does it keep changing? And what about this doll question? Sure Cat and I played with dolls, but none had been terribly special. Why would I ask about a doll? And why would she say there had never been a doll?

Just thinking about that made my skin crawl. Literally. As though millions of creepy long-legged bugs had scattered all over me. I wondered if I would ever sleep again. Maybe I should see if Riverview offered a dream interpretation course. On second thought, maybe I didn't want the dream interpreted after all.

The bell rang. Thankfully. Maybe my next class would do a better job distracting me from my thoughts.

"I can give you my notes." Joe slid his notebook into his backpack. One of Tommy's teammates, he and I usually sat together in class, exchanging notes and gentle flirtation. Even now, after the breakup, he continued to treat me the same as before – one of the few who did.

"Thanks, I'd like that." I started to close my notebook when something stopped me. Something scrawled on the bottom of the page.

Joe said something else, but I had quit listening. Icy fingers trailed down my back, playing my spine like piano keys. My breath hitched in my throat.

What did you do with my doll?

That sentence was scribbled across the page, the writing so large and childish I barely recognized it as my own. Quickly I snapped my notebook shut.

"I'm sorry," I said, taking a few deep breaths. "What were you saying?" The medicine from the inhaler continued to do its magic and my breathing remained normal.

He studied me, his expression full of concern. "I asked if you were all right."

"Yeah, yeah, I'm fine." I stood abruptly, rattling the desk in my haste. I jammed my notebook into my backpack. If I had to look at those words one second longer, I would run screaming out of the classroom.

"If there's anything I can do," he began as we pulled on our coats and walked to the door.

"Your notes would be perfect," I interrupted, keeping my voice light. "I guess I should stop pulling all-nighters." I forced myself to smile. He still looked uncertain, but he smiled back.

"Kit." I recognized David's voice a second before I saw him. I closed my eyes – why wouldn't he leave me alone?

He rushed over, his expression imploring, a covered plastic cup in one hand, a bag in the other.

He thrust them at me. "Kit, I'm so sorry about everything. Can we talk?"

I kept my hands down as I tried to stride past him, anger already coursing through me. At least today I had a football player next to me. "David, what did I say last night? Don't call me – remember? While I'll concede you haven't, this is sort of the same idea."

David matched my pace. "But I have to talk to you. I think you got the wrong impression last night."

"Oh, I bet I did." I refused to look at him.

"You heard the lady," Joe said, leaning over from my other side. "Beat it."

David's face turned red. "This matter doesn't concern you. It's between me and Kit."

"If Kit doesn't want to talk to you, then it's my concern. She doesn't, so I suggest you leave her alone."

"Kit, please, just five minutes. I'm begging you," David said.

"Look buddy, she doesn't want to talk to you. Why is this so tough for you to understand?" Joe strode closer to me, glaring at David.

"I told you this has nothing to do with you." David's eyes were beginning to bulge. "Kit, if I could only have five minutes … "

"Leave her … "

"All right." I held my hands up. "Time out, before someone gets hurt. David, I'll give you your five minutes."

"Alone?"

I gritted my teeth. David looked like a kicked puppy dog. "Fine," I said, against my better judgment. "Five minutes. That's all."

Joe touched my arm. "Kit, you sure?"

I waved him back. "It's okay, Joe. Thanks."

"I'll be right over here." Joe backed off the sidewalk to stand near a skinny, naked tree. I waved at him again as I followed David to an undisturbed area of dead grass next to the psych building.

"Your five minutes are ticking. Better make this fast, I have to get to class." I crossed my arms and glared at him.

David's eyes were on Joe. "Is he your boyfriend too?"

"That's it, your five minutes are up." I started to leave.

He blocked my path. "I'm sorry. That wasn't called for. Breakfast?" He tried again to hand me the food and coffee, but I refused to uncross my arms, only reluctantly deciding to stay.

"You're on borrowed time here."

"I know. I'm sorry." He put the items on the ground. "Look, I was totally wrong. I realized that as soon as it happened. I'm totally at fault here."

I nodded. "Great. You want a medal or something?"

He reached out to touch me, but pulled back before actually making contact. "It's just … I got a little crazy, that's all. I mean, I care so much for you. I feel like we have this connection, this bond. I've never felt this way about anyone before. Then, you lie to me about your plans, I find you with your ex-boyfriend, and I got a little jealous. That's all."

"You didn't get a little jealous, you got a lot jealous."

"I know, I know. It will never happen again. I'm so sorry. I could never, ever hurt you."

"But you did hurt me. And you scared me as well."

He brought his hands to his mouth. "And I'll never be able to forgive myself for that."

I looked away, watching the students shuffle zombie-like to their next class. Against my will, I felt some of my anger drain away. He did have a point. After all, from his point of view, it did look like I had lied to be with my ex-boyfriend. Would I have been any less jealous if our roles had been reversed?

Looming over me. Hissing into my face. "What? I'm not good enough for you because I don't play football?" Shaking me. Voice echoing eerily in the stairwell. Pounding footsteps. "Kit, you know you can't outrun me. Just stop."

I twisted my face away, willing those images to stop. I needed to get away from him, but I had to do it without provoking his rage. "If you had only asked, you would have known I didn't have plans to see Tommy. He just showed up and wanted to be my study partner. We had a fight about it and I left. There was no reason for you to be jealous."

"I know. I know I handled it so badly. It's just that I already care about you so much. Can we try again? Will you give me another chance?"

I studied him. His eyes beseeched me so eloquently. I thought we had a bond as well. And then last night happened and sixty-five roses happened and Bacomb Hill happened. There were many things I didn't understand right now, but I knew one thing – I was done with David.

"I understand better what you were going through last night, and I do forgive you for your … for what happened. But, David, I don't think a relationship is the right thing now, for either of us. I think we need a little space to think things through."

Although David's face had brightened at the beginning of my speech, by the end he looked crushed. "I don't need any space to think things through," he insisted. "I know exactly what I want."

I sighed. "All right, then I need some space. I need to think things through. And I think it would be best if we didn't see each other for a while. At all. That includes showing up unexpectedly at my classes. I thought you understood I don't like commitments or plans. I don't want to be pinned down."

He stabbed his toe into the frozen ground. "You had boyfriends before," he said sulkily. "What's wrong with me? I thought we had a bond. You said we did."

I closed my eyes. Why wouldn't this guy get the hint? "David, I really need some alone time right now. Please. I'm asking you – no, I'm begging you – to give it to me. If you care for me the way you say you do, you'll understand that I really, really need this."

He shifted his weight from one foot to another. "How much time?" he asked grudgingly.

"I don't know. Maybe a week or two."

"A week or two?" He looked aghast.

"David, I need this. Look, I'll give you a call in a week or so and let you know how I'm feeling. Okay?"

He didn't look happy. "I don't have much choice do I?"

I shrugged. "I'm sorry. I really am. I'll call you in a week. All right?"

He nodded. I smiled, a quick, cool smile, before spinning around and dashing over to Joe.

"Everything cool?" he asked as we hurried down the sidewalk.

I peeked over my shoulder. David was still there, standing in the same spot, staring at me. I couldn't read the expression on his face.

I faced forward again. He said he would leave me alone. I could only hope he would honor that promise. "Fine," I said, although I swear I could feel David's eyes burning into my back the entire way to my next class, long after the crowd and the landscape would have swallowed me up from his view.

Chapter 12

"So, you still think David's romantic?"

Elena wrapped a long red scarf around her neck. "Well, not in the conventional sense, anyway. Did he really attack you in the stairwell?"

I rubbed my neck. "Have the soreness to prove it."

She shook her head. "Amazing. He seemed so sweet."

"I think the word you're looking for is sour, not sweet." We headed off to State Street in search of a different place for lunch. Elena had complained she was tired of Union food. It didn't bother me to eat somewhere else, but I didn't know what Elena would get out of it since she only ate salads. How different could a salad be?

"The good news is that you found out about his, uh, other nature before getting too involved with him." Elena clapped her red-gloved hands together. "Man it's cold. I should have gone to the University of Florida."

"Yeah, but then you'd end up sitting next to giant cockroaches in class. I've heard they really mess up the bell curve."

She raised her eyebrows. "On a day like today, I would welcome even giant cockroaches if it meant being warm. Maybe they'd let me join their study groups."

A weak sunlight filtered down, no match for the biting cold wind. Elena's copper-colored curls whipped around her face. I had pulled my dark hair into a ponytail, but the wind had jerked several strands loose, and they blew around my face.

"You're the one who thought a salad made by a different restaurant would taste better," I said.

"And don't think I'm not regretting that decision."

A tree rattled its branches, making me think of the death clatter of old bones. Christ, I was getting morbid. Another thing to thank David for. Several curled up yellow leaves rolled past on the brown grass.

"So, what was it you wanted to talk about a few days ago?" I asked casually, side-stepping around a bundled-up group of people coming toward us.

Elena threw me a sideways glance. "It's nothing, really."

"Even nothings can turn into somethings. Besides, I'm sick of talking about my own problems and you're probably sick of hearing them, too."

She didn't respond. I kept my eyes off her. I didn't want to put any more pressure on her. Instead, I studied Memory Library, one of Riverview's many beautiful, venerable buildings. Two carved off-white columns wound their way past twelve floors and anchored themselves against a gray and black slanted roof. What appeared to be a sparrow was perched on the trim.

"It's just … I don't know. I think I'm being silly."

"If you don't say it, then we won't know if you're being silly or not, will we?"

"Maybe you're right." Her voice trailed off. We left the campus and started walking up State Street. The mile-long street allowed no cars, only buses, bikes and foot traffic. Bars, restaurants and shops lined both sides of the road. The air smelled delicious – a combination of dozens of cuisines, from Italian, Thai and Vietnamese to Mexican and everything in between.

Elena twisted her hands together. "It's just … I think Brad's losing interest in me."

I looked at her in surprise. "Losing interest in you? Why do you think that?"

She studied her fingers. "Well, he doesn't spend as much time with me as he used to."

"It is football season and he is on the team."

"I know, but it feels different this year. And when we are together, he doesn't seem that interested in … anything."

"But, at the Halloween party, you guys seemed so into each other."

She shook her head, her curls swinging in front of her face. "I know. That was a really good night. Maybe I'm imagining things, I don't know. He just feels … distant to me. Maybe part of it is that I thought we'd be engaged by now."

"What?" I asked, taken aback for the second time. "Why would you think that? You say it like there's an expiration date on it or something."

She laughed a little. "I guess I am being silly. You're right. There probably isn't anything wrong. He just has a lot on his mind with football and classes and graduation coming up. No biggie." She stopped in front of Giovanni's. "How does Italian sound? They have a pretty fantastic salad."

I smiled, but I wondered why Elena had dismissed her suspicions so quickly. Although a bit of a worrier, she wasn't prone to exaggeration. Maybe she did have something to be concerned about. Anyway it didn't matter now, I wouldn't get anything more out of Elena today. She had declared the subject closed.

To study or to drink, that was the question.

Although I really needed to get my butt in gear – I had papers to write, second midterms to cram for, even if I didn't know the exact due dates – I also desperately wanted to go out, get drunk and forget about my reality for awhile.

As I ambled back to my apartment, I tried telling myself that I should study tonight since I would be going to a party tomorrow night. But tomorrow seemed way too far away. Besides, maybe if I consumed enough alcohol, it would disrupt my sleep patterns and I wouldn't dream.

The music of Jane's Addiction greeted me as I pushed open the door. Wonderful. I would get to enjoy the company of Martha.

She stood in the kitchen, fixing Ramen Noodles. She jumped when she saw me. "Sorry. I'll turn it down."

I smiled weakly. "Thanks."

She nodded, clumping out of the room. A woman of few words.

Wandering around the kitchen, I studied her books spread out over every available surface. Both history and philosophy books. Maybe she was a double major.

The volume lowered to a respectable level, Martha plodded her way back to the kitchen and her dinner. She ate standing up, leaning over the counter and peering at an open book.

"So, how's things?" I continued skulking around the kitchen, telling myself I should be studying too.

She looked up, brown hair falling into her eyes. "Behind. Paper and a midterm next week. You?"

"Behind. I probably have papers and midterms due next week as well."

She looked shocked. "You don't know?"

I had been running my fingers down her books, tracing the binding, but stopped when she asked that. "You know, that was supposed to be a joke. But I just realized I actually *don't* know."

Without thinking, I sat down, my mind in a daze. "I know what's left to do in my classes, at least I think I do, but I don't have any concept of when I'm supposed to do it." My voice was filled with amazement. "Come to think of it, I have no idea what went on in any of my classes this week at all."

Martha looked at me like I had suddenly sprouted a second head. "How'd you make it this far?"

I rubbed my face. "I don't know." Crap. How could I justify partying tonight when I had no idea what was going on in my classes? Damn Martha. Now if I did go out I would feel guilty, whereas before, with the week I'd had, I would have felt justified.

"Oh, your boyfriend's been hanging around," Martha said in a dismissive tone, turning back to her books. Clearly I wasn't worthy of her time.

I, on the other hand, was now completely focused on Martha. "Boyfriend?" I asked cautiously, struggling to keep my voice neutral.

"Yeah, boyfriend. The new skinny one, not the football player. Left something for you. On the coffee table."

My head spun, like it had turned into one of those tilting rides at the fair. Putting my hands to my temples, I ordered myself not to panic, not to give in to the spinning, but instead to think this through. Which do I react to first – boyfriend, package or hanging around?

Carefully, I folded my hands in front of me, forcing my hands to move slowly as if that would also slow my brain down. "How do you define 'hanging around' exactly?"

Martha's expression changed to annoyance. "Just because you don't care about your grades doesn't mean the rest of us don't."

I briefly closed my eyes. "Martha, I'm sorry. I'm not trying to keep you from studying. But this is important. He's not my boyfriend."

"Certainly hangs around enough to be one," she muttered to her books.

I must not have heard her right. "What? You've seen him here more than once?"

She sighed loudly. "Every night."

I rose to my feet, my voice getting louder by the second. "Every night? Since when?"

She glared in my general direction. "Are you going to let me study or what?"

I marched up to her, slamming both my hands on her books. I leaned over and looked directly into her face. "Martha." I kept my voice very soft. "This is important. All you need to do is answer a couple of questions and then you can go study until your eyeballs fall out. When did you start seeing David hanging around?"

Martha gawked, her mouth dropping open. After a moment, she closed it. "About a week."

"What time?"

"Don't know. Late."

"How late?"

She shrugged. "Two, three. You should know. After you finished fucking him."

It took every ounce of willpower not to scream into her face that I never fucked him. Instead, I straightened and took a deep breath. "He's not my boyfriend, okay? We dated twice, but we've never had sex and we never will have sex. Just … just be careful if you see him, okay?"

"Careful?"

I rubbed my face. "He's … not what he seems. I don't trust him. I'm in the process of ending the relationship, so you shouldn't be seeing him around anymore. Okay?"

She nodded. I took another deep breath, then remembered the package in the next room.

"One more thing?"

Martha glanced up, annoyance creeping back into her face.

I gritted my teeth and continued. "The package. Where was it? In the mail?"

"The front door. Saw it when I got home. Now, can I study?"

"Yeah. Thanks for everything. I appreciate it." I left her alone with her books, deciding my sarcasm was probably lost on her.

The package was a padded mailer, sitting peacefully on the coffee table, minding its own business. Just like the package with the jewelry. Only my name was written on the front in black marker.

I paced around it, not touching it, then collapsed on the couch. It certainly looked harmless enough. Somehow I didn't think I would find jewelry inside.

My stomach rolled in knots, my head continued its wild spinning ride. Finally I couldn't take it anymore and tore the envelope open.

Inside, a piece of paper was folded around something bulky. I grasped a corner, easing it out and over the coffee table. If it was something icky, I didn't want it touching me.

A few dried white petals fell out, piquing my curiosity. I cautiously unwrapped the paper and found a dead white rose, the petals curling and brown.

I picked up the rose and studied it. Looked like your average, ordinary dead white rose. Odd. I took a second look at the paper and noticed it had something typed on it. I leaned over to read it.

When is a rose officially declared dead? Is it when it's cut from the bush? Or when it's denied water? If it is when it's denied water, how long do you think it takes for the rose to finally die?

I fell back, my blood turning to ice in my veins. I couldn't move, my body had frozen. I could only stare with horror at the dead rose. Was that blood drying on its thorns? No, just a trick of light. Or a trick of my mind.

Martha chose that moment to clump out of the kitchen, arms filled with books. "Going somewhere where I can get something done." I followed her with my eyes, the only part of my body I could move. Like a deer trapped in the headlights, frozen as death loomed in for a final embrace.

As she passed by, she spotted the white rose. "Still sending you flowers. Can't be all that bad." She tramped down the steps, leaving me alone with the rose and Jane's Addiction.

Some time later, I have no idea how long, Brandi found me. I hadn't moved, hadn't been able to move.

She stood in the living room, surveying the scene. I could smell her perfume, rich and musky. "Couldn't Martha turn down that god-awful music? I swear, anyone who listens to that much Jane's Addiction has to be a philosophy major."

I didn't move.

She studied me. "Am I interrupting something?"

I didn't answer.

She took a step toward me, her body hesitant. "Kit, are you okay?"

I still didn't respond. She bent over to pick up the note. "You're certainly getting your share of incomprehensible mail." Her eyes flickered over the objects on the coffee table.

"He's going to kill me." I was surprised at how calm I sounded.

Brandi settled herself in the chair next to the couch, then crossed one leg over the other. "Kill you? Aren't you being a bit melodramatic here?"

"Dead rose. A note talking about death. How do you read it?"

She studied me, wrapping a strand of hair around her finger. "I need a cigarette."

That broke my paralysis. "You promised no smoking in the apartment."

"When I made that promise, I didn't foresee these exact circumstances." Her movements deliberate, she uncrossed her legs, rose to her feet and strolled into the kitchen.

I attempted to follow, but found my body uncooperative from sitting in one position for so long. "But my asthma."

"I'll open a window," she yelled from the kitchen.

"It's thirty below out there."

"It's not thirty below, not even with the wind chill. Just turn up the thermostat. What do you care, we're not paying for heat."

Finally, I got my limbs moving correctly and propelled myself into the kitchen. Brandi was perched on the window ledge, one jean-clad leg propped on the chair in front of her. Smoke from her cigarette curled in lazy spirals through the open window.

"First of all, why do you think it's from David, anyway? It wasn't signed. Maybe it's from your other anonymous pen pal, the one who sent you the confetti."

"No, it's from David."

She took another drag, the cold wind caressing her brownish blond waves. "How do you know?"

"The rose. That's why he sent the rose."

Brandi tapped her cigarette against one of Martha's ugly sunflower plates, the ashes covering the petals like a gray cloud. "The man does have some sort of rose fetish going on, no argument there."

I yanked a chair from the table and dragged it as far away as I could from the smoke. "Plus there's my gut feeling. And I saw him today."

She jerked her head up. "Really? Where?"

"After class. He showed up again." I told her about my encounter, but left out my dream and conversation with Martha. I couldn't talk about those yet.

She pondered my words, sucking in smoke, gazing outside. "Yeah, I'd say it's starting to sound like you have a problem here."

I sagged in my chair. "What should I do?"

Brandi shrugged, putting out the cigarette. "You could tell the police."

"Think that would do any good?"

She picked up the pack and tapped another cigarette out. "Honestly? No. Nothing's been done to you yet. Cops only get involved after the crime's been committed, not before."

I leaned my head back against the wall. "Very comforting."

"However, when you register a complaint, you create a paper trail. A paper trail certainly wouldn't hurt and probably would help in the long run. Same thing goes for collecting documentation."

I rubbed my temples. "Just don't expect them to do anything, right?"

Brandi lit a second cigarette. "Sweetie, I'm not even sure if you have enough to get a restraining order. You might be able to get him in trouble with the university, though. I suppose that's worth a shot. Maybe he'll decide it's not worth getting kicked out of school."

"I can only hope." I started redoing my ponytail. Brandi continued smoking, staring moodily out the window. Her hazel eyes were more green than brown, reflecting her dark green turtleneck sweater. With her long brownish blond hair fluttering in the wind, she looked like a piece of art. A painting – elegant and poised with just a hint of sadness. Her heavy gold necklace glinted between her breasts – a brush of brightness in the otherwise somber picture.

I quit fiddling with my hair. "Brandi, what's up?"

She blew a stream of smoke out of the window. "Nothing I can't handle."

"Brandi, you don't smoke unless you're drunk or there's something wrong. I'm not egotistical enough to think my problems would upset you that much. Actually, now that I think about it, maybe I'm the one who should be smoking."

Brandi half-smiled and held out her cigarette pack. I waved my hand in refusal. "What gives?"

She sighed and turned to the window again. "Chuck asked Violet to marry him."

"What? Where'd you hear that?"

Inhaling a mouthful of smoke, she flashed me that half-smile again. "From the little boyfriend-stealing witch herself."

"Maybe she's lying."

She cocked her head. "Got that rock she's showing off from some-where. And believe me, it ain't no prize out of a Cracker Jack box."

I rubbed my chin. "Wow."

"Tell me about it. He doesn't love her, I know he doesn't. He loves me. Why he just can't … " Her voice broke. Bending her head, she focused all her attention on tapping the ash off her cigarette. A sliver of sunlight caught the blond in her hair, making it sparkle.

"Brandi, I'm so sorry."

She shrugged. "Win some, lose some. That bitch couldn't wait to rub it in, though." She shook her head. "This ruins everything."

"Why? You'll find someone else. Not much doubt there."

She snorted. "When? I'm supposed to graduate in May. It's already November. There's no way I'm going to find someone before gradua-tion."

"Then find someone after graduation."

"Oh, yeah, that's a plan. Where? At my nonexistent job?"

I stared at her, shocked at the words coming out of her mouth, the bitterness in her voice. I knew she was looking for a suitable husband, but this sounded like a conversation I might have had with Clarissa.

"Getting a job is generally an acceptable plan after one graduates from college. Even for women. You may not have heard this, but wom-en can have all sorts of careers nowadays. They no longer have to rely on a man to support them."

"Kit, you don't get it. Careers are all well and good for women with a passion to do something, but I don't have a driving passion. I'm a psych major, what the hell kind of job am I gonna get? Some low-level executive somewhere or maybe even a secretary? If those jobs even exist anymore." She lit another cigarette. "Maybe I'll just continue in school, become a psychologist. Daddy'd get a kick out of that, having a shrink in the family. He's been making jokes about that since I told him my major."

"I'm seeing a whole other side of you I never dreamed existed." I leaned back in my chair, folded my arms.

Brandi turned to me. "What are you going to do after graduation? You're in the same boat I am."

"Hey, I have a double major, English and psychology. I'll thank you to remember that."

"Yeah, double of nothing still equals nothing." She cocked her head. "So, what're you going to do?"

I shrugged. "You know me, never like to make plans. Besides, May's a long way off. I suspect I'll muddle through somehow."

"Yeah, you really don't like to make plans. Kit, I don't get you. Here you were dating the star quarterback. Even if he didn't get picked up by the NFL, he probably could've gotten a comfy job at his father's business. And you break up with him. You were set, and you gave it up. Why?"

I stood up. "Not all of us look at men as potential meal tickets."

Brandi gazed back out the window. "Whatever."

Chapter 13

A loud bang startled me and I spilled my coffee all over the white paper placemat.

I turned around to see an embarrassed guy with a bad haircut picking up his books. He grinned sheepishly, not making eye contact with anyone. I went back to my own mess, mopping up the coffee with a bunch of paper napkins.

After the strange conversation with Brandi yesterday, I had gone to my bedroom intending to study. Instead, I found myself first prowling the room, then the apartment, gazing at the windows, the doors, the locks. Wondering if David was out there, lurking behind a tree or a bush, watching, waiting. Wondering how easy it would be for him to break in. Could I nail the windows shut? Would that even work?

While pacing, my eyes fell on the jeweler's box still sitting on my dresser. I needed to return it immediately. Even having it in the room made me uncomfortable. Visions of him having bugged the box to keep tabs on all my movements swam in my head. Finally I stuffed it in my sock drawer, covering it well.

Somewhere in the middle of that long paranoid night, I remembered my mother had given me two self-defense items before my freshman year: an obnoxious noisemaker and pepper spray. I dug them out of the closet and studied them. Pull out the pin and the noisemaker shrieked a dreadful high-pitched piercing sound. Stopping it required putting the pin back in – not as easy as it sounded. I remember trying it once; the sound bordered on painful, and made my hands shake.

Of the two, the obnoxious noisemaker comforted me more, and I ended up sleeping with it in my hand. I figured if nothing else, it would wake up both my roommates and our neighbors, instantly. Somebody would call the police. I made a mental note to carry both items on me from then on.

But even the noisemaker couldn't provide me a decent night's sleep. I slept fitfully, waking at the slightest sound. Convinced I would open my eyes and find David looming over me, grinning, explaining how he just happened to be in the neighborhood and thought he would stop by and see how I was doing ... I didn't mind, did I?

Nothing quieted my mind – not sleep, not waking more exhausted than when I went to bed, not even my yoga exercises. I went through the motions, but my mind kept jumping about like a skittish rabbit. No wonder I spilled my coffee. I was surprised I hadn't spilled more than that.

I finished cleaning up, then pushed my cup over to the edge of the table for a refill. Since I didn't feel safe at my apartment, I decided to spend the day in public surrounded by people, starting with breakfast at Marty's Deli. David wouldn't be able to do much in front of witnesses. Plus it was Friday. That meant no classes, so no David popping up unexpectedly.

I couldn't believe how much David had contaminated my life. Every aspect had been infected. I couldn't even check email anymore. And forget school. No matter how hard I tried, I couldn't focus on my studies. What's more, I didn't seem to care. Somehow, the fate of my education paled in comparison to dealing with a mad stalker, not to mention the weird sister thing. Still, I kept giving it the old college try. Deep down, I didn't want to fail.

The waitress refilled my cup and took my half-eaten breakfast away. I pulled my books closer, trying to concentrate, but instead found myself jumping at every little noise or movement. A girl with short spiky blond hair walking to the bathroom, a couple of scruffy graduate students wearing unkempt clothes demanding more coffee, the squeak of the door opening. I kept twisting in my seat, convinced I was being watched. I could feel them – eyes watching me, analyzing me, memorizing me. It didn't matter that I couldn't see them, I knew they were there.

Finally I left and headed to the Union. Still, the eyes followed me. I hid in the biggest booth I could find. It didn't matter. The eyes continued to watch me. Whenever I left my table, whether to get something to drink or go to the bathroom, I would feel the eyes burning into me. When I returned, something would have changed. Maybe there would be a different page open in my notebook, or a book upside down, or a pen on the other side of the table.

I vacillated between fear and anger the entire day. Fear that David may actually be there – anger that I was letting him control me, control my life. I refused to run scared from this man. I had spent my life fighting death and I wouldn't allow some jerk to dictate what I did and where I went. He was the asshole here, not me. I shouldn't be the one punished, the one to have my life turned inside out and upside down and everything else. This was his problem, not mine. I should quit letting him make it mine.

But then I would return to my seat and find my cup in a different place, and the fear would take over, rising up and grabbing me by the throat.

At one point, I thought I saw the woman who called herself Cat standing at the back of the Union – almost hidden by the arches, face covered by shadow. I tried going after her, but before I even stood up, she had vanished. I got the feeling she had been watching me, but that didn't make any sense. She talked to me at the party, why wouldn't she talk to me now? I was being paranoid.

No matter what I told myself, I couldn't stop scrutinizing every corner, sure I would find the source of those eyes somewhere. I couldn't stop jerking at every movement, every noise. Finally I gave up on the Union and headed for home. Maybe the apartment would be better now, especially if my roommates happened to be home. Worth a shot.

The afternoon had melted into dusk – the shadows deepening, lengthening. The wind picked up, blowing eerily through the naked trees. I walked faster, berating myself for misjudging the time of day so badly. How could I have let the daylight slip away like this?

Night crept forward. Stealthy. Relentlessly. It covered the earth with its inky cape, giving madmen the advantage of hiding in its dark folds.

Enough of this. I had always liked night. I wouldn't let David ruin this for me as well.

I turned right on Jefferson, then left on Lincoln. As I trotted down these side streets, I noticed fewer and fewer people around. But that didn't make any sense. It wasn't that late. Besides people lived here. Students lived here. Where was everyone?

Then I heard it.

Footsteps. Behind me. Soft and determined. I whirled around, a scream caught in my throat.

No one was there.

I must have imagined it. That was all. I forced myself to turn around, to resume trotting. I wanted to get home and out of the cold as soon as possible anyway.

It was so quiet. Even the wind had died down. My breath came out in short, choppy bursts – agonizingly loud in the stillness. I coughed a couple of times. Explosions. My footsteps sounded muffled, dull, against the sidewalk. Anyone could hear me coming. Anyone …

That noise again. Footsteps. Behind me.

I spun around. No one there. Again. My chest tightened, my breath came out in gasps. This is all in your head, I told myself. Stop being so paranoid.

I could feel my airwaves start to shrink. No, I would *not* have an asthma attack now. I only had a couple of blocks to go. I could do this.

The footsteps. Louder now. Closer. This time I didn't bother turning around. I ran. My breath rasped in my throat. Coughs bubbled up. Just a little farther.

I rounded the corner. A streetlight clicked on in front of me. I jumped, a small scream escaping from my throat. Now my breathing had taken on that familiar wheezing sound. I coughed. Running had made everything worse. I needed my inhaler.

Slowing to a trot, I fumbled for my purse and dug inside it.

I couldn't find it.

Oh no. My chest tightened even more, pain constricting my airwaves, my cough deepening. I stopped, pawing through my purse, keeping one eye behind me, waiting for my unknown pursuer to show himself.

The inhaler wasn't there.

Starting to sob, I tore off my backpack and searched it. No inhaler anywhere.

My wheezing grew louder, more frantic. My gasps turned harsh, violent. Where was my inhaler? I always had it, always. I must have had it today. Desperately, I mentally backtracked through my day. Did I have it earlier? Yes, yes. I pulled it out instead of my wallet to pay for a latte at the Union. At least I think that happened today. No, I wouldn't second guess myself. I had it today. I must have accidentally dropped it or it must have fallen out …

Or someone took it.

I froze, although my hands still dug uselessly through my backpack. Footsteps. Louder. Coming toward me.

I snatched my backpack and started to run, although I could barely breathe anymore. Every gasp was agony. But I had no choice. I wouldn't let him catch me.

One more block. There. My apartment. Finally. Thank God. Sobbing and choking, I ran toward it, not seeing the person in front of me until I crashed into him.

Both of us fell. I would have screamed had I any breath left.

"Kit? My God, what's happening to you?" It was Brad, Elena's boyfriend. I almost cried in my relief.

"Asthma ... attack ... lost ... inhaler," I managed to gasp out between coughs and wheezes. The sidewalk was freezing beneath my jeans.

I don't know if he understood me or not, but he definitely grasped the seriousness of the situation. As I coughed and wheezed and choked, he retrieved our backpacks and dragged me to my feet. He wrapped one arm around me and we staggered to the apartment. Somehow he found my keys and got the door open. The sound of Marilyn Manson greeted us. Martha's music. Brad steered me to the bathroom.

Choking, I collapsed to the floor in front of the cabinet, clawing through extra toilet paper and tampons. God, where was it? Did someone take this one to? Blind, sheer panic had just about engulfed me when my fingers brushed against my spare inhaler. Oh thank God.

Brad tore the packaging off – my hands were shaking too violently – and held the inhaler to my lips. His brow was furrowed, eyes narrowed.

"Thanks," I said when I could speak.

He waved it away, trying to be casual but still radiating concern. "Glad to be of service. I had no idea these attacks could get so bad."

"Usually they don't. I catch them in time. But I lost my inhaler today and didn't notice it until I was walking home. Bad timing."

"I guess." He stood up. "If you're gonna be okay, I better get going."

I nodded. "Yeah, thanks for playing the white knight. Hey, is Elena around?"

He backed away. "Oh, no. I was just picking something up for her. Gonna be at the party later?"

I gave him the thumbs up sign. He smiled and left.

Exhausted, I sucked on my inhaler one more time, then stretched out on the bathroom floor. It felt so good to breathe. I just wanted to stay here for a few moments, enjoying the act of taking deep breaths. I was so tired I was almost numb, my brain a big, out-of-focus mush. But I could breathe.

I think I actually fell asleep there on the floor, my relief so complete. When I became aware of my surroundings again, Brandi towered over me, staring at me with an amused expression on her face.

"Interesting place for a nap. Are we going to party tonight?"

I blinked a couple of times, more refreshed than I thought possible after what just happened. "Hell, yes."

Chapter 14

"About time you guys showed." Elena thrust a plastic cup at me. The stereo blared the current flavor-of-the-week song and we had to shout to be heard.

I swallowed nearly half of my first beer in one gulp. "I have been so ready for this."

"Yeah, Brad told me about your attack today. My God, that's some serious asthma you have. I'd say you qualify as having a week from hell."

"And where's my set of kitchen knives to go with that?"

Elena grinned. She had piled most of her copper curls on top of her head, but a few strands had broken free to frame her flushed face. Her ivory-colored sweater made her eyes seem more gray than green.

Sipping my beer, I nodded my head in Brad's general direction. "How's it going?"

Elena looked away. "Fine." She kept her voice casual, but I could see her jaw muscle tighten.

I changed the subject. "Heard Violet's engaged." I regretted the words the moment they were out of my mouth, sure Elena didn't want to talk about engagements, but she seemed to embrace the topic.

"Yeah. Poor Brandi." She blew her hair out of her eyes, shaking her head. "And Violet's such a bitch about it. I mean, she got him, why does she have to parade it in front of her?"

"Details, details. I only heard a bit from Brandi while she smoked almost an entire pack. And, let's head toward the keg."

"I guess." Elena looked pointedly at my now almost-empty glass. But obliging as always, she filled me in on the details while I filled up on beer.

A strong arm wrapped around me from behind. "Kit, where've you been? I've been worried." Tommy's warm breath against my ear, his muscular chest pressed against my back.

He brushed his chin, covered with faint stubble, against my neck, shooting hot and cold tingles through me at the same time. For a second I allowed myself to lean against him, absorb his strength, his confidence. But it was all an illusion. It could never last. I pulled away.

"I've been right here," I said. Reluctantly he let me go, his fingers lightly brushing my back, sending more delicious chills throughout my body. I took another step away.

"Did that guy really attack you in the stairwell of MRB? After you left me?" His expression was incredulous.

"Maybe 'attack' is too strong of a word," I said hesitantly, seeing murder creep into his eyes. That's all I needed, to have him and his football buddies charge off into the night to beat the crap out of David and end up suspended.

He didn't appear to believe me. "That's the word you used in the Union."

"I was trying to make a point."

"If he didn't attack you, why'd you have to make a point?"

Good question.

"Well, he came on pretty strong," I said weakly.

"Kit, what *did* he do?" He looked exasperated.

"Well, he started yelling, then he kind of grabbed me and shook me ... a little."

Tommy stared at me. "He grabbed you?"

"Yeah, technically ... "

"He shook you?"

"Well, yeah, but he didn't hurt me that much ... "

Tommy scowled. I had the feeling he wouldn't mind shaking me himself. "Kit," he said in a carefully controlled voice. "Why are you defending him?"

"Yeah," Elena piped in. I glared at her. She snapped her mouth closed.

"I'm not defending him. Really. But I'm getting a very strong vibe that you'd like to use this guy as a tackle dummy and I don't think that's a very good idea. Especially right before a game."

He looked a little mollified. "Why didn't you come back in the library? I would've helped you."

"Kicked the shit out of him, you mean." I paused to gulp more beer. "Not that it would've been all bad, but you have to admit it's not the greatest press to have the star quarterback punching out some nerdy graduate student."

Tommy frowned. "Quit worrying about me and my football career. You're what's important. If anything had happened to you … " his voice trailed off and he dropped his gaze, muttering something under his breath.

God, he was gorgeous. I could feel my heart soften even as my electrified emotions jolted through my veins. I sighed loudly, hoping to cover my feelings. "Look, he was between me and the door, and I thought running down the stairs would be better than trying to go around him. I was wrong. I realized that about halfway down. I should've gone back in to you."

He raised his head, locking his dark green eyes with mine. "Yes, you should have."

Those eyes. So poignant, so warm, so sexy. Caressing me, drawing me in. I could feel myself getting lost in their green depths. I forced myself to turn away. "Need to use the bathroom. Back in a sec."

Quickly, I slunk into the crowd. I will not allow myself to get involved with him again, I chanted to myself. I will not allow myself to fall in …

"Hello, Kit."

I spun around. David stood there, smiling, holding a beer.

Anger sizzled through me. "What the hell are you doing here?"

He looked hurt. "Is that any way to greet a boyfriend?"

I gaped at him. How *dare* he have the gall to look hurt. "David, let me make this very simple for you. You're *not* my boyfriend."

He reached out and caressed my arm. "Of course I am. Look at all we share." His voice was so warm, so tender. "I mean, we both lost sisters, we both suffered with Cystic Fibrosis in our families. It'd be a shame if other people knew all our secrets, wouldn't it Kit?"

Did he just say what I thought he did? "Are you threatening me?" My voice rose with each word.

He squeezed my arm. "I would never threaten you. I'm simply letting you know how things stand between us. Keeping the lines of communication open. That's a good thing in a relationship, don't you think?" His nails dug into my skin, hurting me.

"Get your fucking hands off her." Tommy burst in, yanking David's arm off me and pinning it behind his back. David gasped, dropping his beer, his face draining of color.

"Tommy," I said.

Tommy ignored me, tightening his grip on David. At least that's how it appeared, since David's face was ashen, his mouth stretched in a grimace.

"I think you owe the lady an apology," Tommy said. His teammates started to circle us. "And then I think you should leave."

David gasped again and made a squeaking noise. Tears glistened in his eyes, two bright red spots bloomed on his otherwise pale cheeks. I wondered how I ever could have found him attractive. A bully and a coward. Revolting.

"This is between Kit and me," he squeaked out.

Tommy jerked his arm higher and David cried out. "Wrong answer," Tommy said. "Want to try again?"

"Kit, I ... I ... I need to talk to you alone."

"Hey, I don't think you're getting with the program here. Do you need the Cliff Notes?"

"Tommy, please," I said, afraid he might really hurt David. Not that I didn't think David deserved it, but I didn't want anything to happen to Tommy.

"Kit, remember the roses," David squeaked, his voice breaking. Tears spilled down his face. "Sixty-five."

I stared at him, horrified. I couldn't have heard him right. He wouldn't dare. Not in front of all these people. He couldn't. He wouldn't.

"Tommy," one of his teammates said. "I think this guy needs to learn things the hard way."

"No." I stepped forward as David opened his mouth. I saw it then – the expression oozing across his tear-stained, blotchy face. He would say it, in front of all these people. He would announce to everyone I had Cystic Fibrosis. He would do it, not just to save himself, but also to punish me.

David smiled. Weakly, painfully, but nevertheless triumphantly. He knew he had won. I hated him.

"Let him go," I said. "Let me talk to him."

Tommy's eyes burned me. "Kit."

I touched his arm. "Please, Tommy," I said softly. "It's not worth it. Really. Don't put yourself in jeopardy over this."

Tommy's eyes narrowed, his mouth flattened. I let my eyes plead with his. The muscles of his jaw worked. "Fuck," he spat, releasing David. David crumpled to the ground.

I stepped toward Tommy. "Thank you," I tried to say, but he stalked away.

The mood of the crowd had shifted. Rather than thirsting for David's blood, they now wanted mine. One by one, their expressions melted into disgust before drifting away.

I deliberately turned my attention to David, refusing to give anyone the satisfaction of seeing my devastation. Choosing David over Tommy? Now who was humiliated?

"What do you want from me?" I hissed as he steadied himself.

He whipped his head toward me, eyes smoldering. "Leave with me now."

I recoiled from his hot eyes. "No. Talk now."

He seized my arm. "I said leave with me now." I jerked my arm away, knowing I could no longer count on anyone for help. I was on my own.

"I'll step outside with you for a minute, that's it." I marched to the door. People stepped out of my way without seeing me.

I stormed outside. The icy air burned my cheeks, but I barely felt it – the heat of my fury keeping me warm.

I faced him. "We're alone. Now talk, you fuck."

He advanced on me, stuck his finger in my face. "Don't you ever talk to me like that again."

I slapped his finger away. "I'll talk to you any damn way I please. Now, what do you want?" His odd salty spice smell made me gag.

He glowered at me, lips pressed together so tightly his mouth disappeared. Tears still streaked his face, wet and shiny under the street lamp, but his eyes were black with fury. Suddenly he paused, shook his head and closed his eyes. His expression smoothed itself out. I blinked a couple of times, wondering if I had seen what I thought I did.

"Isn't it obvious? You. I want you."

"Well, you can't have me," I snapped.

He cocked his head. "Oh, but there's where you're wrong. I can."

"What makes you think you can?"

David smiled smugly. "Because I'll tell."

I swallowed, struggling to control my emotions. I felt nauseous and angry at the same time. "Tell?"

"You know. Tell everyone you have Cystic Fibrosis."

Anger won out. "Let me get this straight. You'd tell everyone one of my secrets in order to keep me from breaking up with you?"

He shrugged, his smile growing wider.

I folded my arms across my chest. "Go fuck yourself." I strode past him, returning to the party.

"Kit, I wouldn't kid myself if I were you," he called.

I snapped my head around. "I will not be a hostage to my disease," I shouted. "That's something I've always refused to do. And I won't be one in this situation either."

"It worked in there."

I didn't answer. I had no answer. He was right, of course. Damn him. My fury was so great I felt like I'd choke on it.

"Why don't you think about it?" he said, his tone suddenly warm and intimate. "I'll call you soon, okay?"

"Don't bother." I stomped back to the party, ready to strangle him if he said one more thing to me. Luckily for him, he let me go without another word.

night went well, wouldn't you say?"

I glanced up to see Brandi pouring herself coffee in a rich, understated blue mug with Techron Industries on it in silver. Her father's business. "Yeah, real well." I went back to brooding into my own coffee.

"Just remember, you did it to yourself."

"Gee, thanks for the support. It's so nice to have your roommates on your side."

Brandi sauntered over to sit at the table. Like me, she wore a bright-red UW sweatshirt and had pulled her hair back in a ponytail. "I'm only telling you because you seemed a bit clueless last night. I thought maybe you needed a little help figuring out what was going on." Her eyes watched me over her mug, more green than brown, looking like pieces of chipped ice.

I continued to pick at my toast, not bothering to answer.

Last night had been a complete and utter disaster. After returning to the party, almost everyone ignored me. Tommy especially wanted nothing to do with me. The only person who acknowledged my existence was Elena.

"Kit, I don't get it. Why'd you do that to Tommy?" she had asked.

"I didn't want Tommy to get in trouble. I was trying to protect him." Even to me it sounded lame.

The way Elena studied me made me feel like a freak in a sideshow – a two-headed monkey or the world's stupidest human. "That's not exactly how it looked."

Obviously.

Finally, after several unsuccessful attempts to talk to Tommy, I had called a cab. I spent the rest of the night huddled in my dark bedroom with a bottle of cheap red wine. I kept my pepper spray, noisemaker and cell phone all within easy reach.

Brandi banged her mug on the table, the noise loud enough to yank me out of my thoughts. "Here's a wild and crazy thought: maybe if you'd let Tommy and the rest of the football team beat the shit out of David, then maybe you wouldn't have a problem with him anymore."

"Then Tommy and the rest of the football team would be in trouble for beating the shit out of David. That's why I stopped it." I crumbled my toast, a fine layer of crumbs covering the pale white and gold plate. Brandi owned this plate.

Brandi's eyes went wide. "That's why you stopped it? Who the fuck do you think the cops would believe, David or the star quarterback?"

"What are you talking about?" I said tiredly. "People would talk, the cops would hear … "

"About what? Do you really think people would choose a scum like David over Tommy?"

I sat up. "And turn this into some sort of conspiracy? No thank you. The truth always comes out on these things anyway."

"What, are we in some made-for-TV movie or something? Truths get buried all the time. Besides, David is scum and Tommy would've been doing you a huge favor. Especially after that scene you threw in the Union. How do you think it looks – you crying that David won't leave you alone, and then turning on Tommy because he tries to take care of it?"

I studied my half-eaten, half-crumbled toast. Of course that's how people would see it. They didn't know what David had over me. Brandi was right. Truths did get buried all the time.

"I know I handled that whole scene badly –" I began.

"File that under 'duh.'" Brandi picked up her mug, the silver rim winking at me.

"And I want to make it right," I continued. "I screwed up. I knew it the moment I did it. Now I just have to get Tommy to talk to me again so I can apologize."

Brandi shrugged. "Why would you want to do that? You're the one who wants to break up. I think you got your point across pretty damn effectively last night."

I sagged in my chair. Oh, God, what have I done?

Brandi laid her fingers flat against the table and inspected her bright red nails. "Coming to the game?"

"That's why I have my lucky sweatshirt on."

She stood up. "Hope for your sake it is lucky. We're meeting the gang in a half hour."

I nodded, wondering what kind of reception I could expect.

***

Chilly. That about summed it up. In fact, I think the weather may have been warmer than the greetings.

I ended up being pushed off to the side, basically sitting by myself. I hunched over, my arms against my knees, breathing in the smells of stale popcorn, hot dogs and cigarettes, and alternated between hating David and feeling sorry for myself. For the first time, I regretted not pledging when I had the chance. If I had, I could expect at least some loyalty. Since I hadn't, I wasn't really one of them. But Tommy was. Therefore, Tommy had their support. And I got to sit at the end of the bench, miserable, and watch Tommy play probably the worst game of his life.

Two interceptions, a dropped snap and what seemed like dozens of incomplete passes. I had never seen him play so badly before. What made it even worse was my sinking suspicion that I was at least partly to blame.

"I'm surprised you showed." Elena bustled over. She plunked down next to me, her stylish black coat buttoned all the way up and a purple-brown scarf wrapped around her copper-colored curls.

"I'm surprised I did, too."

The offense fell short of the first down by two yards. The people around us groaned as the kicking unit ran out.

"Tommy doesn't look too good." Elena rubbed her purple-brown gloves together.

I sighed. "No, he doesn't."

She bumped me with her shoulder. "Well, I'm sure it has nothing to do with you."

I looked at her in surprise. "Why would you say that?"

"Because, if he was still pissed off, he'd be playing the game of his life. What better sport than football to let out all your aggressions?"

I half-smiled. "Never thought of it that way."

She smiled and patted my leg. Defense took the field, determined to keep Minnesota from moving the ball. The fans helped by chanting "defense, defense."

"I think Brad is cheating on me."

It took a moment for her words to sink in. I was still stuck on "defense, defense." Besides, of all things she could have said, I least expected to hear that. My mouth dropped open. "What?"

Elena kept her eyes on the game. "You heard me." Her voice was flat, emotionless.

"Yeah, but I can't believe you said it."

She didn't answer, just concentrated on the game.

I tried a different tactic. "Why do you think he's having an affair?"

She finally looked at me, her eyes as dead as her voice. "You don't believe me."

"No, no, of course I do. It's just … hard to believe. He seems so crazy about you."

The song "Who Let the Dogs Out?" burst out of the sound system. People around us started singing and dancing along.

Elena raised her voice. "Yeah, in public he does. In private, different story."

Her face seemed to crumble, fold in on itself. I put my arm around her. "How long has this been going on?"

"I don't know. At least six months. I kept thinking it was all in my head, because he could be so sweet, especially in public. But then … things just kept getting worse. More and more he made excuses about not wanting to spend any time alone with me. We haven't had sex in I can't even remember when. And then about a week ago, after the Halloween party … " Her voice broke. I hugged her.

"It's okay, you don't have to tell me if you don't want."

She straightened. "No, I need to say it. I need to tell someone. I found an earring under our bed the other day. And … "

"It's not yours," I finished.

Elena shook her head.

"Oh God, Elena. I'm so sorry this is happening to you."

She sighed. "Yeah."

I hugged her again. "Have you said anything to him yet?"

Her eyes darted back to the game. "No. I haven't figured out how to bring it up."

A couple of Asian students, arms filled with popcorn and drinks, wiggled their way in front of us. One of them spilled popcorn on my lap – the perfect distraction. I brushed off the kernels, making a point of not looking directly at Elena. "Do you have any idea who she is?" Below my lashes, I watched her.

Elena's face went very still, her mouth straightened into a thin line. "No."

I went back to the popcorn. Elena had never been a good liar – clearly she didn't take after her lawyer father.

"Six months this has been going on?" I said, brushing off the last of the kernels. "Oh, Elena, you should've said something."

She shrugged. "I didn't want to believe it. I kept telling myself everything was all right and I was just imagining problems. And at the Halloween party he was so sweet, I was sure everything was fine between us. Then, two days later I found that earring ... I felt so stupid. I finally decided I couldn't keep lying to myself anymore."

The game was nearing the end of the first half. Minnesota had to kick the ball back to Riverview. A black-haired guy in front of me yelled: "Now do something with it, Niccels." Niccels being Tommy, of course.

"Have you decided what you're going to do?"

Elena wrapped her arms around herself. "No. Not yet. What do you think I should do?"

"Talk to him," I said simply. A paper airplane landed in the hair of an African-American woman in front of us. She put her hand up, discovered the plane, then turned around to glare at us. I held my hands up. "Don't know anything about it." She scowled, scanned the seats and went back to the game.

"You're probably right." Elena sighed again.

I stood up. "Listen, I need to use the bathroom before the halftime mess. I'll be right back."

Elena nodded as I eased my way into the crowd already forming in the aisles.

It still blew me away. Brad having an affair. Unreal. Especially the Brad I knew – the Brad who doted over Elena. The idea of him cheating on her seemed completely out of character. But then, what did I know – I who have had my life taken over by a kidnapped sister and a crazed, obsessive stalker. Sure, I could be an objective judge.

The crowd grew thicker as I climbed the steps, bodies pressing against me from all sides. It took all my effort just to keep moving. A couple of people jostled me and I would have fallen if not for the crush of bodies around me.

At least Elena had kept me from brooding about my own problems, even if only for a short time. Besides, being here made me feel safe. What could David do to me surrounded by all these people? Two people, one in a yellow and purple ski jacket and the other in a long green coat, crashed into me, again almost knocking me over.

Actually, when I put it that way, was I safe? Sure, tons of people surrounded me, but did that really keep me safe? Jostled about by thousands of strangers? David could easily hide in the crowd, easily watch me. Maybe even grab me when I least expected it.

A cold numbness began to fester in my stomach. My chest tightened, my breathing started to hitch. As I fought my way to the bathroom, I began studying the faces around me. Strangers everywhere. Nobody I recognized at all. In a crowd of people, I was completely alone. Would anyone react if I started to scream?

Coughing slightly, I reached into my purse for my inhaler. My gloved hands found my noisemaker instead. Relief washed over me. Maybe people wouldn't react to my screams, but they sure would notice this thing.

As expected, a line greeted me at the bathroom. People constantly bumped into me as I stood there, clutching my noisemaker to my chest. It felt like a talisman, warding off evil, like a cross or holy water. A noisy new age talisman.

Eventually, a vacant stall appeared. I took my gloves off, shoving them into my coat pockets. My hand touched something odd, something that didn't belong there. It made a crunchy noise. Puzzled, I pulled it out. It was a folded piece of paper.

Cold, slimy dread lodged itself in my stomach. I unfolded the paper with now trembling fingers. A number and a word.

65 roses.

That slimy, sick feeling rose out of my stomach to settle in my throat. I could taste it there. I was going to throw up. My breathing turned to gasps, and I started coughing.

He was here. Worse yet, he had managed to get close enough to slip this note in my pocket without my knowing it. How could this be? I had been *looking* for him. Granted, the stadium was packed, but shouldn't *something* have clued me? What if he hadn't wanted to put a note in my pocket? What if he wanted something else? Would I have sensed him before it was too late?

Slowly, I refolded the note and put it back in my pocket, resisting the urge to tear it into shreds and flush it down the toilet. Brandi's paper trail comment loomed somewhere in my mind, although it sounded more like a whisper next to the fear screaming in my head.

Suddenly I was angry. I had had enough. I told him I wouldn't be held hostage to my disease and, by God, I wouldn't be. If I had to tell everyone personally, I would, just so I could get this creep out of my life.

In fact, I could start with Elena. Elena would be perfect, especially since she had just told me something personal. I could share this, make her feel like revealing secrets was a two-way street.

But even as I thought it, I realized Elena shouldn't be the first. I would make her second. Someone else deserved to be first.

Chapter 16

"Is Tommy home?"

TJ folded his arms and stared down at me, his face as still as stone. "And if he is?"

I knew he would be. It was Sunday morning. Tommy always slept in for his big day of watching professional football. He claimed he studied while he watched, but studying on Sunday simply meant keeping his books open in front of him, as if the words would just hop off the page and into his brain between plays. "Well, then I'd like to see him."

TJ didn't move. One of Riverview's beefy offensive tackles, his job was to protect the quarterback. Apparently he felt that job extended off the field as well. I had the impression he would like nothing more than to toss me down the hall – probably with one arm – and slam the door in my face. I shifted from one foot to the other and attempted my most alluring smile. No reaction.

"Can you at least tell him I'm here? Let him make his own decision about whether he wants to see me? After all, he is over twenty-one."

A slight scowl fractured his stony expression. "He doesn't always think too straight where you're concerned."

Great. Since there didn't seem to be any way I could push past him, I had to come up with Plan B. Maybe I could throw stones at Tommy's bedroom window like some high school Juliet.

Luckily for me, right then I heard Tommy's voice from somewhere behind TJ's bulk. "Hey. Who's at the door?"

TJ's face fractured further, but he stepped aside. Tommy stood by his bedroom door, clad in jeans and an unbuttoned shirt, showing just enough of his broad chest and flat stomach to make me weak. His blond hair stuck up in short tuffs, like he had just fallen out of bed and into some clothes.

He froze when he saw me, his green eyes dark and forbidding. I tried my alluring smile on him. Again, no reaction. Alluring smile definitely needed some tweaking. "Tommy, I'm here to explain. Everything. Can I come in?"

He crossed his arms and leaned against the wall. "How do I know it's not just more of the same doubletalk shit you've been feeding me these past couple of weeks?"

Eyeing TJ, who still hovered protectively near the door, I took a step inside the apartment, praying I wouldn't end up getting tackled. "Tommy, I swear I'm here to tell you everything. No secrets, bare my soul, the whole bit. And, I promise, if you don't like what I say, I'll go away and you'll never have to see me again."

He watched me cautiously, his face a mixture of emotions. He wanted to believe me, I could see that, but he had also been hurt, badly, and didn't feel he could trust me. I dared another step, locking my eyes with his. I could see the hunger there, the pleading, the pain. The electrical currents sizzled between us, causing goose bumps to race down my arms.

Closing his eyes, he banged his head against the wall and sighed. He opened his eyes, and without looking directly at me, gestured with his head for me to follow him. My breath came out with a gasp. I hadn't realized I had been holding it.

TJ grumbled as Tommy strode into the kitchen, still without looking at me. "Coffee?"

"Sure."

Behind me the front door slammed shut, making me jump. "I'll be in my room watching the game," TJ said, shoving me slightly as he lumbered past. At least I think he meant it to be slight since I didn't actually fall down.

Tommy glanced up and nodded. The unspoken part of that communication probably went something like: "If you need me to throw her out, just yell."

TJ closed his door as I removed my coat and sauntered across the living room. I had chosen an outfit I knew he liked – a long, dark blue turtleneck sweater, a short black skirt, black tights and long black boots. I left my hair long and loose, also the way he liked. As a finishing touch, I used foundation to cover the circles under my eyes – thanks to my nights of broken sleep – and added eyeliner and mascara to my usual blush and lipstick. Hopefully I looked better than I felt.

So far, it appeared to be a waste. Tommy refused to so much as glance at me. Picking my way through the mess I normally associated with guys' apartments – papers and dirty dishes strewn everywhere – I leaned against the stove. An empty pizza box from Uncle Frank's Pizza sat there, the red drawing of Uncle Frank's face smiling up at me.

Tommy kept his eyes fixed on a puddle of spilled cream as he handed me a brown mug with the words "I'd rather be having a beer" on it.

"Not much room to sit here." He surveyed the dirty dishes piled on the small round table. A torn tee shirt was draped over one of the chairs.

"Living room's fine." I carried my coffee to the living room. He followed me.

I chose the olive green chair closest to the television. A football pregame show was on. In one fluid motion, Tommy sat down in the brownish orange sofa, scooped up the remote from the cluttered coffee table and turned the television off. Impressive move.

He sipped his coffee. "So, talk."

Perching on the edge of the seat, I crossed my legs and balanced my mug on my lap. "I'm not exactly sure where to start." I gave a little self-conscious laugh. "This was easier in my head."

Tommy didn't answer, simply drank his coffee and waited.

I took a deep breath. Might as well get it all out in the open. "I have Cystic Fibrosis."

His face went blank. "You have what?"

"Cystic Fibrosis. It's a genetic disease that causes my body to produce too much mucus. It's the reason I have asthma, because the mucus gets into my lungs. It's also why I have to take pancreatic enzymes – digestive enzymes – because the mucus interferes with my digestion and I can't digest fats."

Now he looked puzzled. "Isn't Cystic Fibrosis the disease that … " his voice trailed off, his confusion deepening.

I studied the inside of my coffee cup. "Chances are the disease will kill me, yes. Sixty percent of people with Cystic Fibrosis don't live past their twenty-fifth birthday. Even those who do … ." I raised my head to meet his eyes. "My life expectancy is not great, even under the best of conditions. It appears I have a fairly mild case, but I'll never die of old age."

Tommy leaned forward and put his football-shaped mug on the coffee table, after first moving a bill from Riverview Gas and Electric and a *Sports Illustrated* magazine. "Cystic Fibrosis," he repeated to himself.

I rushed on. Now that I had started, I needed to get all of it out. "I'm very susceptible to bronchitis and pneumonia. Even a bad cold could very quickly become life-threatening. As a child, I came pretty close to dying once. My mother somehow managed to nurse me back to health. Kept me out of school for a couple of years, tutored me at home. She took such good care of me I hadn't had another serious attack since, but it's only a matter of time."

He rubbed his forehead with his hands. "Why didn't you tell me?"

I reached out to push aside an empty Chinese takeout carton so I could put my cup on the table as well. "I didn't tell anyone. It wasn't just you. I didn't want anyone to know. People treat you differently when they know you have a terminal disease. Sometimes you're stuck with all kinds of pity, but a lot of the time you get shunned, mostly because people don't know what to say. Sometimes they act like you have leprosy or something. I'm not contagious. It's a genetic disease, but some people can't get that through their heads."

Tommy raised his head, his hair now even more mussed up than before. "But still, you should have told me."

I looked down at my hands – the skin was dry, chapped. "That's why I broke up with you. We were getting too close, and I knew I'd have to tell you. And I didn't know how you'd react. I know I'm pretty normal now, but this will change, as much as I hate to admit it. And it's not pretty either. How could I ask you to take this on? You, with your golden future? You don't need to be shackled with some slowly dying girlfriend." There. I had said it. The truth. I was terrified to look at him. What would be his reaction?

I heard him let his breath out. "Is this why you resist taking care of Brandi's cat? And why you won't make any plans beyond a day or two? Because you're afraid you may end up in a hospital?"

"Yes."

He slumped back into the couch. "Wow. Of all the things I thought you'd tell me, I can honestly say I never guessed this."

"There's more, if you want to hear it."

"More." He said it almost as a laugh, but there was no humor in it. He stared at the ceiling. "You might as well. I'm pretty much numb from shock, so I think I could hear anything right now."

I settled myself in the chair, feeling a strange sense of calmness. Now that I had told him about my disease and he hadn't run screaming from the room, I felt like maybe I could confess everything.

And I did, starting with Cat's disappearance as a child all the way up to Halloween night. I talked about the strange letters and how David had tried to blackmail me. I even told him about my dreams and how the church dream had been transformed.

He was silent during it all. For me, the effect was cathartic. I hadn't discussed my disease with anyone since I walked out of a support group in eighth grade and informed my mother I wouldn't be returning. The more I talked, the more I wanted to unburden myself. It felt the way it did when, as a child, I tripped on a gravel road, skinning open my leg. The wound became puffy and infected. Rather than tell my mother, I squeezed the greenish puss out of it myself – disgusting, but on a deeper level it felt good. Cleansing. Purifying. Like I was finally ridding myself of a dark and evil curse.

When I finished, I felt lighter, clearer, healthier even. But then I glanced at Tommy and my positive mindset died. He looked ill.

I stared down at my lap. "I'm sorry. I probably shouldn't have told you everything."

Tommy rubbed his face, ran his hands through his hair. "No. No, I'm glad you did. I'm just a little … overwhelmed by it all."

I reached for my coffee, now cold. Maybe this wasn't such a good idea. Maybe Tommy really wouldn't be able to handle it. Oh God, what if I was right after all?

He pulled himself to his feet, his movements slow and labored, as if carrying a huge weight. "Give me some time to digest this. I'll call you."

He'll call me. Right. Where have I heard that before? I placed my coffee on the table and picked up my coat, not trusting myself to look at him, sure he would see the devastation in my eyes. "Sure, whenever you're ready." I tried to keep my voice bright, but I knew I sounded fake. Miserably fake. "I know it's a lot to handle."

He nodded, running his fingers through his hair again. Keeping my hands at my sides so he wouldn't see them shake, I strode past him. "See you."

Opening the door, I reminded myself that I would respect my promise. I would stay out of his life. I would not beg. This was his choice. I would allow him to make it and save both of our dignities.

His arm shot out and hit the door, blocking my exit. I kept my eyes focused in front of me. "Kind of hard to leave with your hand there."

"Kit," he murmured, leaning down so his face was close to mine. I could feel the heat of his breath on my cheek. "Look at me."

Closing my eyes for a moment, I willed myself to relax, to rein in my emotions. When I felt as under control as I could be under the circumstances, I opened my eyes and tilted my face toward him.

His eyes were a mixture of emotions, so jumbled I could barely read them. Sadness, shock, confusion, but affection as well, although maybe that was wishful thinking on my part.

"I want you to know, I'm glad you told me."

I nodded, unable to speak. The tension between us was unbearable. He dipped his head slightly, as if he was going to kiss me. I couldn't move, even my breathing stopped. The thought of those warm lips against mine, drawing me close, full of anticipation and promise, shook my very being.

Suddenly, abruptly, he straightened, leaving me reeling. "See you."

It happened so quickly, I felt unbalanced, as though I might tip over. My breathing started again, sounding harsh and violent. My worst fear realized. Complete and utter rejection.

"Yeah," I said, and yanked open the door. I just wanted to get out of there and away from him.

I managed to keep myself under control until I stumbled into the frigid, still air. The sun shone, adding no warmth, mocking the cold. But once outside, I could no longer contain my tears. They coursed down my cheeks, leaving trails of burning heat, then pure ice in their wake, matching my emotions tear for tear.

Chapter 17

Tommy's reaction almost made me lose my nerve, until I pictured my friends first hearing my deep dark secrets from David. That kept me going.

First I went to Rocky's Pizza for a slice of vegetarian pizza and a small salad. Anything to keep my strength up, although I didn't much feel like eating. Then it was off to Elena's.

Her reaction was pure, vintage Elena. "Honey, you should have told me," she cried, throwing her arms around me, almost causing me to burst into tears again. "I can't believe you carried this burden all by yourself for so long."

Her response soothed me, nourished my poor, hungry soul. Until then, I had no idea how badly I wanted that reassurance, how much I needed that support. Even so, I couldn't tell her about Tommy, knowing I wouldn't be able to control my tears if I did.

Next, I went in search of Brandi. I found her studying at the Union. And, again, what I expected I received – pure, vintage Brandi.

"Aren't you a little old to still be hanging around with Cystic Fibrosis?" she asked, looking me up and down.

I started to laugh. As odd as it seemed, Brandi's reaction reassured me. Never have to worry about her pitying me.

I felt so much better. At least, just as long as I didn't picture Tommy and his confused face and slumped shoulders … no, I wouldn't go there. I wouldn't think about him. I couldn't. It was better this way. Better for him to find out now. I refused to keep stewing over it.

Relief had replaced my anxiety, and I was suddenly aware of just how exhausted I was. All those nights of broken sleep. No wonder. I decided to go home and study. Maybe take a nap first. In fact, once I got myself and *Evelina* settled on the couch, I realized a nap was definitely in order.

Bang, bang, bang.

Startled, I tumbled off the couch, flinging my book across the room. Oh, God, David has just shot me.

Bang, bang, bang.

No, he's shooting his way into the apartment. I fumbled for my noisemaker and pepper spray, trying to clear the sleepy cobwebs from my brain. Have to get help. Have to scare him off. I went to pull the pin, my fingers big and clumsy from sleep.

"Kit? It's me Tommy. Are you in there?"

My hand froze. Was David impersonating Tommy to trick me into opening the door? But, what about the gun shots? Does Tommy have a gun? Now what do I do?

Luckily for Tommy, I finally woke up enough to piece everything together. No gunshots, no David, just me being paranoid and Tommy banging on the door.

"Kit?"

"Yes, I'm here," I called out. "Hold on a second." I stumbled to my feet, skirt tangled around my legs, attempting to straighten myself out. Not enough time to go to the bathroom so I glanced in the mirror Brandi had hung in the hallway.

Evelina had landed right there. I scooped it up before opening the door.

Tommy stood there, his red and blue ski jacket thrown over a rumpled Packer jersey, his manner uncertain.

For a moment we just stared at each other. He broke the silence first with a hesitant voice. "I was thinking … maybe if I saw those letters, I might have some ideas about what's going on."

I couldn't answer him right away. The bright, shining edge of relief had cut through my doubt, my anxiety. Did this mean he would accept my disease, could accept my disease? Did I dare hope?

"You think?" I asked, attempting to sound casual. My knees felt too weak to hold me up. I leaned against the door, trying to mask it.

He tilted his head, studying me. Then he smiled, brilliant and golden, lighting up his whole face. My breath caught in my throat. "Yeah. I think."

***

"Any bright ideas?"

Tommy studied the items laid out on the kitchen table: the note that came with the confetti, the letter accompanying the dead rose, the tiny message I found in my jacket yesterday and the rose pin. He shook his head. "Nothing immediately springs to mind."

I moved to stand next to him, breathing in his scent of snow and cold and Irish Spring soap.

Tommy fingered the first note. "'Kit Cat. First there were two, then there was one. Soon there will be none.' It sounds to me like she thinks something's gonna happen to you."

"Yeah, that's kind of what I got out of it."

"But, it also sounds like you can stop it. Discover the truth. What truth do you think she's referring to?"

I shrugged. "Not really sure. Maybe who kidnapped Cat? Although why that would stop anything, I don't know."

He pulled one of the chairs over, flipped it around and straddled it backwards. "What do you know about your sister's kidnapping?"

"Not much." I started pacing. "It happened while I was in the hospital. I had pneumonia and a pretty high fever. Don't remember too much about that period in my life."

"What did your parents tell you?"

I didn't answer for a moment, instead leaning over to rest my elbows on the dark yellow kitchen counter. "Would you believe nothing?"

"Nothing?" Tommy sounded puzzled.

My hands squeezed into fists. I pushed them against my forehead. "We never talked about it."

"Never?"

"Oh God, Tommy, don't make this harder than it is." I straightened, resumed my pacing.

"I'm not, but I am confused. I mean, this is a pretty important event, and families generally discuss important events."

"Not mine." I paced around the counter, my voice flat, devoid of emotion. It felt strange, unnatural almost, to be talking about this, but I had promised I would tell him everything. "My first memory after being sick was lying in the hospital bed and asking my mother where Cat was. She had a strange, almost despaired expression on her face and told me we'd talk about it later. A few weeks later, when I was home recuperating, I asked her again. She told me Cat had been kidnapped. Then, her face just … .shut down. Closed off. I never asked again."

Tommy stayed silent. I kept walking. How could I explain to him the emptiness I felt watching my mother's face flatten? At that moment

I knew, knew with absolute certainty that in my mother's heart, the wrong child had been kidnapped. The pain had been unbearable. I had also understood (or sensed) that my mother would always take care of me – make sure my illness stayed under control, that I did my home-work and didn't stay out too late – but in her heart, I would always be second. A far, distant second. I would always be the sick child. The wrong child.

Folding my arms across my chest, my back to Tommy, I blinked back tears. We had never spoken about it because I couldn't bear to hear her say what I had known all along. Because once said, it would harden and crystallize, shattering my already bruised heart.

Taking a few deep breaths, I wrestled my emotions under control for the second time that day and turned back to Tommy. "Anyway, that's the long way of saying I don't know much."

Tommy studied me, his expression full of sympathy and something else I couldn't read. He opened his mouth, closed it without saying anything, then angled his head toward the notes. "Well, I guess it's one place to start. What happened to Cat, I mean."

I nodded, making my way back to the kitchen table. He continued to examine the objects. "As for David, have you filed any sort of formal complaint yet? To the school or the police?"

I pulled a chair out and sat down. "No, not yet."

He reached out to the dead rose, but didn't touch it. Instead, his hand hovered above it, like he was casting a spell. "Don't you think it would be a good idea? I mean, this guy sounds like he's threatening your life."

"Yeah, Brandi and I talked about it, I just hadn't gotten over there yet." It suddenly occurred to me that he had sent that rose on Thursday, only three days ago. It seemed a lot longer than that.

Tommy's hand then floated over to the jeweler's box, hovered above it for moment, before snatching it up. Snapping open the box, he stud-ied the pin, his face growing stiller by the second. "I thought you said you were going to return this to him."

"Christ, Tommy. I don't see how you can be jealous right now."

He tossed the box back onto the table. "I'm not jealous. It's just with everything that's happened, I'm surprised you still have it."

"Oddly enough, it's because I haven't had a chance to return it."

He folded his arms across the back of the chair, staring at the open box, now lying on its side, diamonds glinting in the light. "It's a pretty expensive piece of jewelry."

"That's already been established."

He chewed on his bottom lip, eyes never leaving the pin, almost like the sparkling stones had hypnotized him.

I rolled my eyes. "Tommy, what's the problem here?"

Arms still folded, he drummed his fingers against his bicep. "Well, I don't know. Maybe it's because you've spent the day telling me what a psycho this guy is, yet it somehow slips your mind to return an expensive gift to him."

"Tommy, what are you accusing me of?"

"I'm not accusing you of anything. I simply don't understand why you'd want a reminder of that psycho lying around."

"I don't want a reminder of him lying around. I told you, I haven't gotten around to returning it."

"The last time I looked, the post office was still accepting letters and packages for delivery."

I gaped at him. "You think I should *mail* it back?"

"Why not? Then you wouldn't have to see him, and you'd have one less reminder of him around."

I paused and took a deep breath. Then I sat back in my chair and crossed my legs. "Why does the fact I haven't returned this piece of jewelry threaten you so?"

His mouth dropped open. "What are you talking about? It doesn't threaten me."

"Then why are you so fixated on it?"

He threw his arms up. "Because if you really didn't like this guy, it would have made sense to have already returned it."

"So, you think I might actually have feelings for David, after everything I've told you, based on the fact I didn't return a piece of jewelry fast enough to meet your timeline requirements?"

That stopped him. He paused, mouth half open to argue, and pondered my words. Then he smiled. "Okay. Maybe you have a point."

I rolled my eyes. "Maybe I have a really good point."

He leaned forward against the back of the chair. "All right, all serious now. You should definitely go to the police and the school and anyone else we can think of and file some formal complaints against this guy. Immediately. Tomorrow. I'll go with you."

"You don't have to go with me." I said, but I was touched. I had spent so much of my life distancing myself from people, I had become used to doing the important things alone. Having someone offer to help felt strange but right at the same time, like trying on a new pair of shoes that you knew would feel great once you got used to them.

"I'd like to help." He locked his eyes with mine. Caring mixed with lust. The shivers started up my spine and I broke the gaze. Before we got involved again, I needed to make sure he fully understood my disease and all its implications. I didn't think I could bear igniting our relationship again, only to have him leave because the disease demanded more than he could give.

Tommy swung his right leg off the chair and stood up. "I should get going. But, I'll see you tomorrow after classes, right?" He looked at me expectantly.

I nodded. "Tomorrow. We'll get it done."

"Right." He scooped his jacket up, putting it on as I walked him out. I opened the front door and the cold wind rushed in, stinging my stocking-clad legs. Pausing for a second, he gazed into my face. His eyes were hungry, desperate to say something. But at the last moment, he changed his mind. "See you," he said, and without waiting for an answer, disappeared into the night.

Chapter 18

Nibbling on my toast and peanut butter, I listened to Martha clumping around, getting ready to face her Monday. At least that's what I assumed she was doing. So when she burst in the kitchen and started yelling, I was totally unprepared.

"You said he was going to stop hanging around."

Oh, no. My stomach dropped to the ground – I could almost hear the sickening thud it made when it hit the tile. "What?" I asked, trying to pretend she meant someone else, an axe murderer maybe.

Martha stomped toward me, her normally pale face flushed an unattractive pink color. Her mousy brown hair looked even more wilted than usual, flattened against her face and neck. "That guy you're dating. You said he was going to stop hanging around."

Brandi chose that moment to saunter in the kitchen, a circular brush in one hand, hair still damp. "Shouting first thing on a Monday morning does not bode well for the rest of the week."

In the space where my stomach used to be, a cold knot of ice had formed. "He will."

Martha glared at me, leaning across the kitchen table, the flush staining her face now spreading down her neck. "How can you be so sure?"

Brandi tapped the brush against her other hand, gazing at both of us. "Now, children, play nicely. What gives?"

Martha pointed her finger at me. Her nail was ragged, bitten off. "Her boyfriend keeps hanging around here."

Brandi's eyes widened, the expression suddenly wary. "*Boyfriend?*"

I stared at the white and gold plate, realized I still held the piece of toast I no longer had an appetite for, and made my hand let go. It dropped to the plate with a tiny plop. "Uh, she's talking about David," I mumbled.

"*David?*" Brandi now advanced on me. "David's been hanging around here?"

"Every night," Martha said.

"Every night?" Brandi repeated, her head swiveling as she tried to keep her eyes on both of us at the same time. "How long has this been going on?"

"Little over a week. She," Martha pointed at me again, "told me that it would stop."

"She told … Kit, you knew?"

"Uh … " I started to say, but Brandi interrupted me.

"And you didn't think I might like to know about this?"

"Well, actually, no," I said.

"*No?*"

"Brandi, I thought he'd stop doing it. I didn't want to worry you."

"Have you reported him yet?"

I looked at my plate again, the crumbs dusting the surface. "I will today."

"Oh. Translated, that means a big fat 'no.'" Brandi began stalking back and forth across the kitchen.

Martha's stain darkened to a reddish pink. "You haven't done anything yet to stop him?"

"Look, I'm trying here … "

"How do you expect me to study?" Martha's voice grew louder. "How do expect me to concentrate when every night I come home to find him lurking around? Even if you don't care about your grades, you should show some consideration to the real students around here."

"Christ Almighty," Brandi groaned. The ice knot tightened, twisting itself painfully inside me.

"Last night too?" I asked in a tiny voice. The expression on Martha's face was all the answer I needed. The ice knot suddenly doubled in size.

"Kit, you've got to do something here," Brandi said.

I pushed back my chair, so abruptly it tipped over, hitting the wall with a bang. "I am. Today. I'm registering a complaint with everyone I can think of." I scooped up my plate and walked to the sink, leaving my chair awkwardly balanced against the wall. "I'll try to get a restraining order as well."

Brandi leaned over the counter until her head was in my field of vision, her hazel eyes hard. "You better," she said, her voice quiet but full of steel.

For a moment, I couldn't move, the harshness in those eyes so intense it paralyzed me. "You knew David was following me. Why so surprised now?"

She leaned closer. "Because now it's my problem, too."

I stared at her, so shocked at her words, her attitude that I dropped the plate into the sink. It made a cracking noise that normally would have disturbed me, but these weren't normal times. I didn't even glance at the sink, instead pushing my way past Brandi. "I have to get to class."

Martha's voice, even more high pitched, followed me out of the kitchen. "I can't focus like this. Get him to stop. I need to be able to study."

"I said I'd take care of it. Quit worrying," I shouted back, grabbing my coat and books and running out the door. I decided to put my coat on outside. That cold out here felt cleaner, fresher, more honest than the chill inside the apartment.

***

"Now let me get this straight," Detective Jenkins said, leaning back in his chair until it creaked, folding his arms across his substantial belly. The buttons on his untidy white shirt strained at the effort. "You're saying a David Naughton has sent you these things." He gestured to the dead rose and two notes. "But not this one," his other hand waved over the confetti note.

For the thousandth time that day, I regretted bringing the confetti note to the station. At the time, I thought it might help my case, show that someone else thought David was dangerous. Just the opposite – it appeared to be weakening my already weak case.

"Yes."

His chair squeaked again as he rocked forward. "How can you tell? None of these are signed."

I ran my hands through my hair, resisting the urge to pull a handful of strands out. The sounds of keyboards tapping clashed with the hum of human voices, everything from low murmurs to shouts to laughter, added to my headache.

It hadn't been a good day. I should have just stayed in bed. I had spent most of it devising avoid-David schemes that now appeared to have been a total waste. At first, I had thought they were working, but in retrospect it all seemed too easy. Like he hadn't even tried to see me.

I gestured toward the messages on the detective's desk. "That note sounds like the same kind of warning I got from the girl at the Halloween party. And the other notes definitely sound more like David."

"So, it's just a feeling then?"

I wanted to scream. "It's more than a feeling. I've had encounters with both these people." My headache worsened. Everything about this place was making me crazy. It even stunk – old, burnt coffee and sweaty, unwashed bodies. Next to me, Tommy put a comforting hand on my arm.

"I'll take these and dust them for prints." His tone clearly said he didn't expect to find any. "Anything else to report?"

"One of my roommates has seen him hanging around outside our apartment every night."

Detective Jenkins nodded, took a few notes. "Where exactly has he been hanging around?"

"I don't know. You'll have to ask her." I didn't think I wanted to know exactly where.

He wrote a few more things down. "Anything else?" He didn't sound very convinced.

I chewed on my lip. I had already told him about David following me to classes and attacking me in the library stairwell. "Isn't that enough?"

"Well, to be frank, Miss Caldwell, what we're missing is hard evidence."

"Evidence?" I gestured toward the notes. "What's this? A ham sandwich?"

"As I said, we'll dust for prints, but as of right now there's no proof these came from the person you're accusing."

I slammed my hands on my lap. "What about him attacking me in the stairwell?"

Detective Jenkins sat back. "Your word against his. Where's a witness? A medical report? Even a bruise?"

Christ, I couldn't believe this. "But, my roommate has been seeing him outside our apartment."

The detective raised his voice. "And we'll get a statement from her. I realize it's frustrating, and it's not that we're not sympathetic, but you haven't brought me enough to charge him. What about answering machine recordings? Other witnesses? We need more if we're going to make an arrest."

Brandi warned me. I should have listened. "Whatever."

"Stalking cases are difficult to prove," Detective Jenkins continued, as if I hadn't said anything. "You need to be very diligent about collecting evidence. There are some excellent resources on the Internet and in the bookstore about stalking, including what constitutes evidence, how much you need, etc. I suggest taking a look at them."

"Thanks for your help."

His expression hardened. I guess my tone was a bit too sarcastic.

"I'll write up my report, interview your roommate and get you a case number," he said, his voice a couple of degrees cooler. "Once you have more evidence, bring it in and we'll see what we can do."

I stood. "Fine. I'll start collecting."

He stood as well. "Finals are coming up, aren't they?"

I looked at him suspiciously. "And that has what to do with my stalking case?"

He shrugged. "Just making conversation. How're your grades?"

"They're fine. What does any of this matter to you?"

He placed his knuckles against the top of his desk and leaned on them, rocking back and forth. "It's just that at about this time of year, we get a certain number of false reports from students, usually students looking for some reason to drop out." His lips twisted into what I think was supposed to be a smile, but ended up being a sneer. "It's procedure to ask."

I wanted to reach across the desk and strangle him. "This is not an attention stunt. I'll get that evidence and be back."

"Good." He rubbed his hands together. "Glad we got that settled." He turned his attention to Tommy. "So, you think you guys will win the Rose Bowl a second year in a row?"

I didn't even try to hide my disgust as I stalked out of his office.

Tommy caught up with me as I paced outside. "Well, that could've gone better."

I strode down the hallway. "You think?"

"We'll just have to get some more evidence, that's all." He shot me a crooked grin. "I guess it's a good thing you made copies of those notes before you brought them."

"Guess so." I ducked to get out of the way of a female cop striding determinedly down the hall, my thoughts sliding to the black jeweler's box still sitting safely in my purse. I had intended to hand it over to the cops for evidence, so it puzzled me that I hadn't. Why this strange reluctance? What could I possibly gain by hanging on to it?

Enough of this. I'll analyze it later. With effort, I forced my thoughts back to the present. "I think we missed a big opportunity back there with my story. We should have told him David was bothering you instead of me. Probably would have garnered more reaction since we couldn't have the quarterback destined to take the team to the Rose Bowl irritated by a stalker."

Tommy chuckled. "Yeah, but he'd never believe it. No self-respecting quarterback gets irritated by stalkers."

I sighed. "I just can't win. Brandi warned me about this. She didn't think there'd be much the police could do."

We had reached the lobby and paused to put on our jackets. "Yeah, well unfortunately she was right. Let's go file a complaint with the school."

***

Student Services was nearly deserted when we walked in – only a couple of Korean women and a red-haired guy with a terrified expression populated the narrow hallway. After reading the descriptions above the windows, I chose the one marked "Harassment." Good as place as any.

The worker barely glanced at us, continuing to furiously pound at her keyboard. "I'd like to file a complaint," I said, leaning over the window. The fluorescent lights added a greenish tinge to the white cinderblock walls and white tile floor.

"We close in fifteen minutes," she answered, eyes never leaving the computer screen. She looked to be middle-aged, with blond hair rolled in tight sausage curls and small silver reading glasses perched on her nose. Her desk was devoid of any personal items save for one framed photograph of a young man in a suit.

"Well, then. We'd better get started," I said.

She looked at me then, peering over the glasses, her lips pursed in disapproval. "It takes longer than fifteen minutes to do the paperwork."

"I'm pretty speedy."

Her frown deepened. I sighed. "Can we at least start, or let me see the paperwork or something? It took me longer than I thought to file a complaint with the cops and I'd like to get something done today."

She studied me, considering. "What kind of complaint?"

"I'm being stalked."

Her eyebrows lifted. "Student or teacher?"

"Student."

"Have you talked to the police about it?"

"Yes, I just finished doing that. Now, I want to file a complaint with the university."

Taking off her glasses, she closed her eyes and pinched her nose for a moment. Leaving her glasses to dangle on a silver chain around her neck, she heaved her considerable bulk out of the chair and gestured for us to move to the door. Opening it, she ushered us inside. I caught a whiff of her floral perfume.

We followed her through a maze of desks, people and filing cabinets – tons of filing cabinets.

"You'd think with computers they could get rid of some of those," Tommy whispered to me. I nodded, stepping aside to avoid a man in a wheelchair using one of the cabinets. Everything seemed to be coated with that same unhealthy greenish glow.

Our guide held open a door to a small room furnished with four chairs, a table and a computer. She gestured for us to sit then disappeared for a moment. When she returned, she had several sheets of paper with her.

"Like I said, we close in fifteen minutes, but we can at least get some of the basics done." She closed the door and bustled over to the chair in front of the computer, eyeglasses jingling on the chain. The floral perfume permeated the small room – I had to concentrate to keep from coughing "You'll also have to meet with the dean of Student Services. Call his secretary tomorrow to get an appointment."

Introducing herself as Eileen Livenson, she laid one of the forms on top of the pile, balanced her glasses on the tip of her nose and uncapped a pen. "Name?" She poised her pen at the top of the form.

"Kit Caldwell," I said, breathing out of my mouth. I wondered why she would handwrite the forms when a computer sat right there. Oh, well, bureaucracy.

She wrote it down, using quick birdlike strokes, before turning to Tommy. "Are you a part of this complaint as well?"

He shook his head. Eileen adjusted her glasses to look at me better. "You do realize there are parts of this process you'll need to do alone. For privacy purposes."

I nodded, trying not to roll my eyes.

"Student identification number?"

I supplied it and the rest of the information for the top half of the form. When she finished, she moved the pen decisively to the second part. "Name of the student you are filing a complaint about."

"David Naughton." I helped her spell the last name.

"Address?"

"Not sure, somewhere on North Main, maybe 141 or 151?"

Eileen turned to the computer and typed in the name. A moment later, she frowned. "The only David Naughton I have in here is a freshman who lives in a dormitory, Loggin Hall. Could that be him?"

I shook my head. "No, I was at his apartment. And he's a grad student in engineering, not a freshman."

"Are you sure you have the name spelled right?"

"Yes, I saw the name when I went to his apartment."

Her brow furrowed. "Are you sure he's a student here and not at Riverview Technical College?"

"Are you sure you're using that computer right?" First that stupid cop and now this. I was the victim here, for God's sake. Didn't anyone get that?

Her eyes narrowed. "There's no need to get defensive. I'm on your side." Her tone had cooled to frosty. Under the table, Tommy put his hand on my knee, gently squeezing.

I took a deep breath and almost choked on the perfume. "I'm sorry, it's been a rough day. Look, I know that address was either 141 or 151 North Main Street. Can you do a reverse search using the address and see what name pops up?"

She tapped a few keys on the computer. "Not without an apartment number."

I thought for a moment. "I think it was 5D or something. Definitely five something."

Eileen eyed me, but obediently tapped away at the keys. Watching the screen, her eyebrows suddenly went up a notch. "Well, this is interesting. There is a David who lives at apartment 5D at 141 North Main Street, and he is a graduate student in engineering. But his last name is not Naughton."

I held my breath and counted to five in my head. No, I would not strangle Eileen Livenson, no matter how attractive that prospect became. "What is it?"

"Terry. David Terry. T-E-R-R-Y," she spelled.

Tommy shot me a sharp look. I shrugged back, my hands in the air, an "I have no idea" expression on my face.

"I wonder how you got that name wrong," Eileen mused, still studying the screen. "Doesn't sound anything like Naughton. Are you sure this is the David you want to make a complaint against?"

I pressed my fingers flat against the table to prevent them from balling into little knots and taking matters into their own hands. "This man has been stalking me. Did it occur to you that perhaps he'd tell me a wrong name to prevent me from making a complaint against him?"

Eileen took her glasses off and pinched her nose. "I don't know. We don't have many students coming in here to complain they're being stalked by other students."

"Look," Tommy interrupted, flashing his most charming grin and squeezing my knee again. He had probably seen my hands looking like they may do something regretful. "It's closing time anyway, so why don't we stop for the day? We'll go make sure David Terry and David Naughton are one and the same, then we can finish this tomorrow. Sound like a plan?"

Eileen looked relieved. "Yes. I think that's an excellent suggestion. The windows open at seven-forty-five in the morning and we close at four-forty-five. Come back anytime between then."

Tommy thanked her as he helped me to my feet and escorted me to the door. At the last second, I broke his hold.

"Can you look up one more name for me? Please?"

Eileen glanced pointedly at her watch. "It's … "

I stepped forward. "Please? Just tell me if she's a student or not. That's all I want to know."

Eileen's eyes darted between the watch and me. She let out a long sigh. "What's the name?"

"Cat Caldwell."

Eileen gave me a funny look before typing in the name. Tommy tried to catch my eye, but I kept my gaze on Eileen.

"No," Eileen said after a moment. "No Cat Caldwell."

Although I expected that answer, I felt my heart sink anyway. "How about Catalina Caldwell?"

"No, no Caldwells except for one. A Kitrina Caldwell." She said this in a voice oozing with disapproval. Oddly enough, the tone didn't match the expression in her eyes, which regarded me warily.

"Thanks," I said, as Tommy gripped my arm and dragged me outside.

"What was that Cat thing all about?" he asked, letting go only after we both stepped into the cold winter sunlight.

I looked at him in exasperation. "The woman at the Halloween party. Don't you remember?"

He glared at me, equally as exasperated. "Of course, I remember. I just couldn't believe that's what you were trying to check. I mean, you really think she was your sister? And even if she was, she was kidnapped when you were seven. Why on earth would she still be using your parents' last name?"

I gazed at the sky, too aggravated to admit he was probably right. "This day totally sucks. Nothing is going the way it should. Why the hell does no one believe me? And why the hell did David lie to me about his name?"

Tommy shoved his hands in his coat pockets. "Don't know. It's probably what you said, he was planning on stalking you and didn't want you to know his name."

I frowned. "Yeah, I know I said that but something just doesn't feel right." In fact, the more I thought about it, the more pissed off I got.

Tommy pondered. "Does the name Terry mean anything to you?"

"Should it? No, I've never known any Terrys."

He stomped his feet. "Well, then maybe he was trying to fuck with your mind. Sounds like it's something he enjoys doing."

A fat gray squirrel ran up the side of a trashcan sitting on the street, studying the contents in its quick, sharp way. Its movements were not entirely unlike Eileen Livenson, although it weighed a lot less. Hordes of students meandered past it, but the squirrel paid them no heed.

"You know." I spun on my heel to face Tommy. "I really would like to know why David lied to me. In fact, I'd like to know so much I think I'll go ask him." I stalked past both him and the squirrel. The squirrel, finding nothing decent in the trash, darted off in search of other treasures.

Tommy hurried to catch up. "Hey, slow down there. I'd like to know that as much as the next guy, but do you really think this is a good time to be asking?"

I kept right on marching, eyes fixed straight ahead. My anger simmered right below the surface, threatening to turn into a rolling boil. I knew I would focus on nothing else for the rest of the day, so I might as well confront David now. "As that crazy old saying goes, there's no time like the present."

Tommy's long legs fell into stride next to mine. "What if he's not there?"

"Then, we'll wait."

I didn't look at him. I knew I sounded borderline fanatical, but I had reached the point of not caring. I wanted answers and I wanted them now. To Tommy's credit, he didn't argue, just silently accompanied me to my destination. If I hadn't been so agitated, I would have admired his response. As Brandi said, and kept saying, he certainly did seem to be a keeper.

Chapter 19

This time I didn't need any help breaking into the red and white brick apartment building. Someone had propped the security door open with a rock. Before going in, I studied the list of apartment numbers in the directory, looking for David's, desperately needing confirmation I hadn't dreamed the whole last name thing.

When I finally found it, I couldn't speak – rage and confusion mingled in explosive concentrations inside me.

Tommy saw it, too. "David Terry," he read. "But I thought … " his voice trailed off.

I stepped forward, putting my hands on either side of the directory. The piece of tape that had read "David Naughton" was gone. In its place, in the same type as the other names, was "David Terry."

"Tommy, I swear. He had David Naughton here last week," I said, my eyes glued to those words.

"I believe you," Tommy said, his tone of voice skeptical even as his words were reassuring. Great. My one ally had started doubting me. I wanted to kill David.

Whipping around, I flung open the security door and strode inside. "Are you sure you want to do this?" Tommy called from behind me.

"Very," I answered, heading for the stairs, too agitated to wait for the elevator.

This time, I kept my stride in check so as not to create another coughing fit. With every step I climbed, my anger also rose a notch. Why would he lie about his last name? Actually more than a simple lie. To be so calculating as to change the directory. What had he expected to accomplish? Did he think I would never find out? And why did he remove the tape? Exactly what the hell kind of game was David playing?

I wished I had never set foot inside that Halloween party – I could have lived the rest of my life quite happily never knowing David, never meeting the woman who called herself Cat. What kind of insanity had I gotten myself into?

I managed to keep myself under enough control so that I was only coughing a little by the time I reached David's apartment. Better than I expected. I pounded on the door.

Tommy wisely stayed to the side, so as not to be seen through the peephole. I didn't appreciate how shrewd that was until I saw David's face when he opened the door.

"Kit," he exclaimed, a smile stretching across his features. Then he saw Tommy and the smile disintegrated, replaced by shock.

"We need to talk." I took advantage of his hesitation to muscle my way inside the apartment.

Tommy grinned at David. "Nice to see you again, buddy." He shoved David aside, slamming him into the wall next to the door. For the first time, I saw fear dart across David's face.

"I could have you arrested for that," he said.

Tommy shrugged as he shut the door behind him. "For what? You fell back against the wall. Where's the crime?"

"How about for breaking and entering?" David snapped back. "This is my apartment and you're trespassing."

Tommy smiled at him pleasantly, crossing his arms and leaning against the door. "Gee, I thought a David Terry lived here. Isn't your name David Naughton? How can it be trespassing when it's not your apartment?"

David hesitated, his expression melting into confusion. I stepped into his line of vision. "Why the hell did you lie to me about your last name?"

David transferred his bewildered expression to me, before comprehending my words. His features smoothed themselves out. "What are you talking about?" A smug smile twitched at the corners of his mouth.

He knew. He knew exactly what I was talking about. I could see it in his eyes. He had deliberately set out to deceive me about his last name, for reasons I would probably never understand, and now he would continue to lie to me about it.

Right then, I fully understood the expression "seeing red." I actually did see red, almost as though a red veil had draped itself across my vision.

"You ass." I struggled to keep my voice under control, to not scream at him. "You know exactly what I'm talking about. You told me your name was Naughton."

He shifted his position against the wall, his whole body relaxing. Obviously, we were back to playing his game again. "Now, why would I do that? It doesn't make any sense. I mean, that's something you can look up for yourself, so it wouldn't make any sense to lie about a last name. Now, would it?"

I stalked toward him, coughing a couple of times. "You put a piece of tape on the directory downstairs with the name Naughton on it." My voice grew louder on each word.

He pretended to look surprised. "Why would I do a thing like that?"

That did it. My control disintegrated. "Because you told me your name was Naughton," I screamed. "Why? Why would you tell me your name was Naughton when it's Terry? Why? Tell me." I started coughing.

"You should take better care of yourself," David said in a concerned voice. "Take some deep breaths. Try not to let yourself get so stressed out, especially over such small things. It's clearly not good for you."

"What's clearly not good for me is you," I gasped, choking back the coughs.

David's eyes turned cold, flat. "I'd be careful what you say."

"Hey." Tommy stepped between us. "Are you threatening her?"

David focused his eerie, empty eyes on Tommy. "Threat? What threat? I just told her she should be careful. It probably wouldn't hurt you to follow the same advice."

"What the ... " Tommy advanced toward him, but I clutched his arm. David smiled, a smile even colder than his eyes, a smile that sent chills through my body. Suddenly I knew David was quite capable of cold-blooded murder. No question about it.

I dug the jewelry box out of my purse. Now I knew why I held it back from the cops. "Here." I threw it at him. "I don't ever want to see your face again. Ever. Don't come near me, don't call me and quit hanging around outside my apartment. Consider this goodbye forever. And no, we can't be friends."

The jewelry box bounced off his chest and hit the floor. He watched it, the sinister smile slipping a notch. I pushed Tommy toward the door.

"Sixty-five roses," he called out. I turned to look at him. His smile had transformed into a sneer – an ugly, calculating, horrifying sneer.

"He knows." I paused to smile triumphantly at David. "In fact, the whole school knows. Goodbye, David." I yanked open the door and slammed it shut behind us.

"Get me out of here," I hissed to Tommy, afraid if I said much more I would collapse into another coughing fit. My chest burned, every breath wheezing and shuttering out of me. Tommy put his arm around me and helped me to the elevator.

Despite the agony I was in, I refused to break down, refused to let David see my weakness. He had already seen too much of it. Even if it killed me, I would not give in to my disease.

Outside, I still didn't let my guard down. He could see me from the window. I kept a tight rein on my coughs, refusing to let them come out and play, as I staggered to the nearest restaurant, Tom's Sub Shop. Once inside, I stumbled to the bathroom and proceeded to hack from my lungs all the stress, frustration and rage of the day.

Finished, my body exhausted and sore, I stayed on the floor, leaning against the stall. Luckily, nobody else had walked in to witness my humiliation. Everything hurt – head, chest, throat. On top of that, the mucus had a worrisome green tinge to it. Wonderful. The beginning of an infection. The perfect end to a perfect day.

All right, enough of this. Time to pull myself together. Standing up, I splashed water on my face. Did my forehead feel warmer than normal? No, stop right there. I did *not* have a fever. This was just a reaction to my horrible day.

Tommy waved as I tottered out of the bathroom. He was sitting at a booth with two cups in front of him. The rest of the restaurant was empty except for one employee, a woman cleaning up the sandwich area. A gold nose ring gleamed against the soft chocolaty brown color of her skin.

"Hot tea with lemon and honey." He gestured to the cup as I slid into the cracked red vinyl booth across from him. I smelled cold cuts, tomatoes and onions mixed with that distinctive tea scent. "Always tasted good when I was sick."

"Thanks." I took a sip, the warm liquid soothing, coating my aching throat. "It does help."

He flashed me a quick grin before turning his attention to his own tea bag. "Well, I'd say that was on the major intense side."

I continued to drink. "Gee, you think?"

He laughed a little. "Okay, understatement of the century. But, seriously, I'm worried about you. David doesn't seem … entirely stable."

"Another understatement. Are you going for the record?" I tried to keep my voice light despite my seesawing emotions. On one side, warm and soft at the idea of Tommy worrying about me. On the other, cold and edgy because I too was worried about me.

A tinkling bell rang, announcing the entrance of a young red-haired freckled woman, loaded with books. She studied the menu for a moment before marching up to the counter and ordering.

Tommy continued to dunk his tea bag, eyes fixed on his mug. "I'm serious."

I sighed. "So am I. Why do you think I went to the cops and the university today? Why do you think I'm carrying around pepper spray and this obnoxious noisemaker? I'll give you hint – it's *not* because I'm having fun here."

He didn't look reassured. "But he's hanging around your apartment, he knows your class schedule. And look at how he acted today. I mean, this is a real problem."

"Tommy, you're not telling me anything I don't already know." I sipped more tea as the red-haired woman started arguing with the employee. Something about mayonnaise, but whether she wanted it or not, I wasn't sure.

He drummed his fingers on the table, next to the steamy circle his mug had made on the plastic red-and-white checkered tablecloth. "And the way he lied to you first about his last name and then lied to you about lying to you. He could be capable of anything."

"And your point is … "

His eyes flickered at me. "Okay, you're right. But, Kit, you gotta understand. This is all new to me. And, I've never seen anything like this – this blatant manipulation. It's kinda scary."

"Tell me about it," I murmured into my tea, trying to block out the throbbing aches coming from my head, chest and throat. They seemed to be conducting an orchestration of pain with different scores. Each ache had its own unique rendition to torment me with.

"And the worst part is that it doesn't make sense," Tommy continued. "Why would he lie about his name? Something so easily caught. It's weird. And how does this Cat person fit into all this? Even if she knew what David was capable of, how would she know you and he would meet? And why be so vague about it, why not tell you straight out this guy has some serious issues?"

I closed my eyes. "I don't know, Tommy. I really don't." What I almost added, but didn't, was that right now I didn't care. I was too exhausted, too drained and in too much pain to care about the "whys." I just wanted to crawl into bed and sleep for a week.

Maybe some of that came across in my tone, because Tommy finally focused on me. "We should get you home, Kit. You don't look too good."

"I don't feel too good either," I said, finishing my tea.

"We should get dinner too. Are you hungry?"

I nodded, although I wasn't. But I should be, I hadn't had that much to eat. "Don't you have football practice?"

"Had it this morning. Coach made a few changes," he said quickly. A little too quickly, I thought, then chastised myself for being so paranoid. Why would Tommy lie to me about football practice? I was letting David get to me.

"Do you want a sandwich here or go somewhere else or just go home?" he asked

"Whatever." I was too tired to make any decisions.

Tommy slid out of the booth. "I'll take you to your apartment."

I nodded, allowing him to help me out of the booth and into my coat. He even took my books for me.

"Been a long time since a guy carried my books for me," I joked as we headed out the door. The red-haired woman, looking vindicated, finished paying for her sandwich.

"Been a long time since I offered," he answered, flashing his grin.

Chapter 20

Back at the church. Back at the graveyard.

The wolves were howling, louder now. The bell rang – low, melodious and discordant against the eerie calls of the wolves.

"Ah, there it is," Cat the seven-year-old said. She walked next to me. Our parents, in front of us, headed purposefully toward the graveyard, ignoring us both.

"There what is? My doll?" I craned my neck forward, trying to see around my parents.

Cat looked at me, sighed. "Forget the doll, Kit. It's not about the doll. The doll is here to distract. It will only get you in trouble."

"How can it get me in any more trouble than I'm already in? Besides, the doll will protect me. It would never hurt me. Why won't you give it to me?" My voice rose, sounding more like a child on the verge of a temper tantrum. We turned the corner of the church and the graveyard appeared. My breath hitched in my throat, coughs bubbled in my chest.

"I can't give you what I don't have. Besides, it doesn't matter. Do you understand? That doesn't matter anymore."

"Why don't you make any sense?" I said, suddenly exasperated, suddenly an adult. "You used to make sense. Why don't you anymore? What did the fairies do to you?"

Cat's face turned stark white. "Oh God, Kit. You don't want to hear about the fairies. The fairies are evil. Pure evil. That's why you have to save the innocent. It's all up to you."

"Fairies aren't evil," I said, confused. "Fairies are good."

Cat glared at me. "If they're so good, why did they take me away? I was happy, I wanted to stay with you, but the fairies came and took me away. I didn't want to go. Kit, you gotta believe me, I didn't want to go!" Her voice changed, becoming plaintive, frantic.

"I believe you," I said, alarmed by the change. Cat looked ill, her face so white it was almost featureless, contrasting with the intensity of her glassy blue eyes.

"Promise me, Kit. You'll save the innocent."

"I promise," I said, willing to say anything to reassure her. The freshly dug grave slid into my view, surrounded by people, surrounded by the evil Being. I began coughing in earnest.

"You promised, Kit. Don't forget."

Cat's voice was fading away. I tried to turn, but my head refused to move. I was staring, transfixed by the grave, the people, the evil. My coughing became choking and I collapsed, gasping like a fish, but not before seeing it. The evil shadow. It looked like it was gathering itself up, molding itself into form. A recognizable form.

A human form.

I woke with a gasp and a shudder, so violent I fell out of bed and toppled to the floor, banging my shoulder hard against the nightstand. Wheezing and coughing, I reached for my inhaler, but found myself twisted in blankets instead. The cold fist of panic gripped me, and I thrashed around in the dark, disoriented, unable to breathe. David was in the room watching me, waiting for me to settle down enough so he could pounce on me, hold a pillow over my face or maybe slash me with a knife …

I wrenched my arm free. Desperate, I flung it up to my nightstand, knocking stuff everywhere. Finally, my fingers closed upon the familiar plastic device and I shoved it into my mouth, sucking the medicine in fiercely.

Moments later my breathing quieted, and with it, my thoughts. Here I was, lying on the floor, dripping with sweat, knotted in covers and convinced David was hiding in the shadows of my room. Pathetic.

Sighing, I snapped on a light and finished untangling myself. Three in the morning. Great. Another night of broken sleep. Much more of this and I'd be sick in no time, probably end up in the hospital. Wonderful. Instead of David showing up unexpectedly at my classes, he could show up unexpectedly at my bedside. Maybe I could convince the hospital to lie about me being a patient. Better yet, maybe my parents would spring for a guard. I didn't think Riverview's Finest would volunteer for the task. Not after yesterday's reception.

Stripping off my soaked tee shirt and sweats, I donned a fresh pair, then went to the bathroom to wash my face. At this rate, I should probably wash an extra load of laundry this week. More fun.

After cooling myself off, I took Tylenol PM to ease my aching chest and hopefully relax me. Unlike other times, tonight I was determined to get more sleep. I couldn't keep this up. I absolutely had to sleep – my health depended upon it.

I stripped the bed, changed the sheets and retrieved all the items that had fallen to the floor in my frantic search for my inhaler. One was the obnoxious noisemaker. Good thing I didn't set that off. What a great way to top off the evening.

Everything set, I climbed back into bed. Now to relax. If I was lucky, I could get four good hours of sleep and still make it to my first class.

The light from a streetlamp slanted across my ceiling, turning my chair into a hunched monster and my desk into a crouching demon. Enough – I had to stop this. I could only think about pleasant things. Not David or Cat or that stupid church dream. Not school or Tommy. Didn't leave much. Maybe a meditation chant. A meditation chant would be safe ... maybe even put me to sleep.

I started the familiar routine – deepening my breathing, stilling my mind, focusing on different areas of my body. Tightening, relaxing, tightening, relaxing. Imagining each area getting heavy, relaxing, emptying my mind ...

My mother taught me to meditate. She taught me yoga as well, long before those activities were considered cool. I was eight – weak, in pain, but alive. Barely, unbelievably, amazingly alive.

My illness had almost killed me. I had both bronchitis and pneumonia – my fever raged as high as 105 degrees. I have almost no memory of that time other than the nightmares. Strange, terrifying fever-induced nightmares gripped me night and day. However, as bad as those nightmares were, in the end I wished they had never let me go.

I don't think I ever fully recovered from that period of my life. I'm not talking physically, but emotionally. Imagine – one day I was healthy, living in Milwaukee and playing with my sister. The next I was in Riverview. No longer healthy but contaminated, marked by the cold decaying kiss of death. No longer a twin, but sister-less. No longer with the parents I remembered, but strangers. These new parents were detached, unapproachable and full of sorrow. I had awakened from one incomprehensible nightmare to another. Or maybe I never did wake up. Maybe the nightmare had simply changed. Much like my church dream.

Overall, I think that experience shook me in ways I still can't comprehend – never mind how my helpless child self felt experiencing it, tossed about by baffling waves of mysterious adult contradictions. Perhaps that's the reason I never made plans more than a day or two ahead – not because of my disease but because of the lesson I learned. The lesson about the strange unpredictability of life.

My mom kept me home for two years. At least, I eventually learned to call it home. In the beginning, it was as unrecognizable as everything else in my life.

My mother taught me how to control my stress and to strengthen my lungs. She took me walking and dancing, anything to get me exercising.

"Just because God gave you weak lungs doesn't mean they have to stay weak," she would say as we marched around the block, as fast as my faltering breathing would allow. "Strong lungs equal strong bodies. My cousin Stella had Cystic Fibrosis, but she never allowed that to stop her. She rode horses and went swimming as often as she could. And she lived to a ripe old age."

My mother never actually told me what that ripe old age was, nor did I ever ask. If she wasn't telling me about Stella, she would recite stories of other CF patients she had read about in one of the zillions of newsletters she received.

"I just read an update about Jessie. Remember him? He was sick as a child, just like you, but he's still doing well. He just wrote another article for the CF Foundation about the latest research findings."

Her words flowed over me, rich and decadent, suffocating me in their soft folds. It was all I could do to focus on putting one foot ahead of the other, breathing one breath after another.

She bought me humidifiers to moisten the air I breathed, fed me both food and supplements. She taught me to manage my weight. Although thin, I was never underweight or malnourished, nor did the weight wither off me like some of the kids I knew with CF.

"There's no reason why you can't live a relatively normal life," she would tell me over and over. "CF patients are living longer and longer. You just have to know how to take care of yourself."

Last but not least, she home-schooled me – doing such a good job I ended up ahead of my class.

Actually, everything she did was a total success. The doctors marveled about her management of my health. For someone with CF, I was in extremely good shape.

My mother was able devote so much time to me because she worked at home as a freelance writer. She had a few high-level corporate accounts that paid well and gave her plenty of flexibility to take care of me. My father held the lofty position of vice president of sales at Duncan Industries – an international company, one of the largest employers in Riverview other than the university. Together, they brought in a sizable income, and as their only child, I benefited from all the privileges income could buy: travel to exotic places, plenty of extracurricular activities, full ride to college.

From the outside, we looked like the perfect family. Both parents with highly- successful careers, a lovely home, a beautiful, bright child. What more could anyone want? Yes, indeed, we had the perfect life all right, to match our perfect house. Our elegant, tastefully-decorated house my mother loved to show off to anyone who came by. Just don't look too closely at the door in the corner, back where the light bulb has long since burnt out and the spiders have taken over. No, that door certainly does not lead to a stinking, rotting carcass masquerading as a daughter dying of CF and another daughter's ghost. No, no door at all. Just like no photos of Cat, anywhere at all in that lovely home.

And now, facing one of the worst situations of my life, I had no one to turn to. Trying to talk to my parents now, after all the things we had never discussed? How could I go to them, when I was the "wrong" twin? Forget it.

I especially couldn't let my mother know how badly my health had deteriorated. Having three violent congestion attacks in two weeks wasn't good. Normally my attacks mirrored asthma attacks, not these congestion-filled embarrassing episodes accompanied by green-tinged mucus. Because of the nature of my attacks, I had always been able to pass them off as severe asthma. In reality, I had mild asthma and mild CF. Together, I could call it bad asthma.

Other than my childhood near-death experience, there had been only one other seriously ill episode. It was also the night I knew my sister had died.

It was April. I was sixteen. I woke with a start – the fairy dream again, but it was different this time - more intense. I sat up in bed, gasping and coughing, tears cascading down my cheeks, when I sensed a presence in the room. Not a person – a presence. I felt the distinction.

Tears drying on my face, I worked to get my breathing under control while scanning the room. Nothing out of place, nothing I could hear beyond my own loud gasps, but I knew something was there. Watching me. Waiting for me to calm down. I was no longer alone, yet I detected no sense of threat.

Then I smelled it. Chlorine. So strong and sudden I ended up coughing again. My room smelled exactly like an indoor swimming pool - exactly like that day so long ago at the YMCA, when I was six. Cat.

I'll always take care of you, Kit. Except she didn't. The fairies took her.

Sitting in my bed, tears still drying, I felt a feather-light touch stroke my cheek, my brow – a kiss, faint, but full of power. And I knew, in that instant, a secret I couldn't voice.

Cat was dead.

The fairies took her and now they killed her. I knew it deep within my bones. My sister had come to say one final farewell, the farewell that had been denied to her so long ago as I lay dying in the hospital room.

I also knew, in that moment, that I should have gone first. I should have been there to welcome her. I should have been the one taken – death had been standing right by my bedside, waiting for me to take my final gasp.

Yet something had diverted death, caused it to move on, to find someone else to caress in its cold, hollow arms. And somewhere in the confusion, the fairies had snuck in and snatched my sister. Just as death had been sidetracked, death had sidetracked everyone else – leaving my sister vulnerable to the fairies and leaving me behind, trapped in a damaged, dying body. Death didn't do anyone any favors that day.

The night I knew my sister died, the night she came to say goodbye, I cried as I never had before. I cried for the guilt, the loss, the could-have-beens, the should-have-beens. I cried until I could no more. Then I lay there, head pounding, chest aching, until my alarm went off and I could safely get up and take my shower.

I had to take special care with my appearance. I couldn't let my mother know how little I slept, or how much I cried. I couldn't tell her Cat had visited me. I couldn't tell her the Golden Twin was dead.

Banging down my breakfast plate, she hovered above me, arms crossed. "What's wrong? Didn't you sleep well?"

I picked up my fork. "Nothing's wrong. I slept fine."

Her eyes bored into me, small gray stones, almost as if she could look right through me. "You're getting sick, aren't you?"

I filled my fork with eggs. "No. I'm fine."

With sudden, jerky movements, she uncrossed her arms and slapped her hand against my forehead.

My fork hit my plate with a clatter. "Mom."

She ignored me. "You don't feel warm."

I wrenched myself away. "Because I'm not."

She put her hand under my chin and yanked my face up. "Was it clear or was it tinged green or yellow?"

Why do you care about the mucus, I wanted to scream. My sister is dead. But I couldn't do it. I couldn't bear to see her face collapse again, the way it had when she told me Cat had been kidnapped.

I could feel her distancing herself from me. *The wrong twin had been kidnapped.*

"God, Mom. Will you leave me alone so I can eat? Everything's fine. Everything's normal."

She didn't believe me. But she let me eat.

I wished I could tell her. Tell someone, anyone. But who would believe me?

Instead I internalized it. Brooded over it. Dwelled on it, and nothing else.

Grief became my constant companion. I went to school and came home. I did nothing else. I stopped eating, stopped sleeping.

A part of me, the intellectual part, insisted I was overreacting. For all I knew, for all anyone knew, Cat had been murdered long ago. If she hadn't been, why would she have been killed now, at this particular time? Even if she had been killed now, why would she come visit me? How would I "instinctually" know about it? We were fraternal, not identical twins. Those kinds of eerie "knowing" things only happened to identical twins. Besides, whatever kind of bond we had would have been broken long ago. We hadn't seen each other for nearly ten years.

No matter how logical my intellectual side was, it couldn't persuade my emotional side. I knew. Simple as that. Never mind that I found nothing about it in the newspaper. I knew. Cat was dead. She had died that night. No amount of arguing could persuade me otherwise.

So, after two weeks of not eating and not sleeping, I ended up with a 102 degree fever, hacking up green mucus.

"I knew you were getting sick," my mother muttered triumphantly as she pumped me full of antibiotics and the richest food she could find – I had lost almost ten pounds.

"What did I tell you about controlling stress?" she said, taking my temperature. "You can't afford to let stress get to you. I don't care what's going on in your life. Stress will kill you. You have got to keep it under control."

I nodded, too sick to argue. Life is out of our control. How could I possibly keep stress under control when the fairies could appear at any time and steal someone away?

Ever since then, I had believed Cat to be dead. Yet someone who resembled her had spoken to me at the Halloween party. I had seen that same person at least one other time on campus. I had even asked the woman in student services to look up Cat's name. Why would I have done that if I thought she was dead? Was I starting to question myself after all these years? Better yet, why did my heart sink when Eileen confirmed what I already knew?

Maybe because I didn't want to believe it. Maybe because in my entire life I never wanted to be more wrong about something. Maybe because I wished more than anything to see Cat again, or if that weren't possible, to at least know what happened to her.

The fairies are evil. Pure evil. Could that be true? Oh, God, what if it was? All these years my sister had been trapped by evil, and all because I didn't have the good sense to die when I was supposed to.

The Jack Nicholson line from the movie *A Few Good Men* flashed through my head: "*You can't handle the truth.*" Could I handle the truth about Cat? Did I really want to know what happened to her? Was the truth even being offered to me? Or was it only an illusion, simply a coincidence that I met two of my tormentors on the same night?

As I started coughing again, I wondered if perhaps I had missed the most fundamental question of all: would I even live long enough to get to the bottom of all of this?

Chapter 21

Lunch tray in hand, I searched the packed Union for a place to sit. I chose the Union specifically because it would be crowded, and it didn't disappoint. Of course, now the problem became finding an empty table. Constant challenges.

Ducking through the crowd, I spotted Brandi with three of her sorority sisters. Since Brandi and I hadn't spoken since the kitchen encounter, I thought it best to eat somewhere else. As luck would have it, Tammy, one of the sisters, saw me and waved me over. Reluctantly, I returned her greeting. Now I had to sit with them. If they saw me sitting alone, they would think I was snubbing them.

"Hey." I nodded to Brandi, Tammy, Bridget and Jamie as I dropped my tray next to Tammy. While the others greeted me in return, Brandi studied the salad on her plate.

Oh well. I doused my fries with ketchup before biting into my fish sandwich, only half listening to the conversation.

"So," Tammy turned to me. "How are *you* doing, Kit?"

I shrugged, my mouth full of fish. "Fine."

"No, really." Jamie's black curls danced as she tossed her head. "How are you doing?"

I swallowed, eyeing them. "Fine. Why, don't I look fine?"

The three sisters exchanged a look between them. "We heard you have Cystic Fibrosis. Is that true?" Tammy asked.

Oh, God. Like I needed this. I stared at them – eyes bright, curious, yet with an edge. Almost predatory. "Yes."

All three spoke at once.

"I can't believe it, you look so healthy," Jamie said.

"Why didn't you tell us?" Tammy asked.

"We could have helped you," Bridget said

I put my sandwich down. "Look, I didn't tell anyone. It's not something I like to talk about."

"Well, yeah," Tammy said. "But we're your friends. We want to help."

Were they? The thought appeared out of nowhere, shooting though my mind like an electric shock. I tried dismissing it. Of course they were my friends. I've known them for the past three or four years. But the longer I studied their sparkling, edgy faces, the more I wondered.

"It's not personal. Me not telling you, really. I just got into the habit of not telling anyone. Since sixth grade I haven't talked about it. But maybe I made a mistake. Maybe I should have said something."

That look again. Then Jamie faced me, her smile just the tiniest bit patronizing.

"We were talking, the four of us." She nodded around the table, although Brandi had yet to look up from her salad. "And we thought maybe this year for our spring community project, we could raise money for the Cystic Fibrosis Foundation."

I felt my face freeze. Oh, God, I was about to become a sorority house's cause. This was exactly the reason why I begged my parents not to tell anyone I had CF in high school. Visions of me being splashed on posters danced before my eyes. I saw myself being trotted out for press conferences, surrounded by the sorority sisters, all with sympathetic and pitying expressions on their faces. "Kit is so sweet, so special," I could hear them saying. "I just can't believe she has such a horrible disease. Of course once we found out, we just had to get involved." Could my life possibly get any worse?

I forced my stiff face to smile. Focus on the fact they want to raise money for the foundation, I ordered myself. "I think that would be great." I hoped I sounded at least somewhat pleased.

Brandi glanced up, caught my attention and rolled her eyes. I raced to cover my mouth with a napkin, hiding my grin. At least Brandi understood.

Apparently I hid my feeling better with the others, because they enthusiastically started to outline their plans for me. Only half-listening, I nibbled on my food and tried to think of a plausible reason why I couldn't be a part of their fundraiser. Health problems? How ironic would that be? At least my mucus didn't look greenish this morning. Maybe last night was a fluke. Or, better yet, maybe I imagined it. Well, I wouldn't take any chances – before going home I planned to purchase a bunch of over-the-counter cold remedies. Even without the green mucus, I didn't like the heaviness I now felt in my chest.

I selected another fry to smother in ketchup, nodding all the while, when out of nowhere came, "Hello, girls. May I join you?"

I froze, the fry hovering somewhere between plate and mouth. David stood there, holding a tray of food and smiling, as though everything was just peachy in the world. Yes, apparently everything could get worse. A whole lot worse.

Brandi whipped her head toward me, eyes accusing. "David, how nice to see you." Her voice was sugary sweet, but her eyes continued to bore into mine. "But you don't want to sit here. Girl-talk, you know. You wouldn't be interested."

"Of course I'd be interested," David insisted. "I'd love the chance to get to know Kit's friends better."

Bridget, Jamie and Tammy sat there as motionless as I was, their eyes round and perplexed. I could almost see the questions written on their faces: "Isn't this the guy who crashed the party and attacked her in the library? What's he doing here? Is she still dating him after all that? What does Tommy think about all this?"

I couldn't move, couldn't react in any way. My emotions had taken over – rage, fear, helplessness – so powerful in their intensity they had paralyzed me. It didn't help that I found myself strangely fascinated at the interplay between Brandi and David.

David moved to the empty spot and set his tray down. "You don't mind, do you?" he asked warmly.

Brandi's arm shot out, knocking his glass of Coke all over his food. It was a good shot, she even got soda on the chair.

"Oh, I'm so sorry," Brandi said, still in that sugary sweet tone. "This chair is taken. You don't mind, do you?"

David fixed his gaze on his burrito now soaked with Coke. An angry red flush began creeping out of his blue turtleneck shirt and up into his face. A vein throbbed at his temple. "You stupid … " he began, his voice soft and menacing, still staring at his ruined lunch.

That broke my paralysis. "David, it's over. I already told you it's over. Find somewhere else to sit."

His chin jerked up, fixing his hot eyes on me. "I need to talk to you," he hissed.

"We have nothing to talk about."

He pounded his fist against the table. Plates and silverware rattled together. "I say we do."

His eyes tore into mine. Suddenly my anger took over, sweeping aside the other emotions like rafts in a storm. How dare he talk to me like that?

I folded my arms in front of me. "I'm not going anywhere with you. We're done. If you don't leave right now, I'm going to call campus police."

His eyes glittered. "Empty threats. You didn't before."

I returned his gaze, matching rage for rage, before bursting from my seat. I ran toward the cashiers. "This man is threatening me," I yelled. "Call campus police. He won't leave me alone."

Behind me, I heard David swear, but I kept going, yelling the whole time, my voice echoing crazily against the decorative arches. People had started to look up, mouths gaping open, words drying up. Finally I reached one of the cashiers. She had frizzled brown hair and dark-framed glasses and looked unable to deal with this situation.

"What?" She sounded like I had just woken her up.

"Call campus police. That man is threatening me." I turned to point at David, but he had already disappeared into the crowd.

"Good, he's gone now." I faced the cashier.

She eyed me cautiously. "Do you still want me to call campus police?"

Suddenly I realized everyone around me was wearing that same cautious expression. The other cashiers. The African-American man, his money in hand, waiting to pay for his lunch. The group of Vietnamese students standing by the condiments. Nobody spoke. An eerie silence descended, broken only when a new song started. Barenaked Ladies. Appropriate.

"No, that's okay. Thanks anyway." I slunk back to my table, careful not to make eye contact.

"What was that all about?" Tammy asked, her voice sounding more gossipy than quizzical.

Brandi was more to the point. "What the fuck was he doing here? I thought you were going to report him."

Conversation resumed in the dining hall as I slid into my seat. "I did report him. Yesterday. But I have to go back today because he told me the wrong name."

Brandi looked like she might burst. "What? I didn't get that."

I now understood the saying about wishing the floor would open up and swallow you. "He told me his last name was Naughton. It's Terry. I need to fix that today."

"You what? You mean you didn't yet? And why the fuck would he give you a wrong last name?"

"I don't know. I asked him that last night and he claimed he never did. I had classes this morning. I was going to straighten all this out this afternoon."

Brandi stood up so fast she knocked her chair over backwards. "You're going now. And I'm going with you."

I got to my feet more slowly. "Gee, Brandi. I'm almost touched by how much you don't care."

Brandi made a face at me. "Don't give me that shit now. This is way out of control. If you're not going to fix it, then I will. Sorry I wasn't PC enough for you yesterday."

Tammy, Jamie and Bridget now watched this exchange, eyes open, mouths closed. Enough gossip to last them for a good couple of weeks. "Catch you guys later." Brandi snatched up her tray and headed toward the assembly line clean-up.

I tried to smile, but it felt pretty deflated. "Sorry for this," I said lamely. "I'll see you later."

They nodded, eyes glittering with a cold sort of excitement.

Brandi was waiting for me at the door. "Let's get this over with."

"You don't have to go with me," I said, amazed at how bitter I sounded. "You made it clear yesterday how much you don't want to deal with this. I'm a big girl. I can take care of it all by myself."

"Don't be an idiot. For God's sake, Kit, you know me." She snatched my arm and started propelling me toward the front doors. "The reason we get along so well is because I don't have to watch myself and you don't get so offended. You know I care about you. I said the things I said because it suddenly sunk in that this guy wasn't simply an asshole, but an unstable, possibly violent, possibly dangerous asshole. And there isn't a whole lot I can do about it. I'm not even sure there's a whole lot you can do about it. And that makes me mad. So, let's go and at least give me the illusion we have some control here."

We reached the front door. Brandi dropped my arm to jam hers into her coat. "We clear?" Emotion had added color to her face, a brightness to her eyes. At that moment, she looked like Joan of Arc reborn.

I put my coat on as well. I knew a backhanded apology when I heard one. "Completely."

***

I swore I would never again tempt the fates by asking if things could get any worse.

Needless to say, changing David's last name on the complaint forms did nothing to improve my case. Not to mention my credibility.

"You had the wrong last name?" Detective Jenkins asked, bushy brown eyebrows crawling up his forehead like fuzzy caterpillars.

I tried to explain, but even to my own ears I sounded lame.

He nodded a few times, made a couple of notes in the file, and smiled dismissively. At least he didn't ask me about my grades again.

Unfortunately, Brandi wasn't much of an ally. Despite his obvious admiration of her well-endowed breasts, I think he missed talking about the Rose Bowl.

Not wanting to repeat that experience at the university, I avoided Eileen, registering my complaint with a woman my age, probably some student fulfilling a work/study program. She snapped her gum during the entire process, but didn't question my story. Usually I couldn't stand people who snapped their gum, but this girl I loved.

Afterwards, Brandi and I went to the store so I could stock up on flu and cold remedies; then we went home. I needed to buckle down and get some studying done. But before I did that, I thought I had better check my email. I hadn't done that for awhile either.

Staring at my inbox, I now remembered why it had been awhile. I had messages from David waiting for me. Great.

However, a quick scan revealed something very interesting. David had sent me two emails. The one on Friday was from his Yahoo account. The one he sent me yesterday after my visit was from his university account, which of course listed his correct name.

Hah! Finally some proof. Why else would he have set up a Yahoo account except to hide his true last name?

The one on Friday read: "I understand you need your space, but please remember how much I care about you. I think you may be The One." One what? One to run up hills with? One to lie about one's last name with? Oh, please.

Yesterday's was more to the point. "Don't come here with HIM again." Well, he didn't have to worry about that, since I didn't plan on returning to his apartment ever again.

Hello, girls. Mind if I join you?

David with his tray, smiling like the executioner before lowering his axe.

God, why couldn't he leave me alone? Why did he refuse to listen to what I kept telling him? Did I have to literally whack him on the head before he figured it out? Or is this how he got his rocks off, by deliberately misunderstanding me? Now that I was involved in this mess, would I ever be free of him?

Actually, the more I thought about it, the more I realized I had better take a hard look at my own contribution to this situation. What the hell was I thinking about when I started this relationship? And why did it take me so damn long to figure out David was bad news? I had plenty of warnings, both from that stranger and from David himself. That evil glint in his eyes the night of the party – monster eyes. I should have run like hell right then.

The more I thought about it, the more I realized I didn't know who I was angrier at – him or me. Nobody can take advantage of you without your permission, one of my mother's favorite Ann Landers' quotes. She was right. I let him in, I ignored the warning signs, and now I had to pay the price. Stupid me.

Well, I could sit here all night berating myself, or I could try to figure out what to do about it. I started by printing out both emails to add to my paper trail. Disgusting task. I could barely touch the paper. Then I scrolled through the rest of my emails, finding nothing of interest until the last one.

It had no return address. I almost didn't read it, sure it was another one from David. But no such luck.

Kit Cat.

Two dangers for two little girls. But one is gone.

Kit Cat.

Two dangers for one new little girl. Soon that girl will be gone.

Kit Cat.

Two dangers for one new little girl. How long will it take for that girl to be gone?

Kit Cat.

Take a closer look at that, because the truth will set you free.

Oh, God. I started to cough, my lungs rattling painfully. This was getting weirder and more frightening by the moment, and I still didn't have the faintest idea of what was going on.

It's the only way you can set yourself free.

Hands shaking, I printed that email as well, adding it to my growing pile. What truth? Setting myself free from what? David? Why would they be related?

The innocent depend on you. You must save the innocent, because by saving the innocent you save yourself.

What innocent? What little girl? Were they one and the same? And what on earth did this have to do with me?

It's the only way you can set yourself free.

Suddenly, almost violently, I found myself hitting reply and pounding out a message.

"Enough with the riddles already. What's going on? What are you trying to tell me? What truth? What girl? This whole mystery thing is getting real old, real fast. Call or email me or something. Just explain yourself."

There. Maybe that would result in some sort of explanation. I could only hope.

I sat back and immediately found myself smothered by the soft fuzzy blanket of exhaustion. I didn't think I had the strength to even pick up a book, much less absorb the information in it. All I wanted to do was fall into bed and into a dreamless sleep – no churches, no graveyards. Tomorrow would come soon enough. Probably much sooner than I wanted.

Chapter 22

For better or worse, our apartment now resembled a maximum-security complex.

Munching on a bagel with cream cheese, I contemplated the barricaded window in the kitchen. "They did a good job."

Brandi leaned against the counter, alternating between sipping coffee and filing her perfectly shaped nails. "Something needed to be done."

"I suppose our security deposit is toast now." I studied the strips of plywood now nailed to the window.

Brandi snorted. "Yeah, like *that* keeps you up at night."

Jezzy strolled into the kitchen, leaping into the chair next to mine. "Guess I hadn't thought of it quite in those terms."

Brandi examined the nail on her left index finger. "Why aren't I surprised?"

Last night, she had brought in three guys to secure the apartment. Because I had already taken a large dose of Nyquil on top of being exhausted, the event was a bit fuzzy in my mind. What stood out most was my incredible relief after they finished. I slipped easily into sleep for the first time since this whole nightmare began.

Unfortunately, one decent night of sleep hadn't made that much of a difference. I was still tired and blurry, my chest was tight and sore and I had hacked up more mucus than usual. I should just go back to bed.

Martha stuck her head through the kitchen door, resembling a twisted jack-in-the-box. "He's still out there," she announced.

The food in my stomach became a hard lump. I gazed sadly at my half-eaten bagel. "Thank you for the update." Not to mention thanks for ruining my appetite. So much for getting even a bagel down.

"You said he was going to stop."

I pushed my chair back from the table. "He is, Martha. It's just taking a bit longer than I expected. The cops should be calling you for a statement any day now."

"How'd you expect me to study?"

I dumped my plate in the sink, then turned to face her. She looked worn out. Black circles stained the delicate skin under her eyes and her hair seemed oilier than usual. A pang of guilt hit me. Great. Just what I needed, another emotion added to the mix – guilt for the stress this situation was causing my roommates. God was I sick and tired of this.

"I don't, Martha." I folded my arms across my chest. "To be perfectly honest, I don't expect you to do a damn thing, except tell the cops what you've seen. Believe it or not, I'm doing everything in my power to make this situation go away. I'll even lay odds that I'm more stressed about it than you are, although you may have trouble believing that. And, to answer another one of your burning questions, I am not trying to keep you from your precious studying. Nothing would make me happier than to have you able to study until your brain leaked out your ears. Because then at least, you'd be leaving me alone."

Martha gaped at me. With every word that dropped from my lips, her eyes grew rounder and her mouth grew wider. In the eight months we had lived together, I had never spoken to her so rudely. That was Brandi's department. I had always strived to be pleasant. She had enough strikes against her, why make things rougher? But no more. No breaks today. I'd had it.

With obvious effort, she closed her mouth and gathered her dignity together. "If you're having that much trouble controlling the situation, maybe you should move out," she said primly.

Now it was my turn to gape. "Move out? Move out? You've got to be kidding me."

She looked indignant. "Am not. Look at this place." She jerked her arms up, fingers twitching sporadically. "Brandi doesn't feel any safer here than I do. You brought the problem to us, so the right thing is for you to leave."

I stalked toward her, getting right into her face. "Right thing? You want to talk about the right thing? We *allowed* you to move in here. We're doing *you* a favor. *You* never signed a lease. *You* have some pretty limited rights here!"

She held her ground, folding her arms in front of her, pinching her lips together. "Two against one. You lose."

I snapped my head around to Brandi. She held her hands up, palms out. "Oh no. You're not dragging me into this."

"You already are into this. She," I pointed to Martha, "dragged you into this. What's this two against one shit?"

Brandi backed up. "There is no two against one. I'm not taking sides here."

"What?" I couldn't believe this. Brandi wouldn't take my side against Martha? Had I fallen into some alternate universe while I slept? What the hell was going on?

"You two work it through. Leave me out."

I stepped toward Brandi. "You want me to move out?"

Brandi tugged her hands through her hair, avoiding my eyes. "I didn't say that. I said for you two to work it out. I'm not taking sides."

I closed my eyes, pushing my hands against the top of my head. "I don't believe this. You of all people, Brandi."

"You should move out," Martha piped in again, her voice squeaking on the last word.

I snapped open my eyes. "Well, it's not going to happen so you can quit saying it." I jerked away from the counter and shoved my way past her. "I'm out of here. See you guys later."

Martha didn't try to stop me as I marched down the hall and into my bedroom. Once there, door firmly closed, I realized I had no intention of going anywhere. I could feel coughs gathering in my ever-tightening chest and I cursed myself for my weakness. I didn't have the energy or the stamina to handle any more crises today. David could spend the day searching for me. All I wanted to do was lie down in my new Fort Knox-style bedroom and sleep. So that's exactly what I did.

To my surprise, I fell asleep immediately and slept a dreamless sleep most of the day. I woke in the middle of the afternoon, feeling more refreshed than I had in a long time. Now for some nourishment. I moseyed toward the kitchen and promptly ran into Elena.

"What the … " I gasped, jumping back and letting out a little scream.

Elena had been stretched out on the couch, but now she scrambled to sit up, her copper-colored hair falling over her face. "God, Kit, are you okay? I'm sorry, I didn't mean to scare you."

I took a deep breath, pressing my hand against my chest. "I'm fine. I just thought I was alone, that's all."

Elena blew her hair out of her eyes. "I guess I should've let you know I was here."

"What *are* you doing here? Aren't you supposed to be in classes? And how'd you get in?"

Elena reached over to the coffee table and jingled her key ring. "I kept it, remember? And I don't have classes Wednesday afternoon, so I thought I'd come over and keep you company."

"How did you know I was here?"

She shrugged. "I didn't. I heard you weren't feeling well, so I thought I'd come over and see if you took a sick day."

I ran my hand through my hair. How was it that my movements were so easily tracked in a school of forty thousand students? Paranoia rears its ugly head. Nevertheless, deep down, I was glad to see Elena.

"An occasional sick day never hurts."

Elena briskly rose to her feet. "How 'bout some breakfast? I make a mean omelet."

"I think all my eggs are hard boiled."

She waved her hands dismissively, bustling past me to the kitchen. "I picked up some non-hard boiled eggs, plus other breakfast goodies."

"You didn't have to do that," I protested, but I was touched.

"It's nothing. Don't worry about it."

I followed her into the kitchen and watched her haul food out of the refrigerator. Eggs, bacon, package of hash browns, biscuits, sausage, cheese, butter, onions, tomatoes. "Nothing? That looks like something to me."

She pulled a frying pan out of the cupboard. "Everyone needs comfort foods when they're sick. My mother always made me breakfast foods, even for dinner."

She chatted while cooking, filling me in on the latest gossip. Light, mindless things. Nothing about Brad or my situation. I sat at the table – she refused to let me help – listening and relaxing. Such a relief.

After we ate, she chased me into the living room to rest while she cleaned up the kitchen. I had just settled on the couch when I heard a key turning in the lock.

Great. Brandi or Martha. I didn't want to see either one of them. A few moments later, Brandi sauntered up the stairs.

She stood for a moment on the landing, surveying the scene. "Is the mole in the kitchen?"

I shook my head. "Elena."

She nodded, started toward the kitchen, then stopped. She must have seen something in my face. "Oh, come *on*, Kit."

"Come on what?"

She put a hand on her hip. "Not taking your side does *not* mean I was against you."

"It was the mole, Brandi. You refused to take my side against the mole."

"Christ, Kit. Have you considered that maybe I think she has a point?"

"Oh, so you want me to move out too?"

"Don't be absurd. I never said that. I want the same thing you want. I want David to leave you alone. Christ, Kit. Do you think I've had a decent night's sleep since he started pulling this crap? What if he decides to attack me to get to you? Or what if he does break in and attack you? How am I supposed to stop it? Just because you're the target doesn't mean you're the only one suffering here."

I slapped my hands against my thighs. "So what do you want me to do about it? Don't you think I'd stop it if I could?"

Brandi rolled her eyes. "Is this stupid thing you've got going an act or has your IQ dropped in the past week? Of course, I know you'd stop it. Of course, I know you don't want anyone else to suffer. But Kit, that's not the point. The point is this has become a real problem. And we have to figure out some way to solve it."

I slumped against the couch. "Tell me something I don't know."

"You asked and I'm telling you. Martha has a reason to be scared. So do I. So do you. That's where this is coming from. I can see both sides. I know you're doing everything you can. But that doesn't change the fact we're scared."

I pressed my lips together. Brandi was right. But I still felt betrayed she hadn't taken my side. "At least you could've defended me on the whole moving out issue."

Brandi tossed her hair away from her face. "Martha's a loser. Don't let her get to you." She went into the kitchen. As I heard her greet Elena, someone knocked on the door.

I froze. *David.*

God, Kit. I forced myself to take a deep breath, my chest aching. You're getting way too paranoid. Besides, it's not like I'm alone here.

Knock, knock, knock. I dragged myself to my feet and to the door, more apprehensive with every step. Peering through the peephole, I saw Tommy.

Oh no. I looked like shit. Although I had taken a shower this morning, my hair was probably flat after sleeping on it all day. Not to mention the sloppy sweats and no makeup. Maybe I should go try to make myself more presentable first. No, I couldn't leave Tommy out in the cold waiting for me. Besides, it's not like he hasn't seen me looking rumpled before. Of course, those were under more enjoyable circumstances. Christ, Kit, let's not forget we aren't dating anymore. I opened the door.

"So, you *are* home," Tommy said.

I ran my hand self-consciously through my hair. "Yeah, thought I'd play hooky today. Come on up."

"Anything new?" he asked as we reached the living room.

"Yeah, I got a couple of emails," I started to say as Elena and Brandi came in. While they greeted Tommy, I disappeared into the kitchen for a glass of water.

"Kit's had some emails," Tommy was saying as I reappeared.

"Emails?" Brandi raised her eyebrows at me.

"Yeah. This whole thing has now followed me into cyberspace."

"Well, look on the bright side," Brandi said. "The worst an email can do is lock up your computer."

"Yeah, and with my luck it would happen between the time I finished a paper and before I saved it."

"Wait a minute," Elena broke in, raising one of her hands. "Need some explanation here. Fill in, please."

I hesitated, wondering where to even start. So much had happened. It was hard to believe not even two weeks had gone by since the Halloween party.

"You might as well start at the beginning," Tommy said. "Maybe she'll have some ideas."

He had a point. Among the three of us, we muddled through the story. I also brought out my paper trail folder for inspection.

"This is unreal." Elena shook her head as she flipped through my printouts and letters spread out on the coffee table.

"He used a different email account until he knew I knew his real last name. Doesn't that prove he lied to me?"

"Doesn't prove a damn thing." Brandi skimmed over the papers next to Elena.

I frowned. "All right. Let's try this again. Do you guys now believe me?"

"I believe you," Tommy said.

"It doesn't matter if we believe you," Elena said. "It's what we can prove."

I slumped. "Now you sound like the cops."

"Talking and thinking like cops is what's going to get you out of this," Elena said, separating the papers. "Now, let me get this straight. You believe these are from David."

I nodded.

"And these," she waved her hand over the other pile, "you think are from this Cat person."

"It's the only thing that makes any sense."

Elena studied the sheets. "Well, it seems to me this all somehow leads back to your sister's kidnapping. What do you know about it?"

I shrugged. "You know as much as I do."

Elena pursed her lips. "Who would know more? Your parents?"

I folded my arms across my chest. "I'm not asking my parents about this."

"Why not?"

I looked away. My mother's face danced before my eyes. "Cat has been kidnapped." Her fallen, dead expression, like collapsed bread dough. The realization the wrong daughter had been taken.

"I just can't," I said. "It's not something we can talk about."

Elena chewed on her bottom lip. "But, if it will help ... "

"What about the Internet?" Tommy interrupted. "Maybe we can find something there. Look through the newspapers or something."

I shot Tommy a grateful look. "That's a good idea."

"I have a bigger screen," Brandi offered, leading the way to her room. Elena and I sat on Brandi's rose-colored bed while Tommy stood behind Brandi. The room smelled oddly of hairspray, perfume, nail polish remover and cat litterbox.

"'You must save the innocent, because by saving the innocent you save yourself,'" Elena read from the paper trail folder, then nudged me. "What do you think it means?"

I shrugged, picking at a dark green throw pillow. "Your guess is as good as mine."

"'Two dangers for one new little girl,'" she mused. "But, what does it all mean?"

"*Milwaukee Journal's* a bust," Brandi said. "Only goes back couple of years."

"What about the *Riverview Times*?" I asked.

Brandi tapped the keyboard. "One year."

"What about missing children sites?" Tommy asked, hovering over Brandi's shoulder.

"They're not going to list children missing from the mid-eighties," Brandi said. "Those sites weren't online back then, and they wouldn't waste their time putting those kids up when they have more than enough new ones. Besides, all those kids would be adults now."

"Worth a shot, though. Don't you think?"

Brandi turned back to the keyboard. "Whatever." But as she predicted, the search yielded nothing.

"What about the police?" Elena said. "They must have a file."

"That's a great idea," Tommy said. "You think they'd be online?"

"Not the case files," Brandi said. "Especially not case files that old."

"But you can do background checks online."

"And who would we be doing a background check on?" Brandi asked. "Cat? She would've been seven at the time, and a victim. What exactly do you think we'd turn up?"

"Okay, okay. So, does that mean we'd have to go to Milwaukee?"

"Maybe," Elena said. "But maybe they'd fax the file to us. I could at least call and find out which station handled the case to save us from running all over Milwaukee."

"They'd tell you that information right over the phone?" Tommy asked.

"A second ago, you thought it'd be online. Now you're questioning the dependability of the phone?" Brandi asked.

"They'd tell us if there was a file for sure," Elena said. "Whether they'll give me much more information, I don't know. So yeah. We might actually have to go down there in person."

"Cool. Road trip," Tommy said.

"You don't mind calling?" I asked Elena, wondering if I should be the one doing it.

"Naw. I used to do that when I worked at my father's law practice over the summers. I'm experienced."

I smiled a little. "Thanks."

She smiled back and patted my leg as Jezzy strolled into the room, taking a moment to check everyone out. Elena followed the cat's movements with her eyes. "Jezzy's still here? I can't believe Martha hasn't raised some serious cat objections by now."

"I'm not sure Martha even knows the cat's here," I said.

Elena frowned a little. "Really? I thought she was allergic?"

"She's allergic to roses," Brandi said. "She's made that extremely clear. As for cat allergies, I haven't heard a peep."

"Roses? Who's allergic to roses?" Tommy asked.

"My thoughts exactly," Brandi said.

"Wait a second," Elena interrupted. "You mean to tell me that Martha has lived here eight months and doesn't know you have a cat?"

"There's a lot of things Martha doesn't know, but should," I said. "For instance, she doesn't know that since her name is not on the lease, she has no right to make demands."

"Besides," Brandi added. "The cat's smart enough to stay out of her way. Something the humans living here haven't figured out yet."

Elena gazed at Brandi's barricaded window. "Oh, Martha," she said, shaking her head and sighing.

"Aren't you going to tell us how sweet she is once you get to know her?" Brandi asked.

Elena made a face. "I gotta go. I'm really behind." She stood, then smoothed out the silky bedspread. "Can I come back and make copies of all those? I want to think on it some more. Maybe come up with some other ways to get info."

I nodded, standing up as well. "Be my guest. Thanks, Brandi."

"Glad to be of service." Brandi tapped some more on the keyboard as the three of us left the room.

Elena collected her books, put her coat on, then leaned over to give me a hug. "We'll figure this out," she said in my ear. "Don't worry."

I didn't answer, just returned her hug.

"Get some rest." She let go of me and turned to leave. Tommy walked her to the door and locked it behind her.

He didn't come up immediately. Leaning his back against the door, his blond hair fell across his forehead as he turned his face toward me, his green eyes connecting with mine. "Can we talk, or are you tired?"

Uh-oh. This sounded serious. "No, we can talk if you want."

He came up the stairs two at a time. I backed up to the couch – he settled for the chair.

My water still sat where I left it on the coffee table. I reached over to take it, more to give my hands something to do than because I was thirsty. "Well?"

Tommy studied his hands. "I've been doing some research. On Cystic Fibrosis."

Oh no. I knew this discussion was coming, I just hadn't expected it so soon, not with this nightmare whirling around me. I tried to read his expression, get some idea where he was heading, but couldn't. "Yes?"

"I learned a lot of things, including that it is a pretty dreadful disease and it seems to be more of a 'childhood killer.'" His voice broke off again.

"Yes, that's true. So, what's your point?"

He met my eyes. "It's just … you seem pretty healthy. And you said you had a pretty mild case. With all the advances in treatment, you could be fine."

I stared at him. "Tommy, I'm not fine. I have Cystic Fibrosis."

"Yeah, I know that. But you could live a long time with it."

I closed my eyes. If he only knew what exquisite torture he was putting me through. "Tommy, I'm not going to live a long time. That's not open for discussion."

"Why are you being so negative about this? Some of the information I found was very encouraging."

"Encouraging, yes. Miracles, no."

He gazed at the ceiling. "I don't get you, Kit. It seems to me, with your level of health and the advances being made, there's no reason why you couldn't have a future. A long one."

Oh no. Serious denial issues here. Translation: there's no reason why we can't have a future. He just didn't get it.

The summer before my freshman year in college, my doctor handed me a diary written by a woman who had died of Cystic Fibrosis. I had no intention of reading it, but somehow found myself flipping through the book anyway. Morbid interest, probably. What I discovered horrified me. Died at forty-three. At thirty-three was on oxygen most of the day and night. Constant focus on treatments, coughing her way through her final ten years of life. Forty-three years old. A time when normal people were in the midst of careers and children. Did I mention she was divorced as well?

No, Tommy didn't get it. I could see so clearly what he thought that it might as well have been written on his forehead. Maybe I would get a few more colds than normal. Maybe I would cough a bit more than normal. He had no idea what it would really be like. I had no idea what it would really be like. And, to be honest, there were times when I seriously wondered if I wanted to live long enough to find out.

Healthy people have no idea what horrors haunt the chronically sick person. Our disease follows us around like an uninvited, unwelcome, but very persistent companion – constantly leering over our shoulders, grinning, smelling of rotting meat and decaying teeth. We're never sure when it will decide to come close, draping emaciated limbs over our shoulders, breathing stink and garbage into our lungs. We don't know how long it will remain content simply hovering in the background, rattling chains of despair and depression.

Why would I ever want to introduce Tommy to this festering corpse nicknamed "CF"? Tommy deserved a healthy girlfriend – one who could bear his children and grow old with him. He hadn't a clue what he was inviting into his life. What would happen after he made its acquaintance? Would he be able to deal with it? Or would he just leave? While I wouldn't blame him for doing so, I knew I couldn't handle it. It would break my heart. And that would probably kill me even faster than my unwanted companion would.

"Tommy, you're living in a dream world," I said. "There is no happily ever after here. I have Cystic Fibrosis. Get used to the idea and start looking for another girlfriend."

He snapped his head up, anger sharpening his features. "What the hell is that supposed to mean? I'm trying to be supportive here. Cut me some slack, why don't you?"

"You're not being supportive, you're being foolish." I banged my water glass on the table, amazed at the words gushing out of my mouth. I didn't think I had been looking for a fight, but like hot oil, the anger just poured out of me. "You have no idea what it's like to live with this thing. You, with your perfect life and golden future. You don't need a girlfriend with the kind of baggage I drag around with me."

He pounded his fist against the chair. "Who are you to tell me what I need or don't need?"

"Tommy, get over yourself. The worst that's ever happened to you is maybe your hair didn't always look perfect."

"Christ, where the hell is that coming from?" He was so furious he was actually shaking. "How arrogant can you be? You think that having Cystic Fibrosis gives you the right to judge other people's problems? How dare you?"

I held my hands up. "What then? Tell me. What's your skeleton? Your black secret? Do you even have one? I certainly wouldn't know."

"Just because secrets aren't as obvious as diseases doesn't mean other people don't have them."

"Well then, what is it? You know mine. What are yours? You cheated on an exam? Got drunk and drove home? Or maybe it was something more serious, like your sister got knocked up at sixteen?"

Tommy leaped to his feet, so fast the chair flew backwards and hit the wall. "That's it. I don't have to listen to this shit."

I leaned back and waved my hands at him. "Can't handle the truth, huh? Thought so. Just go."

He stalked over, snatched up his books and jacket. "Kit, sometimes you can be a real bitch."

"Don't slam the door on your way out." I called after him, as he pounded down the stairs and slammed the door shut.

Breathing heavily, I stayed where I was, trying to collect myself. I didn't like what I had done, but I hadn't seen any other way. I couldn't get back together with him now, not when he had such denial issues. It wouldn't be right for him or me. Besides, he would probably end up leaving me anyway, so might as well be sooner than later.

I heard Brandi's door open and her soft footsteps on the carpet. "I see you and Tommy are getting along splendidly."

I sighed, rubbing my face. "You heard?"

"Not actual words, but tone of voice, yes."

"It's never going to work between us. I wish he'd get that through his thick skull."

Brandi didn't answer, just examined me with heavy-lidded eyes and crossed arms.

I stood up. "Well, he'll figure it out soon enough. Right? I should go get some studying done."

Brandi continued to stare, her expression unreadable. "Whatever."

What the hell was up with her? Still on Tommy's side no doubt, but there seemed to be something more. I decided not to pursue it. I had enough incomprehensible things happening in my life right now, I saw no need to add any new ones.

Chapter 23

Thursday didn't start out particularly well. I discovered I had a paper due that day in my eighteenth century lit class that was worth one-third of my grade. A paper I hadn't even started to write yet, because I hadn't even finished reading the books for it.

Things went from bad to worse when I realized the professor was one who defined an "on-time" paper as one turned in at the beginning of class. Professors anal enough to do that tended not to be the most lenient on granting extensions, especially without an exceedingly good reason. I had yet to decide if I had one.

Well, nothing ventured, nothing gained. Flashing my most charming smile, I approached Professor Markham after class.

"Let me guess," he said, before I could even open my mouth. "You weren't able to finish your paper by today. Should I try to guess the reason now?"

Great. A sarcastic, anal professor. My luck just kept getting better and better. "It's a pretty original excuse."

Professor Markham's expression stated he had heard them all before. "I'm waiting."

For a moment I considered using Cystic Fibrosis as my excuse, something that had never occurred to me before. The thought horrified me. What had David turned me into? "I'm being stalked," I said. "By another student. I've registered a complaint with the university if you need verification."

That did surprise him. His eyes behind his thin wire glasses widened. "Really?"

"Yes. It's been going on for several weeks now. I haven't been able to focus on much else."

He pondered this. "Why didn't you bring this to my attention before?"

I studied him, chewing on my bottom lip. How open should I be? I decided to lay everything on the table. "To be perfectly honest, the deadline caught up with me. I haven't been paying as close attention as

I should have. It just sort of dropped in my lap." I let my hands flutter helplessly to my side.

"I've announced it a couple of times these past few weeks."

"I'm sure you have, but it just didn't sink in. This guy, he waylays me after class. I end up focusing on ways to get from class to class without running into him. I know I should have brought it up before, but I really wasn't thinking. If it makes any difference, I know I didn't handle it right and I'm sorry."

Professor Markham picked up his pointer and tapped the table with it. "Monday," he said at last. "By noon. My office. Do you know where it is?"

Relief blossomed inside me. "Yes, yes I do. Thank you so much."

"Get it in by then and I won't penalize you. Fair?"

I nodded, thanking him again and turning away before he could change his mind. As I hurried to my next class, it hit me that now I had three and a half days to finish a book and a half and write a ten-page paper. Lucky me.

By the time I had walked into the door of the apartment, I'd about had it with being an English major.

Spending the afternoon skimming a book and trying to decipher my meager class notes was not my idea of fun. I finally broke down and bought the Cliff Notes. I hated to do it – I always felt like it was cheating, but there was no other way. On top of that, I appeared to be coughing more than usual, even with my day off yesterday. Not a good sign.

I needed some fun. A party would do the trick. Maybe I would even run into Tommy. Although I didn't want to get back together, I missed having him around. Maybe I could apologize and get us back on the friend track. Actually, I should apologize anyway; I knew I'd been a bitch. Tomorrow would be soon enough to start writing.

Brandi sauntered into the living room just as I walked in. "Oh, you're here," she said. It didn't sound like a good thing.

"Yes. After all, I do live here, so it does make sense to drop in from time to time." I made a point of examining her outfit. She wore her party clothes – tight jeans, red clingy mohair sweater, delicate gold chain. "Isn't it awfully early to be all dressed up?"

She looked uncomfortable. It was an odd expression for her. It didn't suit her at all. "I'm heading over to the sorority house."

I was baffled. "Now? I'm not ready yet."

"Well … technically, you're not invited."

My mouth dropped open. "I'm not what?"

She picked some imaginary lint off her sweater. "Invited. At least not until this David thing gets sorted out. They don't want David showing up again and causing a scene."

I gaped at her. I'd never not been invited to a party before. "I'm really not invited?"

"Just until you get this David thing taken care of. Look at it from their point of view. They don't want any trouble. Okay? I'll catch you later." Brandi brushed past me and headed down the stairs. Stunned into silence, I watched her go,

How could this have happened to me? And so quickly? It didn't even make sense.

I headed for my bedroom for lack of somewhere better to go. Unable to sit, I paced my room, shedding my coat and purse between laps, becoming more agitated with each step. It seemed wherever I went or whatever I did, David lurked somewhere in the background. I hadn't been paying attention to my classes because of him. I had started getting sick because of him. And now, he had managed to alienate me from my friends and roommates. What next?

During one of my laps, I booted my computer up and logged on to check email. Surprise, surprise. A message from David. Exactly what I wanted.

It was simple, just four words, all caps.

WE HAVE TO TALK.

Bullshit. I was done talking. Suddenly I couldn't stand to be in my apartment for one more minute. I grabbed my purse and coat and stalked out of my room.

This time I met Martha on the landing. She still wore her coat and had her books clutched to her chest. I breezed by, not saying a word.

She watched me, her face a blotchy red, her nose running.

"He hasn't stopped," she called after me.

I stopped, my hands clenched into fists. Deliberately, I turned to face her. "Have you given your statement to the police yet?"

She frowned. "I need to be able to study."

I folded my arms. "I take that as a 'No, they haven't called.'"

She sniffed. "No, they haven't called."

"Have you thought about calling them?"

"Why should I do that?"

I took a couple steps toward her. "Maybe because once you tell the police David's been hanging around here, *maybe* they'll take me more seriously and *maybe* they'll jump on this a little bit faster. A little help here would be nice."

She sniffed again and shifted her gaze to her feet. This was just too much. I whirled around and stalked out of the apartment.

I marched toward the State Street bar scene. Although early for the bars, it was late enough to be dark, but I didn't feel the least bit frightened. So what if he's following me. In fact, I think he *should* come after me. I'd *love* a chance to pepper spray his face and kick him in the crotch. *Just you come after me, David. I dare you.*

I stopped first in Marshall's and had a couple of beers. Then on to the Turn Key for a few more and a few shots to keep the beers from being lonely. Next I tried the ever-popular Bear Claw for a couple more. Finally, I ended up in Tanner's, nursing a beer in the corner and brooding.

I still couldn't believe I hadn't been invited. And all because of that asshole David. I was so sick of him affecting my life. Of no longer feeling safe. Losing my concentration. And, probably worst of all, being treated like a leper by my friends. Nothing to do with my disease. Oh no. All because of David. My new plague. One that seemed infinitely worse than my grinning decomposing companion. I was beyond tired of it.

Worse yet, nobody wanted to help me. Everywhere I went, people greeted my story with skepticism. Even the cops and the university. Sure, I had registered complaints, but so what? Unless someone somewhere followed through, those complaints were worthless. And I had absolutely no confidence that anyone would do anything. Why would they – they clearly didn't believe me.

A guy who looked like a young Denzel Washington bumped into my chair, spilling beer all over my jeans. "Watch where you're going,"

I yelled as he melted into the crowd. I mopped up my lap, muttering to myself.

The bar had started filling up – crowds of people who knew each other. Smells of perfume, beer and smoke saturated the air. All those people laughing and drinking and having a good time. Everyone, that is, except me. All alone in a bar on a Thursday night. All because of David.

Suddenly I found myself getting up, shoving my way through the crowd, heading for the exit, without any clear idea of what I was going to do. Wrapped in a cocoon of cold fury, I just kept hearing the words "enough is enough," over and over in my head. If nobody else would help me, then I would just have to help myself.

If you need something done right, do it yourself. I had never appreciated the truth and beauty of that statement until that moment.

Back at the apartment. Opening the door. I needed to get something.

A weapon.

But what weapon? What did we have in the apartment?

A knife.

Yes, a kitchen knife. Something sharp. Something big.

For a second I was appalled at my thoughts. Was I really going to go after David? With a knife? Who was this person I was becoming?

But I wasn't going to hurt him, I told myself. I just needed something to protect myself. And to make sure he took me seriously. That's all.

I wasn't really going to use it.

It took only moments to select the perfect one. I also grabbed a dishtowel to wrap it in and a bottle half filled with wine. I knew I might have to wait.

Close door. Lock it. Off to do what needs to be done. What should have been done long ago.

Before approaching the security door, I located his window. At least I thought it was his window. Dark. Probably out looking for me. Let's see how he likes having the tables turned.

I checked the security door. Still not fixed. Perfect. Crossing the street, I stationed myself behind a couple of dumpsters, then opened the wine. Asshole. He had no idea what he was coming home to.

The more I drank, the blacker my thoughts became, stinking of garbage. The cold seeped through my jeans. Why didn't I stop this before? Why did I let it get this far? Why the fuck was I letting him ruin my life? An icy numbness reeking of rotting food pressed against my face. I hunched my shoulders, sinking lower in my seat, trying to stay warm while not breathing in the stench. Occasionally I would stroke the knife, furtively, through the towel. At one point, I could feel the blade bite into the fabric, hear the delicate tearing noise. Yes, definitely sharp enough. Although I struggled to keep them under control, coughs continued to trickle out of me at odd intervals.

I had finished the last of the wine when I saw a familiar figure trotting down the street. David. No question about it.

Hands in his pockets, he waltzed up to the security door, opened it, and disappeared inside. I waited long enough to see the lights go on in his apartment – hah, I had remembered right – then crept across the street to the door, leaving the empty wine bottle by the dumpster. The streetlights glistened, soft and unfocused, casting strangely- shaped shadows.

I held the knife under my jacket. My legs had stiffened during the wait, the cold settling inside the ligaments and tendons. The lobby tipped and swayed. I blinked a few times to clear my head, then pushed the button for the elevator. Amazingly, I felt calm and focused. My rage was so great it had vaulted to another level – sharpening my senses to a thin burning beam of light concentrated solely on one thing: David.

Inside the elevator, the buttons danced a little jig. I had to wait until they were done before I could push David's floor. I didn't feel drunk, not at all. But I did feel strange, like I had just stepped into a different dimension. One where I was the victor and he the victim. He picked the wrong girl to screw with. In a few minutes, he would know it.

Before I reached his door, I removed the towel and hid the knife behind my back.

David opened almost immediately. "Kit. I didn't expect to see you this late."

I tried to smile, but my face felt brittle, hard. Just seeing him started my anger boiling. "Can I come in?"

"Of course." He held the door open. I eased inside, keeping my back to him. While he shut and locked the door, I backed into the living room.

He finished and came toward me, a bright smile on his face. "I knew you'd come around."

God, I hated that smug expression. I could taste my anger, my disgust, bitter and rotten. It was all I could do to not spit on his clean floor. "You're right. I have finally come round." I whipped the knife out, brandishing the tip at him.

He stopped, the smile dying on his face, his eyes widening. "Kit? What the … "

"Ya'know, I think I'd like to talk right now." I waved the knife and swayed toward him. The room tilted, black clouds buzzed around my head. My anger bubbled, boiling over. He backed up a step. "I'm gettin' the idea you just aren't hearin' what I'm telling you. So I thought I'd come over and explain one more time. You see, I don't want you 'round me. *At all.* Period. End of story. That means I don't want you sendin' me roses, dead or alive, packages, letters, emails, nothin' at all. It also means I don't want you hangin' 'round my apartment, stoppin' by my classes, followin' me to parties or callin' me on the phone. Is this makin' sense to you?"

He put his hands up, backing up more. "What are you talking about? I don't do that."

The room dipped. Did I hear him right? "Excuse me?"

He shrugged. "What you're saying. I don't do those things."

What the hell was going on here? "What do you call showin' up at my classes? The Union?"

"I happened to walk by while you were leaving class. And the Union- I was eating lunch there. You're reading into way too many things that quite simply aren't there."

"Readin' things into … what about the emails I received? The roses?"

"You're right. I did send you roses once. But that was before we broke up."

I gawked at him, the room tilting again. "*What?*" This couldn't be happening. How could he say such bold-faced lies?

"Look, I know you're taking this badly," he said, his voice ev-er-so-reasonable. "I know you didn't want to break up. But I told you it wasn't working, and it's not. You have to stop this."

My anger, white hot, ripped through my body. I advanced on him. "*You* did not break up with *me*. I've been tryin' to break up with you! You've been stalking me."

His face twisted into an expression of sympathy. "If it makes you feel better to tell yourself you broke up with me, that's okay. I know you're hurt and I want to do what I can to help. But this other fantasy that I'm *stalking* you, you have to stop that." He laughed in disbelief as he said the word "stalking."

I started shaking, the knife wavering back and forth. My ears burned with his lies. Who the hell did he think he was, making up realities to match his fantasies? How dare he stalk me and then pretend it was all in my head? "You know damn well what you're doing. I am *not* livin' in a fantasy world."

His face took on a long-suffering expression. "Of course you're not. You're just a little confused and hurt right now."

That did it. "You *are* stalking me. Admit it," I screamed, flying at him. I slammed into his chest, pushing him against the wall, trapping him there. Jerking the knife up, I pressed it against the soft vulnerable skin of his neck. "Say it."

"Kit ... "

I pushed the knife in deeper. A thin line of blood appeared at the tip. "Say it. Say you're stalking me."

Our faces were close, so close I could smell his stinking, rotten breath. It stunk like the garbage had. I stared into his eyes and finally, finally, I could see it, almost hidden in his depths. Fear. Power surged through me, mixing with the burning rage, exploding inside me.

I pushed the knife further. Blood trickled down his neck. "Let me explain somethin' to you." I dropped my voice to almost a whisper. "I *will* slice open your throat. Admit you're stalking me and that you're going to stop."

He swallowed. His Adam's apple bobbed up and down. The fear intensified, but I could see more. Humiliation. Rage – its embers burning in the depths of his eyes. Power gushed through me.

"Well, what's it gonna be? The choice is yours."

He closed his eyes. "I was stalking you."

I nudged the knife. "And?"

"And I won't do it anymore."

"Ever?"

"No." He opened his eyes. Rage flared again. "I'll leave you alone from now on."

I studied the dark emotions swirling in his eyes. Would he really leave me alone? Or was he just saying it so I would leave? Maybe I should kill him. No question he would leave me alone then.

A single drop of blood dripped down his neck, staining his green sweater. Yes, killing him would solve my problems, wouldn't it? I envisioned cutting into his neck, one flick of the wrist to slice through tendons, nerves and blood vessels. The blood would spray out of him, hot and thick. He would make a gasping sound, grabbing his neck with his hands, staring at me with eyes filled with shock and disbelief, even as he sank, dying to the floor. Satisfying.

But what about the police? A distant, sober part of my brain stepped in. You really think you're going to get away with it?

I took a deep breath, coughed a little. To be honest, no. I didn't think I would get away with it. Nobody believed my stalking story, so self-defense was out. Besides, I wasn't a killer. Despite my feeling right now.

Almost reluctantly, I stepped back from David. He didn't say anything, simply put his hand to his neck and watched me. I wondered if he knew how close he had come to dying. I wondered if he saw death in my eyes, burning with a vengeance.

I pointed the knife at him. "Remember what you promised. Stay away from me." Not turning my back to him, I eased my way down his short hallway. The locked front door stopped me for a moment, I had forgotten about it, but I managed to undo it and step outside without turning my back to him. His body didn't move, only his eyes followed me as I gently closed the door.

Still on a high, I ended up at several more bars before returning to my apartment, consuming more than my share of beer and shots. I remembered mumbling to someone, some stranger, whose face remained perpetually blurry, that I was celebrating. I had taken care of an annoying problem. Need something done right, only yourself to depend on, or something like that.

I don't remember when I stumbled home, knife shoved in my purse. I crashed on the bed and almost immediately passed out, even with the bed violently spinning.

Pounding woke me up. At first, I thought it was my in my head. Boom, boom, boom. Each boom exploded into sharp daggers that buried themselves into the soft vulnerable areas of my brain. Boom, boom, boom. Eventually, I realized the booms were actual noises coming from the direction of the front door.

Wincing at the light, I stumbled through the apartment to the source of the noises. Peering through the peephole, I saw an older man with a mustache wearing a suit.

A man in a suit? Who would that be? I unlocked the door and opened it.

"Miss Kit Caldwell?" The man wore dark sunglasses. I had never seen him before.

I blinked a few times, the bright light tearing into my skull. "Yes?"

"Is that you?"

Like I needed this right now. "Am I speaking a foreign language here? Yes."

He thrust an envelope at me. "You've just been served." I took the envelope automatically, still not sure what had just happened. He pivoted and strode down the stairs.

Standing there, holding the envelope, blinking painfully in the light, I began to get a bad feeling I had just been duped. "Wait a second," I called to the man's ramrod straight back. "What do you mean served?"

"Open it and read it." He didn't turn his head or slow his pace. Now I felt stupid.

Slowly, I rotated the envelope in my hands. It was from the Riverview Police Department. Could this be about my complaint? Were they actually taking me seriously? Through shaking hands, I ripped open the envelope and yanked out the piece of paper.

It was a restraining order. Against me. Ordering me to stay away from David Terry.

Chapter 24

"You did what?"

Elena stared at me, astounded. We were in an empty classroom in the Humanities Building. I had always liked the Humanities Building. As official sponsor of music and art students, it presented many interesting and odd-shaped rooms in which to study, or in this case, discuss restraining orders.

"At the time it seemed like a good idea," I said lamely.

If anything, Elena's expression became even more shocked. "You're trying to tell me you actually thought going after David with a knife would be a *good* idea?"

I worried a corner of my notebook. "Well, I'd had a few drinks first."

Elena started shaking her head. "I don't believe this."

I didn't either, which is why I went in search of Elena as soon as I pulled myself together. After finding her at the Union, we headed over to humanities since I didn't want to discuss this in public.

Elena tapped her pen against the desk. "Why didn't you call me last night?"

"Because you were at that party. The one I wasn't invited to."

"You shouldn't have listened to Brandi. You should've come. Then you wouldn't be in such a mess."

I rubbed my temples. Although the headache had faded, it still hurt. "If I'd known that I was going to get myself into such a mess, I would've come."

Elena shook her head again, then picked up the restraining order. "So, this talent for getting into messes – have you always had it or is it a recent development?"

I made a face. "I wish I knew. You know, what I don't understand is how he even got a restraining order on me. I mean, I registered two complaints against him. Wouldn't they at least call me or something? Get my side of the story?"

Elena frowned. "I know. That doesn't make sense. Or how fast he got it. I mean, it's his word against yours. Unless … "

I perked my head up as she trailed off. "Unless what?"

She pondered, her expression considering. "I'm going to check on something," she said abruptly. "I think you should stay here and rest. You don't look too good."

I coughed. "I don't feel too good."

She half-smiled, slipped her jacket on and disappeared out the door. Her books remained, piled precariously on a chair.

I studied the closed door, contemplated my tight chest and pounding head, then decided to visit the vending machines. If nothing else, it would be a distraction.

Settling on two cans of 7-Up, Fritos and trail mix, I headed back to the classroom to make myself comfortable on the table. Luckily I had brought my bag with me so I had a makeshift pillow.

It took Elena a while to return. I had started to drift off when the squeak of the door opening jerked me to a seated position.

She hadn't come alone. Tommy stood behind her. My stomach knotted. I had trouble breathing – my breath had gotten stuck in my tight, sore chest.

We stared at each other, his green eyes dark and hooded. He wore his football jersey, the red accenting his blond hair. My nerve endings started sizzling, tingling down to my fingertips.

I crossed my legs, attempting to put on my best Brandi's I-don't-give-a-shit look. "What are you doing here?"

His stony expression never wavered. "Elena asked me."

Elena studied us both, swiveling her head from side to side. "I think we need a time out. Right now, we have to focus on Kit's immediate problem, which is this restraining order, not your unresolved issues. Unless you don't want to hear what I found out at the courthouse."

That got my attention. "Are you kidding? What?"

She paused dramatically, making sure she had our full attention. "Well, for starters, there's a little matter of proof. And I'm not just talking about the bandage on David's neck."

A cold prick of fear jabbed my spine. "Proof?"

Elena crossed her arms and studied me, eyes unreadable. "A videotape."

Silence. The cold spread throughout the lower half of my body. "A videotape?" I asked in a weak voice.

Elena sighed, shedding her jacket and pulling up a desk. It rattled in protest as she dragged it over. "Apparently he videotaped the entire encounter."

I closed my eyes. This couldn't be happening. "Oh God."

Tommy slid behind another desk. "Videotaped? How could he have done that?"

Elena shrugged. "I guess he had a hidden camera set up in the living room."

My mind spun, stuck in a replay of last night. Every move, every word recorded for the world to see. "Oh, my God, now I see why he said those things."

Elena looked at me sharply. "What things?"

My headache roared back with all its hangover glory. I rubbed my temples. "That he never stalked me. That he'd broken up with me and I couldn't accept it."

Tommy stared at me. "He said that?"

I nodded miserably.

Elena plucked her bag from the floor and rummaged through it. "Well, that explains a lot."

I stopped rubbing my temples and looked at her. "It does?"

"Yep." She pulled out a file folder and opened it. "It says you threatened David with a knife, insisting he was stalking you. He tried to reason with you. You then held the knife to his throat and ordered him to admit he was stalking you. It was only after he did that you left."

Tommy's eyes popped open. "That's what happened?"

I stared at the ceiling, feeling more and more like a freak. "More or less."

"Jesus, Kit. You could've been killed."

I smiled – a cold, humorless smile. "Not likely. I'm the one who had the knife."

"Oh, yeah. Like it would have been so tough to disarm a sick, drunk woman half your size."

"Hold on. To your corners," Elena interrupted, holding her hands up. "I think we're getting a wee bit off the track here. Yes, Kit did a stupid thing and it could've ended up much worse for her. But, to be honest, what did happen was pretty darn bad."

I slunk down in my seat. "Thanks for the pep talk."

Elena shot me a look. "Kit, I don't think you're quite grasping the severity of this right now. Let me put it to you this way. You filed a complaint against David based on the hard evidence of a few emails that any attorney who passed the bar could defuse without breaking a sweat, and on some anonymously sent packages. You also didn't have his last name right when you first made the complaint. And the detective assigned to your case hasn't been able to get a hold of Martha to verify your story."

"He hasn't even tried," I muttered, my stomach filling with ice. "There's been no messages or anything on the answering machine. I don't even have a stupid case number yet."

"Whatever. Still a black mark on your side of the board. Now, on David's side, he has a videotape showing you in his apartment threatening him with a knife unless he admits that he's been stalking you. He has charmingly explained to the court that *you* are actually the one stalking him, and part of *your* strategy is to make the authorities think he is the one stalking you. And, unfortunately for you, this videotape backs up his story and not yours. Becoming clearer to you now?"

The ice had started overflowing, flooding the rest of my body. "Yeah. Bad. I got it."

"I think it's pretty safe to say that your credibility has left the building. Actually, it's probably packed its bags and is on an airplane headed to Miami right now." She sighed. "Wish I could join it."

I buried my head in my hands. "What should I do?"

Elena sighed. "I'm not really sure. Let me make a few calls, see what I can find out."

"Wait a second," Tommy said. "You guys are focusing on the gloom and doom for what reason? It's not like we don't have a case here. Remember, we're the good guys. We have plenty of witnesses who have seen David being a violent asshole. Like me."

"Yeah, won't that neutralize the whole bad thing?" I asked, perking up. "I mean, we do have a bunch of witnesses. Like Martha. And Brandi. She was there when he showed up at the Union along with Bridget and Jamie and what's-her-face."

Elena tapped her pencil against the desk. "That helps. We're going to have to get all those people to testify for you."

"I'll testify," Tommy said. "The way he was when we confronted him about the last name issue. He's clearly unstable."

"But, did he admit anything, though?"

Tommy paused. "Well … "

Elena brushed her hair out of her face. "That's what I thought."

I went back to rubbing my temples. "Wonderful."

Elena ruffled through the file. "No one ever said being a good guy would be easy. Switching gears, why do you think he took the time to set up a hidden camera in the first place? How could he have known this would happen?"

"I don't see how he could," I said. "Although he is pretty paranoid."

"And manipulative," Elena added. "But still. To have the foresight to turn it on even. Seems pretty extreme."

I glanced at Tommy. He appeared to have developed a sudden fascination with the wall. "Tommy?"

He snapped his head around. "What? I agree. He's paranoid."

I eyed him. "Is there something you're not telling us?"

"What? No. Why would you think that?" He shifted in his chair.

Elena studied him, equally as suspicious. "'Fess up, Tommy. What're you hiding?"

Tommy tried to look offended. "Why'd you think I'm hiding something?"

"Because you're a shitty liar, that's why," I said.

Now he did look offended. "I am not."

"Tommy, just spit it out and be done with it," Elena said. "This isn't the time to be hiding things."

He picked at a scratch on the desk surface. "It's nothing, really."

"If it's so nothing then why don't you say it?" I said.

He sighed. "It's just … I think I know why he had a hidden camera in his apartment."

I leaned forward. "And, the reason is … "

"We … sort of had a little … chat with him."

"We?" Elena asked.

"Chat?" I asked.

Tommy's eyes darted around the room before settling on the ceiling. "Me and some of the guys on the team. We happened to run into him near his apartment and told him it'd be better for his health if he left you alone."

I sat back. "Ah. Just happened to run into him at his apartment."

Tommy started to grin. "Well, it was easy once I knew where he lived."

"Was this Tuesday?" Elena broke in.

Tommy's grin slipped a few notches. "Ah … "

Elena rested her forehead on her hand. "So that's where Brad was."

"Well … "

"This is just super," I interrupted. "Now you and I can have matching restraining orders."

"Oh, he didn't actually know it was us," Tommy said.

"He didn't?"

"No, we wore ski masks."

I stood up and began pacing. "And why does that not reassure me?"

Tommy folded his arms across his chest. "Look, there's no problem here. He can't prove anything or I'd have heard about it by now."

"He was probably hoping Kit would lead you back there and you'd slip up and say something incriminating," Elena said.

"Then he could get you kicked off the team and off your football scholarship," I said. "Nice going. Instead, I get a restraining order."

"Oh, now it's my fault you decided to get drunk and stupid last night," Tommy said.

Elena held her hands up again. She was starting to resemble a referee. "All right, all right. At least we know now why he was taping last night."

"And we also know that you better watch yourself." I pointed at Tommy. "He's obviously looking for a way to screw you too."

"You know, I think you're probably the last person in this room who should be giving out dealing-with-David advice," Tommy said.

I stalked back to my coat. "Whatever. I'm outta here." I was sick of the whole mess – sick of talking about it, sick of being in the middle of it, sick of this constant bickering with Tommy and sick of the heavy, clogging feeling in my chest. And if that weren't enough, I still had that stupid paper to write this weekend.

Elena looked like she wanted to say something, then changed her mind. She paused, bit her lip. "I'll call you once I know more."

I started to cough. Damn chest. "Thanks," I said when I could. I didn't look at her, focusing instead on gathering my things.

She slid out from behind the desk and came toward me. "We'll get through this, okay?" She squeezed my arm. "The good guys always win in the end, right?"

I opened my mouth to say something sarcastic, but then saw she was teasing me. "Yeah, right." I half-smiled and moved to leave, making a point of not looking at Tommy as I passed him. "Good luck tomorrow."

"Thanks," he muttered. I didn't touch him, but that didn't stop the electricity from sizzling between us. Would I ever get over him?

Chapter 25

Back when I was a senior in high school, I took a class called Efficient Reading. It was a college prep course, covering things like speed reading and time management. It also covered study skills, giving such helpful advice as transferring notes to three by five index cards so you could study at all times, even while brushing your teeth. Most of that was wasted on me, since I've never even owned three by five index cards, much less studied while brushing my teeth. I wished it had covered other important keys to success, such as: the time to discover you're having a midterm is NOT when the teacher's assistant is handing you the exam.

Worse yet, the exam was essay format – not multiple choice, where I at least had a shot at guessing the right answer. Dreadful way to start out the week.

The weekend prior, I had alternated between forcing myself to work on my lit paper and stuffing myself with over-the-counter cold remedies. Although I managed to finish the paper, my war on disease was about as successful as the war on drugs – along with a tight chest and cough, I now had a runny nose. Definitely a cold. Great.

Flipping through the test, I wondered if I could fake my way through it. But no, I hadn't paid enough attention in class for even that. I could talk to the professor about retaking it. Of course, then I would be stuck in the same situation as my eighteenth century lit class – trying to cram with crappy class notes and zero concentration.

And what about my other classes? Was I going to walk into all of them this week only to find I had papers due and exams to take?

It hit me then that I could fail all my classes. In fact, that was more of a possibility than passing them. I had never been in this position before. I had always been a good student, never great, but good. And now for the first time, I was staring at a midterm where I didn't know the answer to a single question, while carrying a paper not worth the ink it was printed with. How did I manage to do this to myself?

On top of that, I saw no way out. Even if I buckled down and did nothing but study for the rest of the semester, which I knew I couldn't do under present circumstances, I didn't think I could salvage my grades. It looked like I had only one option – and I didn't much like it.

Wanting to hide my lack of preparation, I stayed at my desk, fretting and listening to the sound of pens scratching on papers for nearly the entire hour. I then nonchalantly shoved my blank exam in the middle of the pile before escaping for the door. Humiliating.

Almost as humiliating as having to drop my classes, I thought while heading over to the admissions building. I never thought I would ever be in this situation. I felt like such a loser.

Arriving at admissions, I discovered yet another problem. I couldn't drop all my classes. In fact, because it was so late in the semester, I couldn't even drop one class without permission from the dean of students. Great. I still needed to talk to him about my complaint, but now with this restraining order and David's videotape ... would he even believe my side of the story?

I had another option. I could get extensions on my classes without involving the dean. However, I would still need permissions from each of my professors to do that. And I would still be stuck finishing the classes at some point. This was definitely falling into one of those no-win situations. Damn David.

I stood by the chipped gray counter filled with a variety of administrative forms, including the class-extension forms, chewing on my bottom lip and stewing, until a series of coughs bubbled up in my chest. Enough. If I had to make a decision of this magnitude, the least I could do is get some nourishment into my body. I wondered if it was too early for a beer.

No, coffee would be better. And food. No beer, no matter how tempting. Besides I didn't think the bars were open yet and I certainly wasn't going to my apartment for a drink. Talk about feeling like a loser – deciding between dropping my classes and asking for extensions over a beer on a Monday morning. That sounded like the beginning of a bad Lifetime movie. I decided a latte and bagel at the Union was a much better choice.

While waiting in line to pay for my double latte and toasted bagel and cream cheese, I felt someone staring at me. A woman stood across the room, near the table where I dumped my books. Long golden curls drifted past her shoulders, framing pale, delicate features and huge dark blue eyes. Cat. No question about it.

I tried to sidestep out of line, but a huge man blocked my path. He was in the line next to mine, paying for a tray filled with egg sandwiches, bacon, hash browns, a cinnamon roll and a large cup of coffee. His dark blue sweatshirt stretched painfully across his back. I attempted to weasel past him, but his considerable bulk was wedged between the two cash registers. Cat had started drifting toward the door.

"Hey, you," the cashier yelled at me, snapping her gum, as I searched for another way around. "You gonna pay for that or what?"

I looked at my tray, then back at Cat. She had almost reached the entrance. "Or what." I deposited my would-be purchases next to the cashier.

Her mouth shaped into an "O." She started to say "You can't do that," but I was already pushing my way out of line.

"Wait, Cat," I yelled, frantic, waving my arms. "Wait."

But she had already drifted away. I caught a glimpse of her long curls floating in a sea of backpacks and winter coats – then she was gone.

I fought my way past a Middle-Eastern man balancing a tray filled with food and books, past a couple of African-American women collecting napkins and silverware, and sprinted to the door. Of course, there was no sign of her. I ran all the way to the entrance, searching everywhere, even peering outside, but no luck. She had vanished – disappeared into void, leaving no trace of her presence. Like a fairy.

Actually, that turned out to be not entirely true. When I returned, I found a crisply folded note sitting on top of my backpack. Picking it up, I smelled freshly cut grass and wildflowers. Just a hint, incongruous against the odors of hamburgers, burritos, beer and smoke.

I unfolded the sheet of paper. Two photos slid out and fell to the floor. I saw a flash of blond hair, a bright smile, before they skidded under the table.

Suddenly I couldn't breathe. My chest ached, excruciatingly tight, my lungs squeezed by a giant hand.

Photos. Dare I look? Did I even want to know?

My hand crept toward the photos as my knees buckled beneath me. Kneeling down, my fingers curled around the edges of the photos, the texture smooth and glossy beneath my fingertips. I pulled them toward me.

Blond hair. Blue eyes. Huge smile for the camera.

Cat. As a child.

I went cold, my hands numb, ice emanating from the photo.

Closing my eyes, I took deep breaths, struggling not to cough, willing myself to stay calm. After a few moments, my breathing steadied. I forced my eyes to open, to better examine the photos.

It wasn't Cat. Not even close.

I stared at the photos, perplexed. Someone must have switched them when my eyes were closed. That could be the only explanation.

Oh, God. I can't believe I just thought that. I burst out laughing, toppling over, tears springing to my eyes. It's official – I had lost it. Both paranoid and hallucinating. What a piece of work. I laughed so hard I started coughing.

It took awhile to get my breathing back under control. Once I quit laughing, I had to deal with the coughing. But, eventually I managed it, even with all the furtive, cautious looks people kept shooting me. Yep, another student succumbs to the pressure of college life, those expressions said.

If they only knew the truth.

I got up from the floor and sat in the chair, wishing I had that latte. But there was no way I'd face that cashier again. She would probably spit in it while I dug my money out to pay.

I laid the photos on the table, then realized I still clutched the paper they had been wrapped in with my other hand. Unfolding it, I laid the paper next to the photos.

Kit Cat. Take a look at that.

Tick Tock. Time is almost out.

The words had been torn from a magazine, resembling a ransom note. Made sense. My peace of mind had been kidnapped – naturally, I would need to answer a ransom note to get it returned – hopefully intact.

Back to the photos. The girl was young, seven or eight, with blond hair and blue eyes. That's about where the resemblance to Cat ended. This girl had a thin, sharp face, pale skin and a slight overbite. She was pretty, but pretty in a waif-like, wispy way – not like Cat's soft, golden beauty.

One photo showed the girl close up, smiling, a posed studio shot. The second had been taken outside. An older woman accompanied her, holding her hand as they walked away from a building. The girl wore a little black coat and a red and white striped hat. Her bony wrists poked out from the too-short sleeves. She had turned her head, staring up at the woman. The woman also wore a black coat, which matched her black curly hair and black-rimmed glasses. Her mouth was set in a straight line. She wasn't looking at the child, rather she stared at her feet as she seemed to yank the poor girl along.

I pushed the photo away. I didn't want to look at it anymore. It made me uncomfortable and edgy. I didn't like that woman, nor did I like the way she dragged that poor little girl with those horribly thin wrists.

Oh for God's sake, I had to stop this. I had enough things in my life making me uncomfortable and edgy – I certainly didn't need to be reading things into a photo left by some woman claiming to be my kidnapped sister. She was probably some nutcase working with David to try and drive me crazy.

Suddenly exhausted, I sank down in my seat. I buried my face into my arms and alternated between pretending the world was normal – I had never gone to that stupid Halloween party in the first place, much less met David or seen Cat – and that the world had disappeared into nothingness.

***

I spent the rest of the day trudging around campus in search of my professors. After my earlier "face-to-face" with insanity, I no longer had any doubt about what I needed to do. Although I still didn't feel comfortable asking for extensions, I thought I would have better luck convincing my professors than the dean of students. The dean may already know about the restraining order, but university bureaucracy probably hadn't moved fast enough to attach the restraining order to the complaint, if my professors even called to check.

Actually, my professors were quite sympathetic (about time some-body was!). They all granted me extensions without a fuss. Even the professor whose exam I had just flunked told me I could retake it whenever I felt up to it. She actually treated me like I was the victim in the situation. What a concept.

To be fair, I think my coughing and general sad state of health helped my cause. I could honestly claim that the stress of being stalked had caused my illness. Although I didn't mention CF, I knew I looked horrible.

I decided not to approach my eighteenth century lit professor. He had just given me an extension on my paper – I didn't want to press my luck. I just shoved my paper under his door and slunk away. After all, I reasoned, I now only had one class, his class, to concentrate on. I could do it.

I stopped at the Tavern for dinner – a cup of chili topped with cheese and onions, and a cheeseburger with all the works and onion rings – before heading for home. Except for some snacky foods, I hadn't eaten much all day.

By the time I started walking, dusk had fallen, along with the temperature. I wrapped my scarf around my neck, protecting it from the bitter cold wind, and broke into a trot.

Long shadows stretched out across the sidewalk. I jumped as a flier advertising a bar band called *Meat Locker* flapped loudly – it hadn't been attached well to the side of the building. Another flier flew across the street, this one announcing some sort of peace rally, the dry rattling noise sinister and eerie. A man wearing a bright red ski jacket brushed against my arm as he ran past. I caught a glimpse of wild hair and equally wild eyes before he vanished into the night.

All right. I needed to get a hold of myself. At this rate, I would never make it home – instead I would be found crouched in the doorway of some building, eyes darting and body jumping.

Squaring my shoulders, I focused my eyes straight ahead and sped up my pace. I forced my mind to empty, concentrating only on my pace and destination.

My face felt numb, my lips chapped and dry. It would be good to get inside and out of the cold, I thought. Never mind the rest.

Finally my apartment came into view. Coughing only slightly, I increased my stride. Almost there.

"Hello, Kit."

I let out a short scream. A man stepped out from the shadows of the neighboring putrid green rental house.

Instinctively I backed away, ashamed of having screamed. It was probably Brad or someone else from the football team. No one to be scared of. "Who's there?"

"You mean you can't recognize my voice?" The man replied, his voice teasing. I took another step backward, slimy tendrils starting to curl around my stomach. The man continued toward me, the light from the street lamp slanting across his face.

David.

I suddenly became aware of just how desolate it was. Where was everyone? "What are you doing here?" I croaked. "You have a restraining order against me. Why are you outside my apartment?"

He cocked his head. "Why, I do! That means you have to leave." His voice still had that teasing quality to it.

The hairs against the back my neck started to squirm furiously. Something wasn't right. I mean, really not right. I made myself stop retreating. "What the hell are you talking about? I can't leave my own apartment."

"Didn't you read the fine print? If I show up in a public place, you have to leave."

God, is that what it said? "My apartment isn't a public place."

He spread his arms out wide. "We're not at your apartment. This certainly is a public place." His voice went up, the teasing continuing. With horror, I finally realized what I had been sensing. He was using the teasing to hide something else in his voice, something darker, more sinister.

Madness.

"Fine." I started to stride past him, refusing to let him see the terror threatening to seize my limbs. I couldn't let him sense any weakness. Like a predator, he would pounce.

He stayed in front of me, still in that teasing mode, preventing me from passing.

I stopped, folded my arms. "Can't leave the area if you won't let me."

He pointed behind me. "You can go that way."

I bit my lip. Could he smell my fear? Now what do I do? The words darted through my brain – the best defense is good offense. Besides, most predators back off if the prey attacks them. I forced myself to take several steps forward, to get right into his face. "Just because you have a restraining order doesn't mean you can tell me where I can go. So, get out of my way."

He clapped his hand against his chest and staggered back a step. "Oh, Kit. You break my heart. Can't we put this behind us and start again?"

A shadow covered his eyes. I desperately wished I could see them. Maybe then I would know if I had only imagined the madness I was hearing, or if it was real. "David, as I already told you, we're done," I said with more bravado then I felt. "I don't want anything more to do with you. In fact, since you have me saying that on tape, why don't you go home and watch it over and over again until you get the picture?"

His face grew still. "There's no need to get nasty, Kit."

Oh, God, did I push too far? Too late to back off now. I had to keep this charade up or he really would see my terror. "Me, nasty? You're the one who put the restraining order on me."

"That was only because you filed complaints against me."

I held my hands up. "Fine. We were both wronged. Now, would you please step out of my way so I can go home?"

His jaw worked, but he didn't move. I stayed where I was. What would I do if he didn't get out of my way? Could I get my pepper spray in time? Or would it come down to a physical fight? Did I even have a chance against him?

The wind had died down, the night growing more still, more silent. Keenly aware of just how alone we were, I struggled to control my breathing. How did he always pick the times when I was alone? Did he have a sixth sense about it?

After what seemed like forever, he stepped aside and gave me a playful flourish. I closed my eyes, my breath wanting to rush out of me in a whoosh, but I restrained it. I hadn't realized I had been holding it until then.

I nodded at him and started forward. Not too fast, I warned myself.

He fell into step beside me. "I really wish you'd be more open about talking things out."

Oh, God. I increased my pace. "David, has it occurred to you that ambushing me outside my apartment isn't helping your stalking case?"

He flung his hands out. "Who's seen me?"

Oh, God. Oh, God. The silence was agonizingly loud in my ears. Where was everyone? Why couldn't one person appear, just one? Maybe he had some sort of supernatural powers gifted to him by the fairies. Maybe that's why Cat knew about him. The fairies had kidnapped him, too. Oh, God, stop it. I was a heartbeat away from hysterics. I forced my eyes straight ahead. My apartment building was the next one. Almost there. My chest tightened even more, but I had to stay calm. I needed to buy time. "Are you *sure* no one has seen you, David?"

"I am. And I know what you're doing right now, because I know you." His voice dropped, became intimate. "I know you better than you know yourself, Kitrina."

I wouldn't let myself look at him. "Nobody calls me that."

"Why? It's a beautiful name."

I didn't answer. We were in front my apartment building, just steps away from the walkway leading to my door.

"You know what else I know about you, Kitrina?" He leaned closer, his foul breath grazing my cheek. "I know you like knives."

I snapped my head around. His face was close, close enough to kiss me, but still his eyes lurked in the shadows. His stinking breath nearly overwhelmed me.

"Get away from me." I tried to sound menacing, but my voice shook and I coughed. His lips curled into a smile.

"Got your attention, didn't I?"

I glanced at his hands. They were empty.

For now.

I started up the walkway, David matching my step, stride-for-stride.

"David, I mean it. Leave me alone," I said, my voice firmer. My hand crept toward my purse.

"Why? You came after me with a knife. What's so different now?"

Oh, God. This was so out of control. My hand dipped into my purse, frantically searching for a weapon as my eyes stayed glued to his hands. Why wouldn't he stop walking with me? I coughed again. My hand found my wallet.

"Bye, David. We're on my property now."

He cocked his head. "What are you doing?"

"Searching for my keys." My fingers scrambled furiously. Nothing, nothing. Why couldn't I find something? My hand closed around my cell phone. No good, he would never give me enough time to use it. I touched a pen. Would that work? Could I actually use it as a weapon?

We neared my door, David continuing to walk right next to me. Oh, God. I had to stop this before we reached my apartment. I couldn't take the chance he would force his way inside after I unlocked the door. Taking two quick steps forward, I whirled to face him then stopped, putting my free hand against his chest, my other hand still in my purse. "We're done here. It's time for you to go. Now."

He kept moving, pushing me backward. "What if I don't want to?" His eyes caught a sliver of light and they gleamed.

Oh, God. Oh, God. My fingers brushed against my wallet again. "Well, you could always stick around until the police arrive and then explain how you're so terrified of me that you followed me home."

He looked disgusted. "The police aren't coming, Kit. I expected more from you." He cocked his head. "Need help finding your keys?"

My fingers grazed against plastic. Finally. Oh, shit, no. That's my inhaler. I backed up. "No, I'm just fine. Just leave."

He took another step forward. "I can hear them in there. Why don't I help you?"

My fingers curled around a cylinder. I found it. My pepper spray. I whipped it out. "Why don't you just go?"

He stopped, hands outstretched, still empty. "Whaddya got there?" The teasing note was back in his voice. I stepped toward him, my other hand grabbing my keys.

"Leave right now, or you'll find out."

He backed up. "Interested in adding an assault and battery charge to your restraining order?"

"It won't be assault and battery because we're on my property," I said through gritted teeth, pulling my keys out, stifling a cough.

"You don't own it."

I moved away from him, toward the door. "No, but I rent it, you asshole. And if you're smart, you'll get out of here fast, because the first thing I'm doing when I get inside is calling the police."

"And who do you think they're going to believe?"

My back brushed against the door. "Oh, you want to stick around and see for yourself?" Still facing him, I reached around and fumbled for the lock.

He retreated to the sidewalk. "Kit, why do you insist on making this so difficult? You know we're meant to be together."

Shaking. I couldn't get my key to fit. "David, for God's sake, will you just go?" I coughed out.

He continued to stand there, a dark shadowy figure on the sidewalk. "Our history, Kit. Nobody will ever understand what you've been through. Not like me. You belong with me, Kit. One day you're going to figure that out, but I may not be so willing to take you back when you do."

"If I could be so lucky," I muttered. Why couldn't my damn key work?!

"What did you say?"

"I said I'll take my chances," I yelled. What was going on with this key? If I could only turn around and see what I was doing, but I didn't dare do that with him mere feet away.

"What's going on here?"

Brandi. I almost collapsed with relief. She stood at the corner of the yard, elegant in her long green wool coat and leather gloves. My fashionably dressed savior.

"Brandi. Why hello! It's so nice to see you." David shifted toward her and held his arms out, as if to hug her. I took advantage of the diversion to focus more on unlocking the door.

Brandi stepped toward him. "What are you doing here?"

"Why, I'm here to see Kit." He waved an arm in my direction.

Brandi moved closer. "You have a restraining order against her. Why would you want to see her?"

David backed away. "She asked me to."

"I did not," I yelled before I could stop myself. I was ready to explode with frustration, rage and terror.

"So what if she did?" Brandi continued to advance, her voice heavy with sarcasm. "Is that what you're going to tell the judge, that even though you were so frightened of Kit you had to get restraining order? That you still came over to her apartment when she asked?"

David teetered backward. The light from a streetlamp fell across his face and for the first time I saw uncertainty reflected there. Ha! Maybe this wouldn't go his way after all.

"You don't understand," he floundered.

"You know, I think you're finally right about something," Brandi said. "I don't understand. Maybe it's because the facts in this case don't fit the bullshit story you're spitting out."

I gave up on the key and went to help Brandi. David now had a stricken look on his face. "But that's not true. Kit and I love each other. This is just a misunderstanding."

"Oh right. Big misunderstanding," Brandi said, her voice filled with disgust. "Game's over, David. You lose. There's a witness now. So why don't you get the hell out of here before you have to give that pathetic explanation to the police."

David looked at each of us, his features melting into anger. "This isn't over," he spat and strode into the darkness.

"Unfortunate but true," Brandi sighed, turning toward me. "Why didn't you go inside and call the police?"

"Because I couldn't get the stupid door open. My key doesn't fit."

"That's odd. Here, try mine while I keep a lookout." Brandi dug through her purse.

"You were absolutely incredible. I can't believe you were able to chase him off."

Brandi handed me her keys. "All talk and no backup. He's a bully at heart. His particular brand of torture comes from twisting the truth around. When you're the only witness, he can do that. But when other people step into the picture, poof."

"I gotta get Martha to talk to the police." I headed back to the door. Brandi's key didn't turn either.

"What's taking so long?" Brandi yelled from the sidewalk.

I jiggled the key. "I can't get yours to work either."

"Christ Kit. Now you can't work a door anymore." Brandi sauntered over. "Here, let me try. You keep an eye out for Hannibal Lecter."

"I only wish it was Hannibal Lecter. At least he was polite. And funny." I stepped away so Brandi could try.

She fiddled with the key. Same results. "What is going on around here? Maybe Martha's home." She banged on the door. "Martha. Get your butt over here and open up!"

"I have my trusty noisemaker if you think that would get her here faster," I offered.

Brandi rolled her eyes. "We'll try that if she's at the library or something. Martha!" She pounded on the door a second time.

"I'm here, I'm here," Martha muttered, her voice muffled. "No need to make such a fuss."

I heard the click of the lock, then the door swung open. Martha's red plaid shirt was rumpled, her hair tucked in big hunks behind her ears, black circles stained the skin beneath her eyes. "See, door's open. Everything's all right."

Brandi pushed her way past her. "Everything is not all right. My key doesn't work."

"Neither does mine," I stepped in as well.

"That's because I changed the locks," Martha said.

Brandi, who had started up the stairs, stopped in mid-stride. "What did you say?" she asked, her voice deceptively quiet as she turned to face Martha.

"Changed the locks," Martha answered almost cheerfully, as she shut the door and bolted it.

Brandi leaned a hip against the banister and folded her arms across her chest. "And why, pray tell, did you do that?"

"Because she needs to move out." Martha pointed at me.

My mouth fell open. "You have got to be kidding," I stuttered, flooded by so many emotions I was almost speechless.

Brandi stepped back down the stairs. "But, I was locked out too."

"Oh, well, I was going to give you a key," Martha said.

Something inside me snapped when she said that. Stress, anger, frustration, panic and terror collided and exploded.

"Martha, you bitch!" I yelled, trying to ignore images of David looming over me with a knife, helpless in front of my locked front door. "I could've been killed out there! David was threatening me with a knife. And I couldn't even open the door to my own apartment."

Martha looked unfazed. "Told you he was dangerous."

"He had a knife?" Brandi asked, a hint of fear in her voice.

I ignored Brandi. "I know he's dangerous, you stupid cow. What, you think I'm an idiot or something?"

"You haven't done anything about it," Martha said.

God, did I want to slap her. "I've made formal complaints about him, to the police and the university."

"Oh, yeah, I know about those. They called me." Martha said, almost indifferently.

There was that feeling again – that feeling that I had wandered back onto some illogical world without knowing it. How could I be having this conversation? "You talked to them? And you still changed the locks?"

"I told them I didn't know anything." Martha brushed past Brandi and clomped up the stairs.

"You did what?" I didn't believe what I just heard. "You told the police you didn't know anything?"

Martha continued clumping up the stairs, her back to me. "Yep."

Unbelievable. My mouth opened and closed, but no sound came out. I could only stand there, gaping at a large wrinkle on the back of Martha's red plaid shirt. Brandi's eyes met mine, her expression as shocked as I was. I clapped my hands to the top of my head, as if to keep it from flying off.

"Martha, what the hell were you thinking?" Brandi asked.

I heard a buzzing noise in my head – the sound of my credibility flying away no doubt. Sucking in my breath, I struggled to keep from screaming. "Why did you do that?"

Martha leaned over the mud brown banister, hair hanging down, the circles under her eyes even more pronounced. "Because that's not going to make the problem go away."

I felt like I might burst. I bounded up the stairs, bringing up a few coughs in the process. "What do you mean it's not going to make the problem go away?" I said, between coughs. "How else is the problem going to go away?"

Martha planted her hands on her hips. "You leaving will make the problem go away. Going through the law will take too long."

"For you, maybe. It's not going to make the problem go away for me."

Martha shrugged. "You should have thought of that before you dated him."

A veil of red descended before my eyes and I lunged at her, slapping her across the face.

"Kit, stop it," Brandi yelled, yanking me back.

Martha put a hand to her cheek, now as red as her shirt, her eyes as round as pebbles. "I can't believe you did that."

"And I can't believe you," I screamed, thrashing in Brandi's arms. "You're standing in judgment of me? You bitch! You have no rights here, none. I can have you thrown out tomorrow!" I exploded into a coughing fit, wrenching away from Brandi.

Martha rubbed her cheek. "No, you can't."

"Yes, we can," Brandi said. "We've been through this. Your name isn't on the lease. Our names are. We can throw *you* out. You can't throw us out."

Martha turned to Brandi, a hurt expression on her face. "I thought you were on my side here."

"I wasn't on *anyone's* side before, but after that stupid stunt you pulled changing the locks, I'm definitely *not* on your side."

"But you're an innocent victim here, too."

"So is Kit," Brandi said, as I struggled to get my coughing under control. "Do you really think she asked for this, even if she did date the guy a couple of times? She's trying to do something about it, and then you screw it all up by lying about it."

Martha began to look uncertain. "But, I thought … "

"No, you didn't think, that's the problem," Brandi interrupted. "Yes, going through the system will take longer than if she moves out, but her moving out is *not* an option here. My God, Martha, have you no compassion?"

Martha's eyes grew rounder at same time as her mouth flattened. "Don't you see? Every time I come home, I see him hanging around outside. What if he attacks me? I can't stand it anymore. I just want the problem to go away."

"Newsflash, Martha. I want it to go away too, probably more than you do," I said, finally getting my coughing under control. "Do you have any idea how it feels to be the one he's waiting for?"

Martha collapsed, landing on the couch, legs folding under her like a rag doll. "I can't concentrate like I used to. My grades are slipping. This is ruining my life." Her body slumped over, arms draped over her knees, hair trailing over her face.

"It's ruining all our lives," Brandi said quietly. "Especially Kit's."

Martha didn't answer, burrowing further into herself. As pissed as I was, I still couldn't help feeling a little sorry for her.

"Give me a key." I held my hand out. "How the hell did you get the landlord to agree to this anyway?"

Martha paused, straightened, her hair falling away from her face. I could see the creases under eyes, the folds sharper and deeper than I remembered. "Said I was Brandi. Told him we were being stalked." She folded her arms across her chest.

"I want a key now, and if you ever do anything like this again, I will have you evicted." I closed in on her.

"No," Brandi said flatly. "That's not good enough. Tomorrow, you're going to call the police and tell them the truth. And, if you don't, we will have you evicted."

Martha's eyes darted up at us. "Just wanted the problem to go away," she muttered.

"Yeah, you said that," I said, exhaustion creeping through my veins like a dark, liquidy drug. I flopped on the chair and blew my nose. God, I felt awful. Both my head and chest ached. I could even taste my sickness, it coated the back of my throat like a wooly blanket.

Brandi turned to me. "Now, what's all this about a knife?"

Chapter 26

After debriefing Brandi on the entire David encounter, which she handled very well, considering … I decided to take a very long, very hot shower. I was dizzy with exhaustion and every part of my body hurt.

The shower loosened the mucus in my lungs and eased my aching head. Hot raspberry tea with lemon and honey soothed my sore throat. I followed that with an array of cold remedies and went to bed. I refused to allow myself to think.

As tired as I was, I couldn't fall into a deep, restful sleep. I instead remained on the shallow edges, tossing and turning. Disconcerting images danced through my subconscious – floating knives, David grinning under a streetlight with eyes as black as a freshly dug grave, Cat flying away with the fairies. When I dragged myself out of bed at eight o'clock, I swore I felt more tired than I had the night before.

Brandi sauntered in while I played with my bagel, trying to decide if I had the nerve to attend the one class in which I hadn't received an extension. There was no question I ought to go, but that didn't stop David's grin from leering up at me every time I made a move to get ready.

Brandi seated herself across from me. "Don't worry about going to the police. I'm filing a report today."

She looked pale and drawn, eyes drooping. Her appearance shocked me. "I should, too. After I go to class."

Brandi shook her head. "Just call it in. I'll tell you after I've filed, then you can call and add to it. If they ask why you didn't do it earlier, tell them you have CF and you were too sick to do it before now."

I smiled slightly. Not too far from the truth.

"Besides," she continued. "It's probably better if a formal complaint came from someone other than you right now. I'm getting Martha down there as well."

I poked at my bagel. "I get the feeling you think I should stay here today."

She narrowed her eyes. "Don't you think that'd be a good idea?"

I know you like knives.

I stared at my bagel, now crumbled into something barely recognizable on the hideous sunflower plate. Brandi was right, but the idea of spending the day cooped up in my apartment because of David twisted my insides. And then I would have nothing to distract me from seeing his distorted face grinning, the madness within shining through ...

I stood. Time to get my mind off this before I made myself crazy. I boiled water for tea, took more cold medicine and stretched out on the couch. I'm not hiding from David, I thought. I'm just taking another sick day.

I spent the better part of the afternoon dozing in front of daytime television, feeling like I had hit the epitome of laziness. Eventually I decided I'd had enough, so I turned off the television and checked my email.

I hadn't done it for several days, mostly because I thought if I saw some smug message from David there, I would throw my computer out the window. As expected, he had sent me several messages. I decided to pretend I hadn't seen them, and didn't open them.

Equally disturbing though were the two emails from the university. The first appeared to be routine, requesting me to make an appointment with the dean regarding my complaint. The second, sent yesterday afternoon, was more menacing.

"We have recently received information regarding your complaint against David Terry. Please call our office immediately to schedule an appointment with Dean Barnow."

They had to be referring to the restraining order. Lovely. Well, I knew I'd have to deal with this sooner or later, I just had hoped it would be later.

It amazed me how David, the attacker, had managed to get the wheels of justice furiously turning for him, whereas I, the victim, could barely get a courtesy call. What did that say about our justice system?

No, I wouldn't go there. It would only make me angry, and I had enough things standing in line to make me angry. Today was a day about resting and healing. God knows I would need all my strength and then some in the coming weeks.

Speaking of strength, I picked up the phone to call the police department. I wanted the cops on my side before I saw the dean. Then maybe I could finally get this mess straightened out.

The police, however, had a different interpretation of the facts. Detective Jenkins explained that he had spoken to David, seen the videotape, and discovered I had received extensions on all but one class. His tone left no doubt as to which one of us he believed. I hung up, seething, amazed at how fast I was becoming the stalker and David the victim.

I took a quick shower, dressed and blow-dried my hair so it wouldn't freeze in the cold. I had to get out of the apartment. And why shouldn't I? It was the middle of the afternoon – the sun was shining, people were shuffling to and from class, work and studying. Nothing to be afraid of. Nothing at all.

I put on my coat and walked to the door. David wasn't out there. He couldn't be. He had classes to attend, a life to live. He couldn't be out there, hiding in the next building or behind the garbage dumps, waiting for me to leave so he could pounce …

I know you like knives.

I rubbed my face, then went back upstairs to call a cab. This was an insane way to live. I shouldn't let him control me like this. He was in the wrong. I shouldn't have to change my life. None of those thoughts stopped me from dialing.

I told the driver to take me across campus to Franklin Street. David wouldn't be able to follow a cab across town on foot. Besides, there was a café there, The Wagon, which served breakfast all the time. Breakfast sounded good to me right now. It also happened to be across the street from the stadium, and Tommy would be finishing practice in an hour or so. Not that I was going to see him or anything. I just liked the food at The Wagon.

I ordered a huge breakfast – cheese and mushroom omelet, bacon, hash browns and English muffin – and managed to polish most of it off between jumping at every noise and eyeing every person around me. Pretty pathetic.

Maybe I would go watch Tommy practice for a bit. It would be a good distraction for my mind, plus the fresh air would be good for my health. Seemed like a good idea all around.

I had always loved watching Tommy play. A natural athlete, he exhibited grace and dexterity on the field. Combined with his obvious pure enjoyment of the game and a body that all that padding couldn't hide, he was quite a sight on the field (even for those who didn't like football).

I found a seat near the field and settled in to watch, hugging myself to keep out the cold, trying not to peer at every person who strolled by. It was clear and crisp – a perfect autumn day. The sun sparkled on the trees, a few still clinging to some vestiges of color – dark rust, rich orange and bright gold. In the distance, the taller campus buildings stood out in bold relief against the dark blue sky. The air smelled clean and sharp, a combination of apples, wood smoke and dried leaves. No question about it – autumn was by far Wisconsin's most spectacular season. Its beauty could almost make me forget how much I actually hated the season. How much it reminded me of death.

With a shiver, I recalled Halloween, getting out of the cab and catching a whiff of the night. The scent of autumn, heavy and thick. Then, too, the thought of death had crossed my mind. And still I walked merrily into that party.

Maybe the reason autumn made me think of death wasn't some general, philosophical mindset – the change of seasons and all that. Maybe it was personal. My own death. I would die in autumn. And somehow I had sensed it all these years.

My chest spasmed and a huge, mucusy coughing fit erupted. As if my body was verifying what my mind had always known.

No. I had to stop this right now. My priority should be finding a way out of the mess I was in, not morbid thoughts of death. Unfortunately, with a mad stalker after me and my body deteriorating by the day, the idea of my death no longer seemed farfetched. In fact, death might be right down the street, perhaps in a bar having a couple of beers to warm up from the cold before coming to find me. Death had been distracted once. It wouldn't twice.

Maybe it didn't matter. The thought came from nowhere, startling me. Why would I think that? What a horrible thought.

But there was truth in it. I felt it.

Maybe it didn't matter. I turned that statement over in my mind. Examined it from different angles. *Maybe it didn't matter.* Finally allowed myself to finish it.

Maybe it didn't matter because I wasn't bothering to live anyway.

I sucked in my breath. I wasn't bothering to live anyway.

The pieces suddenly clicked and there was my life – spread out in front of me like a dissected frog. By not discussing my disease, I had never analyzed my feelings about it. Worse yet, I had been deceiving myself about it. Back when I did attend support groups, an issue that had come up was how most CF children rebelled against their disease at some point in their lives. What usually happened was they quit taking care of themselves – ignored their treatments, refused to exercise, that sort of thing. That had never happened to me. Other than overdoing it on the partying, I had always taken meticulous care of my health. My mother had drilled that into me. Besides, I had always refused to be like other CF patients.

But I *was* just like them. I, too, had rebelled. Just in a different fashion. Rather than refuse to take my pancreatic enzymes or do my daily lung-clearing exercises, I had refused to live. Instead of embracing life, embracing love, I had drifted.

Some people are accused of possessing death wishes. What I was doing was far worse. I had spent my life drifting. Drifting, until the one day I would drift into death.

At that moment, Coach Barrymore blew the whistle, ending practice. Not a second too soon, I thought, getting to my feet. Definitely needed something else to think about.

I trotted down the stairs leading to the locker room, still shaken by my discovery. The guys were already filing in – a few nodded to me, most ignored me. Still on that black list apparently.

At last, I spotted Tommy. He had taken his helmet off and his hair clung to his face, dripping with sweat despite the cold. My heart made an odd lurch as I stared at him, watching him rub his neck as he spoke to the guy next to him. God, was he gorgeous. God, did I miss him.

"Tommy."

He glanced up, saw me. His expression hardened.

"Tommy, can I talk to you?" I pleaded, trying not to sound too desperate. A couple of his teammates glanced over, saw me, and hurried into the locker room.

Tommy closed his eyes for a moment, shook his head, then made his way over to me. "What?"

I stamped my feet, trying to warm them. "I'd like to talk to you."

"You're talking. What do you want?"

I sighed. Guess he had decided not to make this easy.

"Look, I'm sorry about the other night. I didn't mean to sound like a bitch. It's just ... look, you more than anyone know what's been happening to me. My life is coming apart at the seams. And it keeps getting worse. I really need a friend right now. I'd like it to be you. But, as for the other stuff, I can't focus on that now. I have no energy for anything else except dealing with all this crap. I can't even deal with school. I've gotten extensions on all but one of my classes. So, can we call a truce? Once I get some control back, then we can talk, but can you just be my friend for now?" I ended my speech with a few rumbling coughs. Not planned, but they did a nice job of underscoring my illness.

His face tightened, his eyes narrowed. "What do you mean, things getting worse?"

I stamped my feet a second time. "I'd tell you, but I'm freezing and you need to take a shower."

He drummed his fingers against his football helmet, studied my red cheeks and running nose. "Yeah, okay. I'll meet you at The Wagon in about a half hour."

"Okay," I said, even though I had just left there. That's all right, I could have a cup of tea and warm up while I waited. I could even check my purse for the thousandth time to make sure all my weapons were accounted for and my cell phone was set to auto-dial 9-1-1.

***

"This is getting really weird." Tommy flipped through the photos and latest Cat message. We were walking to my apartment. Tommy thought I belonged in bed, and he didn't even leer when he said it. I must look like death if I couldn't sexually interest a twenty-one-year-old male. Not a comforting thought. Not to mention a huge blow to my ego.

"Tell me about it."

He used one photo to tap on the other one. "I guess she must be the innocent we keep hearing about."

"You think, Sherlock?"

He smiled. "Am I being too obvious, Watson? Well, how about this? Did you notice she's in Minnesota?"

I looked over his shoulder. "No. Where'd you get that?"

He showed me the photo of the child and adult. "See. Right here. The Minneapolis School for Special Children."

I leaned closer. There it was, right at the top, nearly cut off. "You're right. I guess I was too busy looking at the girl."

"It's a tough burden to carry, being a genius, but I do it because it needs to be done." He attempted to look both noble and martyred at the same time.

I snorted. "Genius. Right. If you're a genius, you'd know what it means."

"All in good time, my child." He tried to sound ancient and wise, but then he saw my expression and burst out laughing, ruining the effect. "No clue whatsoever. I don't know why a child in Minneapolis would have anything to do with you being stalked in Riverview."

"Not to mention what any of this has to do with Cat being kidnapped," I mused. "Nothing makes any sense. I keep getting pieces, but it's like I'm getting pieces from different areas of a jigsaw puzzle, so nothing fits together."

"Or you're getting pieces from different puzzles," Tommy remarked, taking back the photo.

I glared at him. "Oh, that's a comforting thought."

He shrugged. "You said it. None of this makes any sense. And why would it all fit together anyway? Seems like completely different problems."

I sighed. "You're probably right."

We walked along in silence. An Asian man with thick glasses wobbled by on a bicycle, riding on the wrong side of the street, his worn brown coat billowing out behind him. On the corner, a younger man with a long curly beard and John Lennon glasses argued passionately with a tiny, bird-like girl with long stringy dirty blonde hair and an oversized black overcoat. She appeared to be crying.

"I haven't been exactly fair either," Tommy said suddenly.

I jerked my head around, wondering if I had missed some part of the conversation. "Excuse me?"

"To you. I haven't been fair to you." He stared straight ahead, eyes fixed in front of him.

"What are you talking about?"

He paused, cut his eyes at me. "You. What you always say, that I don't share things. You're right, I don't. And that's not fair to you."

Where did this come from? "So you're planning to share now?"

He shoved his hands into his pockets. "Well, not exactly."

I dropped my arms to my sides before my hands could reach out and throttle him. "Tommy, just spit it out. What are you trying to tell me?"

He sighed. "I thought this would be easier."

"What? What would be easier? You're making about as much sense as Cat right now."

"Hey, at least I'm not doing this in an email." He half-smiled at me.

"At least an email I can delete," I retorted. "If you want to say something, say it or drop it. I'm not in an analyze-y mood."

"Okay, okay." He shoved his hands deeper in his pockets. I was surprised he didn't tear the fabric. "I've been doing some thinking. About things … us … things. I know I haven't told you about myself the way you have. And that isn't fair to you. But … " His voice dropped off and he stared at the sidewalk.

"But," I prompted, sidestepping a tall, skinny guy swinging a backpack like a lethal weapon.

"But there are things about me. Things I'm not proud of."

I turned away so he couldn't see me roll my eyes. What did the golden boy have to be ashamed of? Whatever it was, it couldn't be this big of a deal. "So what do you want me to do about it if you aren't going to tell me?"

"That's not it. I'm doing this all wrong. It's just that … I tried telling someone once, and it didn't work out. At all."

We passed a bus stop. A stern-looking woman stood waiting, gripping the hand of a little blond-haired girl, reminding me of the photo from Cat. "And that has what to do with me?"

"Kit, this isn't easy for me."

"I should say not." My voice had developed an edge, echoing the glow of anger beginning to burn inside me. "You're making that painfully clear. Nor is it easy for me. Because what you seem to be saying is because you had a bad experience confessing your sins to someone once before, you're not willing to trust me. Despite the fact you know all of my deep dark secrets."

His expression tightened. "Don't make this so difficult."

"Me making this difficult?" I stretched my arms out. "How is this suddenly my fault? I didn't bring this up, you did."

"I know. I wanted you to understand."

"Understand?" I stared at the sky in exasperation. "Understand what? You didn't tell me anything."

"Yes, I did." He took his hands out of his pocket and balled them into fits. "It's not that I don't want to tell you about myself. It's just that I can't right now. It needs to be the right time."

First he insults me, then he tries to make it up by turning it into some sort of romantic gesture even though he hasn't shared anything. Couldn't anything in my life be simple and straightforward? My anger burned a little hotter. "Whatever, Tommy."

He sighed. "I'm not very good at this."

"Understatement of the year."

He faintly smiled. "Look, I'm trying here. Can't you give me some points for that?"

"No, but I'll give you a bit of free advice." I stopped in the middle of the sidewalk and waited for him to turn and face me. "Next time you feel like sharing nothing, share nothing." I waved at him. "Thanks for walking me home. I'll catch you later."

His expression transformed into a mix of puzzlement and irritation. "But you're not home yet."

"I'm a couple of blocks away. I'll be fine."

Now he looked impatient. "Kit, I was trying to tell you something."

I clasped my hand to my heart. "You were? I had no idea."

"That's not fair."

"Tommy, you told me nothing and you damn well know it." I said, my anger getting the better of me. "I'm sick and tired of games and riddles and trying to decipher the real meaning of what people are doing or saying. You of all people should know that, yet you pull the same crap on me."

He scrubbed his hands through his hair. "I wasn't trying to do that."

"Then what were you trying to do? Tell me I wasn't good enough to share things with? That you had a bad experience once and you think I might do the same thing to you?"

"Fine." He backed away, his hands in the air. "I give up. Good-bye, Kit."

I didn't say anything, just watched him stalk off in the opposite direction. I told myself I was in the right, he was the one being a wishy-washy jerk. I still felt my anger burning inside me, hot and righteous. Yet, I couldn't help thinking how final that good-bye had sounded. In fact, I thought about it the rest of the way to my apartment.

Chapter 27

I pushed my empty mug across the bar. "Another," I said to the bartender, a scrawny African-American guy wearing a stained white shirt. He nodded, substituting my mug for a clean one and filling it with Miller Light. Behind me a couple of pale, exhausted guys wearing faded old tee shirts played a game of pool. The snapping and rolling noise of the balls was in direct contrast to the creepy mellow strains of Pink Floyd's "Comfortably Numb" playing on the loudspeaker.

I had no business being in the Bear Claw. None. I should be home resting. Not sitting on a cracked bar stool suspiciously eyeing everyone who walked through the door and jumping every time the pool balls smacked together. But between my argument with Tommy, the skepticism of Detective Jenkins as to my status as a victim, and not being invited to yet another party, I knew I couldn't stand being alone in the apartment.

"It's just a birthday party," Brandi had told me, poised at the top of the stairs. "Guy Halloram. He's turning twenty-one. Just a few beers at the house then off to the bars. No big thing."

Right. No big thing. Unless you weren't invited, of course. I swallowed more tea, trying to hide my expression.

Brandi put her hand on her hip. "You look like crap. Think of this as a gift, not a punishment. If you were invited, you'd go, and you belong in bed." She left the rest unspoken, but I heard it anyway.

Where you're safe.

I know you like to play with knives.

"Thanks, Mom. I'll keep that in mind," I said.

Brandi shrugged. "Only trying to help. I'm not kidding. You do look like hell. You don't want Tommy to see you like this."

"Newsflash – Tommy has seen me like this. Today even." Yeah, and he couldn't wait to get me into bed … to sleep. Brandi was right again. I drank more tea. Maybe I could drown my sorrows in tea – people always tried alcohol and it didn't work. Maybe the trick was in some nonalcoholic beverage.

"Oh, so you two lovebirds are finally back together?" She glanced in the hallway mirror and fluffed her hair.

I swirled my tea around. "Not exactly."

She stopped in mid-fluff, eyeing me. "Not exactly?"

"Don't ask."

"Whatever." Brandi picked up her purse and headed down the stairs. "Get some sleep."

"Yeah, yeah." I called out, fully intending to crawl into bed as soon as I finished my tea.

That intention didn't even make it to an empty tea cup. I found myself dressed and out the door fifteen minutes later.

Except I hadn't much improved my circumstances, sitting there alone in the Bear Claw. All it did was increase my sense of loneliness and isolation. After a few more beers, I would probably feel *really* sorry for myself.

The door opened and Elena walked in, shaking out her copper-colored curls. She spotted me and headed over. "Thought I'd find you here." She slid onto the bar stool next to mine.

I barely glanced at her. "Why aren't you at the party?"

"Why aren't you in bed?"

I studied my half-empty, glass mug. "Because I'm wallowing in self-pity. People take your wallowing much more seriously if you're nursing an alcoholic beverage than if you're lying in bed."

"Glad to see none of this has affected your sense of humor," Elena said dryly. "I have news for you."

"Oh?" I drank more beer. "Good or bad?"

"Unexpected, I'd say."

I turned to look at her. "You're pregnant?"

She laughed, but there was no humor in it. "Hardly. You need to have sex to get pregnant."

A pang of guilt hit me. I had been so wrapped up in my own problems, I had forgotten about hers. Nice friend I was. "Oh, things are that good between you and Brad? Did you finally confront him?"

Elena became very busy pulling her gloves off and loosening her scarf. "No. With everything you're going through and finals and papers coming up and playoffs on the line, the timing hasn't seemed right. But that doesn't mean things are all Mr. and Mrs. Cleaver either."

"No, they probably wouldn't be." An image of Brad rescuing me the day David stole my inhaler popped into my head. What was Brad doing there anyway? I think I asked him but now I couldn't remember his answer. "I'm not sure the Cleavers had sex. Ever."

A wry smile touched her lips. "On second thought, I think things *are* all Mr. and Mrs. Cleaver."

"Yeah, that's better." The music switched to David Bowie's *Changes*. Must be seventies night.

"Back to my news. Do you want to hear it or not?"

Half my brain was still puzzling over why Brad would be at my apartment without either Elena or Tommy there as well, but I nodded. "Why not?"

"There's no record of Cat being kidnapped."

I attempted to put my mug down and tipped it over instead, the beer oozing its way down the bar. "What?" I couldn't have heard her correctly. At any moment, I expected the theme song from *Twilight Zone* to drown out David Bowie.

"Cat. Kidnapped. No record."

My brain finally caught up to the conversation. I quit pondering Brad and his motives and signaled the bartender for another beer and a bar rag. "Cat. My sister Cat." Maybe another beer would make this more comprehensible.

"Yes. Your sister Cat. You *were* in Milwaukee, right?"

Definitely needed another beer. "What are you talking about? Of course she was kidnapped. Otherwise what would've happened to her?"

"Well, according to the Milwaukee police department, there is no record of a Catalina Caldwell being kidnapped in the eighties."

The bartender plopped another beer in front of me. I drank half of it in one swig. "Maybe I got the year wrong."

"I had them check the entire decade. No record."

"No record? I don't understand."

"Are you sure it was Milwaukee?" Elena pressed.

"Well, yeah, I think." I swirled my beer around in its glass. "I was in a Milwaukee hospital at the time. I don't remember my parents taking a trip then, but I'm probably not the right person to ask. There isn't much about that time I do remember."

Elena sat back on her bar stool. "They must have gone somewhere else. That's the only explanation."

"Or maybe the Milwaukee police department put her file in the wrong place. Did you check missing kids?"

Elena twisted her glove in her lap. "Kit, I had them check under anything I could think of that would cause a child to go missing. That included missing, runaways and murder."

"Murder?" I bolted upright, sloshing my beer. "No, she wasn't murdered. She was still alive … " My voice trailed off. Somehow I didn't think Elena would put too much stock into Cat's spiritual nocturnal visit five years ago.

Elena put her hand over mine. "I know this is hard. But that is a possibility. However, there's just no record of her, Kit. At all."

My mind reeled. "So, she just disappeared without a trace and my parents never bothered to call the police?"

Elena held her hands up. "That's what it looks like. Unless it happened somewhere other than Milwaukee."

"Or she really was kidnapped by the fairies." The dim light of the bar deepened the amber color of the beer, making it glow.

Elena shrugged. "Maybe she was. Although I'd put my money on the police misplacing the file over a fairy kidnapping."

The fairies are evil. Pure evil. I shuddered, clutching my mug like a lifeline. "You think the police really could have misplaced the file?"

"Anything's possible, although that's pretty doubtful. But you never know – cops are human and humans do make mistakes."

"Maybe it is time for a road trip to Milwaukee. We could look through old copies of the *Milwaukee Journal.*"

Elena nodded. "Yeah, that's one way to do it. But there's another way. An easier way."

"What? The Internet doesn't work. Files don't go back that far."

"I'm not talking about the Internet, Kit. I'm talking about your parents."

I picked up my mug and poured the remaining liquid down my throat. "If you knew my parents, you'd know that wasn't the easier way."

"Why not? What's so hard about talking to your parents about this? Don't you want to know the truth?"

The truth. *Cat's been kidnapped.* My mother's flat, empty expression. I stood up, threw a couple of dollars down for a tip. "Funny thing about the truth, Elena," I said, sliding on my coat. "Sometimes you get way more than you bargained for. Sort of like pulling a rabbit out of a magician's hat. Before you know it, you have dozens of rabbits hopping out of that stupid hat, going who knows where and doing who knows what."

Elena studied me carefully. "I'm sure what you said would make perfect sense to someone, somewhere, but unfortunately I'm not that person. So talking to your parents is out. Which, I guess, means road trip is in."

I nodded, adjusting my gloves and striding toward the door. "Precisely."

Elena followed me outside. "So, now where're you off to?"

I didn't answer, instead tipping my head to stare into the sky. The night was still and cold. Stars sparkled brightly, like chips of ice embedded in blacktop.

The cold made me cough a couple of times. Both my head and chest hurt. I should go home. "Not sure."

"Come with me to the party."

I took a deep breath, sucking in the smells of snow and cold tinged with the stink of car exhaust. "I don't go where I'm not invited."

"You're invited because *I'm* inviting you. Come on. I know you aren't going home, even though it's where you should be. Come to the party for a few hours, then get some sleep."

A couple with their arms around each other stepped past us. "It'd be good to see Tommy," I hedged.

"Good. It's settled then." Tucking her hand through my arm, she led me down the street.

Why didn't I just go home? I wondered, only half listening to Elena's chatter and trying to stop myself from jumping at every shadow. I used to be so much more responsible about my health. What had changed?

Everything. The word rattled around in my brain, almost like it was surprised at being there. But the moment I heard it, I knew it was the right word. Everything had changed. Especially me.

"David wouldn't dream of showing up," Elena said in my ear as we walked up the porch steps. "He knows he'd get his ass kicked. Don't worry about it."

I know you like knives.

I shivered. "That wouldn't deter him. He probably wishes he would get his ass kicked so he can line up more restraining orders." But if Brandi was right and he didn't like witnesses, he wouldn't appear.

"Well, think of the bright side. If he does, there's no way he'd be able to show his face here again." Elena held the door open for me. I ducked inside, the moist warmth slapping me across the face.

I stepped into the landing, opening my mouth to answer her, but suddenly those words developed wings and flew out of my wide-open mouth with no assistance from me.

Standing in the corner next to the staircase were Tommy and Brandi. Actually, standing wasn't exactly the right word. One step removed from making out would be closer. Brandi had her face turned toward Tommy, staring intently at him. His head was bent forward, close to hers, one arm against the staircase.

Elena bumped into me, peering forward. "What are you ... Oh, my God!"

I found myself paralyzed, gawking, unable to believe the scene unfolding in front of me. Tommy and Brandi? This was completely unreal.

Then, right before my stricken, disbelieving eyes, Tommy leaned forward and kissed Brandi on the mouth.

Chapter 28

Elena clapped her hands over her mouth. "What the hell are you two doing?" she shouted.

Both Brandi and Tommy jerked their heads toward us, looking as shocked as I felt. I wanted to open my mouth and say something, but my mouth was already open. So, I closed it and realized I couldn't remember what I was going to say. Not that it mattered. Words couldn't adequately express the chaos of emotions inside me. Escape was a much better solution.

Whirling around, I pushed my way back out the door, ignoring calls to come back, that it wasn't what it looked like. Yeah, that's what everyone kept telling me, that nothing was how it seemed. Too bad I didn't believe them.

A cold damp wind greeted me outside. I half-heartedly wrapped my scarf around my neck as I ran down the street, my chest already aching with suppressed coughs.

It didn't take me long to run out of steam. I was in no shape for running, which I would have remembered had I been thinking straight. After two or three blocks, I slowed to trot while hacking my lungs out. My head pounded. My eyes swam with tears, whether from coughing or the massive spear of betrayal piercing my soul, I didn't know. I couldn't remember the last time I had felt this miserable.

"Kit, wait." It was Brandi, running to catch me.

I tried to run again, found I couldn't, and kept right on coughing. "Go away. I don't want to talk to you," I yelled, between coughs.

"Kit, come on. It's not what you think."

"It never is."

Brandi finally caught up to me, out of breath, hair hanging in her face. "You're going to have to deal with me sooner or later. After all, we live together."

"Maybe I'll take Martha's advice and move out," I said bitterly.

"Don't be absurd." Brandi fell into step next to me.

I was so angry I couldn't even speak, only cough. "Me absurd?" I spat when I got my hacking under control. "I'm not the one seducing my roommate's boyfriend."

"I am not seducing Tommy. If you'd just let me explain … "

"Explain? Explain why Tommy was kissing you." The image of Brad rescuing me shot through my head and everything clicked. "You're sleeping with Brad, too, aren't you?"

"What? Brad? What are you talking about?" Brandi looked at me like I had started yelling at her in Yiddish.

Now it all made perfect sense. "That day David stole my inhaler. Brad was here. At our apartment. I couldn't figure out why, until right this moment. Because you're sleeping with him."

"I am *not* sleeping with Brad."

"Then why the hell would he at our apartment without Elena?"

"Well, he wasn't there because of me."

"Likely story. First Elena's boyfriend and now mine. What, you're so bitter you can't hold onto your own man you need to go after everyone else's?"

Brandi blew her hair out of her face. "First of all, according to you, Tommy isn't your boyfriend. And second, that was a shitty thing to say."

"Not to be confused with the shitty thing *you* did."

"I didn't *do* anything. If you'd just let me explain … "

"Save it." We were nearing the apartment. I tried to get ahead of Brandi, but my chest felt like it had knives sticking out of it. All I wanted to do was lie down and die.

Brandi tried again. "Kit … "

I whirled around. "Let me spell it out, since you don't seem to be grasping the obvious here. I don't want to talk to you. I don't care about your explanations. I just want to be left alone. Maybe tomorrow I'll feel like listening, but not tonight."

Brandi chewed her lower lip, folding her arms across her chest. "Fine." She turned and started marching in the opposite direction.

"Fine." I resumed walking toward the apartment. Then I saw the shadow.

Someone was there. Standing on the stoop in front of the door.

A man.

David.

My heart leaped into my mouth, nearly choking me. "Brandi," I cried in a strangled voice. I knew I was in no condition to face him alone.

Brandi didn't stop. "What?" she called over her shoulder.

"David," I gasped, trying to speak loud enough to get her attention without attracting his.

Brandi froze, then turned, long hair spilling out of her coat. "What did you say?"

I backed toward her, pointing to man. "Look. David."

Brandi came forward. "Christ, that guy doesn't give up, does he?" She stalked toward David, while I struggled to keep up. "Hey. What is your mental block? Or did you never learn that no means no?"

The man spun around on his heel to face us. It wasn't David. This man was older, gray at the temples, heavy jowls, thickening skin, squished facial features.

Brandi stopped. "Oh, shit," I heard her gasp.

The man came barreling toward us. "Who are you? And where's my daughter?"

Brandi swallowed. "She's not here, Mr. Jamieson."

Jamieson? Oh no. This was Elena's father.

Mr. Jamieson kept coming, his purposeful strides eating up the distance between us. "Well, then, where is she? Studying?"

I think for the first time ever, Brandi was at a loss for words. "Ahh, yeah."

Covering for Elena was a lot easier when her parents only made phone calls or sent letters. We had never discussed the possibility of a surprise visit.

Mr. Jamieson halted in front of us. I towered over him. Much shorter than I expected. "I need to speak with Elena immediately. Where does she usually study?"

Brandi looked at me, shifting her weight from one foot to another.

"It depends," I answered. "She has a few favorite spots."

Mr. Jamieson's eyes darted back and forth as he studied each of us. "You are her roommates, I presume?"

"Yeah, I'm Kit and this is Brandi."

"I see." He looked us over a second time. "And which one of you is being stalked?"

My eyes widened. How did he know that?

"Uh, who told you that?" Brandi asked cautiously.

His expression became impatient. "That's immaterial. I'm sorry that one of you is being stalked, and if I can offer any legal expertise, I'd be happy to do so. But we can talk about that later. What needs to be accomplished immediately is getting my daughter out of here. I can't allow her to live in a situation where she might get hurt. Her mother has been a wreck about this ever since she heard. Now, if you don't know where she's studying, when do you expect her home?"

"You know what?" Brandi said brightly. "I'll go find her."

I shot her an expression that said: *Right, leave me alone with him.* Brandi shrugged. *What other choice do we have?*

"Excellent idea," Mr. Jamieson said, moving toward the door. "In the meantime, I'll start collecting her belongings."

Brandi and I exchanged looks again. "I'm sorry," I said. "You want to do what?"

He folded his arms across his chest and tapped his foot – the picture of exasperation combined with impatience. "Come on now. I haven't a lot of time here."

Slowly I started toward the door. "Mr. Jamieson, I think you should wait out here while Brandi goes to get Elena."

"I'm not waiting out here. Who do you think pays for this apartment? Now let's go in."

I shot Brandi a *help me* look. She shrugged again, mouthing "try to keep him occupied."

Another figure materialized out of the darkness. "Uncle Ed?" Martha's voice squeaked out, echoing in the night.

Mr. Jamieson circled back. "Martha? What are you doing here?"

Martha's mouth opened and closed, but nothing came out.

Brandi started trotting away. "I'll go find Elena. See you in a bit." After a few steps, I saw her break into a run. I launched into another coughing fit.

Mr. Jamieson regarded me with something resembling alarm. The expression didn't quite work on his face – maybe his features were too thick and heavy for it. "Good heavens. You sound terrible. Have you seen a doctor?"

I waved nonchalantly, like coughing my lungs out was no big thing. I wondered how long we could realistically keep him on the front step.

"So, what are you doing here?" Martha asked, her voice shrinking.

"I'm here to fetch Elena. I won't have her be a part of this stalking situation."

"Oh," Martha said.

Mr. Jamieson clapped his hands. "Now move along there. You, Kit, that's your name, right? You shouldn't be outside with that cough anyway."

"Uh, actually fresh air is supposed to be good for colds," I said, creeping my way toward the door.

"Don't be foolish. You should be in bed. Now, chop chop."

Martha shot me a terrified look. I shrugged in return. What the hell was I supposed to do? Her uncle was obviously hell bent at getting inside the apartment. Short of tying him to the streetlight, I saw no other way to keep him outside.

I took my time digging through my purse and pulling out my keys, stretching it out as long as I dared. Mr. Jamieson watched me, shifting from foot to foot.

"Martha, you can go home now," he said as I fiddled with the keys.

"No, that's okay, I'll wait for Elena," Martha said.

"Suit yourself." The moment I unlocked the door, he strode in. "Now, where's Elena's room?"

"Mr. Jamieson, why don't you have a seat? Would you like something to drink?"

He ignored me and started searching through the apartment. I followed him at first, asking him in as many ways as I could think of to wait, but to no avail. Eventually, I gave up my ineffective stalling techniques and sat on the couch, watching him alternate between opening every door and demanding explanations from Martha.

"Is she sleeping on the couch?" Mr. Jamieson asked, shutting the door to the linen closest. "I don't understand. Where are her clothes? Her stuffed animals? Why doesn't she have a room? Is she sharing a bedroom with one of you? Martha, what is going on here?"

Martha muttered something.

"Speak up, girl." Mr. Jamieson snapped his fingers in front of Martha's face. When that didn't produce the desired results, he was off again, rechecking every room in the apartment.

The front door flew open, right as Mr. Jamieson finished investigating Martha's room for the third or fourth time. Elena and Brandi rushed in. Elena's coat was open, sweat beads dotted her cheeks that had somehow managed to be both pale and flushed at the same time. Several strands of copper hair stuck to her sweaty chin. She was panting.

"Daddy. What are you doing here?"

Mr. Jamieson ran up the steps, taking two at a time. "Elena, where are your belongings? We're leaving immediately."

Elena stared at her father, opened her mouth to answer, and burst into tears.

Chapter 29

The rest of the night went downhill from there.

Amid much crying and recriminations, Elena spilled out the entire living-arrangement story. If I hadn't felt so sorry for her, I might have laughed at Mr. Jamieson's expressions. He kept vacillating between relief Elena wasn't living in a stalking situation and anger about whom she was living with. Eventually, he regained control of the situation – collecting Elena and herding her out the door.

"That was fun," Brandi said as the door closed behind them.

I disappeared into the bedroom without answering.

"Oh Kit," I heard her sigh before I shut the door.

I spent another night tossing and turning and another morning waking with a splitting headache and aching chest. Every time I sucked air into my lungs, a dangerous-sounding rattle reverberated deep in my chest. My old friend CF no doubt had decided on a more intimate acquaintance. Lucky me.

Pulling on a pair of torn blue sweats, I went to check out the kitchen. The apartment was empty. Good. I didn't think I could deal with either of my roommates right now.

Glancing at the kitchen clock, I saw it was already past noon. Much later than I normally slept. I put the kettle on the stove to boil and took out bread and peanut butter. Only think about food. No disturbing thoughts before breakfast. That would just be asking for heartburn.

The doorbell rang. I froze. David. My stomach shrunk to the size of a walnut. I was alone. What should I do?

First, take a deep breath. I did, only to be rewarded with a coughing fit. While I struggled to stop, the doorbell rang a few more times.

The person at the door didn't necessarily have to be David, I thought, forcing my stiffened legs to hobble into the living room. I picked up the portable phone. That's what peepholes are for. So I can see who's there before I open the door. And if it is David, I can call 9-1-1 right there without him even knowing I'm home.

The doorbell continued to buzz as I crept down the stairs. Persistent little bastard. My palms were so slick with sweat I nearly dropped the phone. I peered through the peephole.

Not David. Thank God. I was so busy sighing with relief it didn't register for a few moments who was standing there.

Mr. Jamieson.

Sighing, I unlocked the door and opened it, but not before I put the chain on. Paranoid to the last. "Mr. Jamieson," I said as politely as I could muster through the crack. "What can I do for you?"

He face sagged. Like he had gotten about as much sleep as I had. He wore an expensive-looking overcoat that seemed a bit too thin for the weather. "I'd like to come in."

"Why?"

The question surprised me almost as much as it did him. Before David, I probably would have let him in without question. No more.

"Why?" he repeated.

"Yes, why? Neither Elena nor Martha are here right now, so why do you need to come in?"

"I need to collect some of her belongings. She didn't take everything when she moved in with that no-good, loser boyfriend."

Christ, not again. Have him digging around the apartment a second time. What if there was something here Elena didn't want her father to see? What happened last night was bad enough, I didn't need to make it any worse.

"Look, Mr. Jamieson," I said as reasonably as I could. "I'm not feeling very well right now. Why don't I get her stuff together and you can come by later with Elena and get it, okay?" I tried to emphasize the Elena part.

"I'm here now, so why don't you let me in and we can get this done." When he said it, it wasn't a question.

Obviously he didn't hear my emphasis. Now I was annoyed. Why couldn't anyone respect my wishes?

"Mr. Jamieson, you need to come back with Elena, all right? I don't feel comfortable letting you in without her."

His expression sharpened, turned more wolf-like. "You're the one being stalked, aren't you?"

This just kept getting more and more annoying. "Mr. Jamie, fail to see what that has to do with anything."

"It's the reason why you won't let me in."

I tapped my fingers against the doorframe. "All right, fine. You win. I'm the one being stalked and I'm not going to let you in."

"Why don't you let me in and maybe I can help you?" He licked his lips and smiled, looking more and more like some sort of predator.

Now I definitely wasn't letting him. "Mr. Jamieson, come back with Elena." I started to shut the door.

"Wait." He stepped closer to the door. "You can't keep me out. I pay the rent."

I stared at him. "Now, Mr. Jamieson, you're a smart lawyer. I don't think I need to tell you that the names on the lease are mine, Brandi's and Elena's, not yours. And since Elena is over eighteen, she is considered an adult in the eyes of the law. And that means you have no rights here, regardless of whether you're paying the rent or not."

His eyes widened. Now his expression looked more like a goggle-eyed fish, amazed it had been caught. I took advantage of his surprise and shut the door.

I had no sooner started up the steps when the doorbell rang again. What is this man's issue? I opened the door a crack.

"Look," Mr. Jamieson said. "I'm sorry you're being stalked. But I didn't come here to waste my time. If you won't let me in, would you at least bring her belongings to me? Three boxes, labeled, in Martha's room."

Christ, what on earth could be so important? Maybe I could call Elena on her cell phone, ask her what this was all about.

"Fine," I said to Mr. Jamieson and shut the door again. While walking down the steps to Martha's room, I dialed Elena's number.

Her answer was curt. "Give him whatever he wants. I don't care anymore." She hung up without saying goodbye. What was that about? Was she mad at me? Things just kept getting better and better. I opened the door to Martha's room.

My first impression was the odor – sweetish, like pot, but smokier, with darker undertones. At least part of the scent came from various kinds of incense strewed about her dresser. A white bra lay draped over her boom box.

It was an understatement to describe the place as a mess. Books, papers, dirty dishes, clothes everywhere. Empty pizza boxes and Chinese takeout cartons poked out from underneath the unmade bed. Screwing up my nose, I picked my way across the room. I had been in fraternity houses cleaner than this. She couldn't even carry some of trash out to the dumpster? Unbelievable. Brandi better never get a whiff of this or she would be calling the Orkin man.

Elena's things had been stacked in the corner. Good thing she had left her belongings in boxes, otherwise they probably would have found a way to join the party on the floor and no one would have seen them again.

A heap of wrinkled shirts and a pair of green cotton underwear with a hole in the crotch lay on top of the boxes. The shirts appeared to be clean – the underwear not. Incredible. Maybe I should have let Mr. Jamieson in – he could have dealt with Martha's dirty underwear. Next to the boxes stood a small wooden filing cabinet with an opened box of tampons and an empty bottle of Cooks champagne stacked on top. The bottle caught my eye. Martha's drinking champagne? This bears closer scrutiny.

A couple more bottles lay in front of the cabinet. Not champagne, though. Red wine. Cheap red wine.

I picked up the champagne bottle. There was a faint smear of soft pink lipstick on the neck. Martha's wearing lipstick? Hard to picture. Maybe she had a lesbian lover who wore lipstick. Actually easier to picture than Martha wearing lipstick.

The top drawer of the filing cabinet stood partway open, just begging to be looked into. I leaned over to oblige it. After all, I reasoned, I hadn't actually *opened* anything, so I really wasn't snooping. Moreover, that drawer *wanted* me to look into it.

Scholarship info, school records, tax receipts. Files everyone had. Normal stuff. Boringly normal. But then, I noticed a file with Brandi's name.

Puzzled, I pulled it out. Why would Martha have a file with Brandi's name on it? Surely she couldn't be the secret lover. Besides, that wasn't Brandi's shade of lipstick on the bottle.

The file contained only a couple of sheets of paper. On top was a photocopy of a check. Made out to Planned Parenthood. And signed by Tommy.

Tommy kissing Brandi. Oh, God. I sunk to my knees, my legs unable to hold me up anymore, my mouth dry and sandy.

I forced my stiff fingers to turn the sheet over. Paperwork from Planned Parenthood swam before my eyes. Focus, Kit. I blinked a couple of times. Patient: Brandi Sanders. Services rendered: pregnancy termination.

Pregnancy termination.

Abortion.

Brandi had an abortion.

And Tommy paid for it.

Tommy was the father.

Tommy kissing Brandi.

Oh, God. I squeezed my hands together so hard I crumpled the file. Oh, God. Tommy kissing Brandi.

A coughing spasm jerked me back to reality. Christ, I was having a nervous breakdown in Martha's room surrounded by her dirty underwear and unopened mail. I dragged myself to my feet and stumbled out of her room.

Shutting the door, I leaned against it, trying to focus my thoughts. Tommy kissing Brandi. I couldn't get that image out of my head.

The doorbell rang, making me jump. Mr. Jamieson. I had forgotten about him. As I went back in to fetch the boxes, a part of me wished I had just let Mr. Jamieson get them himself. Then I could have remained happily ignorant.

***

Some time later, I'm not sure how much later, Brandi came home.

She stood at the landing, studying me. I was sitting in the easy chair, staring at nothing, the papers laid out on the coffee table in front of me.

She took a hesitant step into the living room. "Up for a chat?"

I didn't look at her, merely waved in the direction of the coffee table. She looked down, read the papers, looked at me.

"How'd you find them?"

"Does it matter?" I asked tonelessly.

She sighed, sat on the couch. "I guess not." She pushed her coat off, fished her cigarettes out of her purse.

I watched her fiddle with the pack, saw her eyes linger on the boarded up window.

"Just smoke the damn things if you want to so much," I said.

She half-smiled. "Yeah, what does that say about me? Smoking in front of someone with Cystic Fibrosis?"

"I sit in smoky bars. I go to smoky parties. It's pretty hypocritical of me to tell you not to smoke in front of me."

She tapped her pack again, extracting a cigarette. "Well, when you put it that way … " Fumbling for her lighter, she lit up.

"So." I winced as she sucked the smoke deep into her lungs. Just watching her made me want to cough. "Ready to explain?"

She studied the ceiling, slowly exhaling smoke from her nose. "Tommy and I did date. For about three months. Four years ago."

I rubbed my face. Maybe I didn't want to hear this. "How come you never told me?"

Brandi shrugged. "It was the summer between freshman and sophomore year. Most of the gang had gone home for the summer. Tommy and I were basically the only two on campus. Tommy stayed because of some special football camp or something. I think he was making up a class in summer school as well, I can't remember now. I stayed because Ellen was in detox – again – and I didn't feel like dealing with her. I don't know where you were, since you're usually here in the summer."

I did. I was home recovering from too much partying. Too bad I hadn't learned my lesson by now.

"Anyway," she continued. "Tommy and I started going out to bars and movies and such mostly because it was convenient. We really didn't know anyone else. I suppose it was inevitable that something would happen between us. And one night, it did."

She sucked down another lungful of smoke. "I won't bore you with the details, but suffice to say in those couple of months of sleeping together, I fell in love and he was having a good time."

Brandi paused to tap some of the ash off her cigarette onto the glass coffee table, pointedly not looking at me. "The rest of the story is even more clichéd. I got pregnant, accidentally, but I still used it. I think deep down I actually expected him to propose once he found out I was pregnant. But, alas, that's not how the real world works. A gentleman to the end, he offered to pay for the abortion. I accepted his offer once I got it through my thick head that was all I could expect from the relationship."

My head was pounding now, so hard I could hear the ringing echoing in my ears. "I can't believe neither one of you told me." My voice seemed very far away.

Brandi shrugged. "Neither one of us told anyone. I was so embarrassed by the whole mess, and ashamed, and pissed off, and still half in love with him. I couldn't believe I'd fallen so hard for someone who didn't love me back. After awhile, the only emotion left was anger. And revenge. That's why I kept a copy of the check and the paperwork. I figured one day I could find a way to use it against Tommy. But, as it turned out, it bit me in the butt again."

She bit her lip, studied her cigarette. "Chuck was the first man after Tommy I fell in love with. And he loved me, too. But then he found out about the abortion. At heart he's still a good Catholic boy. It didn't help that Violet lost no time comforting him."

"Oh, Brandi," I said, sick with emotion. On one hand, I felt so bad for Brandi. On the other, so betrayed by her. By both of them. "You should have told me. Either you or Tommy. Especially once we started dating."

"Yeah, and to think I got to watch you break his heart when I was expecting him to break yours. I figured once he did, you and I would commiserate and figure out a way to get even with him. Instead … well, I was just so pissed watching you throw away something I would've sold my soul for."

This was too much. I massaged my pounding temples with my fingers. If only my headache would stop, maybe I could think. "But that kiss … Are you two still seeing each other?"

Brandi let out a bark of laughter. "Are you kidding? He's nuts over you and he was never that way about me." She stared straight into my eyes. "What you saw was a pity kiss. That's it. I finally told him why Chuck broke up with me. He'd always suspected it. And, to his credit, he seemed to feel genuinely bad about it. So, he gave me a kiss. That's all."

I watched the smoke drift down to the mud brown carpet, trying to digest what she had told me. Did I believe her? It seemed so unreal. But then, my whole life seemed unreal right now. Why should this be any different?

"I have to go take something." I stood up and headed to the bathroom. Everything hurt. My head, my chest. I needed something to dull the pain.

After swallowing several pills, a few extra than what was prescribed, I returned to the living room. Brandi was staring at the ceiling, blowing smoke straight up in the air.

"What I still don't get," I said, leaning against the chair, "is why Martha had that file."

Brandi exhaled, smoke billowing out. "Now that's an interesting story. Much more interesting than my pathetic tale." She tapped the ash off her cigarette and lowered her chin to look at me.

I opened my mouth to speak when I heard a key turn in the lock.

"Speak of the devil," Brandi said, as Martha clumped up the stairs.

Except that it wasn't Martha. Well, it *was* her, but *not* her. She wore a short silky white dress, nylons and high heels. She had on makeup – soft, natural looking makeup – and her hair was up in a French twist.

My mouth dropped open. She looked amazing. Not beautiful exactly, but arresting. My head reeled.

Brandi, noticing my expression, shifted her body so she could see Martha. "Well, well," she said, her voice cool and dangerous. "So, that explains how you did it."

Did it? I glanced at Brandi, but her attention was on Martha.

Martha sniffed. "Saw no reason to hide it anymore. Elena's moved out."

"Hide what? What are you two talking about?"

Brandi stretched, slowly and languidly, before rising to her feet. "What are we talking about, Martha? That's a very good question, isn't it?"

Martha gnawed her lip. "Thought she knew."

"No, she doesn't know. She's pretty much clueless. In fact, she's so clueless she thinks I'm the one sleeping with Brad."

I started. "What?"

Martha stared at me. "You think Brandi's sleeping with Brad? Too much." She began to laugh.

I whirled around to Brandi. "Are you telling me that Martha is the one who's sleeping with Brad? Martha?"

"Among others," Brandi answered dryly. She shot Martha a disdainful gaze. "Many others."

"But I'm the one he truly loves," Martha said, getting her laughter under control.

"Oh, right. If you believe that, you're even stupider than I imagined."

I threw my hands up in the air. "Wait one second. *You knew?* You knew all this time Brad was cheating on Elena and didn't say anything?"

Brandi shrugged. "I had my suspicions. The talk about him was never good. But there was never any proof. Unfortunately for Elena, he's a bit smarter than your average cheating guy – he stayed away from mutual acquaintances."

I pointed to Martha. "She's a mutual acquaintance! She's her cousin, for God's sake."

Brandi transferred her "You're an idiot" look to me.

"And other than those presently here and accounted for, who else in our little circle of friends knows this?" I shook my head, rubbed my eyes and started pacing. "This is so out of control." As I passed Martha, I caught a whiff of her perfume. Light and flowery.

Of all the things I had experienced in the past few weeks, this by far had to be the most bizarre. I snapped my head around to face Martha. "And you. Of all people. Elena's your cousin. Your *cousin*. How could you do this to her?"

Martha pursed her soft pink lips together, her blue-gray eyes darting back and forth between Brandi and me. I was amazed at how large and expressive her eyes had become. A little makeup could do wonders.

"You don't understand." Her voice was flat and expressionless. "She got everything handed to her. Always did. I had to work and work and work. I got nothing handed to me. Not like her. She gets a college education with everything paid for. Me, I need scholarships and loans and I still have to work. It's not fair."

I cocked my head. "Not fair? You're telling me about not fair?"

She made a face. "Oh, you. It'll work out for you, just like it'll work out for Elena. She'll find someone else. Brad's mine."

"Brad's not yours anymore than he was Elena's," Brandi said. "He doesn't want a relationship. With you or anyone else. He only wants one thing. And you're a fool if you keep giving it to him."

Martha lifted her chin. "He says I'm the best he's ever had."

Brandi rolled her eyes. "Oh, please. You believe that shit? Honey, let me give you a bit of advice – he says that to everyone. You deserve to be dumped."

"You don't understand," Martha burst out. "He loves me. He really does. Why should Elena always get the good ones? I want someone to love me, too. I deserve it."

"Martha, I can't believe I'm saying this to you, but Brad is not one of the good ones," I said. "Trust me, you could do better than some guy who gets off screwing his girlfriend's cousin. Do you honestly think these are the actions of a man who has a high opinion of women?"

Martha violently shook her head, tendrils of hair whipping around her face. "You don't understand what we mean to each other. How he feels about me. He loves me."

Brandi slipped another cigarette between her lips. "Whatever." I heard the click of the lighter and Brandi's sharp intake of breath.

"You're smoking? In here?" Martha squeaked.

Brandi blew out a cloud of smoke and smiled coldly. "And you're going to say what about it, Miss Marijuana-Fiend?"

"Am not a marijuana-fiend," Martha said.

Brandi gestured with her cigarette. "Whatever. Aren't you off to meet Brad? Make sure you ask him what kind of relationship you can expect from him now that Elena's out of the picture."

"Already saw him," Martha muttered.

"Well," Brandi drawled out. "You must be so excited, talking about when you can move in now that Elena's gone."

Martha became very interested in her scuffed white pump. "Didn't get around to talking about it."

"What?" Brandi said. "Didn't quite hear you there."

Martha raised her head, eyes burning, mouth flattened. "Said we didn't get around to talking about it."

"Oh," Brandi said, nodding and sucking down another lungful of smoke. "I'm sure you will." She smiled, a cruel smile, and blew a steady stream of smoke at Martha.

Martha muttered something and clumped down the stairs again. Amazing. She sounded exactly the same in heels as she did in her usual heavy brown boots. Guess the old cliché is true – you can take the girl out of the country, but you can't take the country out of the girl. After a moment, we heard the front door open and close.

"Well." Brandi sat back down. "That was entertaining."

I kept staring at the top of the stairs. Even through the smoke, I could still smell Martha's light, flowery perfume. Kind of what you would expect fairies to wear. "You didn't have to throw it in her face." I faced Brandi. "She knows. Deep down, she knows."

Brandi shrugged. "She's a fool and she's sleeping with her cousin's boyfriend. Not to mention all the shit she did to you. Why would you defend her?"

I couldn't answer. There was something so, well, pathetic about Martha. Watching her face when Brandi dug in, I almost felt sorry for her. Like watching someone kick a mean, mongrel, half-starved dog.

Brandi abruptly put out her cigarette out and stood up. "Let's get out of here. I need a drink and, by the looks of you, you could use one too."

"Yeah, but with the amount of medicine I'm taking, I probably shouldn't have one."

"One beer isn't going to hurt. Might help you sleep."

I shrugged, too drained to argue and I really did want that beer. "I still don't get how Martha had your papers in the first place."

"I would've thought that was obvious." Brandi tripped down the stairs. "I caught her with Brad."

"Really? Where?"

"Here." Brandi handed me my coat. "I skipped a class, came home to pick up something, can't remember what now, and found them on the landing. Brad about to leave, Martha in this little nighty thing. Ugh. Can't tell you how scary it was. Not just the nighty, although that was pretty scary, but the whole situation. Anyway, despite the fact I told them this was none of my business and I don't do tattle-telling, Martha decided I still needed to be encouraged to keep my mouth shut. So, she dug through my things, found what she needed and made copies. Quite the little blackmailer, our Martha."

"But that doesn't make any sense. The file was sitting there in plain sight in an open filing cabinet."

Brandi slid her coat on. "And you were in her room for, what? Needed to borrow a cup of sugar?"

"Mr. Jamieson wanted me to get the rest of Elena's things."

"Ah." Brandi adjusted her scarf. "She told me she had copies, multiple copies, in safe places. At first I was so furious I almost did go straight to Elena, but then I decided it was better to wait and see what happened. I knew it had to come out, eventually. And, once it did, we'd vote Martha off the island and that'd be the end of it."

Brandi held the door open for me and I stepped out, the wind immediately cutting into my cheeks. "Would you really have not told Elena? Even without the blackmail?"

Brandi became very busy locking the door. "There are a lot of women out there who know their husbands or boyfriends are cheating on them and are dealing with it in their own way. When that's the case, getting involved does more harm than good." She straightened, dropped her keys in her purse. "I wasn't sure if Elena was one of those women or not. So, no, I probably wouldn't have told. But that wouldn't have stopped me from dropping a few hints, in case she wasn't that kind of woman. Now, where to?"

"Just as long as the beer is cold and plentiful, I don't care," I said. "This is not a week to be picky about drinking establishments."

Chapter 30

"Your stupid stalker ruined my life."

Startled, I spilled one of the beers I was collecting from the bar, just missing the guy with a goatee and brown flannel shirt next to me. "Join the club, Elena."

She slammed her fist on the bar as I attempted to pick up the glasses a second time. The goatee guy shot me a worried look. Probably afraid I would ruin his favorite shirt.

"My father is furious," Elena said. "Threatening to cut me off. My mother is hysterical. What am I going to do?"

At least now I knew why Elena was mad at me. "Have a beer. On me." I gestured for the bartender to pour another one.

"This isn't funny, Kit." Her face was red and swollen, her eyes bloodshot.

"I didn't say it was. I think you need a beer. No joke. C'mon. Brandi's over there waiting." The bar door opened and two African-American women walked in. I found myself holding my breath and forced myself to exhale.

Elena's eyes flickered in Brandi's direction. She pulled a wadded up rag of a tissue from her pocket and blew her nose. "I don't know what to do. He's threatening to cut off all my funding."

"With one semester left before you graduate? He may be angry but he's not stupid. Tell him you'll move back in with us. That should make him feel better." I weaved my way across the bar, dodging knots of people having a few quiet beers while the Eagles played mournfully in the background.

"Right. You're the ones who let me move in with that loser in the first place. I'm sure he'll be leaping at that chance. Not to mention the whole stalking thing."

"Elena, you're blowing this out of proportion. He's not going to cut you off because it'd be stupid."

"You don't know him."

I sighed, reaching the scarred wooden table and putting the drinks down. The table rocked slightly. "Okay, let's say the worst happens and he refuses to give you a single dime. You can get a job, get student loans. That's how other people make it through college. You only need one more semester. Worse comes to worse, maybe you'll have to work full time and go to school part time next semester and finish this summer. So what? You'll get through. And you won't be under your father's thumb. Wouldn't that be nice?" I sat down in the uncomfortable chipped wooden chair across from Brandi, taking another quick peek at all the guys in the bar. The one by the darts had David's build, but his hair was the wrong color and style. I squeezed my purse. Yep, everything in order – phone, pepper spray and noisemaker on top in easy reach.

Elena hiccupped. "You're not being very sympathetic."

I scooped up my glass and drank, the table rocking, sloshing the beer sitting on the table. Suddenly I realized I had reached the end of my resources – nothing left for politeness. Survival. That's what this was turning into. "And you need to ask why? I'll trade places with you in a second. A tenth of a second. You know you can always live with us." I rubbed my chest – it still hurt despite the pain medicine.

"Yeah." Brandi finally spoke as she reached for her glass. "We have a room available and everything. It's downstairs, but it should be cozy once we get the current tenant out."

Elena slid into a chair. "Don't kick Martha out," she said heavily. "She has enough problems."

Brandi glanced at her in surprise. "You're awfully generous considering she's been banging your boyfriend."

Elena slumped in her seat. "Yeah, well. What does that say about me? I wanted to marry someone who preys on lonely, vulnerable women. Martha wasn't the first, and lord knows she won't be the last, but she probably was the most vulnerable of them all."

"Still." Brandi arched her eyebrows over her glass. "Aren't you taking this forgive and forget thing a little far? You can't tell me you're all right with her doing this."

"No, I'm not." Elena pulled a glass toward her and drank. "But you have to understand our families. Martha's mom, Aunt Bev, was wickedly jealous of my mother her entire life. Mom was beautiful, second runner-up in the Miss Illinois pageant and married well. Aunt Bev, the older and less attractive sister, didn't marry so well, at least not in her estimation. Uncle Fred works in a factory. Makes good money, but he's no lawyer." Elena sighed. "Of course, what Aunt Bev doesn't know is Mom's life is hardly perfect. Daddy's been cheating on her forever, and Mom puts up with it because she likes the money and lifestyle. Not to mention how Mom's never gotten over losing the Miss Illinois pageant. She's convinced it's because the one who won slept with the judge. Then, there's me – such a disappointment – her only daughter not even making first cut in the Miss Illinois pageant."

"None of that's your fault," I said. The guy by the pool table really looked like David. No, his hair was too long and he wore wire-rimmed glasses. I checked my purse again, just to be on the safe side.

"No, but Martha's been weaned on my aunt's hatred and jealousy all her life. Is it any surprise she'd do this to me? And me, seriously dating a guy who can't be faithful, although as pre-med he'll probably make good money one day. I mean, my God. Is this the most pathetic thing you've ever heard?" Elena finished her beer. "However, I don't think Daddy's ever slept with Aunt Bev."

"Quite the consolation," Brandi said dryly.

Elena shrugged. "Maybe I should hope Daddy cuts me off. Maybe I'd quit making the same mistakes."

"My advice – take the money. Chances are you'll make those same mistakes anyway, might as well have the money while you do it," Brandi said.

"Just what I needed to hear. Thank you, Brandi." Elena got to her feet. "Going for a refill."

"Bring back a pitcher," Brandi said. "We need it."

I nodded, although I planned only to nurse this current glass of beer. I kept hearing the echo of Elena's words. Was I repeating the same mistakes my parents made?

***

The church loomed in front of me. I followed my parents as they walked around it. My breathing hitched, my chest burned.

"It's all here," Cat said next to me. "Everything you need."

I opened up my mouth to answer, but coughs flew out instead. I coughed so hard I couldn't walk, but still I continued to move forward. Moving closer. The wolves howled, the bell rang.

Hot pains burst through my chest. Fire searing the soft flesh of my lungs. Hungry. Eager. I put my hand to my mouth and it came back red and dripping. Blood. Coughing up blood. The pain in my chest sharpened. My head burned. Fever most likely.

"I'm dying," I said to Cat.

Cat shrugged. "You always knew you had come here to die."

Come here to die. Come here to die.

The graveyard was up ahead. The newly dug grave. The people around it. The dark shadow. The wolves howled louder. The bell rang faster.

"It's time," Cat said. "Finally. The time has come."

The dark shadow gathered itself. Blood leaked from my mouth. Helpless, I floated closer.

"You have no idea how long I've waited," Cat said.

I was almost on top of the people gathered around the grave. They turned their blank faces toward me. Doctors, nurses, lawyers, judges, executives, psychologists. Some of the faces I recognized – my doctor as a child, the nurses who had administered medicine and cooled my burning body while I lay dying in the hospital, even the woman in the photo Cat gave me. All had wings, like fairies. With a start, I saw my parents had joined them. My parents with their flat eyes and empty faces. They turned to look at me, no recognition in their expressions. They, too, now had wings.

I collapsed on the grave, fresh dirt filling my mouth. I tasted the coldness, the dankness, the grittiness. My blood soaked into the ground, darkening it.

Ashes to ashes. Dust to dust.

The dark shadow loomed over me. I spat bloody mud out of my mouth, coughing. I was burning up. I was dying.

Slowly, I tilted my head up. Into the shadow. Into the darkness. At first, I couldn't see anything but the black. I blinked a few times and the details sharpened abruptly, like focusing a camera.

It was David. David towering over me. Grinning. Holding a knife. He had been waiting for me.

Now I understood.

David was death.

Death had finally caught up with me.

At last.

Cat knelt next to me. "It's all real, Kit."

I stared at her. "What's real?"

She smiled, held her arms out. "All of it, Kit. All of this."

David leaned closer, grinning, raising the knife.

I crashed back into reality, thrashing on the bed, tangled in the sheets, my breathing harsh and violent. Before I could get myself under control, I exploded into a ferocious coughing fit, complete with green mucus. Oh, God, here it is. Infection. My body was on fire. Maybe I should go to the hospital.

Once I calmed down, I decided the diagnosis wasn't quite that bad. My temperature was at 99.6, elevated yes, but hardly hospital-worthy. And the mucus wasn't as green as I first thought. Definitely getting worse. Definitely should call a doctor. Definitely should be taking better care of myself. If I had my head on straight, I would be doing all these things. However, I hadn't had my head on straight since Halloween.

Staying as quiet as possible, I splashed cold water on my face, changed into clean sweats and a tee shirt, swallowed a couple of Tylenol and went back to bed. Elena was sleeping on the couch and I didn't want to wake her. After splitting a couple of pitchers with Brandi, she couldn't bear to return to the one-room apartment her father had dug up for her. So, she took over our couch instead. Tomorrow morning should be interesting.

As for me, I had tried calling Tommy a couple of times last night. Both his apartment and cell, but he didn't answer either. I desperately wanted to talk to him, to hear his voice. I wanted to tell him I understood now and I thought I might be willing to give us a try, just as long as he still wanted to. I wanted to say so many things, but I kept getting his voicemail. I didn't leave any messages.

Crawling back into bed, I didn't expect to fall asleep again after the horror of that nightmare – a nightmare that should have required copious amounts of alcohol to explode into existence instead of the measly half glass of beer – but almost immediately I dozed off. Dream free. Thank God.

When I woke again, it was midmorning. I felt much better – still, I should go see Dr. Jones. I could already hear him yelling at me for not making an appointment sooner. But what if he threw me in the hospital? There I would be – helpless, exposed. Perfect prey. Perfect for David. No thanks.

I left my bedroom in search for some breakfast and was greeted by a strange sight – Brandi and Elena in the living room, books scattered everywhere.

"Morning," Brandi said.

"How're you feeling?" Elena asked.

"You mean, other than like I've been hit by a Mack truck?" I rubbed my chest. "Actually, I'm better. So, what's up with the study party? Classes cancelled today?"

Elena and Brandi exchanged looks. "Well, we're both pretty behind, and we thought it'd be better to get caught up here than – ah – go to class," Elena said.

"I see." I went to pour myself some juice. Stupid explanations aside, I had to admit, it did make me feel better knowing they were there.

"Tommy's coming over," Brandi called out. "You called or something last night? He should be here shortly."

"Thanks." Maybe I should take a shower before breakfast.

"Kit." Martha stood at the doorway. She looked terrible, her face as red and swollen as an overripe tomato.

"Hey," I said, not really sure what to say, but figuring that was safe.

She looked down at her feet, her lank brown hair falling forward. "Can I talk to you for a second?"

I leaned against the counter, loaf of bread in one hand. "Go ahead."

She shuffled further into the kitchen. "I … I didn't mean to make any trouble for you."

I folded my arms, awkwardly because of the bread. "Okay."

Martha raised her head, peeking at me from between strands of hair. "I spoke to the police. Told them everything. Even why I lied in the first place."

"Thanks," I said, but inwardly I sighed. No wonder Detective Jenkins didn't believe me, hearing words like "I lied because I wanted the problem to go away faster than it would through the court system. I lied because I wanted her to move out." Still, she meant well. That counted for something.

"Also, I … I didn't mean to sound like such a bitch yesterday. I … I know you have Cystic Fibrosis. I didn't mean it."

"I know, Martha. It's okay."

Her puffy red-rimmed eyes stared at me a moment longer, then she started to shuffle out of the room.

"Martha," I called. She turned, hair still in her face.

I smiled. "Hey, thanks. For going to cops, for putting up with all this stalking crap. I appreciate it."

She paused, staring, then smiled back. I sucked in my breath. Incredible. Her smile illuminated her entire face, making her as attractive as she had been last night, even without makeup and with disastrous hair.

"You really should smile more," I said. "You look gorgeous when you do."

She ducked her head, probably blushing although with her face so red it was a tough call, and shuffled out the door. I went back to making toast.

After eating, I jumped in the shower. I made it fast so I would be ready when Tommy arrived. While getting dressed, I turned on the computer to check my messages.

They took awhile to download. Probably got on some spam list. I pulled on jeans and a sweater, combed my hair and glanced at the screen.

One hundred and fifty new messages.

All from David.

One hundred and fifty messages from David.

Prickles of ice trailed down my arms. My breathing caught in my throat. He had sent me at least twenty just this morning. What did this mean?

The doorbell rang. Tommy. At least it had better be Tommy. God did I want to see him. Dropping my comb, I hurried out of the bedroom and to the door.

Brandi was in the kitchen fiddling with the coffee pot. Elena and Martha were nowhere in sight.

"Kit, wait a second. I'll go answer."

"It's probably Tommy." I rushed past the kitchen and headed for the door. "I'll look through the peep hole first and let you know if you need to call 9-1-1."

"That's not funny," Brandi yelled.

"It's not supposed to be," I called back.

I peered through the peephole, but saw nothing.

"Who's there?"

I pressed my face to the door. "No one."

Brandi appeared at the head of the staircase. "Get away from the door."

I backed up and she came down the stairs. "Here." She handed me a canister of pepper spray. "It's mine. You stay back, but be prepared to spray. I'll open." She unlocked the deadbolt, but left the chain on. Slowly turning the knob, she eased the door open a crack.

Her face turned pale. "Oh, God. Jezzy!!!" Slamming the door shut, she slid the chain off and flung open the door. "Call the cops, Kit. How could he do this?! To a helpless cat who never did anything to him? Goddamn him!!"

I didn't move. I couldn't move. I couldn't even breathe. My eyes were locked on the small, bloodstained bundle on the front stoop.

Definitely a cat. Definitely Jezzy. She had been stabbed repeatedly. Dried blood matted her fur. The knife used had been stuck through a bloodstained note, then jammed into her chest.

Brandi let out a strangled cry as she bent to touch the cold, dead fur. One blank green eye stared unseeingly at the cold gray sky. Brandi's fingers hovered above the animal, but couldn't make contact. She jumped to her feet and ran past me.

Mesmerized by the horror, I knelt down, studying the torn and crumpled note. It was all black and red – blotches of red and smears of black ink.

Look what happened to this CAT.

Wouldn't it be a shame if it happened to a KITten?

I was so cold, so cold. As cold as the matted fur, the dried blood, the dead, unseeing eye. The knife glinted dully at me. I started to shake.

"Kit. Come back inside." Elena had her hands on my back, so warm, gently guiding me inside. "You're sick enough. You don't need to be out here making it worse."

"But the cat," I said, my voice hoarse and cracking. "We have to bring it inside. We can't leave it out here."

"I know. I'll get it. It's evidence so we don't want to touch it."

Evidence? I shook my head. Not evidence, I tried to say, but I couldn't form the words. It's Jezzy. She's cold. It's not right to leave her out there all alone in the cold covered with her own blood. She was such a beautiful cat, such a proud cat. It's undignified to leave her out there. Unseemly.

Brandi stood at the top of the stairs, a warm breathing Jezzy in her arms. "It's not Jezzy," she said. "Not Jezzy!" She buried her head in the cat's fur. Jezzy, however, appeared to be less than thrilled with Brandi's open display of affection.

"But." I pointed to the door. "But … the cat … whose is it? Where did it come from?"

"And how did he find a cat who looked so much like Jezzy?" Brandi asked darkly.

Jezzy had had enough of Brandi and leaped out of her arms with a sharp meow. I caught a glimpse of disgruntled green eyes before she stalked off.

"Kit, let's get you all the way inside." Elena steered me up the stairs. I let her do what she wanted, my body limp and mechanical – no thought, no control. And so cold. So very, very cold.

Look what happened to this CAT.

She wrapped me in a worn red blanket and sat me on the couch. So cold. Never be warm again.

"Kit, drink this." Elena pressed a mug into my hand. Automatically, I took it and sipped, nearly choking on it.

"Ugh. How much sugar did you dump in here?"

"You're in shock. Sugar's good when you're in shock. Drink up."

Grimacing, I took another swallow. What a way to ruin a perfectly innocent cup of tea. But, at least it had managed to break through my paralysis.

By the time I had drained the mug, my shaking had calmed down. "Guess you were right about the sugar."

Elena smiled, but her eyes remained worried. "I'm right about a lot of things. Now if only people would listen to me."

"Gee, we don't think too highly of ourselves at all," Brandi said, her voice a pale, blurry copy of her normal sarcastic tone.

Elena touched my forehead. "When you're feeling a bit calmer, we should call the police."

"Why?" I said dully. "What're they going to do?"

"You have to report it."

I put my empty mug on the coffee table. "I'm sure there aren't any fingerprints on … it. The police already believe David's the victim. They might even think I did it and am trying to blame it on David."

Brandi sat down heavily on the chair. "I wish I could say you're wrong, but after their reaction to this last complaint …"

I shrugged. "And even if they did suddenly start believing me, so what? Even if they give me a restraining order against him, what will that do? It's only a piece of paper. It's not going to protect me if he comes after me with a knife."

Elena twisted her hands helplessly. Her fingers were short and stubby, an odd contrast against the elegant way she carried herself. "Kit, you have to keep building a case against him. Eventually they'll have enough to charge him with something."

"Would that be before or after he kills me?" I asked, my voice soft although I really wanted to scream.

Silence. Neither Brandi nor Elena looked at me. Brandi started twisting her hair. Elena began straightening books and papers strewn about the living room floor.

"Okay, Kit,' Brandi said, breaking the silence. "Do you honestly think it's going to go that far? I know the cat was bad, but it's still a big jump to murdering a person."

I rose from the couch. "I want to show you something." I led them into my bedroom and the hundred and fifty emails from David.

At first, they didn't say anything – just stared at the screen. Then Brandi reached out and started opening them.

Why won't you see I'm the only one who will ever understand you?
Our shared past binds us together in ways no one will ever comprehend.
Why do you keep fighting the inevitable? We belong together. Forever.
I know you love me. Why won't you just admit it?

The same thing. Email after email. The same crap spewing out. But the last was by far the worst.

If I can't have you, well, you already know the answer to that, my love. We're destined to be together. Forever.

"Oh, my God," Elena breathed.

"You've got to be kidding me," Brandi said.

"I think it's safe to say he's getting worse," I said.

"What's all this about a shared past?" Elena asked. "I thought you said you didn't know him before?"

I collapsed on the bed. "I didn't. We just have similar childhood experiences. His sister died of Cystic Fibrosis. I have Cystic Fibrosis and I had a sister kidnapped. As you can see, he's deluded himself into thinking this means far more than it does."

"So, this is at least part of the reason why he's so fixated on you," Elena said.

Once again I cursed myself for showing up at that Halloween party in the first place. "Unfortunately."

As if she read my mind, Elena said, "I'm so sorry I ever introduced you two in the first place."

I began wrapping myself in my blue and green plaid comforter, feeling cold again. "You and me both."

"Wasn't Cat your sister's name?" Brandi broke in.

"Yes. And yes, that's what he's alluding to in that note."

"But you said he never knew you," Elena said softly. "How would he know if she's dead or not?"

I wrapped my arms around my knees and started rocking. "Lucky guess. I'm sure she's dead."

The doorbell rang. All of us jumped.

"It's probably Tommy," Elena said, although she didn't sound too sure.

"I'll get it." I unwrapped myself from the comforter.

Elena headed toward the door. "I'll come with you."

She scooped up the pepper spray and phone in the living room, as well as insisting on going down the stairs first.

It was Tommy. His eyes darted between Elena and me. "What the …"

"Oh, God, Tommy. It's been a nightmare," I said.

"It must've been."

Elena recited the morning's events as we trooped through the apartment.

"Believe it or not, I found a couple of emails not from David in this mess," Brandi said as we walked in the bedroom.

"Are these good emails or bad emails?" I asked, curling up on the bed.

"Well, one doesn't seem too good. It's from the university. They urgently want to talk to you about your complaint, especially with recent developments."

I slumped on the bed. "Figures."

"And, there's this one. It's from some anonymous address, but it seems to be a reply to one you sent."

Anonymous address? I sent something to an anonymous address?

Oh God. *Cat.* I tore off the bed and threw myself in front of the computer.

There are two kinds of death in the world.

One is quick. That death is destined to be yours.

One is slow. The body remains alive but the soul is dead. That death is destined for a new little girl.

The clock is ticking. Tuesday is when the new little girl will meet her death.

How long will it take for you to meet yours?

The truth will set you both free. The truth about the first little girl.

What are you going to do about it?

The blood drained from my face. I closed my eyes, trying not to shake.

Look what happened to this CAT.

"We can do a trace," Tommy said. "Find out who this person is. Find out exactly what the hell they're talking about."

"That'll take too long," Elena said. "I don't think we have that kind of time."

"What about a court order or something?" Tommy argued. "When are the cops getting here? Once they see the cat and these emails, they should do something."

"Ahh," Elena said. "Kit, where's your file?"

I had rewrapped myself in my comforter. So cold again. I untangled my arm long enough to point to my book bag. Elena headed over to investigate.

"What do you mean, 'ahh'?" Tommy asked. "You did call them, didn't you?"

"Kit didn't want to call the police," Brandi said. "And after what happened the last time she called them, I can't say I disagree with her."

"What?" Tommy whirled around to look at me. "What do you mean, you didn't call the police?"

"Tommy, they aren't going to do anything." I burrowed myself deeper in the comforter. Green and blue. Like the ocean. I felt like I was drowning in an ocean, except my ocean was a freshly dug grave and the howling of wolves. "They think he's the victim here. I told you their reaction when I tried to report him hanging around the other night. He'll have to actually attack me before they take it seriously."

"This is bullshit."

"Welcome to our justice system."

Tommy started pacing. "Kit, you have to report it. It's stupid not to."

Maybe I needed another cup of tea. Why couldn't I warm up? "What's stupid is to keep depending on the police to fix this. If I want this fixed, I need to do it myself."

"So, what do you plan to do?"

The phone rang. Everyone jumped.

"Don't answer it," I yelled, flinging myself off the bed, erupting into a coughing fit. "Nobody answer it." I coughed.

I ran to the living room and stared at the answering machine. I was sure it was David. I wanted the call recorded.

I heard the others behind me, but I didn't turn. I just focused on the answering machine.

There was a click, then Brandi's voice inviting callers to leave a message. Another click. Then an unfamiliar voice.

"This is Catherine Cook with the dean's office. We need you to call us as soon as possible to schedule an appointment regarding your complaint against David Terry. It's urgent we speak to you right away. It's come to our attention that he's placed a restraining order on you and that you've received extensions on four of your classes. Our office is here to help you. No matter what's going on, we can help you get through it. Please call as soon as you get this message."

Silence, except for the clicking of the machine. I turned. Brandi, Elena and Tommy stared at me, mirror images of concern plastered on their faces.

Elena broke free and rushed forward. "You could bring those emails and the … the cat. They'll have to believe you then."

I had already started shaking my head. "You heard her. They're already convinced I'm in the middle of some breakdown."

"But you can't fake those emails," Elena said.

"Well, you could," Tommy said. "If you knew how to log in as David."

Brandi punched him. Elena glared at him. "Tommy, that's not helping," Elena said.

Tommy rubbed his arm. "It's the truth. I'm just telling you what they could argue if they wanted to. Not that I'm saying we shouldn't call the cops."

I turned back to the answering machine. A couple of coughs bubbled up in my lungs, leaving a trail of burning acid. My head pounded.

Look what happened to this CAT.

If David doesn't kill me, this infection might.

I rubbed my chest.

Miss Caldwell, I have seen the videotape and have spoken with David about his side of the story.

The cops believe David. They think he's the victim.

Promise me, Kit. You'll save the innocent.

Our office is here to help you, no matter what is going on.

No matter what.

There are two kinds of death in the world.

What are you going to do about it?

I faced my friends. "There's only one thing I can do," I said calmly. "I'm going to find out what happened to Cat."

Chapter 31

"Look, it's obvious." I sat on the living room floor surrounded by all the papers in my paper trail and the latest email from Cat. "Cat, or whoever, believes that David, this girl in the photo and what happened to Cat as a seven-year-old are all related. So, if I discover what happened to Cat, I should be able to stop David and save this other girl."

"But why would they all be interconnected? It doesn't make sense," Brandi said.

"I know. But this person obviously thinks so, and she seems to have a much better grasp of the situation than I do. I might as well do what she has been suggesting since day one of this mess."

"Does the term 'wild goose chase' mean anything to you?" Tommy asked.

"I don't know," Elena broke in. "Kit may be right. There is something a bit suspicious about Cat's disappearance. After all, there isn't a file."

"Besides," I said, looking hard at each one of them. "Honestly now, what are my choices?"

No answer. Brandi inspected her nails, now painted a dark mauve. Elena shuffled through papers, Tommy studied the ceiling.

I picked up the latest email. "Alrighty then. Let's get down to it. Maybe we should start by tracking down this girl, whoever she is."

"What about that school?" Elena pawed through the papers. "Ah, here it is. The Minneapolis School for Special Children."

I clapped my hands together. "Perfect. That's where I'll start."

"Minneapolis is three hours away," Brandi said.

"And you're pretty sick," Elena said. "I mean, shouldn't you be in a hospital or something?"

"Oh, yeah. That's where I want to be. Sitting quietly in a hospital just waiting for David to show up."

Elena's worried expression deepened. "But going to Minneapolis when you're this sick can't be smart either. Maybe you should at least wait until you're better."

"I can't wait. This thing with the other girl is supposed to happen on Tuesday. That may be significant for me, too. I don't know. I have to go now. Immediately. As soon as I figure out a way to get there."

"I could borrow my roommate's car," Tommy said.

"Tommy, I wouldn't feel comfortable driving your roommate's car all the way to Minneapolis," I said.

"I didn't think you would. That's why I'll drive it."

I shook my head. "You can't go. What about football?"

He shrugged. "I can miss one practice if I give the coach notice. And, if we leave now," he glanced at his watch, "we should make it to Minneapolis by mid-afternoon. Plenty of time to discover what we need and drive back. We could probably even make it back by tonight."

"Great, we can all go," Elena said.

"No, we all can't go. That'll look too suspicious. It should just be me," I said.

"Kit, you're too sick. I'm going with you and that's that." Tommy got to his feet.

"Tommy's right," Brandi said. "It should just be the two of you. David might get clued in if we all go."

"Then it's settled." Tommy snatched up his coat and started down the stairs. "I'll get the car and make a few phone calls. Maybe pack a few things in case we stay the night. Be back in a half hour."

I stumbled after him. "Tommy, wait."

He turned, hand on the doorknob, eyes cautious, watchful.

Probably afraid I'm going to hurt him again. The thought pained me.

I stepped closer. "Brandi told me everything," I said. "I just wanted you to know I understand."

There was still so much I wanted to say, so many unspoken words between us, but I couldn't do it. He studied the dull brass doorknob before meeting my eyes.

"See you in a half hour." He smiled slightly, then disappeared out the door.

I stared at the closed door, feeling strangely empty and unsettled. Taking a deep breath, I coughed a couple of rumbling coughs and returned to the living room.

Brandi was studying the photos while Elena gathered papers. "Tommy's not starting anymore," Brandi said casually.

I paused, hand on the banister. "What?"

"Football. Not starting in football. Missed too many practices. Playing badly in games." She sauntered over, handing me the photos. "No chance to win the Heisman Trophy now."

I took the photos, my thoughts a blur.

She smiled. "Just thought you should know."

I nodded stiffly. Tommy not starting? But football was everything to him. He had a football scholarship. What happened?

"But ... what ... " I stuttered.

"You know the divorce rate is around fifty percent, don't you?" Brandi interrupted.

I stared at her, perplexed. "What does that have to do with a damn thing going on here?"

"Humor me. Half of marriages don't work, right?"

"Right."

"And of those marriages that don't work, how many are because one or the other is chronically sick or injured?"

Understanding began creeping through my mind. "I have no idea."

Brandi smiled. "Neither do I. But Kit, doesn't it surprise you that of the three of us here, you're the one with the most chance of a satisfying, long-lasting relationship? Elena and I are pretty much zeros on the subject, and last I checked, we're the healthy ones here."

"It's more complicated than that ... " I started to say, but Brandi interrupted me.

"Bullshit. It's not more complicated than that. Sure, your disease is horrible. Sure, when you start to get sick, it won't be pretty. Sure, Tommy may leave you then. But you know what, he may *not* leave. He's shown remarkable resilience so far, despite you best efforts at pushing him away. Perhaps you should thank him by giving him a chance."

Elena touched my arm. "As the recent actions of my ex-boyfriend have proven, being healthy is no guarantee of anything positive. Why should being sick be a guarantee of anything negative?"

I didn't answer. I didn't know what to say.

Brandi pushed her hair back. "Come on. I'll help you pack."

Shaken, I followed Brandi to my room. Martha intercepted me, stepping out from the kitchen, a sandwich in one hand. Peanut butter and grape jelly from the smell.

"That school," she paused, licked jelly off her wrist. "It's for wards of the state."

I stared at her, feeling once again as though the last wisp of reality had just drifted away, leaving me in nightmare never-never land. "Excuse me?"

She looked me at me like maybe I belonged in a special school. "The school you were talking about. Minneapolis School for Special Children? A lot of wards of the state go there."

Wards of the state. Could this girl be a ward of the state? "Martha, how do you know this?"

She smiled, sucked up another drop of jelly. "You'd be amazed at what I know."

Still pondering, I thanked her and headed for my bedroom. I noticed she and Elena avoided looking at each other.

***

Tommy insisted I sleep during the drive to Minneapolis. He made a little bed for me in the back seat, complete with several blankets and pillows. He even turned the heat up.

For my part, I took a huge dose of cold and pain medicine. Just for a day. Just to dull the pain. I couldn't be in so much pain if I was going to solve this. It was only temporary. As soon as I returned, I would see the doctor, take better care of myself. Just let me get through this first.

Elena hugged me before I left. "I am so sorry about this," she whispered in my ear. "Call if you need me to do anything, anything at all. I'm going to keep digging here."

"I'll report the … cat to the police," Brandi said. "I'll tell them you left for a few days because of the stress, didn't even see the cat or the emails."

I nodded, tears suddenly glistening in my eyes. What did I ever do to deserve this much kindness? I, who tried to make as few demands on people as possible, in case they started expecting more than I was willing to give. Where did all this come from?

I hadn't expected to sleep at all during the drive. I was way too wound up – images of the dead cat, the obsessive emails, Tommy, what

Brandi and Elena had said, all flashed through my head like some strange, sick collage. But despite everything, I slept throughout most of the trip, only waking when Tommy stopped to buy gas, drinks and a map.

"Well, here it is."

I scrambled over the seat to get a better look. The Minneapolis School for Special Children. Looked exactly like the photo. Even the trees were the same.

Maybe the photo had been taken recently. But that thought was just too creepy and I pushed it away.

Thick pines and blue spruces framed the small, red brick building. Their distinctive scent permeated the car even with the windows rolled up. A brown pick-up truck passed us, blowing big belches of smoke as it went.

"Looks kind of dead."

"Yeah, well, school must be out." I studied the windows for any sign of life. "The teachers are probably still there. Worth a shot anyway." I coughed a few times, deep booming coughs that burned my chest. I dug out my pills and opened my water bottle.

Tommy eyed me. "You don't sound too good."

"Funny, I don't feel too good either." I downed my medicine, tossing down a few extra pain pills for luck.

Tommy watched me carefully. "Those all can't be good for you."

I rubbed my forehead. Definitely a fever. "I'm sure they're not, but I gotta do something. It's only for today – once we get to the bottom of this I can collapse."

Tommy half-nodded and glanced at the building again. "Got a plan?"

"Actually, I do." Martha had given me the initial spark this morning. I rummaged around in the back seat for a notebook and pen.

"And that plan is … "

"Too complicated to get into now." I removed the studio shot of the girl from the paper trail folder and placed in front of my notebook. "You can come in with me, just as long as you know you may have to leave."

"Great," Tommy grumbled, following me out of the car. "Just what I always wanted to be. A sidekick."

"Sidekicks are just as famous as leads. Sometimes more so."

"And that makes me feel so not better about it."

I punched him lightly on the arm. "Hey. Things could be worse. You could not be here at all."

He grunted as we headed up the sidewalk covered with browning needles. We stepped around pinecones and branches. The smell of pine was even stronger out here.

The front doors were open. The building felt oppressively quiet – why did schools in particular seem so hollow and devoid of life when not being used? Empty classrooms lined each side of the hallway. Our footsteps echoed in the stillness.

"Where do we go?" Tommy whispered. He must have felt it too – that reluctance to break the silence.

I shrugged. We kept walking, our footsteps sounding way too loud.

At the corner, I looked into one of the classrooms and saw a woman erasing the blackboard. At last, a person. I tapped on the door.

The woman turned around. "Can I help you?" She looked to be in her early forties. Her brown hair was cut in a bob, framing a creased, round, friendly face with pleasant features and patient eyes.

I took a deep breath. Now or never. "Yes. I'm Kit Caldwell, a social work major at U of M. I'm doing a project for one of my classes, a follow-up on a ward of the state."

She put the eraser down, brushed off her hands. A puff of chalk dust rose in the air. "Oh, of course. You must be one of Professor Green's students."

Amazing, it was actually working. "Yes, exactly. But unfortunately I'm playing catch-up big time. I have Cystic Fibrosis and as you can see, I've been pretty sick, so all I have is her photo."

Behind her round, gold-framed glasses, her eyes widened. "Oh, you poor thing. But no background sheet?"

I hung my head, looking as abashed and embarrassed as possible. "Uh, actually, to be honest, I lost it. And I don't normally lose things, I'm a very good student and very organized, but I've been so sick and I've torn apart my apartment looking for it and I don't want to tell Professor Green ... "

She came toward me, put her hand on my arm. "Sh, sh, dear. It's okay. I know Professor Green quite well and I wouldn't want to own up to her that I lost my school work either." She patted my arm and smiled. "It'll be our little secret. Come sit down and let me see what I can do."

I shot her a grateful look, then indicated Tommy. "Oh, this is my boyfriend, Tommy. He drove me here, but if you don't want him to stay ... "

She waved her hand. "No, no, that's perfectly fine."

She introduced herself as Maeva Jacobson. "Now, let's see that photo," she said, as we sat down in miniature green plastic chairs around her desk.

I slid it from my notebook and handed it over.

"Why, that's Kayla Benson," Maeva said immediately. "One of our success stories. She's about to be adopted."

I kept my eyes focused on Maeva. "On Tuesday, right?" I said hesitantly.

She tapped the photo. "Yes, I believe it is Tuesday."

I wrote down a few notes, coughed a couple of times. "And do you know the family adopting her?"

"The Terrys? Of course. Kayla's in my class. Gretchen Terry visits her here at least three times a week."

Terry? As in David Terry? I arranged my features in the most neutral expression I could. "They have an older son, don't they?"

"Yes, he's in grad school, I believe. In Wisconsin." She handed me back the photo. "It's such a shame, really. What the Terrys have gone through over the years. So much tragedy. And such good people, too."

I reached out to take the photo, saw my fingers close on the edge of it, but my hand was so numb I couldn't actually feel it. "Tragedy?" I said faintly.

Maeva sighed. "Mr. and Mrs. Terry had three children, two daughters and a son. One daughter died as an infant of SIDS. The other was killed in a car crash about five years ago. She was only sixteen." Maeva shook her head. "So very, very tragic."

David had two sisters? And neither died of Cystic Fibrosis? I dropped my gaze to my notebook, busied myself putting the photo away. I didn't want her to see my face, sure my shock would give me away.

Apparently I wasn't fast enough, because Maeva reached out to pat my hand. "It's so difficult when bad things happen to good people," she said, thankfully misreading my expression. "But as tragic as it is, some good's coming out of it. Kayla will be going to a fine home."

Oh, God. Kayla. I had almost forgotten about her. I raised my head. "Is Kayla happy about it?"

Maeva nodded, her round face breaking into a smile. "Of course, she is. She's a good kid – sweet, smart. And tough. When you look at what she's been through in her short life, it's nothing short of miraculous at how well she's turned out. But all that's behind her now. The Terrys will take good care of her. I think she'll be good for them as well – they'll be able to heal together."

I coughed, so as to have a reason to cover my face. Heal together? Was this woman writing for Hallmark? The state was happily bestowing an innocent girl on a woman who had raised two dead children and one living stalker. This was nothing short of state-sanctioned child abuse. How did it get so far in the system without ringing a few alarm bells?

Maeva studied me, motherly concern radiating from her every pore. "Are you sure you're feeling okay? You still sound pretty sick."

I rubbed my aching chest. "Actually, maybe we should continue this another day. I guess I'm not as well as I thought."

Maeva nodded, helping me to my feet. "You go home and rest. Take care of yourself. Kayla isn't going anywhere, even after the adoption she'll still be attending this school at least until spring."

She walked us to the door, sensible shoes clicking on the linoleum. I shook her hand, thanked her, then hurried out of the school as fast as I dared.

"David's mother is adopting Kayla?" Tommy said, as soon as we were outside.

"Sounds like it."

"Why would she do that?"

"Good question." I jerked open the car door. "An even better question is what really happened to those daughters. David told me his sister died of Cystic Fibrosis, yet Maeva thinks one died of sudden infant death syndrome and the other in a car wreck."

Tommy slid into the driver's seat. "This is getting weirder and weirder. And there's still no connection to Cat."

I pulled out my photo of Kayla and the older woman – the one taken in front of the school. "That's gotta be Gretchen Terry. Look at her. It's so obvious she's a grade A bitch. How could they be giving that poor child to her?"

Tommy shrugged. "Kayla's a ward of the state. You don't become a ward of the state because your family is like the Cleavers. She's an older child and probably dragging around some serious baggage. Her options aren't great."

"I guess." I couldn't tear my eyes off that woman – her stern, unyielding face, her iron grip on Kayla. Two dead daughters. One psychopathic son.

"What I don't get," Tommy was saying, "is why that Cat person would care about this."

I shook the photo. "Because *Gretchen* is obviously a terrible, abusive mother."

"Yeah, but there are plenty of terrible, abusive mothers who adopt children. What's so special about this particular one?"

The stern face. The iron grip. I could almost feel the coldness emanating from this woman.

Two dead daughters. One psychopathic son.

The innocent depend on you.

Two dangers for one new little girl. How long will it take for that girl to be gone?

Two dead daughters.

I glanced up at Tommy. "We so gotta go there."

Tommy looked back at me, a slow grin unfolding. "Yes, ma'am."

Chapter 32

"Not exactly what I was expecting," Tommy said.

The little white two-story house with black trim sat nestled between neatly tended bushes and thick manicured grass.

"Yeah," I said. "Way too cute."

The house had "American Dream" stamped all over it. A house like that could never have sheltered David, the mad stalker. Could never have nurtured him, watched him grow up, kept him safe and sound. Not possible.

"Well, maybe his parents moved here later," Tommy said. "You know, after they sold the Addams Family house."

"Let's hope." We got out of the car and headed toward the driveway.

"What if she's not home?" Tommy asked, as we hiked up the driveway. Perfectly rounded evergreen bushes lined each side.

I shrugged. "What else? We wait."

"Cool, stake out."

"I'll even spring for the doughnuts." We reached an immaculately swept porch, complete with a white wooden porch swing that creaked in the wind.

I rang the doorbell. The swing continued to creak, the sound eerie in this clean, sterile porch. It made me think of a coffin opening – one that had been buried for a long, long time.

The door swung open, revealing Gretchen Terry.

At first I could only stare. She looked exactly like the photo, except instead of a black coat she wore a blue housedress covered with tiny white flowers and a white apron.

She adjusted her black-framed glasses. "May I help you?"

"Are you Mrs. Terry?" I asked.

She pressed her lips together. "What do you want?"

Now that she was actually in front of me, I realized I had no idea what to say. I had been so caught up in the whole house-finding ordeal, I had forgotten about making an after-I-found-her plan. She continued to stare, her eyes cold and calculating. Just like David's, although the color was wrong – brown instead of turquoise.

She stepped back. "Well?"

I was going to lose her if I didn't think of something. "I'm from the state department," I found myself saying. "I'm here about your adoption application."

Her eyes narrowed. "What about it?"

"I need to check on a few things. Could we come in?"

She took another step back. "I've already had my application approved. What do you need?"

"Just a few answers, that's all."

Her eyes grew colder still. "Aren't you a little young to be working at the state department?"

I smiled. "Oh, I get that all the time."

Her lips were a red slash across her face. Like a knife cut. "What did you say your names were?"

I glanced at Tommy. "Mary Smith and Tommy Johnston."

She started to close the door. "Stay right here while I go call the state department."

Ack! Definitely not the right response. Without thinking, I stepped forward and shoved my foot against the door, just stopping it. "Actually, Mrs. Terry, I'm not from the state department."

Her cold eyes glowered at me. "Then who are you and how do you know about the adoption?"

"My name is Kit Caldwell and I'm actually here about your son, David. He's been stalking me ... "

Her face froze. Her eyes turned round with horror. With a strangled cry, she slammed the door shut, banging my foot and barely missing my head.

Hopping backward, I shook my stinging foot. "Mrs. Terry," I called. "We don't want to hurt you. We just want to talk."

Locks clicked, bolts rattled. "Go away," a muffled voice said. "Get off my property before I call the police."

I looked at Tommy. He shrugged.

"All right, Mrs. Terry," I called back. "Sorry to bother you. We're leaving now."

"That went well," Tommy said as we stepped off the porch.

I glanced over my shoulder, trying to see if a curtain twitched. I knew she was watching. "Hey, at least she didn't threaten us with a shotgun." The porch swing creaked again. Rotting coffins. Buried secrets.

"So, now what, Holmes?" We reached the car, me continually stealing glimpses at the house as we walked. I still felt those cold eyes boring into me.

Opening the door, I pondered our options. It certainly seemed like we had hit a dead end. Yet, those two dead children kept haunting me.

"The library, Watson," I said at last. "Using their computers to search through the back issues of the newspaper is probably the fastest."

Tommy slid the key into the ignition. "You got it."

***

Another task that wasn't as easy as it sounded.

Even narrowing the search down to five years ago still meant examining three hundred and sixty-five potential newspapers. After a half-dozen fruitless searches, Tommy had the bright idea of looking only at obituaries. It still took forever.

"I think I found it," Tommy said.

I had taken a break to down more pills. My head was killing me, my fever was up and I had started coughing again. Death had to be preferable to this.

"Where?" I craned my neck to peer over Tommy's shoulder.

He pointed. Bethany Terry, age sixteen, died April twenty-four in a single-car crash.

April twenty-four. Something about that date sent chills down my spine. April twenty-four.

"Can you find the article about the death?" I asked, as Tommy pressed the button to print the obituary.

"Nothing wrong with trying." He started tapping the keys.

I sat back and rubbed my face. April twenty-four. I would have been sixteen as well.

Then I remembered: the sharp scent of chlorine. The feather-light touch on my cheek. Come to say good-bye.

"Here it is," Tommy said, pointing at the screen. "Look, there's even a picture of Bethany."

I leaned over to look, but I already knew what I would see. The headline blared "Teen Killed in Car Crash, Alcohol Suspected." Underneath a photo of a pretty, blonde teenager smiled at us.

It was Cat. No question about it.

Chapter 33

"They must've kidnapped Cat. That's all there is to it," I said.

We had moved to a more secluded area of the library – a corner near a window. The gray day was melting into night. We sat facing each other in two brownish orange chairs, a small square table between us.

Tommy tapped the newspaper article lying on the worn table. "But this girl's dead. She can't be the one you've been seeing around campus or who's been sending you emails and photos."

I propped my elbows on my knees and rested my head in my hands. "But it looks just like her."

"You haven't seen Cat since you were seven. How do you know what she'd look like at sixteen? Or at twenty-one for that matter?"

"She's my sister. Besides, she looks just like the girl I saw at the Halloween party and at the Union."

Tommy slid back in his chair, his legs sprawled in front of him. "And we're right back where we started. She can't be the girl you've seen these past few weeks because she's dead."

I rubbed my forehead. "It's got to be Cat. The Terrys must have kidnapped her." Shocked, I jerked my head up, understanding turning my blood to burning ice. "Oh, my God, Tommy. The Terrys kidnapped Cat. It rhymes with fairies. See, I was right all along. She was kidnapped by the fairies!"

Tommy took a deep breath. "Kit, be real for one second. How would you know she had been kidnapped by the Terrys? Don't you think if anyone knew who'd kidnapped her, they would've gotten her back?"

"But, Tommy, if they kidnapped Cat, it would all make sense. Why Cat wants me to stop this adoption, because she knows firsthand what crappy parents the Terrys are. And why she warned me away from David."

"So, you're telling me her ghost has been haunting you?" Tommy stared at the ceiling. "A ghost with an email address and the ability to take recent photos? Not to mention this girl looks like she's our age, not sixteen. I know there's an X-Files out there about ghosts aging, but still."

The smell of chlorine. The touch of a feather on my cheek. Now I knew. She really had come to say good-bye.

Cat's ghost had already visited me once. Why did it seem so strange she would return a second time? Her ghost wandering around made as much sense as anything else did. Maybe more.

On the other hand, as much as I hated to admit it, Tommy did have a point. How could a ghost send me emails and photos? And she did look older than the picture in the newspaper.

"It's the only explanation that makes sense," I argued.

"But you said Elena found no police file. If Cat was kidnapped, where's the file?"

"Maybe she wasn't kidnapped in Milwaukee. Maybe it was here. We should talk to the police here."

"It also doesn't explain why Mrs. Terry threw a fit when she heard your name or why David fixated on you."

"Au contraire, Watson, it points to their guilt. Cat would've been old enough to tell them her real name. She may have even talked about me."

Tommy leaned over to fiddle with the articles. "I still think you're reaching."

"And I still think we should go to the cops and see if they have a file on her."

Tommy held his hands up. "Fine. We'll go." He started to stand up.

"What's with the attitude? Do you have a better idea?"

He shoved the articles at me. "Did you even read this story or are you so convinced you're right you don't want to look at anything else?"

"What the hell is that supposed to mean?"

He stood, backed away. "Maybe it means now that you're on this kidnapping kick, you're not willing to consider any other angles."

"That's not true. I just think it makes the most sense."

He pointed at the table. "Just read the article. Need a bathroom break, back in a minute." He strode off.

Glaring at his retreating back, I snatched the article off the table. How dare he accuse me of being close-minded. Covering the photo with my hand so it wouldn't distract me, I started reading the text.

Teen Killed in Car Crash, Alcohol Suspected

A local teenager was found dead in a single car crash early Sunday morning.

Bethany Terry, 16, was driving down a deserted section of Bolt Road when she apparently lost control of her car and hit a tree, killing her instantly.

Highway patrol officers Dick Macy and Christine Yorlet discovered her body at 4:12 a.m. Sunday morning.

"She had been dead for several hours by the time we got there," said Yorlet. "It's such a shame."

The cause of the accident is unknown, although alcohol was found in her system.

In her junior year, Terry had been an honor student and yearbook editor.

"She was always such a good girl," said Gretchen Terry, her mother. "I've never had an ounce of trouble from her before. I don't know how this could have happened."

Police have a launched a full-scale investigation.

"It's a bit peculiar," said Detective William Reynolds, the investigator assigned to the case. "There's nothing on or around that road. Why she would be driving down it at that time of night doesn't make a lot of sense."

If anyone has any information about this crime, please call the Minneapolis Police Department at 555-3487.

"It IS a bit peculiar, wouldn't you say?" Tommy leaned over the chair, having returned while I had been reading. "And especially after meeting the poor, grieving mother, I'd say it was more than a bit peculiar."

I chewed on my lip. "But this doesn't change the fact the woman could still have kidnapped Cat."

Tommy looked pained. "Back with the kidnapping. Kit, I'm not going to pretend I know who you've been seeing around campus, but don't you get it? The Terrys may have murdered Bethany. At the very least, don't you want to know what happened to her?"

Two dead daughters. One psychopathic son.

One murdered daughter. One psychopathic son.

The fairies are evil. Pure evil.

Yes, I certainly did want to know what happened to Cat. Every last detail.

I stood up. "Well, then let's go and see if Detective Reynolds will talk to us. And, while we're at it, we can check out kidnapping cases for Cat."

***

By the time we reached the station, it was past seven o'clock and very dark.

"Probably should've called," Tommy said glumly, as he pushed open the station doors. "Probably done with his shift and gone home."

As it turned out, Detective Reynolds's shift had ended a few hours ago. However, he had stayed late to cover for a fellow detective whose wife was in the hospital. Better yet, he was more than happy to talk to us about the case.

"The Terry case. Yes, I remember it." He gestured for us to take a seat, his every movement slow and deliberate. His desk was an explosion of papers, files and a monthly calendar desk blotter covered with scribbled notes and coffee stains. Framed photos of smiling children stood in a corner, next to a coffee cup with the words "World's Best Grandpa" on it. With his smooth, dark complexion and thick, black hair, he didn't look old enough to be a grandpa. "Sad. Very sad. What's your interest in it?"

I eyed Tommy. "Her brother," I said, nearly choking on the word, "is stalking me." Tommy had made me promise not to bring up the kidnapping until after we had discussed the accident.

His eyebrows went up. "David?"

My mouth dropped. "You still remember his name?"

"There are some cases that never leave you. This was one of them."

"Why?" I asked, rubbing my chest and trying not to cough. I had doped myself up again, but the drugs hadn't kicked in yet.

He half-smiled. "Many reasons." His speech was as slow and deliberate as his movements had been. "The main one being how this case stunk to high heaven and we were never able to prove anything."

I leaned closer. "What stunk?"

"Everything. Bethany had been at a party until a little before 11 p.m. By all accounts she left that party in a good mood. Yet, we found her five hours later in the middle of an unfinished subdivision. The car was checked out, no mechanical problems that we could find. Her blood alcohol was very low, like she had consumed one, maybe two drinks at the most. So, what made her crash? Better yet, why was she on that road in the first place?"

He adjusted himself in his chair, sitting back, stretching his legs out. "Then there were her injuries. They weren't consistent with the crash."

"Consistent?" Tommy asked.

Detective Reynolds folded his hands across his stomach. "Her injuries weren't consistent with the damage to the car."

I put my hand to my mouth. "Oh, my God."

Detective Reynolds reached over to pick up his coffee cup. He half-waved it at us. "Kind of nasty this time of day, but I'd be happy to get you some."

I wanted answers, not coffee, and especially not bad coffee. I shook my head politely. He nodded, drank slowly, then put the cup down.

"But what really did it was the family," he continued. "There was something hinky about them from the beginning. First, the mother. In here every other day with some new theory. First, it was that we made a mistake, her daughter would never have been drinking. Then it was Bethany's friends – her friends were a bad influence. Then it was some stranger who had abducted her and caused her to lose control of the vehicle."

He straightened his desk blotter, leaned back again. "Not that that's so unusual, grieving mothers with theories. But there was something odd about her. She was so frantic about it, nearly in a frenzy. And when we tried to question her or the other family members, she went ballistic, said she'd sue everyone for false accusations." He pressed his fingers together, hands forming a triangle over his stomach. "At the time none of them were suspects. We were simply asking routine questions."

"The father wasn't much help, deferring to his wife on every issue and question. Then there was David."

Detective Reynolds rotated his mug, took another swallow of coffee. "Shifty. Very shifty. Never a straight answer – hell, never a straight look even. I'd bet my pension he's up to his eyeballs in it."

Sounds like David. Even listening to this account secondhand sent eerie shivers through me. "So what happened? Why wasn't he arrested?"

He shrugged. "No proof. Just suspicions."

I gestured with my hands. "But, but you had proof. The injuries."

He shook his head. "They weren't conclusive, just suspicious. No, there was nothing. We couldn't charge the Terrys with anything. And it rankles me to this day."

Nothing. The police could do nothing. Cat was dead and they got away with it. The perfect crime.

I didn't think I could hate David anymore than I already did, but at that moment the rage burned inside me. How could they do that to Cat? What kind of monsters were they?

The fairies are evil. Pure evil.

I wondered if Cat had suffered, if she had known their intentions, if she had seen her death reflected on their faces before the final blow.

Now they wanted a new little girl to play with.

Detective Reynolds stretched back in his chair, steepling his fingers again. "So, tell me more about how David is stalking you."

I gave him the shortened version, but I did include how David had managed to destroy my credibility. The detective didn't interrupt, simply alternated between nodding his head and drinking his coffee.

When I finished, he pondered for a bit before speaking. "Your story is certainly consistent with my dealings with David. I'm sorry you got tangled up with him in the first place. If you'd like, I'd be happy to call the Riverview police and share my experiences with them."

"You'd do that?" After weeks of living in a cloud of doubts, second-guesses and outright disbelief, I was deeply moved that someone not only believed my side of story, but was willing to help me.

"Of course. I do have an advantage over the investigators in Riverview since I've had prior experience with David. Although, even without my help, I'm sure they would have figured out David's true nature eventually."

Ah, eventually. That was the key. With my luck, eventually would come when Riverview's finest were standing over my murdered body.

I glanced sideways at Tommy. He shrugged. "Uh, I was wondering if I could share something else with you," I began.

"Go ahead."

"Well, I think that there might be a … more personal reason why David chose me to stalk."

Detective Reynolds leaned forward, his face narrowing. "I'm listening."

I took a deep breath. This was harder than I had expected. "You see, I had a sister, Cat. She was kidnapped when I was seven. And the thing is, Bethany looks like her."

He paused, considering. "So, you think the Terrys kidnapped your sister and raised her as their own?"

"Okay, I know it sounds a little crazy and a little paranoid, but it actually makes sense. David told me he lost a sister to Cystic Fibrosis as a baby. I have Cystic Fibrosis, which is another reason why I think he latched onto me. But, anyway, now I find out he has another sister, Bethany. He loses that sister at sixteen. And now Mrs. Terry is in the process of adopting a ward of the state, a little blond girl named Kayla."

Detective Reynolds reached down, selected a pen and began jotting notes. "You say she's about to adopt another girl?"

"Yes, on Tuesday the adoption will be final. Kayla Benson. That's the little girl's name. But, back to Bethany, I really think she's my sister, Cat Caldwell. Can you find out if there's a police file on her kidnapping?"

He continued to scribble on a piece of paper. "To be honest, the kidnapping doesn't ring any bells, but I'll check it out."

I filled him in with as much of the kidnapping details as I remembered while he took notes. I even told him about my meeting with Mrs. Terry.

After I finished, he pondered his notes before looking at me. "I'm glad you came in today, Miss Caldwell. Why don't you go get some rest? Check into a motel and let me see what I can dig up."

I nodded, my body going limp with relief and gratitude. Finally, some official help. A police officer who actually believed me. Even more amazing, he wanted to help me find the truth. For the first time since this nightmare began, I felt like things would work out for me.

Tommy and I both stood up, thanking him. He stood as well, shaking our hands.

"I don't suppose I have to tell you two to be very careful," he said. "You're dealing with someone very dangerous, who's quite possibly violent and homicidal. Watch yourselves."

"But how could he possibly know we're here?" I asked. "He's probably in front of my apartment building in Wisconsin right now."

Detective Reynolds's face became grave. "I'm not trying to unduly alarm you, but you did visit his mother. I'm sure he knows you're here."

My stomach dropped with a sickening thud. How could I have been so stupid? Of course she would call him. Why did I tip my hand like that? How idiotic could I be?

"All I'm saying is be extra careful," Detective Reynolds said. "He knows you're in Minneapolis, but he doesn't know exactly where, so you're probably safe for now. But he also knows you're investigating him, and he's probably going to become even more dangerous. Make sure you check in with me before you return to Riverview."

I nodded, thanking him again, but more subdued than before.

Two dead daughters, one murdered. One psychopathic son.

And now that son knew I was on to him.

***

We didn't speak in the car. I was too busy trying to force my numb brain to process all the information thrown at me today, but Tommy just seemed preoccupied. He kept glancing in his rear view mirror.

Finally, I couldn't stand it anymore. "What's with the rear view mirror love affair?"

Tommy stared into the mirror, pressed his lips together. "I think there's a car following us."

I automatically glanced in the passenger side mirror. Several sets of lights shone back at me. "How can you even tell?"

"I don't know. It's probably nothing. Just paranoia. Forget I said anything."

"Paranoia is catchy," I said with forced lightness. He half-smiled at me, but he didn't stop checking the rear view mirror.

I spent the rest of the trip studying the mirror, trying to see why he thought we were being followed. I couldn't tell, all the lights looked the same to me.

Tommy turned into a lighted Motel 6 parking lot. Pulling into a space, he shut the car off and glanced around. "This fine?"

"Sure."

He looked strained and exhausted. I attempted a smile. "Hey, look at the bright side. At least now we *know* David has some serious issues. Before, we only had a hunch."

He drummed his hands on the steering wheel. "I think I would've preferred being wrong."

Somewhere close by a set of tires squealed and a horn blared. "You think?"

Tommy looked away, running his hands roughly through his hair. "It's just such a shock. This whole day. I mean, I knew there was something off with him, but this goes way beyond it."

Two dead daughters, one murdered. One psychopathic son.

"I know. Believe me, I know."

Tommy studied the steering wheel, his fingers splayed across it. He took a deep breath and gave himself a shake. "Let's get checked in, then we can go across the street and get some dinner."

I nodded, following him out of the car. Although the parking lot was well-lit, the darkness hovered around us, hemming us in. Trees waved their bare branches, menacing silhouettes in the shadows. Our footsteps sounded hollow and exposed. I found myself craning my neck, trying to see everything at once, even though I kept telling myself I was being paranoid. No way could David be out there. Nobody had been following us.

"What about football?" I said, the thought suddenly breaking through the muddle.

He shrugged. "If we leave in the morning, we'll be back in plenty of time."

That explanation sounded way too nonchalant. Brandi's words flashed in my head. I opened my mouth to dig deeper, when an inarticulate cry shattered the stillness. I snapped my head around.

David rushed out of the darkness. His face was twisted in rage. Hot eyes burned with madness. A knife glinted in his hand.

I froze. How could this be? It was like the first time he showed up at my classes. Like my thoughts had caused him to materialize. How long had he been following us? Would I ever get away from him?

Tommy knocked me out of the way just as David's knife slashed toward me. I fell sideways, landing awkwardly on the cement. Tommy barreled into David, knocking him to the parking lot. They landed into a heap of flailing arms and legs.

Stunned, I rolled over. I had to help Tommy. But what could I do? From the tangle of bodies, I could see David raise the knife and plunge it downward.

I screamed and scrambled to my feet. Tommy cried out in pain. The knife was buried in his shoulder. Blood splashed against his blue and yellow jacket, forming a new design.

I ran toward them. David yanked the knife out. As he swung it down a second time, I grabbed it in mid-motion. It felt warm, sticky.

A muffled curse. "Kit, get out of here," Tommy muttered. "Call the cops." I struggled to peel David's fingers off the knife.

David's foot shot out of nowhere, kicking me in the calf. The pain was sharp, unexpected. I lost my grip on the knife. One finger slid across the sharp edge. A sting. More blood. Mixing with Tommy's.

Another kick. More pain. I went down hard. I tasted blood in my mouth.

David stabbed Tommy again, this time in the arm. Tommy gasped as he fought to get the knife. Blood was everywhere. Have to do something. But what?

My purse. I spied it lying on the pavement. I dove for it. Trembling with both fear and rage, I dumped the contents on the parking lot. There. Pepper spray. Noisemaker.

Grabbing both, I ran back to the fight. David had pinned Tommy beneath him and was raising the knife a third time. Aiming for the chest. The kill. I sprayed him in the face.

He screamed, whipping toward me. "You bitch." The lower half of his face was wet, but his eyes blazed with the bright light of insanity.

I saw my mistake then. My hand had been shaking too much. I missed his eyes.

I sprayed a second time, but he was ready. His hand snaked out, grabbed my arm. "Bitch." Twisted my wrist. Pain exploded in my arm. "Sneaking around. Spying on me. Spraying me with pepper spray. I'll show you." He yanked me against him. Squeezing and bending my wrist. Agony. I dropped the pepper spray. God, he was strong. Strength born of rage. Of desperation. Of madness. How else could he have overpowered Tommy?

"Yeah, well you murdered my sister," I hissed through clenched teeth, refusing to show how badly he was hurting me.

His eyes widened, shock penetrating his madness. "How could you know that?" he gasped.

"Detective Reynolds told me. Remember him? He didn't fall for your crap."

David stared at me. Then he began to laugh. A horrible, eerie laugh.

"Kit, you don't know a damn thing," he started to say, but Tommy punched him in the throat, striking him in the Adam's apple.

David's eyes bulged. He made a strangled, garbled noise and dropped the knife. It hit the cement with a clatter.

I lunged for it, falling across Tommy's body. My hands touched the knife, slid over the wet, slick surface.

"No, you don't." David's voice came out as a choked gasp. He snatched my hair, jerking my head up painfully. My teeth clicked together. The knife kept slipping, I couldn't get a good grip on it.

Another head jerk. Hot, bright pain. Tears filled my eyes. I clawed at the knife, just managed to get if off the pavement.

"Bitch." David dragged me to my feet by my hair. "We'll see if your boyfriend can save you now."

He seized my throat.

I plunged the knife into his thigh.

He screamed and let go of me. I fell to the ground, landing on something hard.

The noisemaker.

Tommy groaned. David was staring at the knife poking out of his jeans. Blood spurted out, staining his clothes. He raised his head, mouth twisting uselessly. He didn't look human.

"I can't believe you did that to me." He grasped the knife, as if to pull it out.

I wretched the noisemaker from under me and yanked out the pin. The alarm squealed. David stopped what he was doing, jerking his head to fix his hot, gleaming eyes on me. People started streaming out of the hotel, running toward us.

David followed my gaze. He looked back at me.

"This isn't over yet," he mouthed, then turned and limped away.

I closed my eyes briefly, then struggled to replace the pin. My hands shook so bad it took a couple of tries, but I eventually did it.

Silence. Tommy groaned again. Blood everywhere, his jacket soaked.

"Somebody call an ambulance," I heard someone shout, before realizing I was that someone.

Chapter 34

David's face. Twisted. Laughing.

"Kit, you don't know a damn thing."

Newspaper photo. Cat's face looking at me. "It's all real, Kit. It's all real."

I opened my eyes. Dozens of blue-gray chairs. Gray carpet. White walls. Television in the corner. Hospital smell. Such a dreadful smell. I hated that smell.

For one terrible moment, I was seven years old and dying. Dying in the hospital while the fairies kidnapped my sister.

No, it was the Terrys. The Terrys kidnapped her. And they killed her.

Now it all came back to me. I had fallen asleep in the hospital waiting room.

I stood up and every muscle in my body protested. God did I hurt.

Tommy had been whisked away the moment we arrived at the hospital. They had tried to whisk me away as well, but I kept telling them I wasn't hurt, it wasn't my blood all over my clothes.

"We have to check you out anyway," the Hispanic doctor said, escorting me to a room.

He introduced himself as Dr. Sanchez. Reluctantly, I allowed him to examine me.

"Well, it doesn't appear that you have any injuries," he said, after he had finished poking and prodding me. "But that cough doesn't sound very good."

"Yeah, I'm pretty sick," I said. "Nothing some chicken soup won't cure."

He started writing a few notes. "Have you had a chest x-ray?"

Oh no. Not a chest x-ray. They would never let me out of here if they actually saw the condition of my lungs. "I'm sure I'll be fine."

Dr. Sanchez glanced at me. "The way your lungs sound, I think you should have one."

Oh, God. I couldn't be admitted. Not with David still out there. I'd be dead in no time. "Okay, I'll get one, but let me get one back in Riverview. I'm a broke student and I have an insurance problem. Deal?"

Dr. Sanchez smiled. "Ah, yes. I'm well acquainted with both situations. All right. Just promise me you'll schedule an appointment with your doctor the moment you get back to Riverview."

Relief. I smiled back. "You got it. Thank you, doctor."

He nodded and let me return to the waiting room, telling me he would check on Tommy for me. I had just managed to get myself semi-comfortable when he reappeared, informing me that Tommy was going to be fine, but was pretty drugged up at the moment. I could see him in the morning. I thanked him, then worked on getting more comfortable since it appeared I would be spending the night.

I didn't think I'd fall asleep, but I must have, because that had been another peculiar, unsettling dream.

It's all real, Kit. It's all real.

Whatever that meant. I glanced at the clock, rubbing my chest. A little after 10 p.m. I hadn't slept long.

"Didn't I just tell you to be careful?"

I whipped around. Detective Reynolds was striding toward me.

I closed my eyes for a moment, trying to get my breathing under control. "You scared me."

"I wish I'd scared you more." He looked grim. "Now, what exactly happened?"

I filled him in as best I could. He took copious notes, asked questions when I started losing steam and nodded a lot.

When I couldn't think of anything more to tell him, he closed his notebook with a sigh. "He's upped the stakes, you do realize that."

I nodded.

He ran his hand over his face, his head. "I probably don't have to tell you to be very, very careful. I've already informed the hospital not to tell anyone you or Tommy are here, and I've alerted hospital security of the seriousness of the problem. In addition, I've supplied them with a photo of David. The fact that you've wounded him is something we can track. We'll check hospitals, clinics, and his mother's. I'm also sending out an APB. We're doing what we can."

I nodded again. He studied me, his brown eyes warm and concerned, then reached out to squeeze my hand. "We're going to get him. Don't you worry about that. You just keep yourself and your boyfriend safe until we do."

His hand was warm, comforting. Strong and gentle at the same time. He was a man who kept his promises. And he had promised to help me. I smiled, a real smile. "Thank you."

He ducked his head in a quick nod, squeezed my hand one last time and left.

I settled myself back on my chair. Might as well get some sleep. But every time I closed my eyes, fragments of my life cracked through my subconscious, keeping me awake.

"Kit, you don't know a damn thing."

Why would David say that? What was I missing here?

"It's all real, Kit. It's all real."

Cat had said that in my church dream.

My life has been dominated by two dreams.

In one, the fairies kidnap Cat. In real life, the Terrys kidnap Cat. I knew they did with the same deep-down certainty I had known when Cat died.

After all, she came to say goodbye.

In the second dream, I visit a lonely country church with my parents.

Could that one be true as well?

"It's all real, Kit. It's all real."

Still pondering, I looked at the clock. Only eleven. Elena would still be up. I dialed my cell phone.

***

"I did it," Elena crowed in my ear.

I rubbed my eyes with my fist. My entire body pulsed with pain. "What?"

"What do you mean, what? You know what. I can email it to you but it may be easier if you were able to see a print out. Do you think you could get the hospital's fax number?"

Fax number? Blurrily I stared at the clock. Nearly nine. I shook my head to clear it. "Hold on. I think I'm waking up."

Last night, security had stuck me on a cot in an empty room. While the empty room was nice, the cot was not. I should have stuck with the waiting room chair.

Groaning, I eased myself up. I hurt more this morning than I had last night. "So, you got something."

"With phone numbers. Philip Marlowe would be so proud."

At least somebody was liking this private detective crap. I limped my way to the desk. "Could I have your fax number?"

The woman behind the desk glanced at me, frowning. "Why?" She wore a deep blue sweater over her white uniform, blonde hair pulled severely back in a bun.

"Because I need to receive a fax."

Her frown deepened. "This isn't a hotel, you know."

Christ. How did I always end up with the hard asses? "Look, you know I'm a victim of a crime here. This fax has to do with my case. Can you help me out?"

Her expression softened a touch. "Faxes cost us money, you know."

"I'll pay for it."

She pondered. "All right," she said, rather ungraciously I thought, and rattled off the fax number.

While I waited for the fax to come through, I went in search of a restroom to clear out my lungs.

Green mucus. Streaked with red.

I went numb with horror.

Red. Blood.

I could have pulmonary bleeding. Or a punctured lung. My lungs could be filling up with blood right now.

Or it could be from my mouth. No blood in my lungs at all.

Or it could be pneumonia. Blood-tinged mucus was a sign of pneumonia.

See, all sorts of reasons for coughing up blood that didn't mean pulmonary bleeding. No reason to get myself worked up. No reason at all.

I closed my eyes and breathed as deeply as I could. David was here. I had to stay calm. I couldn't get worked up. Think healthy. There's nothing seriously wrong with me. Nothing.

I washed my face, forcing myself to relax. Just think of solving the case. That's it. Just solve the case.

When I felt I was control, I went to get the fax.

***

"You should see the other guy," Tommy joked weakly.

I decided to refrain from mentioning that I was the one who stabbed the other guy. "Are you sure you're okay?"

He shrugged. "Looks worse than it is."

I found that hard to believe. One side of his face had swollen up and his right arm was in a sling.

Right arm. Throwing arm.

His eyes followed mine. "Yeah, football's out for me."

"Oh, Tommy." I put the faxed sheets on his nightstand and sat on his bed, near his left side. "But you can still try out for the pros, right? I know you haven't been playing well, but they should understand … "

Tommy brushed his fingers across my lips, silencing me. "The pros are out, Kit. They don't want a college student who's already injured. They have enough injuries to deal with as it is."

"But … "

"Don't worry about it. It's going to be fine."

Tears filled my eyes. "No, it's not all right. This is your career, your future. And I'm ruining everything. I'm the reason you were playing badly in the first place, and now this. It's all my fault." I covered my face, struggling to keep the tears from falling.

Tommy sighed. "Kit, you just don't get it. You're the one I want. Why else do you think I'm here? Football's all well and good, but it doesn't mean anything if I can't have you."

I peeked at him from between my fingers. "But, Tommy, it was your future … "

"You're my future."

I dropped my hands. Tears glistened on my palms. "What are you saying?" Could he be saying what I wanted so desperately to hear?

"Just this. I know about your disease. I know it's bad. I know you may not live long or even if you do, you may not be healthy a lot of those days. But I'd rather be with you than not be with you – whether it's six months or six years."

Our eyes locked. I couldn't talk, couldn't breathe. All I could do was drink in the passion of his eyes, the emotion, the caring, the love.

I don't know who moved first, but all of a sudden we were kissing, his one good arm locked tightly around me. His lips were so warm, so right. Nothing had ever felt so good.

"Tommy, I'm so sorry … " I started to say.

"Shh," he whispered, kissing me harder. "It doesn't matter now. This is all that matters. Only this."

I have no idea how far it would have gone if a nurse hadn't interrupted us.

She clucked her tongue. "I'm glad to see you're both feeling better." She moved around the bed, checking his vitals, taking a few notes. I used the time to down more cold medicine.

"By the way," the nurse said, putting the file back. "In about a half hour, the doctor will be here to discharge you. Thought you might want to know." She winked at us as she left.

Tommy locked his gaze with mine. "Well, this probably isn't the best spot for it anyway." His eyes sparkled with wicked promises.

I grinned back, the answering heat whipping through my body. "Yeah, and neither one of us is in the best shape for it either."

He sighed. "Ain't that the truth? Ah well. I've waited this long. I guess I can wait a little longer." He reached for a glass of water, saw the fax. "What's this?"

"Oh, I almost forgot. My big news." I grabbed the sheets and started waving them. "Tommy, I think I figured something out."

He leaned over, trying to look at the papers as I shook them in my excitement. "Looks like a Wisconsin map with a few cities highlighted."

"That's it exactly."

He picked up his water. "And this means … what?"

"Just that I think I know the location of my church dream." I rattled the pages triumphantly.

Tommy didn't look impressed. "Uh, Kit. Hate to impose a bit of reality here, but this is a dream we're talking about. Dreams don't have locations in real life."

"Ah, but this one does." I jumped up and started pacing. "You see, the dream always starts the same. I'm in the car with my parents driving to Milwaukee when we veer off the main highway and into a small town. Last night, I called Elena. She faxed me a map of all the towns between Riverview and Milwaukee and a list of phone numbers of town officials. I called them to ask if they had a church in their town like the one in my dream, only I didn't say I dreamed about it. I said I'd visited there some years before and wanted to return but couldn't remember the exact town. And, lo and behold, Emmitsville has a church just like the one in my dream."

Tommy sat back. "Okay. So, let me get this straight. Based on the fact that somebody in a town called Emmitsville said they had a church similar to one you dreamed about means the dream is real?"

"No. The dream is real because Cat told me it's real."

"Cat? You mean the dead girl in the photo told you the church dream is real?"

"No. I mean, yes. Will you stop being so damn logical for one second and go a little on faith?"

He sighed. "I'll certainly try."

I stopped at the foot of his bed and held my hands up. "Okay. You know I've had basically two dreams all my life. The church dream and the dream where the fairies kidnap Cat. As it turns out, the fairy dream is real. Cat was kidnapped by the fairies, otherwise known as the Terrys, an easy mistake for a child to make. So, now in the last church dream, Cat told me 'It's all real.' Now, do you understand?"

Tommy twisted the sheet. "Kit, what you're arguing is absurd. The fairy dream isn't real. Cat wasn't kidnapped by the fairies, we're not even sure she was kidnapped by the Terrys."

"Semantics, like I said."

"All right, even if we go with that, which is a stretch, that still doesn't make the church dream real."

"It is, Tommy. It always starts the same. We're in the car, driving to Milwaukee, and we stop at this little town with a church in it. In Emmitsville, a town between Milwaukee and Riverview, there is a church exactly as I dreamed it. The man I spoke to said I had an excellent memory, my description was so perfect."

Tommy stared at the ceiling, sighed. "I think I'm going to regret asking this. Let's say the church dream is real. What are you proposing?"

I paused, took a deep breath, coughed a little. "We go there. To-day."

Tommy shook his head. "I was afraid you were going to say that."

"It's the key, Tommy. I know it. Maybe Cat was kidnapped there or something. I don't know. But it's the key. We have to go."

"Kit," Tommy said gently. "If all this is as you say it is, you said you'll die there. How can we possibly go?"

You always knew you had come here to die.

Thoughts cascaded through my mind, all at once.

Coughing blood.

David running at us brandishing a knife.

Green mucus. Fever. Toxins oozing through my body.

David grabbing me by the throat.

If my disease doesn't kill me, he will.

I stared straight at Tommy. "I have to find the truth. I have no choice. We have to go."

Tommy glared back. "Oh, and I have no say in the matter? Kit, look at me. I can't protect you. Hell, I'm not even sure if I can drive."

"I'll drive. It'll be okay. You're not in the church dreams so if you come the outcome won't be the same."

Tommy made a face. "Somehow, that statement doesn't have the ring of reassurance I'm sure you were going for."

I sat on the edge of the bed. "We've come so far. I know this church holds the key. Don't you want to finally know the truth?"

He stared at me - blew air out of his cheeks. "What are we going to tell the cops? They called this morning, they want a statement."

I smiled, knowing I won. "We'll give them one when we return. We'll come back today. Just out to Emmitsville, then back. Won't take long at all."

Tommy shook his head. "Ha – that sounds familiar. My words have come back to bite me."

Chapter 35

For all my bravado, the closer we got to Emmitsville, the worse I felt.

I could feel my fever growing, burning hotter. My coughing continued, despite the cold medicine. Blood poured from my lungs. Toxins flooded my system. The disease was drawing strength from the dream.

It knew it had the upper hand. The medicines were all but useless.

I spent what little energy I had hiding my worsening condition from Tommy.

He had insisted on driving.

"Didn't they give you something for the pain? Something that would make you drowsy and unable to drive?"

He shot me a look. "I didn't take it because I knew this was on the agenda, thank you very much."

I saw beads of sweat already forming on his upper lip. "Driving in pain isn't exactly brilliant either."

"Hand over whatever it is you're taking for your pain and I'll be fine. I've played football in pain, I think I can drive."

"You have only one arm. You played football with one arm?"

He glared at me. "By the looks of it, you're walking around with pneumonia. You want to tell me you're in better shape to drive?"

Point and match. I handed him the keys.

Luckily for us, the cops had brought our car to the hospital last night so we could leave right from the hospital.

Once in the car, I kept twisting around, trying to see who was behind us. "Think David's following?"

"You told me you put a knife in his thigh. He'd first need medical attention, then he'd have to find us. I don't think there's been enough time for all that." Despite his words, I noticed Tommy kept his eye on the rearview mirror more than usual. For my part, I alternated between watching the scenery, watching the passenger mirror and chewing on my lip.

"You know, I'm not rich."

Startled, I looked at him. "What?" I had been trying not to think about the blood I kept coughing up.

"Rich. I'm not rich. Nor does my father run a business. Actually, to be honest, I don't have a father."

"Tommy, why are you telling me this now?"

His hand tightened on the steering wheel. "Because, I ... because you have a right to know."

Because I might not get another chance, was what he almost said. I could hear it in his voice. Loud and clear.

Fear.

I felt it, too.

"Besides," he tried to smile. "I thought it might distract you."

I firmly put coughing up blood out of my mind. "Okay, you're not rich and you don't have a father."

"Actually, to be *perfectly* honest, I do have a father, but he left my mother and me. Destitute, as it turned out. My mother ended up having to do whatever it took to keep food on the table and pay the rent." He paused, switched lanes.

I laid a hand on his thigh. "You really don't have to tell me." His expression had become hard. Chiseled. Granite.

He threw me a quick look. "I want to. Believe me, I've wanted to for a long time." He paused, sucked in another breath. "She became a high-class call girl. A hooker. Well-paid. But still, a prostitute."

I studied the scenery. The bare trees. The dead grass. "Tommy, I'm so sorry."

"That's why I don't talk about my family. It's why I don't go home much to visit. Hurts too much. To see what she did. For me. All for me."

I turned back to him. He stared at the road, his jaw hard, set. Now, I felt even more terrible. "And here I am ruining your chances with the pros. Not to mention your football scholarship."

"Kit, that's not what I meant. I can find something else to do for living. And I can struggle through one more semester of schooling if they do yank my scholarship. That's not the issue. No, I want you to understand why I'm here. I couldn't help my mom. But I can help you. You're what matters. Do you understand now?"

We passed barren farms, dead but for a few stalks of dried wheat. I squeezed his knee. I didn't deserve him.

The least I could do for him was live. Really live. Not just drift, but actually live.

That is, if I could make it through the church dream.

You always knew you had come here to die.

I was already having trouble breathing.

***

The moment we took the turnoff, I knew it was true.

I could almost hear my mother's voice, directing my father down the road, my father spinning the steering wheel. Everything had a hazy, dreamlike quality.

Like I had been here before.

In one hand, I clutched my inhaler. The other I used to direct Tommy.

Just like my mother.

Just like my dream.

Tommy said nothing, merely drove the car. But I could sense his amazement and disbelief as the dream I'd shared with him came to life around him.

The church emerged, as if it had been waiting for us. All these years. Waiting. To welcome me home.

I sucked on my inhaler several times before stepping out of the car. Tommy had already gotten out and was gazing up at it.

"Think it's open? Looks kind of small to have a full-time pastor, but you never know."

"We don't need a pastor," I said, my voice dreamy and unfocused. "Everything we need is in the graveyard." I began to walk, my legs moving without any direction from me.

Tommy jogged to catch up. "I think a living person may be helpful in this matter. You see, graveyards are really good for finding dead people, but not so good at finding kidnapped people. Unless, of course, they're being held in a graveyard, but I think we can safely rule out that possibility."

I continued to be drawn forward. "A little faith, remember? We've gotten this far on it. Besides, we can always find a living person later."

Tommy grunted. I felt my lungs fill with fluid, the coughs gather in my chest, ready to burst out. I kept waiting to hear the bell. Any second the bell would ring. The wolves would howl.

And I would die.

The wind whipped around us, bringing whispers of cold, of decay, of death. Anytime now the bell would ring. Any moment.

I started coughing, blood trickling from my mouth. I slowed to get myself under control.

Tommy stared at me in alarm. "Kit, are you sure … "

I held up my hand to silence him. The bell would toll any second now. I had to be ready.

We approached the corner, began to turn. Any moment, the graveyard would appear, and with it, death. Here's where death has been waiting for me. He's been waiting a long time, but his wait is almost over. The perfect spot, really. Nothing to distract him. Soon, I would be in his embrace. Where I belonged.

We rounded the corner, my breaths shorter and more labored. I had expected to see an open grave presided over by death and surrounded by people, but the graveyard was empty. Silent. Except for the wind rattling through dead and overgrown weeds.

"This doesn't look like it's been used for years," Tommy whispered.

"I know," I whispered back. Long yellowing grasses almost hid the gravestones. A broken down, rusted fence nearly obscured by weeds surrounded three-quarters of it. I wondered why I never noticed the fence before.

Then another part of my brain answered; you've never gotten this far before.

The dried grasses crunched under our feet. I continued to be propelled forward, drawn to one of the first graves beyond the fence. My breathing became shallower and shallower, punctuated by booming coughs.

The stone was barely visible under the carpet of weeds. Falling to my knees, barely able to suck air into my lungs, I reached with trembling hands to clear the grasses away. They made a crackling noise as they broke. The top of the stone held an elaborate carving of cherubs with the words "Our Littlest Angel."

"But … but this can't be right," Tommy said, stepping forward. "This stone is for a child, an infant. Not a sixteen-year-old."

I kept pulling up weeds, my hands moving meticulously, even as the blood trickled from my mouth.

Stone clear, I sat back to study it. But something wasn't right. Not right at all.

Above me, Tommy gasped.

I kept shaking my head. No, no, no, this couldn't be right. I tried to breathe, but the air refused to pass through to my lungs.

"Kit, this doesn't make any sense," Tommy said.

I couldn't breathe. I couldn't breathe. Then, from far away, I heard it.

The tolling of the bell.

Darkness hovered on the edge of my vision. It had finally come, and all I had was more questions – no answers.

"According to this," Tommy said, oblivious to my gasps, "Catalina Caldwell died before she was even four years old. But you said she was kidnapped when you were seven."

I started to choke. The darkness came closer.

"Someone must have carved the dates wrong," he continued. "But you'd think they'd notice and fix something like that."

My hands started clawing up the dead grass, trying to dig into the frozen ground. This couldn't be. Cat had been kidnapped by the fairies. She didn't die this early. I remembered her at seven. I remembered her.

"Finally," a female voice drawled from behind us. "I didn't think you'd ever figure it out."

Choking, I turned my head. There stood the woman from the party. From the Union. The one who looked like Cat.

The one who should be dead.

Chapter 36

"I didn't mean to give you such a scare."

We were sitting in the corner of the Emmitsville Bar. Dark and cramped – the wooden paneled walls were decorated with Packer posters. The bar was empty except for two grizzled men sitting at the bar drinking amber-colored liquid in fat glasses.

As it turned out, the woman's name was Courtney Deborne. Not Cat. Not Bethany. Courtney.

And I didn't die after all. I realized my dream hadn't been predicting my actual death, but something else altogether.

Something even more sinister.

The death of innocence.

I sipped my coffee, heavily laden with sugar and cream. Not my favorite way to drink it, but Tommy had insisted.

"You probably wouldn't have if you'd been a little more forthcoming in your messages," I said.

She tossed her long blonde curly hair. "Ah, yes. I'd thought you'd say that. But I did what I had to do. To save Kayla."

Tommy held his hands up. "Okay, can we back up here a little? How do you know about David and Cat? Some answers would be greatly appreciated."

"Yes, I guess they would be." Courtney glanced around the bar. "I'll try to make this fast. We don't have a lot of time." God, she looked like Cat. I couldn't take my eyes off her.

Tommy looked even more mystified. "Time? Why are we running out of time?"

"You'll understand when I'm done." Courtney took a deep breath. "David is my cousin. For that matter, so is the girl you know as Cat."

"What?" I started to interrupt, but she held her hand out.

"This is a lot to take in, so just let me try to tell it. This story starts the day of your birth, Kit. October 16. You see, my Aunt Gretchen was pregnant at the same time as your mother. Your mother gave birth to two girls, my aunt to only one girl. But, somehow, somewhere, a terrible mistake happened. The hospital switched the babies."

"What? My mom and dad aren't my real parents?" I gasped.

Courtney shook her head. "No, you're fine. Your parents are your real parents. But your sister got switched. With my cousin."

Silence. I could hear the bartender clinking glasses together.

"So," Tommy said slowly. "What you're saying is the person Kit thinks of as her sister isn't her sister. Her real sister."

Courtney nodded. "Yes. The person you think of as Cat is actually my cousin Bethany."

Another pause. "Then, what happened to my real sister?" I asked.

Courtney tossed her head to the side. "You were just visiting her."

A cold wind seemed to blow through the bar right then. I shivered, wrapping my fingers around the coffee mug, trying to absorb its warmth. "My real sister is dead?"

Courtney reached over and touched my hand. "I'm so sorry, Kit. Yes, your real sister is dead."

"But, what ... I don't ... "

"My aunt took home your blood sister, who she named Bethany. Your parents took home my blood cousin, who they named Cat. When Bethany was still a toddler, my aunt discovered she had Cystic Fibrosis."

I sucked in my breath sharply. "She really did have Cystic Fibrosis?"

"Yes. And about a year and a half later she died of it." Courtney paused, glanced around the bar again. "You have to understand something about my aunt. She's just like my mother. Both wanted daughters in the worst way. Perfect little dolls. Living, breathing dolls they could mold and twist in their own image."

Twist? I glanced at Tommy. He raised his eyebrows ever so slightly.

"Anyway," Courtney reached for her untouched soda, visibly trying to calm herself. "After Bethany died, my mother and aunt started talking about it. How could Aunt Gretchen have given birth to a child with Cystic Fibrosis? It wasn't in either family, and as you know, it's strictly a genetic disease. Both parents must have the gene. So, my aunt started to do a little detective work. And, that's when she discovered another woman had given birth to two children the same day she did. A woman who carried the Cystic Fibrosis gene, who had already given birth to one child with the disease ... and one healthy, perfect child."

Courtney paused, tapped her fingers against her glass. I noticed her fingernails – perfectly manicured, long, sharp and painted dark red. "After that, it was just a matter of tests and legalese. The hospital kept it out of the courts, gave both families large settlements. But, my aunt ended up with the best prize of all. A second chance for a perfect daughter."

I squeezed my coffee cup tighter. "Why don't I remember any of this?"

Courtney sighed. "I'm sure it's because your parents kept silent about it until they knew they'd have to give up Cat. By then, you were in the hospital."

An image suddenly burst through my head. Cat leaning over me, clutching a doll. Blonde curls brushing my face. "The Terrys are taking me," she whispered. "Kit, we can't stop them. I'm being kidnapped by the Terrys." The doll's empty eyes staring at me.

I'm being kidnapped by the Terrys.

In my confused, fever-induced condition, I heard fairies. The fairies had kidnapped me.

The doll. The doll knew the truth all along. The doll had heard what Cat really said. But *it wasn't about the doll* – it was the message.

The fairies are evil. Pure evil.

My lips were so stiff I could barely form the words. "What happened to her? Cat … I mean Bethany?"

"Well, as it turned out, my aunt should have let well enough alone. Bethany would never be the perfect child. She was too old when my aunt got her. Too willful. Too independent."

Courtney's hands with their red, pointed fingernails, knotted into fists as she talked. The knuckles turned white. Breathing deeply, she dropped her gaze to them.

"The abuse was never physical," she said softly. I could see her trying to force her fingers to relax. "Always verbal. Emotional. Manipulative. They aimed to break your spirit, never your bones.

"Bethany was having none of it. From the moment my aunt brought her home, it was a battle. She even refused her name, would never answer to Bethany. Only Cat. That's the name she told to people. Drove my aunt absolutely wild."

Courtney smiled a little. "I guess it was easier for her to rebel. She had another place to go. I have no doubt your parents would have taken her back in a heartbeat. And she never got tired of throwing that into my aunt's face. 'You're not my real parents. You just gave me your blood. You'll never be my real parents.' David and I didn't have such a fallback."

David. Now everything was becoming clearer. The manipulations. The deceiving. He learned it from his mother.

"How did she die?" I asked.

Courtney's fists tightened again. "I'm not exactly sure of the details, but this is what I think happened. Cat came home that night from the party. She and my aunt had one of their big, blow-out fights, except something happened this time. I'm not sure if my aunt pushed her or if Cat lost her balance because of the argument. All I know for sure is that she was dead when they put her in the car."

I closed my eyes. Oh Cat. I'm so sorry.

"David helped my aunt hide it. He's the one who staged the car crash. As per her instructions, I've no doubt."

"Okay," Tommy broke in. "This is an absolutely amazing story, but what I don't understand is why you just didn't come out and tell us? Why all the secrecy and notes and shit?"

Courtney paused, eyes dropping to her soda. "A couple of years ago, my aunt decided to try a third time for the perfect daughter. She started going to adoption agencies, but quickly realized it was going to take far too long, if ever, to get a child that way. Then she hit upon the whole ward of the state thing. So, she went through the classes and the paperwork, and eventually found little Kayla Benson."

"Again, this is all very interesting, but it still doesn't answer my original question," Tommy said.

Courtney stared at him. "Isn't it obvious? I couldn't let her do it. Not again. Especially since it was my fault."

"Your fault? How on earth is any of this your fault?" I asked.

Courtney's fist tightened further. I could see a drop of blood glistening on the edge of her fist. "I thought you would have figured that out," she said bitterly. "I am the perfect daughter. *My* mother succeeded, whereas my aunt did not. It literally ate my aunt up inside that she couldn't do what my mother did. And don't think my mother doesn't throw it in her face at every opportunity."

"That's hardly your fault," I said. Now blood dripped from her other fist. I wanted to stop her, but was afraid I would make it worse.

Courtney gave her head a quick shake. "Anyway, I'd been racking my brain for months looking for a way to stop this whole adoption thing. I was starting to get desperate, and then David met you at the Halloween party, and I knew I had my answer."

I tore my eyes away from her bloody hands to look her in the face. "Excuse me? How exactly am I an answer?"

"You can get David to confess."

"What?"

"Get David to confess. To the murders. Once they hear what my aunt has done, there's no way they'll give a child to her."

"Newsflash. David's stalking *me*. He's threatening to kill me. How am I supposed to get him to confess?"

She shot me a coy look. "Oh, come on Kit. David's stalking you because he's obsessed by you. You must've figured that out by now."

"Well, yeah, but that still doesn't mean I can get him to confess."

"He was obsessed with Cat. Actually, it was more than an obsession. He wanted to BE Cat. He wanted another family, a good one, like Cat had. When he met you, it was a dream come true. He could literally have Cat's family."

Tommy broke in again. "I'll say it a third time. Why didn't you just come out and tell us? Why all these riddles and games?"

Courtney finally loosened her fingers. A trail of blood dripped onto the dark wood table. This was so creepy.

"Let me ask you something. If I had just walked up to you and told you what was going on, what would you have done?"

I glanced at Tommy. "Verified it, probably."

She tapped the table with a bloody finger, her nail painted the exact color of her blood. "Exactly. Then, you would have gotten so caught up with what happened to Cat and what happened to your first sister – to Bethany - you would have forgotten all about poor Kayla until it was too late. Wouldn't you?"

Courtney sat back, a triumphant look on her face. Her hands were streaked with blood. What had it cost her to give us the little information she had? What kind of family could twist a child into doing that to herself, without her even knowing it? This went beyond creepy. More like sinister. Eerie. Terrifying.

And terribly sad.

Tommy gave her a strange look. "Well, maybe at first, but you could've talked to us … "

"Yes," I cut in. "You're absolutely right, Courtney."

Tommy now gave me the strange look, but I nudged him under the table. In Courtney's reality, manipulation was king. It probably never occurred to her there was another way to handle the situation.

Blood never lies.

"I still don't know how I'm going to get David to confess," I said.

Courtney shrugged. "That's easy. Cat could get him to do anything she wanted."

"But I'm not Cat."

"That's why we have to hurry," she said, as if she hadn't heard me. "He's still in Minneapolis. I have to bring you there. Now's a good time. He's in pain and on drugs from the knife wound you gave him. Should be no problem."

"How do you know where he is?" I asked.

She looked surprised. "Because he called me, that's why. Think he'd go to his mother with that knife wound? You gotta be kidding. Then she'd know he failed. No, I came and took care of him last night. Waited outside the hospital this morning for you. I was going to talk to you then, but I decided instead to follow you. What a kick. Never thought you'd come here. Shall we go?"

My head was whirling. "Wait. The police said they told the hospital not to tell anyone where we were."

Her look sharpened, became crafty. "I didn't ask the hospital. I asked the night manager at the Motel 6." She started giggling. "Told him I was a reporter. Bought it hook, line and sinker. We should go."

Christ, it was a family of con artists. The Brady Bunch gone bad.

"Wait one more second," Tommy said, struggling to keep a neutral expression on his face. "You said murders. Who else was murdered?"

Courtney stared at him like he was a slow student who had missed the point she had so painstakingly explained three times now. "Who do you think?"

Tommy's mouth fell open. "Uh." He stared at me wildly.

I could only think of one other person in this mess who it could possibly be. "But you said Bethany," I said cautiously, "the first Bethany, died of Cystic Fibrosis."

"And she did. If she hadn't had Cystic Fibrosis, she never would have died."

I must have looked as confused as Tommy, because she uttered a long sigh. "Kit, you of all people should know the answer to this. You inherited Cystic Fibrosis from your parents. Bethany inherited the same genes you did. How could she have died from the disease as a toddler while you're still alive and healthy more than seventeen years later? I told you, she wanted *perfect*."

Understanding began to seep through my mind. "Oh, my God."

She cocked her head, looking so much like Cat at that moment I stopped breathing. "Look, it was never something we talked about. It was something I figured out later, when I realized you were still alive. Why else do you think David's so obsessed with your disease?"

Leaning forward, she touched her finger to the corner of my mouth. Where there was blood. Blood from my lungs. "You're perfect right now. You do understand, right?"

Our eyes locked. David. Sixty-five roses. A rose pin. Yes, now I did understand.

"Oh, and one other thing," Courtney said, as we slid out of the booth. "Thought you might want to see this."

She held out a crumpled photo. As I took it, I could see the scars on her palms, darker red where her blood had soaked in.

I studied it. It was a family photo of the Terrys – Cat, David, Dad and mom - blonde and beautiful. The family resemblance was striking. Now I could see why Courtney and Cat looked so much alike.

"But, I saw Mrs. Terry and she … "

"I know," Courtney cut in. "When she decided to adopt, she did the whole dark thing. Dark hair, dark glasses, brown contacts. Doesn't need either glasses or contacts, by the way. She thinks it makes her look more matronly. People would treat her with more respect as a brunette than a blonde. In reality, I think it makes her look hideous. Don't you agree?"

"Uh, yeah." What was it about Courtney that put me at such a loss for words? "Oh, Courtney, something you said earlier. About David meeting me at the Halloween party. You were there, though. Because I saw you."

Courtney now stared at me like I was slow. "Of course I wasn't there. That's the party where David met you. I heard about it later."

"But ... " I started to say, then stopped.

The smell of chlorine. The scent of wildflowers.

"Don't be afraid, Kit. I'll take care of you. I'll always take care of you."

And she had tried to take care of me, to warn me.

If only I had listened.

Chapter 37

Taking a deep breath, I adjusted my skirt one last time and knocked on the plain hotel door.

"Who's it?"

"It's me. Kit."

Silence. Then shuffling noises, clicking noises – deadbolt thrown back, chain removed.

The door opened.

David.

He stood there, cold eyes raking me up and down, wearing sweats. He smiled. "I knew you'd come."

He held the door open wider so I could slip in, then locked it behind me. Dead bolt, chain, the works. He tested the door a few times, nodding while he did it. I noticed he favored his left leg. A surge of pleasure shot through me. About time something went my way.

After he finished locking me in, he turned and limped to where I stood. "Please, have a seat." He pulled out one of the straight-backed chairs. I sat down, removing my coat and carefully arranging my purse on the table next to a lamp with a light blue shade.

His eyes crawled all over me. Although I desperately wanted to cover up, I forced myself to relax, to smooth my hands over my hips, cross my legs. I wore a black mini-skirt, black pumps, and a tight red sweater with a scooped neck. Courtney had made an emergency stop at the mall. She had insisted on driving us back to Minneapolis, said we both looked like we were going to keel over.

"So." He sat on the rumpled bed, covered with a blue and beige striped bedspread. "What can I do for you?"

I gave him my most charming smile. "Just want to talk, that's all."

"Talk." He studied me. "Just talk, eh?" His eyes continued to creep over me.

Suddenly he leaped to his feet and grabbed my purse.

I stood up, knocking my chair over. "David, what are you doing?"

"Talk. Yeah, right." He limped to the far corner, unzipping the purse.

"Don't, David," I said, sounding panicked. "That's my personal property. You have no ... "

He pulled out a small tape recorder. My voice trailed off.

"So, Kit." He turned the tape recorder over in his hand. "You thought you could trick me."

I didn't answer.

He snapped it off, dropped it on the bed where it bounced a couple of times. "Kit, Kit, Kit. When will you ever learn?"

I eyed the door, trying not to let him see. How much time would I need to undo the locks?

He saw my glance and limped to the edge of the bed, effectively placing himself between me and door. "Kit, why don't you sit down?"

I stood for a second longer, fidgeting, before bending over to straighten my chair. I lowered myself into it. He plopped down as well.

Locked in with a madman.

Two murdered daughters. One psychopathic son. And me. What a fun bunch we were.

"Kit, it would be so much easier if you'd quit fighting it," he said kindly. "You know we're meant to be together. I can read you like a book. Our destinies are intertwined. We have no choice in the matter."

I broke into a coughing fit, the fever burning through me.

His expression didn't show any alarm or concern. Not like Tommy's did. Instead, he looked a little turned on.

Oh, God. Courtney was right. This was so twisted. I've got to be in the middle of a David Lynch movie.

But, no. That's not the way to look at it. It's something I can use.

I leaned forward. "Let me hear you say it."

He looked delighted. "Say what?"

"You know what I want to hear."

"I have absolutely no idea what you're talking about."

"Come on, David," I smiled at him again. "You know it's just us talking. Say it. Just for me."

He shrugged. "Can't say what I don't know."

I coughed a little. "If you care about me as much as you say you do, you'll say it."

"I care about you." The teasing was gone. He began to get agitated. "I care about you!"

"That's what you keep claiming. But, how can I believe it when you won't admit one little thing to me?"

His eyes started bulging. "You're the one who should be apologizing to me. Stabbing me. Sneaking around behind my back. Worrying my mother. How dare you do those things to me?"

"You left me no choice when you refused to be honest. How can we have a life together when you won't be truthful?"

He pointed his finger at me. "You're the one in the wrong here."

"Then talk to me, dammit."

"I don't owe you anything."

This wasn't going as I had hoped. The sheen of madness was back in his eyes. Definitely the wrong approach. Maybe I could brazen it out somehow.

"You tell me we're meant to be together, but then you turn around and lie to me ... "

"Lie to *you*?" Now he jumped off the bed. "When did I ever lie to *you*?"

I made a point of getting huffy. "Well, for starters, about Cat."

"Cat?" He froze. "What about Cat?"

"You *knew* her and you didn't tell me. Don't you think I would've liked to hear you talk about her?"

He relaxed, sinking back onto the bed. "Cat was wonderful. Beautiful. And so full of life. I miss her so."

"So, what happened to her that night? Why would she be driving alone on that road?"

The guarded look was back in his eyes. "How would I know?"

Shit. Too fast. Courtney had told me it would be easy, that he wanted to talk about it. Obsessed with it. Yeah, real easy. "Why wouldn't you know? You were her brother. Probably the closest person in the world to her."

The faraway look replaced the guarded look. "Yes, we were close." Then his look changed again, became craftier. "Finally figured it out, huh?"

"Yes."

He shook his head. "Couldn't believe it when I met you and you didn't know. All that talk about being kidnapped by the fairies when all along she had been adopted by the Terrys. God, are you gullible."

I hung my head. "I know. So, tell me more about her."

He smiled. "She was so wonderful. So wonderful. Kind of like you. You reminded me a lot of her, especially in the beginning," he laughed a little. "Oh, and she talked about you a lot, especially at first. But eventually that stopped. It had to stop, you understand. But ... " his expression became confused.

"But what," I prompted gently.

"She ... didn't fit in. Didn't do the right thing. Mother was never very happy with her. Said your parents ruined her. But I don't understand how. I mean, you're a lot like her." He shook his head. "She just didn't fit in."

I coughed some more. Blood. I made a point of smearing some on my face. "What did your mother do about it?"

He saw the blood, stared at it hungrily. "They fought. A lot."

"And, what did you do?"

He edged a little closer. "Tried to make peace between them. Keep them together."

"Did it work?"

"Sometimes." His eyes focused back on me. "But sometimes it didn't. Sometimes ... things got out of control."

I started rubbing my leg, slowly, sensuously. The blood on my fingers left a trail. "Did Cat get hurt when things got out of control?"

His eyes followed my fingers. I could feel the longing burning in him. "You have to understand. Mother didn't mean it to happen. It was an accident."

I kept my voice soft. "Accident."

"Yeah." His voice was getting higher, more childlike. "One time, she accidentally pushed Cat's face through a window. She didn't mean it, but Cat made her so mad. And another time, she accidentally burned her with a cigarette. She gave up smoking after that. Mother did, I mean. But you have to understand, Cat made her do those things. Just like Cat made her push her down the stairs."

It was all I could do to keep my face composed, to not rush at him, attack him, claw out his eyes. Courtney said the abuse was never physical. Dear God. What sheer hell had Cat gone through?

I bit down hard on the inside of my mouth, drawing blood. Focus on the pain. The pain in my lungs. The pain in my mouth. "Cat got pushed down the stairs?"

"Mother didn't mean it. Really. Cat just made her so angry, she had to. Just had to. But Cat just laid there. She wasn't breathing." He sounded exactly like a little boy tattling. "She wasn't breathing. So I had to take care of it. Mother was depending on me. That detective, he never would have understood. He wouldn't have seen that Mother had to do it. So I made it look like an accident. Like Cat had been drinking and had run into a tree."

He looked down at his lap. "It was an accident." His voice was so quiet, so pitiable. I almost felt sorry for him.

Almost.

Suddenly he put his hand to his mouth. "I shouldn't have called her that."

I coughed again. Blood trickled down my face. "Called her what?"

"Cat. Mother hated that. Her name was Bethany. But when we were alone, I always called her Cat." He looked a little shy. "It was my pet name for her. My special name. Our secret. I could never think of her as a Bethany anyway."

"Why not?"

He shot me a quick look, and now I saw David the adult. "You know who Bethany was. She's the reason why our destinies are intertwined. Why our paths must merge."

"Ah," I said softly. "My sister."

He nodded. "Your sister."

"The one who died of Cystic Fibrosis."

A pause, a hesitation. "Yes. The one who died of Cystic Fibrosis."

I cocked my head, touched the blood on my face. "Did she get sick? Like me?"

He frowned. "She got sick. A lot. Thin too, like you. Actually, thinner. Coughed a lot. But ... ."

"But ... "

"She was sick."

"How?"

His eyes narrowed. Drummed his fingers against his thigh. "What do you mean, how?"

"Exactly what I said. How? One day I'm going to die of Cystic Fibrosis too. Maybe I'm dying now. I want to know first-hand what you saw so I'll know when the time comes."

"No," he half-shouted. "No. I can take care of you. You won't the die the way she did. No. I'll take good care of you."

"But I will die the way she did. I have the same disease."

He shook his head violently. "No. I'll take good care of you."

"But what about Bethany? Didn't your mother take good care of her?"

"Mother ... " he paused, fishing for a word. "Mother tried. But it didn't work. I learned from her mistakes."

"What mistakes?"

"Her medicine." His voice was childlike again. "It made her throw up. Mother said it'd be good for her, but it made her throw up. How could it be good for her when all it did was make her throw up?"

I swallowed. "Then what, David?"

He shook his head hopelessly. "She got thinner and thinner. Always sick. Wouldn't eat, when she did, she'd throw up. Coughed more. Got more colds. Fevers, infection. And always the medicine. But it didn't seem to work. Do you understand? It didn't work."

He straightened. "I won't make the same mistake. I learned. The medicine I give you won't make you throw up. I'll take good care of you, Kit. That's why we're destined to be together."

So many emotions ran through my head. Locked in a room with a monster. A monster who had stalked me, terrorized me, tried to kill me, who would try again no doubt.

And yet he had watched his mother kill both his sisters. Without being able to stop it. He had been forced to live day in and day out with a murderer. A murderer who had nursed him. Raised him. Twisted him. Destroyed him.

David, the perfect son.

"We have enough, Kit." The voice in my ear said. "It's getting too dangerous in there for you. We're coming in."

"Kit?" David was watching me from the bed, lust radiating from him. Leaning over, he reached out a finger and barely stroked my face.

Where the blood was.

The fairies are evil. Pure evil.

Moving so slowly, ever so slowly, he sat back, staring at blood on his finger. He raised his finger to his face, ran the tip down his cheek.

Smearing his face with my blood.

It was all I could do to not scream.

The fairies are evil. Pure evil.

Both of my sisters were dead because of his family. Because they weren't perfect.

And after telling me, instead of showing remorse, he wanted to have sex.

Because I was sick.

He hadn't shown this much interest when I was well.

He had stalked and terrorized me until I became sick. Sent me threatening notes. Killed a helpless cat. Stabbed Tommy.

All for sex.

I stood up, smiling my most bewitching smile. "David, you're right. We are meant to be together. I can feel it. Let's not wait another moment."

He grinned, started to get up, but I waved him down. "Let me do this for you."

He leaned back, his grin turning into a leer.

I pirouetted, my hips moving suggestively. Kicking my chair over, I brought my leg up, resting my foot on the edge of the seat, posing seductively. I ran my hands down my leg. Then slowly, oh so slowly, brought my fingers up, catching the hem of my skirt and tugging it up.

His eyes were mesmerized by my movements. Even the muffled sounds outside the door couldn't break his concentration.

Smiling, I eased my skirt up further.

And exposed the transmitter taped to my inner thigh.

For a moment, he looked confused. Lust had fogged his brain, so he couldn't immediately comprehend what he was seeing.

Then he understood.

He jerked to his feet. "You bitch."

I dropped my leg. "Ha, ha, David. Guess I'm not so dumb after all." I began to laugh.

He limped toward me, rage engulfing the shock and confusion in his eyes. "But I didn't admit to stalking you."

A crash from the door made me jump. The cops to the rescue. I laughed in his face. "I don't care about that. I got exactly what I wanted. And you're going down for murder. Now who's the idiot?"

He slapped me just as another thump rattled the door in its frame. I kept laughing. "Is that the best you can do?"

Fury exploded on his face. I suddenly realized I had gone too far.

Why hadn't the police gotten in yet? They kept banging away … why weren't they breaking the door down?

I tried to back away as he lunged toward me, knocking the lamp over. It smashed against the wall. "We belong together, Kit. And if I have to kill you to prove it, I will."

My back hit the wall. Trapped. He pounced. Foul breath against my cheek.

"Nowhere to run, Kit." He grinned, lust and madness mingling together. "Told you we were gonna to be together." His hands closed around my throat.

I couldn't breathe, coughs straining my chest. I clawed at his face, his hands. Blackness swirled at the edges of my vision. Must breathe. My already sore chest roared with pain.

From outside, I could hear the muffled shouts from the police in between the thudding. "David. Open up. There's no where for you to go."

David grinned wider, leering closer to me. "No one can help you now," he whispered and licked my face. I shuddered, the warm stickiness of his tongue jerking me closer to consciousness for one horrifying second. The pain was unbearable. Agonizing. David was death. My dream was right all along.

"David," the police yelled. "Open up."

Blackness was closing in. My lungs were filling up. I was drowning in my own fluids. My chest wanted to explode with coughs. I couldn't breathe. I couldn't think. David's grin started to fade away. The last thing I would see on this earth. God, I hated him.

Dimly, from far away, came an even bigger crash. I tried to focus, see what it meant, but the darkness swallowed me whole.

Chapter 38

Tommy pulled into the driveway, turned the car off. He drummed his fingers on the steering wheel. "So, this is where you grew up?"

I glanced at the three-story cream-colored, turquoise-trimmed house. "Yeah."

He nodded, eyes on the neat, subtle lines of the house, the manicured yard. "Nice house."

"Yeah." Even on this miserably gray February day, the house still radiated understated elegance.

I studied it. So many secrets. So many words left unsaid. The house was bursting with unexpressed thoughts and emotions. How could I walk back in there?

Tommy, as if reading my thoughts, put his hand over mine. "Do you want to go in alone or should I wait out here?"

He was so good to me. I leaned against his shoulder, absorbing his strength. "No, I should do this alone."

Over the past few months, as I lay in the hospital fighting death a second time, I had come to depend on his strength. He was there with me, through it all, including when the cops stopped by to let me know that, finally, justice had been served. David and his dysfunctional, murderous mother were both in jail. Kayla had been adopted by a new family. Both my sisters could finally rest in peace. And finally, I too, allowed myself to let go, to let myself be carried away by Tommy's warmth, his caring, his love.

Tommy had saved my life in more ways than one. For the first time, I realized what it was like to want to live, really want to live. With everything I had, I fought the pneumonia and a secondary bacterial infection ravaging my body.

And I won. We won.

He leaned over to kiss me. "I'll be here."

I nodded, opening the car door and getting out. A cold gust of wind greeted me, whipping my black dress up. Pulling it back down, I made my way to the house.

My mother stood in the foyer, adjusting her makeup in the mirror. "Oh good, you're here." She wore a stylishly cut black silk dress, her dark hair smoothed into a French twist.

"Tommy's in the car." I watched her dab at her lipstick. So much needed to be said. Did I have the strength yet to say it?

As I pondered, my mother glanced at me in the mirror. "We should have done this long ago."

"Yes, we should have."

She capped her lipstick and dropped it into her purse. "Your sisters deserved better. You deserved better, too."

The wrong twin had been taken.

I didn't answer, couldn't answer. She faced me, a wisp of black hair falling across her forehead.

"I know I have a lot to make up for. I'd like a chance to try."

I couldn't look at her. She seemed so vulnerable, naked almost.

But I saw love, too. Maybe she did love me, after all.

The wrong twin had been taken.

By saving the innocent, you save yourself. It's the only way you can set yourself free.

I was finally free.

I raised my eyes to my mother. "I'd like that."

She smiled, hesitant but real. "We should go. I'll get your father. It's time."

I nodded. Yes, it was time.

Time to pay our respects.

To both of my sisters.

THE END

Michele Pariza Wacek (also known as Michele PW) taught herself to read at three years old because she so badly wanted to write fiction. As an adult, she became a professional copywriter (copywriters write promotional materials for businesses, nothing to do with protecting intellectual property or putting a copyright on something) and eventually founded a copywriting and marketing company.

She grew up in Madison, Wisconsin and currently lives with her husband and dogs in the mountains of Arizona. You can reach her at MicheleParizaWacek.com. *The Stolen Twin* is her first published novel.

CPSIA information can be obtained
at www.ICGtesting.com
Printed in the USA
LVHW052358030520
654931LV00003B/423